continued . . .

"These books are golden! . . . A fresh take on the blood-suckers of the paranormal world."

—Kings River Life Magazine

"*Iron Night* is just as good as *Generation V*. . . . There's plenty of action and supernatural baddies to round out Fort's narrative, but it's Fort's journey, within himself, and with his family . . . that really makes this shamelessly addictive series sing."   —My Bookish Ways

"Ripe with mystery, suspense, and a cast of richly diverse characters that will have you laughing and rolling your eyes at their antics. . . . Brennan has brought back the dangerous and cruel supernatural creatures of old and integrated them into the modern society with nary a hitch."

—Smexy Books

"A wonderful trip through a continuously creative universe."   —All Things Urban Fantasy

Generation V

"I loved M. L. Brennan's *Generation V*. Engrossing and endearingly quirky, with a creative and original vampire mythos, it's a treat for any urban fantasy lover!"

— Karen Chance, *New York Times* bestselling author of *Tempt the Stars*

"Full of vivid characters and terrific world building, *Generation V* is a fun, fast-paced romp of a story that kept me glued to the pages to the very last word. Loved it! Bravo, M. L. Brennan, bravo!"

—Devon Monk, national bestselling author of *Infinity Bell*

"At last, the millennial generation has a vampire to call its own. Brennan's debut blends old-world mystique and the brutality of literature's best vampires to make a sensational coming-of-age story rife with chills and smart one-liners . . . [a] promising series."   —*Romantic Times*

"Brennan has a wholly new, and very deep, take on the vampire mythology . . . a perfect combination of new and old that comes along only very rarely."   —Tor.com

Also by M. L. Brennan

Generation V
Iron Night
Tainted Blood

DARK
ASCENSION

A Generation V Novel

M. L. BRENNAN

A ROC BOOK

ROC
Published by New American Library,
an imprint of Penguin Random House LLC
375 Hudson Street, New York, New York 10014

This book is an original publication of New American Library.

First Printing, August 2015

ISBN 978-0-451-47412-4

Printed in the United States of America
10 9 8 7 6 5 4 3 2 1

Penguin
Random
House

For Devon.

Who let me read all his *Star Trek* novels, helped me roll my first D&D character, beat all the really tough level bosses for me, and sat with me for hours upon hours until we figured out that we had to type "Tickle whale's uvula with peacock feather" at that one point in King's Quest IV.

More recently, when I was behind schedule on this book, he wrote me the following haiku:

Bare slate beckons man:
"Fill the page ere dusk descends.
Words don't write themselves."

You are, without a doubt,
the best big brother anyone could ever have.

ACKNOWLEDGMENTS

I am utterly grateful to Anne Sowards and the incredible people at Roc for letting me give Fort and Suze a fourth outing. This was a book that I've wanted to write for a long time, and I feel so privileged that I got to do it.

Seth Fishman has my sincere thanks and devotion for helping me out at a critical and particularly panic-ridden juncture. Sarah Riley somehow managed to resist punching me in the face when I was capable of little more than whining about how stressed I was about writing this book—during her wedding. Immense thanks also go to Sarah's mother, Marie, for also giving me extremely generous reassurance at a time when there were substantially more important things going on. (For the record: I'm still sorry about failing Bustle 101.) Kudos as well to all of my fellow bridesmaids, as well as the extremely awesome bridesdude.

John Shearer not only read this manuscript in one of its earliest and rawest forms, but gave me many useful notes that helped me keep Fort's trials and tribulations with Scirocco ownership accurate. He also reminded me that a vegetarian should not be eating a bacon-wrapped scallop. For all your efforts at keeping me from embarrassing myself, John, I salute you.

Andrew, Arlen, and Ryan kept me from collapsing on the side of hiking trails in Yosemite National Park and being eaten by bears. I appreciate that, guys. The rest of my family has also shown unending support and enthusiasm for my work, and I'm so lucky to have all of you.

At one point I got extremely nervous about where a particular story element was going and begged Jaime Lee Moyer to give me some feedback. I can't believe how fast she read through the manuscript for me, and I'm still unbelievably grateful for the assurance when I needed it the most. Jaime, I owe you a drink.

Thanks are definitely due to my husband for daily support and belief as well as for functioning as my eternally on-call sounding board, which he handles with grace and humor. And to my cats —those still alive, and those who sadly passed away during the time that I was working on this book: You have no idea what the hell I'm doing when I huddle at my computer for hours each day, but having you with me —sitting on my lap, blinking lazily at me, or knocking random shit off the desk just to piss me off (Shackleton)—makes me feel a lot less alone.

This book would never have happened without all of the readers and fans of my slacker vampire who made their opinions known—and loudly. I sincerely hope that you enjoy this one—you made it happen.

In writing this book and pondering the intricacies of a vampire's digestive tract, I once again owe a great debt to *Dark Banquet: Blood and the Curious Lives of Blood Feeding Creatures* by Bill Schutt. This excellent, informative, and deeply funny book gave me the inspiration for many scenes—one in particular. I'm sorry about that one scene, Anne, but I owed it to Schutt. Because of *science*.

Chapter One

The highway sign indicating my entry into Hardwick Township appeared just as the digital clock display on my GPS clicked over to noon. I'd been driving for four and a half hours by then, enough time to take me from the heart of my mother's territory in Providence, Rhode Island, to its very edge in northern New Jersey. There were a lot of people who would've been surprised to know that I-80 demarcated a line of ownership that had been established with blood hundreds of years ago. Those people would have been even more surprised to learn that the path of this particular interstate had been placed at the direction of a vampire.

Or not. New Jersey politics were rather notorious, after all.

My mother was the vampire in question, and also the reason that I was driving through New Jersey. Madeline Scott reigned supreme in a territory that stretched from New Jersey's border with Pennsylvania up into southern Québec—and like any good leader, she had realized long ago the importance of delegating menial tasks. Today I was on my way to discuss terms and conditions with a group of hopeful immigrants to the territory. Not humans, of course—with few exceptions, humans moved through territories with blissful ignorance. Territory rules and boundaries applied to a much smaller, and more secret global population—the supernatural.

This was normally the kind of task that my older brother, Chivalry, was best at handling—with smooth good looks and the kind of diplomatic skills that would've made Madeleine Albright jealous, my brother was practically tailor-made for these kinds of missions. I was definitely the second string in this particular field, but I was at least an improvement over our oldest sibling, my sister, Prudence.

Her diplomatic skills mostly involved leaving bodies on the floor.

I'd been involved with only one immigration request before, and that was a fairly standard one of a werebear (sorry, *metsän kunigas*—the bears are picky about the terminology) family from Mexico coming in to join up with our local group. It had been back when I was still doing ride-alongs with Chivalry as part of my training. I'd spent most of my life trying to be like the humans around me, and pretending that things like vampires didn't even exist—that had led me to a film studies degree from Brown and then a series of minimum-wage jobs. But last year things had changed, and now I was irrevocably part of the family system, and was even on the family payroll. At my own insistence, I'd kept the minimum wage, even though I knew that my family could pay me marriage-counselor-level hourly rates and never even notice. During one of the periods that the Scirocco had been in the shop, and I'd been relying on the Providence bus system and shanks' mare for transportation, my roommate, Dan, had asked me outright why I didn't just take more money from my family— they'd be happy to give it, and in fact could probably have just bought me a new car from the petty cash account and relied on their fleet of accountants to turn it into a tax write-off. It had been hard to put a lifetime's coil of fear, stubbornness, and tiny private high ground into words, but the best that I'd been able to explain was that taking no more than I would otherwise have been earning on the open market of shitty jobs made me feel like I couldn't be caught by my family's money, or ever build up a style of living that required that money and therefore could put pressure on me to do things that I felt might be unethical. This way, after all, I could always tell them all to go pound sand and maintain my current lifestyle by pouring coffee and cleaning public toilets.

Dan had been so utterly disgusted by what he termed my "bullheaded and bullshit martyrdom" that he'd lent me his car until the Scirocco was fixed. While I hadn't exactly followed his reasoning on that one, I supposed that at least we were both equally mystified by the other's actions.

Today was going to be my first solo effort—and it probably wouldn't even have been happening, except that Chivalry was on vacation with his new wife, Simone, in New Hampshire. The call requesting a hearing for immigration into the territory had come in yesterday, and had cited some emergency as the reason for the short notice. Chivalry had offered to come home early to handle it, but I'd promised to do it myself. Simone was a professional mountaineer, and she'd just finished guiding a group of winter hikers up Mount Washington, so it didn't seem fair to make her cut short her downtime afterward at a fancy and expensive ski lodge. Plus, she and Chivalry had been married for only a month and a half, and most of that had been sucked up with the holiday season. With the new year only a week old, I figured that she deserved a little one-on-one with my brother. After all, it wasn't like she had a lot of time to waste.

So that had all led to me here, in my gray Scirocco, cruising into a rural town (population 1,696) in New Jersey whose sole claim to fame was that the original *Friday the 13th* had been filmed there. Under normal circumstances, I might've been kind of excited. After all, despite the layer of snow on the ground that was old enough to have acquired a nasty grayish crust that removed all picturesque elements from it, the roads were dry, my car was running well, and my partner in crime and new girlfriend, Suzume, was reclining naked in the backseat.

Well, naked other than her natural fur coat. Suzume was a kitsune, and apparently the Scirocco had been built on a scale far too compact for her to willingly spend four and a half hours in her human skin. She had shifted into her other form, which had coal-black fur, amber eyes containing a world of mischief, and a snow-white tail tip. From the soft whuffling sounds emerging from my backseat, she'd been napping for at least the last two hours. Before that she'd been playing with a balled-up take-out bag from Dunkin' Donuts—all that remained of our breakfast of champions.

Normal circumstances didn't apply because the Scirocco's passenger seat was currently occupied by the generously endowed figure of Loren Noka, the family's business secretary and a woman whose air of complete and utter competency left me feeling more than a little intimidated. Her Native American heritage was clearly written across her face, and even though I knew that she was in her late forties, her dark hair showed not the slightest hint of gray. I had almost suffered a near-death experience from sheer shame this morning when she wordlessly lowered her cream linen pantsuit–clad body down onto a subcompact car seat that was not only older than I was, but had been liberally patched and repatched with duct tape in four different colors. And I also had a very bad suspicion that the entire interior of the car was currently coated with Suzume's black fox hairs.

Loren was along on this trip to provide double duty as my chaperone in diplomacy, and also to handle most of the paperwork. Immigration into the territory had co-pious aspects, such as whether my mother was willing to let certain groups or species enter, but the biggest focus was a simple one: money. From the meagerest kobold right up to the elves, every supernatural who lived in my mother's territory tithed heavily for the privilege. We even ran their credit scores.

In exchange, those who lived in my mother's territory were under her protection. It was a very Mafia-style pro-tection, with many regulations on behavior and activi-ties, and the possibility of death-by-Prudence if they violated any of those rules, but it did prevent any group from preying on another. I'd never set one foot outside the boundaries of Scott territory, but given how desper-ate many people were to get in, what was out there couldn't be a walk in the park.

Suzume was along in case ass needed to be kicked at some point. Which, though her current form looked like nothing more than an adorable plushy toy, she knew how to deliver.

Loren must've been following my train of thought, because she glanced over her shoulder and noted qui-etly, "We'll be at the Supplicant House in less than ten minutes. Shouldn't your companion assume a more ap-propriate form?"

"I don't know," I said. "She's a lot more diplomatic the way she is."

A delicately angled black snout immediately inserted itself between the two front seats, and a long vulpine tongue gave my right ear and surrounding hair a thorough slobbering, ignoring my shout of protest. Apparently Suze hadn't been as asleep as I'd thought. The snout withdrew again into the backseat, and Loren restrained herself to a single raised eyebrow as she wordlessly removed a tissue from her purse and handed it to me.

I mopped myself off as best I could, grumbling as I

did. A moment later I yelped again as Suzume leaned forward between the seats again, now entirely human and just as entirely naked.

"I resent your comment," she said. "I have excellent diplomacy skills. In fact, of the two of us, I am the resident champion of diplomacy."

"Yes, Diplomacy. The lying, backstabbing board game that appeals to every innate skill you possess. I'm aware." We'd played it a few times with Dan and his boyfriend. I'd been soundly beaten each time. "Now can you please put clothing on before you cause a multiple-car accident?" Suze's casual attitude toward personal nudity was genuine, but she was also quite well aware that the rest of the planet's population was significantly less casual in response to it. In the passenger seat, Loren Noka suddenly exhibited a new and powerful interest in the rural New Jersey scenery.

Suze smiled at me, the delicate corners of the eyes that were the clearest marker of her Japanese heritage crinkling. "Now, who would expect to see a smoking-hot woman in the backseat of a car this shitty?" With that bon mot, she began a leisurely reapplication of her bra. All of the kitsune had a kind of illusion magic that they referred to as fox tricks—it allowed them to fool all of a person's senses (and sometimes even cameras and technical equipment) into seeing only what the kitsune wanted to be seen. I knew that fox tricks were the easiest when the kitsune worked within what the viewer would normally expect to see—for example, it probably would've been more difficult for her to convince someone that there *was* a naked woman in the back of my car than to convince them that *of course* the woman in that car was wearing clothing—even while she was still functionally undressed.

"Don't think I won't turn the heat off if you take too long," I muttered. If the January chill was what it took to get her dressed, then I wasn't above unrolling my window.

Of course, if I wanted to see Suzume undressed again in a more *recreational* setting, then I knew as well as she did that the odds of me actually following through on my threat were practically zero.

"Hey," Suze said, her voice partially muffled by the turtleneck she was pulling over her head, "any chance we can turn on some actual music? If I have to sit through one more minute of NPR, I might have to punch the next person I see with an *All Things Considered* travel mug in the face."

"You knew the terms when you agreed to come on the trip," I warned her. Suze's preference in music could be best described as "tunes to speed to," and while I normally didn't mind it too much (and in fact had begun to develop an unwilling appreciation for J-pop thrash metal), I'd felt the need to intercede for the sake of Loren Noka (who struck me as more of a smooth jazz connoisseur), and we'd spent the entire drive going from one NPR station to another.

"This is completely unfair. If it wasn't for me, we would've spent the entire trip with nothing but Springsteen."

"I know that it's New Jersey, but they do occasionally play something other than The Boss," Loren interjected.

"No, she's talking about my car stereo," I explained. "When I bought the Scirocco back in November, the radio was broken, and there was a *Born to Run* tape permanently fused into the player. It wasn't exactly at the top of my priority list of repairs, so Suze got me a new system for Christmas."

"And surprised him with it," Suze said. Her voice still sounded a little weird, and when I checked the rearview this time, I saw that she was in the process of wiggling into her jeans. Winter clothing was rough for shapeshifting.

"Yes. She surprised me with it by hiring someone to break into my car, take it to a chop shop, install the new stereo, and bring it back."

Suze leaned forward again and frowned at me. "You're not sounding appropriately appreciative of the awesomeness of my gift presentation."

"It was a great present," I assured her, "and I really was happy to not have to have it installed. I just wish that the installer hadn't permanently broken the passenger door while doing it, and stolen my tire iron, cell phone charger, and flashlight."

"No one likes an ungrateful gift recipient," Suze said.

"They broke the passenger door?" Loren interjected, looking concerned. After all, if the door in question suddenly failed catastrophically, she was on the front lines.

"Not too badly," I assured her. "They just broke the lock pin, so you can't unlock the passenger door without the key anymore."

"So I can't open my door from the inside?" Loren asked.

"No."

"So you now essentially have a kidnapper-mobile?"

"Some people would regard that as an added feature," Suze said helpfully.

"Yes, Suze. But those people would be *kidnappers*." I'd been having this conversation with her since the holidays. A preliminary phone call to a repair garage had also revealed that fixing this particular issue could only be accomplished with a special thread die, so this was probably now going to be a semipermanent feature of the car from now on. That had definitely tempered my gratitude for relief from endless repeats of The Boss. Suzume's helpful suggestion had been to simply leave the door eternally unlocked, but given my lack of interest in allowing the petty thieves of Providence to treat my car as a personal rummage sale, I'd simply gotten into the habit of manually relocking the car on every occasion that I had to let a passenger in or out.

Loren headed off the topic with a polite redirection to the kinds of minimum tithing amounts that we would be looking for in this meeting, and I let myself focus back on the road. The percentages and payoffs had already been thoroughly drilled into my head during a cram session spent with the documents that I'd been sent last night, and Loren had gone over them twice already on the trip. But apparently Loren's back-to-business topic choice was enough to remind Suze about what was waiting for us in a few more miles.

"This is going to be awesome," Suze interrupted, glee heavy in her voice. "It'll be like the whole Victoria's Secret catwalk show."

"How do you figure that?" I asked.

Suze scoffed. "They're *succubi*, Fort."

"Oh. So they're actually—" I looked over at Loren and raised my eyebrows inquisitively. I was living proof that superstition, literature, and Hollywood were not always accurate in presenting the supernatural, so I'd assumed that any particular cultural assumptions I might've had about succubi were likely to be hugely off base.

Loren wiggled a hand in a maybe-yes-maybe-no gesture. "We've never had them in the territory, and they seem to prefer warmer climates, so I couldn't find much information in the files." Irritation crossed her face for a brief moment. Nothing got under Loren's skin like shoddy file-keeping. "Your mother categorized them years ago as completely nonthreatening, and with none in residence, that was rather it. It made for pretty brief reading."

"The Northeast isn't good thong weather. It makes sense that we wouldn't see many of them," Suze noted.

"They're not all female," I pointed out. How much of it was to prove that I'd actually done the reading, I couldn't exactly say.

"Dudes can wear thongs too, Fort. Unlike you, I'm not making sexist assumptions." Suze was using her most helpful tone, which she only used when she was having particular levels of fun.

I pushed onward. Loren's mouth had made a suspicious twitch at Suze's comment, and whether the secretary was struggling not to laugh or containing the urge to throttle the kitsune, I figured that a little more filler would give her the minute to find the strength. "It's like foxes—we call females vixens, but they're still foxes. All succubi are called succubi, but if you need the gendered term you can call the males incubi."

"That's very fascinating, Fort. I'm taking notes, I swear." In the rearview I could see Suze push up her left sleeve to the elbow and solemnly start moving her index finger on the inside of her arm in a writing motion.

It was a sleepy, rural town, heavy on big farming fields covered in snow and a few derelict buildings that suggested that the area had been having trouble hanging on to businesses. It was close enough to wilderness vacationing areas that there were a few motels and one bed-and-breakfast, but that was about it. The GPS led us down several winding two-lane roads that boasted nothing but woods until, like magic, there suddenly appeared a tidy little subdivision. The neat and wholly forgettable and generic sign at the entrance to the subdivision read CEDAR HILLS, and a short road led to a rounded cul-de-sac with four identical houses set around it. They were all modest Colonials, the kind that could be found across the country. All of them were painted a tastefully bland wheat color; all of them were in good condition, with identical driveways and a basic amount of landscaping. And for fifty-one weeks out of the year, these houses were always completely empty.

This secluded little area, existing like a ghost in its community, was where petitioners from the south and west of the country came to wait for meetings with my family. There was a similar setup in Québec for more northern visitors, and I was fairly certain that the subdivision there was identical to what I was looking at now. Our eastern border was a whole ocean, so overseas petitioners essentially had to choose where they preferred flying into—Canada or New Jersey. These tiny wait stations were set just inside our border, positioned for easy expulsion of anyone who didn't make a cut. There was no way for my family to fully police our borders against someone who just drove in—but anyone who did that was risking the death penalty that it carried if a member of the Scott family caught them. My sister had apparently made something of a name for herself over the years with how inventive she could be when it came to punishing trespassers. I'd been told that videos existed of her inventiveness.

There was a large van, the kind driven by church groups and college sports teams, parked in the driveway of the third house, and I pulled the Scirocco in behind it. Whenever a petition call came in, Madeline's local agent would drive over to one of the houses and leave a key in the mailbox. The agent was also the one who was paid to make sure that the houses were always fully maintained, and was paid well for the privilege of asking no questions. One key per group, one house for their stay, and one interview with a member of the Scott family. Decisions were final.

We all sat for a moment in the car, looking at the house. There were blinds in the windows, but we could see them being rustled. At least one of the succubi was watching. I felt a tug in the pit of my stomach. Inside were the representatives of a group that desperately wanted to get away from wherever they came from and come to the presumed safety of my mother's territory, and I was the person who represented my mother and held all that authority in my hands. Maybe it should've made me feel more excited, but mostly it just made me feel awfully depressed and a bit embarrassed.

Loren and Suze were both doing small, surreptitious checks on clothing and hair after the long drive, so I pulled my vanity mirror down as well. What I saw looking back at me was exactly what I'd expected—a guy in his late twenties who wouldn't have turned a single head on the street, either positively or negatively, with dark hair that only with the greatest reluctance would yield to styling gels. I was wearing the khaki and collared button-down combination that Suze had said made me look like I was on my way to a Christian revival picnic, and I'd traded my aging winter parka for a more dignified black wool knockoff-of-a-knockoff jacket that came to mid-thigh, and that from a distance actually looked fairly nice. I'd spent my life trying to make sure that I didn't become like the rest of my family, and while the surface still showed that, I was becoming more and more concerned about the rest of me.

Behind me, Suze made a rude noise and swatted me lightly. "I can actually *hear* your internal demotivating monologue," she said. "The best cologne in the world is power, and right now you're covered in it, so let's head in."

I deliberately didn't look at Loren, and instead just opened the door. The blast of icy January air was immediate. In the car, with the heater cranked and the weak winter sun greenhousing through the windows, it had been easy to forget how lung-bitingly cold it was. After a quick walk around the car to unlock the passenger door and release the women, who were giving me what I felt to be unnecessarily grumpy looks about not having control of their own egress, I stuffed my hands into my pockets and shuddered. With the winter wind biting at us, we headed up the walk at double time, Loren's sensibly low pumps clacking urgently against the slate panels. The door was pulled open as we neared it.

If I'd had any particular personal investment in having Suze's expectations of six-foot-tall underwear models be realized, my day would've received a quick crushing. The figure standing in the doorway was male, average height, but lean in a way that reminded me of a marathon runner, with nothing but muscle, veins, and skin. His hair was black, but with a line of pure white at the roots, as if a recent dye job was growing out. His skin had that particular orange hue of someone who was a fan of spray tanning, with the lighter patches around his eyes and at the corners of his elbows that confirmed it. From his face I would've guessed his age at not more than early thirties, but that felt oddly wrong, though I couldn't figure out why. His clothing was wildly out of season—sandals, shorts, and a thin T-shirt, and the house was definitely not heated to match.

As I stepped over the threshold and into the small foyer, I could see a woman standing a bit farther back. She was also showing the signs of spray-tanning, though hers looked a bit more evenly applied, and if I hadn't caught a glance at the palm of her left hand, I might not have suspected it. Her hair was a midbrown, but had the same line of white rootiness showing at her hairline as the man. Both of them had dark brown eyes.

The man was standing within reach, so I began what I hoped to be a solid, honest handshake, but unfortunately the amount of stress sweat on the succubus's part left the experience rather lacking in vigor—though it certainly made up for that in sheer sogginess. I concentrated on meeting his eyes and carefully resisted the urge to wipe my hand on my pants. "I'm Fortitude, Madeline Scott's son. I'm here to negotiate."

"I'm Nicholas," he responded, and immediately tipped

his head toward the woman beside him, "and this is my wife, Saskia."

"Lovely to meet you," I said, making another round of handshakes. Saskia's hand was drier, though she was shaking hard enough that I felt like I was chasing a moving object. Clearly both were under pressure. My smile must've looked like a rictus by now, but I tried to normalize and continue with introductions. "My companions are—"

"Shenanigans." Suze cut me off.

We all froze. I turned around, completely unsurprised at the sight of the long, carefully honed knife that had suddenly appeared in Suzume's hands. I could feel my muscles tense immediately, and I looked around the room, moving sideways to put myself between Loren and the two succubi, who both looked ready to faint. "What's wrong?" I asked, sliding my right hand into the pocket of my jacket. One of the things I'd liked about this coat was how well the pockets could conceal a .45. It wasn't exactly a regulation holster, but with the safety engaged I wasn't worried about it going off, and I hadn't wanted to let anyone know that I was carrying. I'd gotten more distrustful over the last year.

"This isn't just a representative pair. I smell multiple other recent scents."

I took the gun out and stared at the succubi. "If there's an explanation, I'd recommend that it starts fast."

It was Saskia who started speaking—fast and terrified, never able to take her eyes away from Suze's knife, even though I was holding a gun, and her words tumbled over one another and became incomprehensible.

Loren's hand closed over my wrist. "Look," she said softly, drawing my attention to the small figure that was just barely in view through the open archway that led into the living room. I froze at what I saw.

"Suze, put the knife away," I whispered.

"What—"

"*Look.*"

They must've been told to hide away where we wouldn't see them, but there were a lot of them, so it was understandable that one had managed to slip the leash. Peeking around the corner at us was a toddler.

We ended up in the living room. All of these houses were fully furnished, so there were sofas to sit on, along with end tables, knickknacks, and even books to fill the shelves, though it all came off looking just slightly too much like an IKEA showroom display. I sat on one long sofa, flanked on either side by Suze and Loren. Saskia and Nicholas were on the catty-corner love seat. And between them was their daughter, Julie.

It was hard to look away from Julie. Saskia and Nicholas looked just a little off, but nothing that would've looked particularly unnatural on the streets of a city like L.A., or Las Vegas, which was where they were from. But Julie stood out—she lacked the familiar level of baby chub that I'd always seen before on toddlers, and was a miniature version of the adults, built like Iggy Pop. Like her parents she had only clothing fit for an afternoon in Nevada, but they'd tried to compensate by swathing her in an adult-size hoodie that covered her from neck to knees, the kind sold at highway rest stops—this one had been bought in Illinois, judging by what was written across the front. But I could see her face and her lower legs—her skin was pale, so pale that it was translucent enough to see the blue and purple tracings of the major arteries in her legs and throat. Her lips were the color of old chalk dust. Her hair was pale, and not just the white-blond of some small children before it turns to brown, but pale like the fur on a polar bear, ranging from pure white to a dull cream. And her eyes had just barely enough pigment to be charitably called gray—it was uncomfortable to look at, which was probably why her parents were both wearing colored contacts.

She was the one I was focusing on, but I could've looked at any of the others. Six other children sat around us, from a fourteen-year-old boy down to a two-year-old who was so tightly swaddled in a blanket from one of the upstairs beds that if I hadn't been told, I wouldn't have been able to guess gender. He was held by his father, the third of the adults, though Miro was clearly unable to do anything more at the moment than hold the baby and rock back and forth—though whether that was meant for his son's benefit or his own, I had no idea. The children all had the same pale looks, the traits that the adults apparently covered up later with spray tan, hair dye, and makeup.

And according to what they were telling us, these three adults and seven children were possibly all that was left of a community that had been over fifty members strong.

"It started a month ago," Saskia said slowly, focusing on the children rather than us. "Las Vegas is pretty quiet, supernaturally speaking. Usually it's just been us and the humans, with a few roamers coming through every now and again, but we just minded our own business and kept our heads down and almost nothing ever happened. Then, overnight, there were a dozen skinwalkers walking the floor of almost every casino. Most of us ran as soon as we saw them, figured that they were just in for a convention or something, and that if we would all just take a few days off of work and lie low, then everything would be fine."

"But they started hunting you," I said grimly. I'd had a run-in with a skinwalker before—they were strong, predatory, and vicious, and Suze and I had both had our asses handed to us in a one-on-two fight. Frankly the fact that we'd made it through and even managed to kill it in the end had been more out of luck than skill. Skinwalkers were viciously dangerous, enough to make even adult vampires tread cautiously. A skinwalker had once killed one of Chivalry's previous wives and worn her skin to taunt him—that it had managed to survive for several months was a testament to just how tough and deadly they were.

"Not at first," said Nicholas, his voice choked. He coughed, then continued. "First they put out feelers, left messages. They said that they'd lost their home in Miami, and they needed to find a new place to live. They said"—his mouth twisted horribly—"they said that they wanted to share the city with us. That if we could help them settle in, that they would protect us."

"We're not strong like the vampires or like shifters," Saskia said, her eyes sad and dull. "That's why we ended up where we did, where no one else wanted to live, and where there were enough humans coming and going that we weren't afraid of being discovered. But we're vulnerable. So when the skinwalkers said that . . . we wanted to believe them."

"When did it change?" Loren asked.

"Last week. By then they knew how many of us there were, where we lived, how much money we had . . . they started with the elders. The ones who lived alone. The first night, that's who they killed. Then they left the bodies at the back doors of the ones who would be next."

There was a long silence while I tried to figure out what I could possibly say.

"They wanted us scared." Miro's voice was rusty and strained. He didn't look at anyone while he talked, just rocked his son faster. "They wanted us running, so that they could chase us. When my wife—" He stopped, swallowed, then pushed on. "I was carrying Kirby, and she was behind us. When the skinwalker caught her, he said that we were their housewarming present."

"You're the group that had the children," Suzume said. Her expression was completely neutral, but her eyes were alert, and I could see the wheels cranking in her head. "The group with the weakest and slowest, but you were the ones who made it to safety."

"The rest said that they would give us two days." Saskia wasn't even whispering. The children in the room were unnaturally quiet and still—for a moment I wondered why they'd been allowed to stay, but then I realized how pointless that feeling was. They'd already seen people die around them. It was no use pretending they didn't know. "They would stay in Vegas for two more days, to keep the skinwalkers occupied, so that we would have a head start. Then, if anyone is left"—she choked, and corrected herself—"everyone who *is* left, will follow."

Beside me, Loren made a small sound, softly enough that if my hearing hadn't made some significant steps up during the last few months of my transition to being a full vampire, I might've missed it. It was a sad, despairing sound.

This group had no power, nothing strong to offer. It was quite possible that these three adults were the only ones left alive.

"You're not really here because you wanted to emigrate." Suze's voice was like Joe Friday's—nothing but the facts, ma'am. "You're refugees, and you're looking for asylum."

I slid forward on the seat, not wanting to give either of the women beside me the chance to catch my eye, and I focused on the group in front of me. "Suzume is right. So tell me what you need, and what you can offer my family."

I'd been hoping that they were also carrying all the liquid financial assets of their group—I knew that I'd be making a tough pitch to my family, and I'd been hoping for something to grease the wheels. But unfortunately this group was flat broke. They'd had the cash that they had on them, but had been afraid to use any credit cards in case the skinwalkers knew how to track those purchases. Early in their trip they'd tried to get cash out of ATMs, only to discover that their accounts had been emptied, undoubtedly thanks to the skinwalkers, who'd had ample access to their homes and financial records. None of them had owned a car big enough to transport everyone, so they'd dumped their cars and stolen a church youth group van, swapping its plates as often as they could to try to muddy the trail. The adults had driven straight in shifts, a few times even pressing the fourteen-year-old into service when they were on back roads, stopping only when they needed to put gas in the car. Everything they'd eaten had come from highway rest stations, and they hadn't even dared to spend the money it would've taken to get seasonally appropriate clothing for everyone, just a few pairs of hoodies and sweatpants that they could trade off between the people who had to go outside the car to fill the gas or hit a restroom.

"You need safety—that's clear to anyone looking at you," Suze interrupted. There wasn't anything cruel in her voice, just coldly practical. "But he has to go back to his family and know what to ask for. What kinds of jobs do you do? Where do you need to live? We know you have some need to hunt people—you're going to need to be more specific, though." Even as I winced at her words, I knew that she was right. If it had been up to me, I would've let them in and settled them deep in the territory where the skinwalkers wouldn't dare go, but it wasn't. Even if they'd been a strong, wealthy group with lots to offer, I couldn't have said yes. I was getting information, finding preliminary common ground, and then I'd be going back to my mother to get the real decision.

I could call myself the negotiator, but I had no authority to make deals on. The last time I'd been given that authority, I put a werebear into power that my family would've preferred to see dead—my mother had made it very clear that she wasn't risking a repeat of that.

Suze's questions seemed to calm Saskia down, though, maybe because it gave her something to focus on besides the terror of the skinwalkers' attacks and their frantic race to the Scott border. "We would need a city that has a large transitory population, lots of people who are going to come, then leave again quickly."

"Like Las Vegas," I noted. "Atlantic City is outside our borders, and so is New York City, but we do have the Connecticut casinos like Foxwoods and Mohegan Sun. Are these the kinds of places that would suit you?" Beside me, Loren had slid a pad of paper out of her satchel and was taking careful notes.

Saskia nodded vigorously. "I was a card dealer—I'm not good enough for the big-time high-roller tables, but I had steady work at smaller casinos. Nicholas worked at a car-rental agency at the airport, and Miro was a hotel concierge."

I nodded. Those weren't highly paying jobs but were at least the kind that transferred easily—and with my mother's interest in politics, I was sure that she had one or two people in her Rolodex who could arrange to make sure that open positions could be found. I braced myself, and made my voice get a bit harder. The next part was important. "Now tell me how you feed, and why you need a transitory population."

There was an awkward pause, like the moment at the doctor's office when it's explained that you need to drop your pants for the rest of the exam. It's not unexpected, but it is awkward. Saskia and Nicholas glanced at each other, one of those looks that longtime couples have where they almost seem to telepathically exchange information, and it was Saskia who extended her arm, then turned it over to expose the soft underside.

For a second nothing happened; then I saw a little ripple at her wrist, and something very thin, decidedly sharp, and almost completely colorless extruded itself outward. I had no desire to lean forward, so I was glad that my vision was good. At first it was just a little prong extending an inch from her wrist, but then it lengthened until it stretched up to the middle of her palm, a long, delicate appendage, gleaming slightly with moisture, but drying quickly. And once it was dry, I almost couldn't see it against the skin of her hand because of its translucency.

"It's a feeding prong." Saskia moved her hand slightly, showing how the prong could move on its own. "It's as painless as a tick bite when it goes in, but there's a small venom that goes with it that works within a breath. The venom doesn't cause damage; it just makes the human blank out for about two minutes. If I insert my prong when I'm shaking someone's hand, then they'll just stand there, and I can pretend that I'm talking to them while I feed. If I'm sitting next to someone at a bar and they're wearing short sleeves, I can brush against them and feed. It can be on an elevator, in a lobby—anyplace where it wouldn't seem odd to see two people standing or sitting beside each other for two minutes while one person talks and the other looks completely uninterested."

"And what are you feeding on?" I knew what my family fed on—blood. But my sister had shown me what feeding on a human looked like, and it sure didn't take two minutes. "And since you're talking about quick, chance encounters, I assume that you aren't taking repeat feedings."

"We're feeding on . . ." Saskia looked at Nicholas, who shrugged a little. She gave an apologetic smile. "I've never described it to an outsider before. It's not a liquid as far as we know. We call what we take *daya hipup*. The closest translation to that is 'vitality.' One feeding will leave someone exhausted, but no more than you'd expect after a wild weekend in Vegas. But we need it, and without it we'll sicken and die. And we could take multiple feedings from one person, but . . ." She paused. "It wouldn't be a good idea."

"I'm sorry, but you need to be specific," I said.

Nicholas leaned forward, resting a hand on Saskia's leg. Between them, Julie looked up, as eerily attentive as the rest of the silent children. "The problem is with what we leave behind." He was clearly uncomfortable to be talking about this, but he took a deep breath and continued. "We leave contagion, and sickness. One feeding from us and the human will develop a urinary tract infection within a day or two. A second feeding, or even worse, a third, and the human will end up with something that looks indistinguishable from syphilis, and will act the same way."

"You spread VD," Suze said, almost musingly. "They'll have to update the posters at the bus stops and subway stations."

Nicholas's mouth pressed into an angry line while Saskia immediately said, "We're very careful. We feed on people when they're leaving the casino or the city, not on their way in."

"But is there any way for you to tell which human you or any other succubus has fed on before?" Loren was supremely calm as she asked the question, her pen never stopping its path across the page as she took shorthand of the conversation. I wondered exactly how many of these conversations she'd heard over the years, and how many times she'd listened as humans were described as the entrées to meals. She'd inherited this job from her father—how had he explained to her what his job was, and what kind of family business he'd hoped that she'd step into?

The couple glanced at each other again, and I knew the answer even before Saskia reluctantly said it. "No. No way. But our numbers are small, and only one partner in a pair hunts at a time. There's no way to mark a human in a way that would stick out to another succubus without the human wondering what is going on, so we've mostly relied on the law of averages. In a city like Las Vegas, the odds of a human encountering two succubi on the same last day of their visit was low. The odds of them being fed on by another succubus on a later trip were even lower."

"Pair?" I asked. "Like a marriage?"

"It's not a bad parallel, but not complete either." Saskia looked down at the toddler snuggled between her and Nicholas. "Two succubi become a pair when they've decided to have a child, and the pair stays together until the child is ready to hunt on its own, because the parents are both needed to feed it." She hesitated. "We feed our children with a secondary prong that's under our tongues, but it's not a particularly . . . elegant process."

"I can pass on the demonstration," I assured them. "When can children hunt for themselves?"

"Around sixteen, but usually we continue to supplement them for a little while afterward. They're fully independent at twenty."

They were syphilis-spreading albatrosses. I couldn't figure out whether this was sweet or creepy, but I did remember to shoot Suze a quick look that warned her not to say a word. She gave me a hurt look, clearly indicating that my impulse had been right, and she'd had a particularly choice remark waiting. "The kids don't blend in very well. Even in New England, which as you can see from Fort is known for producing pasty, your children would stick out as pale." That was as close as Suze came to being diplomatic.

"We always homeschooled, at least while they're

young," Nicholas explained. "Even if our babies didn't visually stick out, we needed to keep them home anyway. Prong control isn't reliable for several years, and it's not like we could just provide bagged lunches for what the kids need. Around high school we sent them to public school—for socialization if nothing else."

"So you normally have a two-to-one ratio of feeders and eaters—and now you have three adults and seven children." I said the numbers slowly. "Exactly how well has that been working out?"

"We understood the rules," Nicholas said quickly, almost falling over himself to assure me. The expression on his face, though, clearly said that the honest answer would've been *not well*. "We haven't hunted on the Scott property, and we won't without permission. Saskia, Miro, and I will take turns making small runs into Pennsylvania to hunt enough to sustain the children."

"And in Pennsylvania?"

"It's not even close to ideal," Saskia acknowledged. "We don't know if anyone followed us, but we'd be fools to push our luck. Hunts will have to be fast, and we'll have to feed heavier than we'd like to. We're in a rural area, without a lot of people or movement. We'll try to find truck stops or highway diners, places where people are just passing through, but it will be harder to initiate casual contact—" Her voice had been steadily rising as she spoke, stress and worry bleeding through. Beside her, Julie wiggled and crawled into her father's lap. The movement startled Saskia, and I could see her strain to pull herself back, to soften her voice. She was begging, and it hurt to see it. "We're grateful that the Scotts were willing to hear our case," she said, even as her hands tightened hard on the edge of the sofa. Beside her, Nicholas rubbed their daughter's back soothingly. "It's hard to even say what a relief it is to be able to put the children to bed and tell them that they're safe in this house."

I knew she wanted to say the words, and that she wouldn't let herself. It was Loren who said them, leaning forward slightly. "But you need to plan for the long term," she said. "You need jobs, hunting rights, a place to settle and rebuild. You need an answer."

"Yes," Saskia whispered. Looking down, I could see that the children, who had seemed so still, had been slowly shifting and creeping, and now they were pressed as closely against where the adults were sitting as possible. Those pale faces were sneaking glances at me—me, the person who had the right to just tell them all to leave the house, leave the state, and live or die somewhere where I didn't have to see it or be responsible for it.

I'd spent years running from this kind of responsibility. In honesty, a large part of me wanted nothing more than to tear out the front door—but the last months had shown me the costs of trusting that someone else would come along and handle situations like this one.

They *would* get handled. In a way that resulted in bodies in shallow graves.

"I'll get you an answer," I promised. I wanted to promise more, but I couldn't. If I could be careful, do this right, I could help make things safe for this group—but it meant playing by the rules and doing my best for them. "I'll be meeting with my family tomorrow morning, and I will tell you now that I'll be pushing for us to take you in." I'd run fast calculations in my head—all I had to do to schedule the meeting was to ask Loren to put it on the family calendar (we did e-mail notifications—it was charmingly corporate of us) and we would gather. I could've asked her to push it for that evening, but I wasn't sure whether Chivalry would be back from New Hampshire yet—I knew him well enough to know that if he spotted any antique stores or adorable co-ops or (heaven help us) some hole-in-the-wall art gallery along the road, it would add hours to his ETA. And when I made this proposal to my mother, I wanted to make sure that Chivalry was there as a potential vote in my corner—because I already knew what my sister's response would be.

I wasn't used to having jobs where people relied on me for something important. If I wasn't able to get someone a latte fast enough, or if I was slow bagging groceries, or if I was a terrible telemarketer, no one ever got hurt, because nothing was ever really at risk. That wasn't the case anymore. And the look of desperate hope in their eyes at what I'd said, hope that rested in *me*, was enough to redouble that urge to run for the hills. I devoutly hoped that nothing on my face was indicating to the succubi how much I was longing to go back to my apartment and create a pillow fort to stand between me and the world I'd found myself in.

"We're going to leave several of these financial forms with you," I said, gesturing to Loren's satchel. "I know that you're going to have to leave a lot of blanks, but I want you to fill them out as honestly as you can. We have to run a credit score and a few other things, but Loren and I know that at this point you're almost certainly victims of identity fraud, so don't worry about that. You'll have probably about forty minutes to do that before we get back."

"Get back?" Nicholas looked confused.

"I'm echoing what he said." Suze lifted an eyebrow. "Where are we going that we're heading back?"

"We're going to pick up some pizzas for everyone."

As I'd hoped, it turned out that eerily quiet, horribly traumatized children with feeding prongs in multiple parts of their bodies could still perk up at the word *pizza*.

I'd broken my phone recently, and the one I'd replaced it with was talk and text and nothing else. Suze lived an active lifestyle that was similarly hard on phones, and her phone was barely better than that. Fortunately for both of us, Loren was in possession of the smartest and shiniest of smartphones, and was able to direct us to a local pizza place, where I ordered half a dozen large cheese pies. I'd taken a quick look in the Supplicant House kitchen before I left—there were a few cans of tomato soup, an assortment of cereal boxes, and a bag of rice, things that wouldn't go bad and that could cover one or two meals, but that was it. Pizza was an easy answer for one night, and if they had leftovers, then they'd also have lunch for the next day.

As we stood inside the pizza place, enjoying the heat from the ovens, Loren was her usual quiet, diplomatic self. And Suzume was also herself.

"Fort, what have I told you over and over again about things like this?" She was keeping her voice low enough that the people behind the counter couldn't hear what we were talking about, but it was pretty obvious that this was the early stage of a couple disagreement. "No money, no allies, nothing to offer. We might as well boot them out of the territory now, tell them to run for the Canadian border, and hope for their sakes that the skinwalkers either lose interest or don't like cold weather."

"Nothing is certain." I looked out the front windows. There was a bank across the street—the same kind of bank I had an account at, actually.

"I think that I could place a very reliable bet on how Prudence is going to react when you want to give this group asylum at a cut-rate price." Suze was grim.

"My mother is in charge, not Prudence, and she's surprised us all before." A few times. Personally I was hoping that an argument of asylum now, hugely crippling tithes later was going to appeal to her. "Listen, Suze, do me a favor and pay for the pizzas while I run across the street."

"Wait, you want me to—" Suze saw what I was look-

ing at and groaned loudly. "Oh no. Fort, you are the softest touch I've ever met."

"I'll pay you back next week," I promised as I darted
out the door. There was almost no traffic to speak of in
this tiny little main street, so I walked across the street,
balancing awkwardly on the piles of skuzzy snow left
behind by the plows.

I didn't want to do what I was about to do. Just walking into the bank branch made me grit my teeth, and
picking up one of the blank withdrawal forms was almost physically painful. It wasn't as if I was the kind of
guy who could toss away a few hundred dollars and not
feel the sting of it. But I reminded myself that, thanks to
my brother, my half of the rent was paid up for three
more months. And while the Scirocco had had a number
of expenses when I first purchased it—notably the alter-
nator, the timing belt, the interior fuel pump (that had
actually been a tricky one, because unbeknownst to me,
the Scirocco had been built like a Klingon and had *two*
pumps, one internal and one high-pressure one on the
outside), plus a leaking exhaust manifold, it was at a
point where it ran pretty reliably now. There were some
rust issues, but I could keep buying myself time on those
by just slapping primer paint over them.

There wasn't a line in front of the teller, which I was
grateful for. Too much time and I might've talked myself
out of this. Working for my family plus picking up a bit
of extra with a part-time job had been good for me, and
I'd built up six hundred dollars in my checking account
that didn't have to go to any bill. It had been a very long
time since I had that much in my account *plus* a working
vehicle.

I withdrew it all. Payday was this week, I reminded
myself. I could live on the twenty-three dollars that was
in my wallet. The six hundreds went into my back pocket.

Returning to the pizza parlor, where Suze stared at

me disapprovingly through the window, I wondered how much it cost to get seasonal clothing for seven kids and three adults, plus fill up the van (which had to be a gas guzzler), plus put food on the table for however long it would take me to convince my mother to let them into the territory permanently. Suddenly the six hundred didn't seem like much at all.

Both women were waiting for me. "Ms. Hollis thinks that you're planning on giving the succubi some money. Is this true?" Loren looked curious.

"Just what I had in my account. It's not that much." I hesitated, then asked, "Loren, I'll make sure that you're reimbursed from petty cash—could you give me whatever money you have on you?"

Something flickered across her face. She was surprised—and like a good butler, Loren almost never showed it when she was surprised. "Did that bank have an ATM?"

"In the front." Relief filled me. "Just whatever you can spare right now, and I promise that you'll get it back."

She left. Unlike me, she went to the corner before crossing. It was hard to imagine Loren Noka crunching her way over a snow wall, though even if that was her secret vice, it wasn't as if I could expect her to do it in pumps. As it was, my formal shoes now had a solid coating of road salt that I'd probably have to scrub off tonight. Beside me, Suze just shook her head in disgust.

Loren came back and handed me a folded wad of twenties. "Here's two hundred," she said, then held up a hand. "Don't say anything, Fortitude. I've worked for your family all my life, and I respect them terribly, but . . . they wouldn't have done this, or thought of this. Not even Mr. Scott. So don't say anything." She cleared her throat loudly.

We both looked at Suze. She looked back at us.

A long minute passed.

"Fuck you," she snapped, then zipped her parka up to her nose and pulled on her gloves. She stomped across the street, hopping the snow walls with the perfect balance and grace of a gymnast, and disappeared into the bank. A minute later she was heading back, and then she was shoving the door to the pizza restaurant open with bad temper and pushing two crumpled hundreds into my hands. "I'll be adding a service fee to my bill for this," she warned.

"Thank you, Suze," I said.

"I'm expecting big things in return for this," she said darkly. "*Sexy underpants* things."

I pretended not to have heard her because Loren was standing right there, along with several very curious locals, but I heard and received the message. After all, the car radio hadn't been the only thing she got me for Christmas.

We stopped back at the Supplicant House just long enough to deliver the pizzas and the money to the succubi. The looks on their faces—the creeping expression of a hope that they were terrified to accept lest it prove just another terrible trick, were painful to see. By unspoken consent, the three of us hurried out again as soon as we were able and then we were back on Route 80 and heading for home. None of us spoke much—there didn't seem to be anything that felt right to say. Too much was resting on us.

Even Suze felt it, because we drove for forty minutes in silence before she leaned forward and cued her iPod up for Babymetal.

Chapter Two

Loren lived two towns over from Newport, on the mainland—like a lot of the people who worked in Newport, she had chosen to save money by buying a home outside the tourist hot spots and accepting the off-set of a longer commute and the cost of daily bridge tolls on her way to and from work.

"I'll schedule the meeting as soon as I go inside," Loren promised as she heaved herself out of my low-slung car while I stood beside the door like a particularly attentive date or well-trained chauffeur. Given the current state of my bank account, however, fixing the lock pin had just plummeted down my list of possible expenditures. "Ten a.m.?"

I nodded my agreement—Loren knew what she was doing. I'd originally been in favor of hauling everyone together as early as possible tomorrow to start talking about what the succubi needed, but Loren had advised me against that approach, noting that my brother was driving back home late this evening and would probably be tired, my sister was not exactly known to be a morning person, and my mother liked to watch the morning news shows and got slightly put out when she couldn't. We wanted people in good, pleasantly receptive moods. Ten was late enough in the morning that everyone would've been able to have a leisurely breakfast and gotten a few morning tasks out of the way.

Loren's house was an older Victorian, gorgeously painted and maintained but wedged in on its sides by her neighbors, and she had no garage on the property, just a largish storage shed at the end of her skinny driveway. When I'd picked her up that morning, her compact Honda was parked in front of the shed, and I had wondered how many times during our trip to and from New Jersey she'd regretted not suggesting that she drive us in her car, however economy-sized. Now, though, the Scirocco's headlights illuminated a second car parked behind the Honda—this one was a Volvo SUV. Loren headed up her walkway, taking her keys out of her purse as she went, and I practically leaped back into the heated interior of the Scirocco, grumbling quietly to Suze, "Now, why the hell weren't we driving *that* to Hardwick?" I appreciated the Scirocco's fuel efficiency, but there was something to say for basic comfort, and it had not been a vehicle intended to transport multiple people.

Suze was climbing agilely from the backseat to the front. "That's her wife's car. She needs it to ferry their kids to soccer practice and oboe lessons."

I stared at her. "How do you know that? You just met Loren this morning—how could you know things about her personal life that I don't after working with her since summer?"

"Maybe I'm more approachable," Suze said, stretching out in the passenger seat.

"Really?" In honesty, I hadn't thought much about Loren's personal life before now, for the same reason that I never really spent much time thinking about Alfred's personal life when I watched Batman movies. I'd intellectually known that she didn't just hang herself up in the closet at the end of the evening, and the days of servants sleeping in the attics and having no personal lives were (much to my mother's regret) long over. There were still a handful of my mother's staff who lived on-site and were provided rooms, but Loren wasn't one of them.

Suze laughed at my expression. "No, not really. I tailed her for a few days."

I stalled the Scirocco out in the process of backing out of Loren's driveway. "You *what*?"

"Spied on her, Fort. Don't look so shocked. I pulled her financials while I was at it. Her oldest kid got into an Ivy League school. I hope for her bank account's sake that the younger two go state. Plus, her wife works at a nonprofit, and I have to say, the pay really matches the name."

I blew out a heavy breath and resumed driving, even as my temper spiked. "Is there any particular reason that you decided to violate Loren's privacy, Suze?"

There was a long silence, and when I finally glanced over while we sat at a red light, I saw that she was giving me a long, level stare. After I'd finally made eye contact, she raised her eyebrows a little. Her voice was utterly flat and serious. "Don't be naïve. Loren Noka is loyal to your mother, and to your brother. She's worked for them since she was fifteen, and probably did odd jobs or helped out her dad even earlier than that. But you've only worked with her for a few months—don't think that loyalty automatically transfers. I wanted to check her out."

"You're thinking about a succession," I said quietly. "About what happens when my mother dies."

Her eyebrows arched even higher. "Aren't you?"

I was, of course. That is, I was thinking about my mother's death. Despite popular myths, vampires weren't immortal. We were born, we aged, and we died—though we did have centuries more on the clock than any human. I had always thought of my mother as basically immortal—I was probably like any other child in that respect. It was maybe a little more excusable on my part—my mother had been born before the fall of Constantinople. But she'd been weakening recently, and now it was an open topic throughout the territory—when would Madeline Scott die, and what would that mean for those who lived within her borders?

But I was thinking very little about the territory. I was thinking about my mother. My terrifying, murderous, ancient, powerful mother. Who loved me. My feelings for her were too complicated to just be called love. And it wasn't just her death and its loss—I was standing on the threshold of my transition into full vampire adulthood, but for the moment I was still reliant on my mother for my blood needs. I fed on her, and because of that, I didn't have to feed on humans the way my siblings did. And I really, really didn't want to have to start preying on humans.

And at the moment, I certainly didn't want to have a conversation about any of that. So, without even an attempt at grace, I changed the subject. "You seemed awfully quiet in today's meeting with the succubi."

"Really?" Suze gave a crooked grin. "You're going to go there after that diplomacy crack?"

"You know what I mean. I was the one doing most of the talking. Even Loren asked more questions than you did."

Suze snorted. "Well, talking was your job, wasn't it? Besides, I was doing my job and watching your back. While you were engaging in active listening and figuring out what questions to ask, I was making sure that I was ready to slice anyone who suddenly came after you."

"You talk more when it's you and me out together. Like when we were figuring out the selkie shakedown in the fall. You talked plenty then."

"That's different," she noted. "That's us being our own buddy-cop movie, and it's awesome. I mean, jeez, I got to punch a seal in the face. That was basically a life-time achievement unlocked right there. When we're hunting shit down and policing the territory, there are always good opportunities for violence. With this, though . . . Fort, I hate to say it, but freaking diplomacy and taxes are not exactly my areas of primary interest or, dare I even say it, expertise."

I turned the Scirocco onto the entrance ramp for the highway, settled into the middle lane, and just let habit steer us home. "Yeah, but your grandmother—"

She snickered. "Fort, I'm going to stop you right there. My grandmother figured out my strengths years ago. I definitely got to focus on tussling and being a general badass. Keiko was the one who got stuck with reading stuff like Miyamoto Musashi's *A Book of Five Rings*." Suze's grandmother, Atsuko Hollis, was the matriarch of the kitsune in Providence, and Suze's twin sister was her designated heir. Though Keiko had been up to a few things lately that the White Fox would not have been pleased with.

"But the succubi—"

"You're just setting yourself up for heartbreak, and I wish you wouldn't." For all the harshness of her words, they were almost gently spoken. "You want to help them, but coming to the Scott territory was their Hail Mary move. Your mother hasn't allowed any succubi in before— why would she change her mind now? Because she feels bad for them? That doesn't exactly sound like usual behavior from Madeline Scott."

"You heard what I did—you saw what I saw. Don't you want to help the succubi?" It was that terrible, reluctant hope that had been on their faces when I gave them the money and the pizzas that hurt the most. They hadn't had that when we first showed up. I'd given them a sliver of hope, and now it was resting on me. If I failed, and betrayed that hope, then it would be worse than if I'd just kicked them out of the Supplicant House as soon as I saw them.

Suze made a rude sound. "I'm going to tell you about something very important that I learned about from watching lots of TV shows about spies—it's called compartmentalization. Bad things happen, Fort, and people get hurt. But you need to limit your efforts to the people who are most important to you, or you'll just get burned out or rubbed out."

I glanced over at her. It was past six thirty, and fully dark. I could see only a little of her expression in the lights from the highway and the passing cars.

"Besides," she continued, "if you keep asking me to front money for pizzas and children's clothing, it's going to be like that time that I sent ten bucks to the Humane Society. Fifteen years later and I still get annoying mail from them."

I sighed. "Listen, I'll write you a check when we get back to the apartment. Just . . . don't cash it for about a week."

She poked me in the ribs then, and there was a softness on her face, a smile. "I don't want you to change, Fort," she said suddenly, surprising me. "I'm not trying to nag you into not caring. I like who you are right now, and I'm not going to suddenly try to remake you just because I've lifted tail for you. I just don't want you to end up like a marshmallow Peep in the microwave of the world."

I couldn't help laughing at her analogy, and the tension in the car eased. She slid her left hand comfortably onto my leg, letting it rest there as we drove along, and when I didn't need to shift gears I let my own hand drop down onto hers, holding it loosely. There was a long silence, broken only by passing trucks howling down the highway.

I finally spoke. "Okay, now I really want some Peeps." Why had she chosen an analogy that involved a seasonal snack that wouldn't be on shelves for another three months?

"Oh my God, me too!" Suze immediately responded.

We pulled into the parking lot of my apartment building just after eight. Parking the Scirocco was a delicate endeavor because of the building manager's approach to snow removal, which could charitably be referred to as problematic. Mr. Jennings was not a fan of paying the plow service, and any snow accumulation below four inches was judged by him as insufficient to justify calling the plow guy. Unfortunately for those of us who actually lived in the building, it wasn't unusual during the winter to wake up to an inch one morning, then a few days later another three inches, then another two. Things started getting problematic when the temperature never got warm enough for there to be a melt between snowfalls, and suddenly the parking lot started having some serious snow accumulation, all of which Mr. Jennings insisted was not his problem.

This had resulted in a lot of shoveling on the part of me and my roommate, Dan, given that we were the only able-bodied residents of the building. The ground floor was an upscale women's lingerie boutique that had never had access to the parking lot to begin with, and the second-floor apartment was occupied by Mrs. Bandyopadyay, who was in her eighties and, while still impressively spry and mobile, was not exactly in shoveling shape. So a parking lot that had previously been, if not exactly roomy, but at least comfortably able to handle our two cars plus Mrs. Bandyopadyay's ancient Buick Roadmaster (used only when Mrs. Bandyopadyay had to go to a funeral), plus the cars of our significant others from time to time, had suddenly become exceedingly claustrophobic as walls of snow began to accumulate. Right now we'd been keeping our fingers crossed for a bit of a thaw to bring the snow back down again; otherwise we were going to have to seriously consider spending an afternoon moving one of our snow piles over.

I glanced over at Suze as we pulled into the parking lot. We'd stopped for dinner at a branch of the Newport Creamery on our way back into the city, so both of us were comfortably sated with greasy diner food and excellent milk shakes. It was entirely possible that she would decide to saunter over to her Audi Coupe and head back to her own house in the Silver Lake neighborhood for the night. We hadn't been dating long enough for there to be an automatic assumption of an overnight, and frankly we were still working on navigating the particular ins and outs of this relationship.

One thing I valued about Suze, however, was her appreciation of the straightforward approach. Unlike my previous girlfriends, where getting them into my apartment for some sex and an overnight visit had involved carefully considered bait and the emotional equivalent of defusing a nuclear bomb with five minutes on the clock, Suze didn't mind if I just asked her if she wanted to sleep over. Bless her.

"So," I said. "I believe you brought up the subject of sexy underpants earlier?"

"Hell yeah. I'm on that offer like maggots on roadkill."

"That . . . is not exactly keeping up with the mood I was hoping for."

She grinned. "Put on those underpants I got you and you'll see how fast I can get in the mood."

We got out of the car, the icy night air enough to take my breath away. I shoved my right hand in my pocket, and grabbed my duffel bag with my left—the duffel was where I kept all the particular tools of my trade stashed—a Colt .45, an Ithaca 37 shotgun with the barrel sawed down, and a spare pair of pants (which I learned the hard way was an essential tool of the trade during a never-to-be-repeated incident in Maine). Suze stopped over at her Audi long enough to fish a small backpack out of her trunk—one that I knew from experience contained her toiletries, fresh underpants, and a spare shirt.

"Not that I'm complaining about the result they get," I said, linking our arms together as we walked across the slick parking lot (Mr. Jennings was a skinflint about rock salt too), "and I'm definitely not suggesting that you get more creative, but I'm still not sure how a pair of trunk underpants from Jockey count as sexy underwear. Even if they *are* red."

Suze gave a long-suffering sigh. "Fort, you're the king of the Fruit of the Loom boxer brief multipack. *Clearly* you're not going to get this one."

"I'm just saying that it's kind of annoying that the 'sexy' underpants don't have a fly. It's kind of inconvenient."

She snorted, very loudly, as we walked into the apartment stairwell and began climbing the three flights of stairs to my floor. "Yes, you have to drop trou to pee. How unspeakably difficult for you. I'll cry you a river of sympathy after you spend one day in a thong, panty hose, pencil skirt, and heels, with only a public restroom to pee in."

I dodged the suggestion. "Let me just point out that I very happily wear the sexy clothing you got me, whereas I have yet to see you in what I bought *you* for Christmas."

"And you won't," she growled dangerously, "because I burned it in effigy and salted the earth where the ashes fell."

For some reason she hadn't appreciated getting a T-shirt with WHAT DOES THE FOX SAY? emblazoned across the chest, although her expression when she'd first seen it was priceless. While Suze normally enjoyed depictions of foxes in the media (and in fact still owned the Disney *Fox and the Hound* nightgown that she'd worn as a little girl), she had developed a particular loathing for the viral video that had spawned the catchphrase.

Entering the apartment, we greeted my roommate, Dan, and his boyfriend, Jaison, who were comfortably ensconced on the couch and watching a movie. I could tell at a glance that it was Dan's pick of film—for one thing, Jaison looked mind-numbingly bored. For another, Benedict Cumberbatch (Dan's not-so-secret star crush) was on the screen. And the movie wasn't *Star Trek: Into Darkness*—that rare moment when Dan and Jaison's interests had overlapped into a perfect Venn diagram.

"Taking a break from studying?" I asked Dan as I hung my jacket on the ancient coatrack that had mysteriously appeared in my apartment after Chivalry's first visit several years ago, along with a set of matching dish towels (though the dish towels had long ago been stolen by one of my earlier, former, immensely shittier roommates).

"I'll get another hour in after this is over," Dan said. He was a second-year law student at Johnson & Wales University, and studied more than I had ever even dreamed possible. Of course, my highest academic accomplishment had been a bachelor's degree in film studies, where apart from a few pretty decent film theory textbooks (most of which I'd actually even kept after graduation—one currently helped keep my desk level), most of my homework had involved watching movies—a high percentage of which had actually even been good. Being around Dan was a daily reinforcement of the many reasons why I wasn't interested in getting a graduate degree.

Jaison gave a theatrically heavy sigh and stretched one long arm around Dan's shoulders, a comical look of amusement stretching across his dark-skinned face. He was a general contractor, and while he managed to put more physical work into an eight-hour period than most people attempted in a week, he considered work done when he left the job site. He even held off on returning calls about bidding for jobs or client questions until he was back in his truck and heading to the site the next morning.

The two of them contrasted more than in just their work philosophies and film tastes (Dan tended toward moody dramas of the English variety, while Jaison had quickly become my go-to partner for dragging our respective dates to every geeky film there was—we'd managed to hit *Guardians of the Galaxy* twice before Suze and Dan brokered a rare mutual peace agreement for the sake of boycotting future viewings). Jaison was well over six feet tall and favored broken-in jeans, tees, and sweatshirts, while Dan was barely five-five and spent most of his life looking like he'd just wandered off the pages of *Esquire*. And, of course, there was the small detail that of the four people in the apartment at the moment, Jaison was the only human. And, coincidentally, the only one who was completely unaware that the supernatural actually existed.

Dan was a ghoul—and while he didn't exactly feast on the flesh of humans, he did dine on human organs several nights out of the week. He didn't kill people, of course—none of the ghouls who lived in the Providence community did that. Why go through all the fuss and possible exposure of killing people when people died every day? Ghouls owned local funeral homes and worked in medical pathology, just the kinds of places where they would have plenty of access to fresh human bodies that had no more need of any of their delicious, vitamin-heavy organs. Those were harvested and distributed to the rest of the ghouls—though apparently there were also at least two ghoul-owned butcher shops in the

Providence area. If I'd still been eating meat, I admit that that would've given me pause.

Jaison craned his head back to look at me. "Hey, Fort. Did you see Ninja Kitty anywhere when you came in?"

Beside him, I could see Dan suppressing a sigh. When Suzume and I had started dating, I hadn't quite realized how much time she'd be spending at the apartment in fox form. We'd been good friends for months, so she'd long been a regular fixture around the apartment, and she and Jaison got along well (Suze and Dan . . . that was a different story), but in the past she'd primarily kept to human form, particularly when we weren't the only ones in the apartment. That had changed, slowly at first, then in a big way over the last two to three weeks. Dan and I had actually been worried enough to try to have a serious conversation together about how exactly we were going to explain to Jaison why there was a fox scampering around the apartment.

Our big mistake, of course, had been in asking Suze if she could try to avoid taking fox form when there was a chance that Jaison could spot her. Naturally the very next time the two of them had been in the apartment together, Suze excused herself on the pretext of being really tired, and a black fox had sauntered into the living room and jumped up on the sofa next to Jaison, tail wagging delightedly, ready for a belly rub. It was a good thing that Dan and I had healthy cholesterol levels, because the moment had nearly given both of us heart attacks.

Of course, with Suze's ability to mess with perception, she'd had the situation completely under control. Jaison had been startled at the sudden appearance of a friendly black cat, but certainly not shocked the way he would've been by a fox. We watched as Jaison rubbed her long foxy face and called her a nice kitty, and that was our only hint about what he was seeing. Suze had deliberately not influenced the way that Dan and I were seeing her, which she later admitted to me had been partially because Dan and I both had at least some expectation of seeing a fox in the apartment, and it would've therefore been harder to trick our minds. But mostly because Suze had gotten substantial thrills out of fucking with the two of us.

Thus had been born the fiction of Ninja Kitty, the stray cat who was mysteriously able to enter and exit our apartment at will. And, in the classic tradition of Superman and Clark Kent, the possibility that Suzume and Ninja Kitty could be one and the same was so unbelievably far-fetched that it never even crossed Jaison's mind. Not even Ninja Kitty's noted habit of "accidentally" knocking over Dan's stacks of study flash cards and how often she seemed to find herself sitting on his open textbooks tipped Jaison off. Of course, Dan knew that she was doing it deliberately—but couldn't even hint about it when Jaison was around, marveling at Ninja Kitty's consistency.

"No, haven't spotted her tonight," I answered Jaison.

"I hope she's okay," he worried. "The temperature is supposed to drop below zero tonight."

"I'm sure she'll be fine." Poor Jaison. He was a devoted cat lover, but couldn't have one himself because he lived with his grandmother, who was allergic. The more often Jaison spent time with Suze's alter ego, the more I could see the wheels turning in his head as he tried to figure out a way to convince Dan to adopt Ninja Kitty full-time for him.

"She knows how to get in, Jaison," Suze said, with a blandness utterly at odds with the glee in her eyes. "I'm sure if it's too cold for her outside, she'll show up."

"Given her level of socialization, I bet that she has her own home," Dan said, giving Suze an icy look. "Maybe she's spending more time there."

Before Dan and Suze could fully engage, I plopped down on the sofa and redirected things. "What are we watching?"

"Parade's End," Jaison said. "The British World War One masterpiece about a man who never gets laid. Portrayed by Benedict Cumberbatch."

"Jeez, Fort. Before I broke your dry spell, that could've been the story of your life." Suze grinned and settled herself down in the armchair. It was a recent addition to the living room, obtained after Dan and I agreed that a three-person sofa was not quite up to handling the seating demands of two couples. A few days spent cruising Craigslist, and the assistance of Jaison's truck, and we had a new armchair, tastefully upholstered in acid green corduroy. We were even moderately confident that no one had died in it (the seller had sworn that the tenant whose apartment he was emptying had died in the bedroom, not the living room).

"You people have no appreciation of film," Dan said. "Fort, support me."

"The British cinematic tradition of people staring intently at each other in lieu of actually addressing story elements is a long and noble one, particularly in Masterpiece Theater," I noted.

"Thank you."

"Also, Dan is gay for Cumberbatch."

That earned me a couch cushion thrown at my head by Dan while Jaison and Suzume hooted with laughter.

I woke up the next morning with a substantial crick in my neck, thanks to the black fox that was ensconced in the middle of my pillow. I rolled over to the side and began rubbing my abused neck, grumbling. I didn't deny that my single-size mattress had been making for some tight quarters when Suze spent the night, and I had in fact been considering making the upgrade to a double or even a queen (plans that had now been firmly put on the back burner thanks to my financial support of the succubi), but we did have two pillows. It wasn't exactly necessary for her to take hostile possession of my pillow every time she stayed over.

Also, the truth of the matter was that I'd gone to bed with a naked woman, and waking up next to a fluffy fox was not exactly how I liked to start the morning.

I said her name loudly. Then, with no response, I nudged her slightly. I was rewarded by the lazy opening of one amber eye.

"Suze, I'd like to do some early-morning postcoital cuddling," I said.

Her luxuriously long tail wagged happily, and she rolled over so that she was regarding me upside down, her jaw open and her tongue lolling partially out.

"Rubbing your belly is not exactly what I had in mind." My voice sounded about as dry as the Sahara.

She made a little disappointed sound in her throat; then with a huff she transformed. Between one breath and the next the winter-coated black fox on my pillow was replaced with a naked woman draped over the top of my bed.

Suze quirked an eyebrow. "Spoilsport."

I hooked an arm around her hips and tugged her around and down. "Don't worry," I promised her with a grin. "You'll still get plenty of rubbing."

An hour later I was whistling while I put together a dual breakfast of English muffins, cereal, and orange juice. The stiffness in my neck was still present, but it now seemed like a decent tradeoff for the relaxation of every other part of me. Suze was in the shower, which thanks to our crummy pipes produced a rattling sound that was almost impossible to ignore, but I was determined to hold on to this good mood as long as possible, and I just whistled louder.

Dan came out of his room, slick and put together for another day spent studying the law and surviving the Socratic method of teaching. He shook his head at the sight of me.

"Fort, you need to work on getting more of a poker face. It's a little too painfully obvious that you just got laid."

"I'm just whistling," I defended. "Besides, don't pretend that you're so good at keeping it hidden. You always look smug as shit after Jaison puts out."

"You have no definitive proof of that," Dan said as he pulled on his wool jacket and wrapped his scarf in a perfect just-so knot. Smugly. "Hey, I'm hitting the grocery store after classes. I've got the list, but can you think of anything else we need?"

"I'm out of tofu again."

Dan made a face as he pulled the list out of his wallet and updated it. "You drink blood. I would think that that would make you comfortable with the consumption of meat."

"Wow, that argument is so compelling, and one that I've never heard before. Let me forget the tofu and fry up some bacon." Besides, I only drank my mother's blood. For now.

"The bacon in the fridge is just waiting for you to backslide."

I threw a balled-up paper towel at him, and he laughed as he headed out. My vegetarianism was definitely imperfect—I was never going to give up eggs or fish—and the truth that Dan was certainly aware of was that avoiding meat was an ongoing struggle for me. I'd made the switch to vegetarianism for the sake of a former girlfriend, but before my transition had begun in earnest it had helped suppress some of my more predatory instincts when I didn't eat red meat. It was hard to tell whether it was still true—my instincts had taken control of me once, and I'd attacked one of my mother's employees, James, before Thanksgiving, and had actually bitten him hard enough to draw blood. It had scared the shit out of me (it hadn't done good things for James either, though thankfully he hadn't been seriously hurt), and while I could've just thrown up my hands and assumed that if this was happening, then my meal plan was useless and I should just give in to my cravings (and believe me, my cravings for bacon were hard to ignore at times), but the truth was that it was possible that my vegetarian diet was actually helping me avoid causing more serious damage—and since none of my family members had been either willing or able to give me a definitive answer on that, I was sticking like glue to my no-meat approach.

Not that I still didn't miss hamburgers. And while I'd certainly learned a lot of different ways to prepare tofu, the truth was that it was still pretty far down on my list of preferred meals.

Suze sauntered out of the bathroom then, rubbing her hair dry with a towel and giving me a smile. She'd gotten completely dressed—the sad fact was that the heating system in the apartment was sluggish at best, and no matter how often Dan and I dialed the thermostat up to eighty, the temperature in the rooms never seemed to inch above fifty. We had more than a few suspicions that Mr. Jennings had locked the main heating system. I knew that Mrs. Bandyopadyay relied on plug-in electric heaters in every room and a heavy robe from Land's End.

Of course, Dan and I were manly men, so we just gritted our teeth and wore thermally layered shirts. The lack of exposed skin from our respective partners (and both Suze and Jaison seemed very willing to bitch about the ambient temperature) was the tragic result of Mr. Jennings's suspected parsimoniousness.

After breakfast, Suze headed for the door. Whenever she wasn't working with me, Suze helped out at her family's business, Green Willow Escorts. Not that she actually did escort work herself—while her hugely intimidating grandmother, Atsuko, had been a geisha in Japan during the thirties and forties, she'd moved into a management position when she came to America.

"Getting to beat anyone up today?" I asked Suze as I leaned in for a good-bye kiss.

The kiss was good enough to pleasantly spin my head and make me wish that I didn't have to hurry down to my mother's mansion for the meeting. "Nah, I'm just helping out with scheduling. If I get really bored I might ask Taka if she wants any help with payroll." Then her eyes took that extra foxy gleam that always made me act especially cautious. "So . . . you're working at Redbones tonight?"

I could feel my mouth flatten into a thin line. After having to leave my last part-time job as a dog walker because of how the animals were responding to smelling Suze's scent marks on me, I'd spent a soul-killing week as a telemarketer before picking up my current work. It wasn't the worst job I'd had, but it definitely had its drawbacks. One being just how much Suze was enjoying it.

"Yes," I said reluctantly. "Why do you ask?"

Her smile showed a lot of teeth. "Well, a day doing office drudgery needs something fun at the end of it. I was figuring that I'd swing by and say hello to you while you're working. Maybe bring a few of my cousins."

"How many of your cousins?" I asked, worried, but Suze was already strolling down the hall, giving me a cheerful wave over her shoulder. Shit. Suze had eighteen first cousins, and so far they'd *all* gotten far too much enjoyment out of my job.

A glance at my watch reminded me that that particular problem would have to wait. If I was going to make the ten a.m. meeting that Loren Noka had scheduled for me, I was going to have to leave soon. And since the succubi badly needed for me to bring them good news, it wouldn't hurt to spend a little extra time on my appearance. While neatly combed hair and a clean shirt might not be enough to secure a yes vote from my sister and mother, the truth was that it certainly wouldn't hurt.

At my mother's Newport mansion, we convened the meeting promptly at ten minutes before ten. Loren Noka had put together binders for each of us that contained all of the pertinent information (neatly bullet-pointed) that she and I had collected yesterday, as well as the results of the credit scores and background checks that she must have done in the early-morning hours. It was the kind of presentation that would've warmed the soul of any corporate drone, which made it a strange counterpoint to my mother's sitting room, where this meeting was being held. Antique furniture (though when my mother had purchased it, it was probably new) was upholstered in pink damask and satin, and mother-of-pearl was inlaid into as much of the woodwork as possible. For once the TV, constantly set to the twenty-four-hour-news network, was off.

Chivalry, casual in beige slacks and an argyle sweater, sat beside me, making thoughtful "hmm" sounds of active listening as he listened to my presentation on the succubi. His movie-star-vampire handsome face was carefully neutral, giving me plenty to worry about as I tried to emphasize the few benefits that the succubi had to offer while downplaying their notable issues. Loren had done her best with the documentation, hiding the financial information behind several stock photos that she must've grabbed from the Las Vegas tourism board, but it's hard to fight against numbers, and these were all too clear.

My sister, Prudence, was sitting across from me on the matching love seat, and she was making it very plain from her expression that she was not being distracted by my emphasis on how easy it would be for us to help the succubi find gainful employment in the Connecticut casino industry. She was dressed for a day at her office, where she and a horde of stockbrokers did alchemic things with money and markets and turned profits in ways that I wasn't even sure were feasible, much less legal.

Madeline, our mother, would normally have been orchestrating our meeting from her favorite chair, but that had been quietly replaced several weeks ago by an elegant chaise longue where she could recline in style. She was stretched out on it, the oversize nineteen eighties grandma glasses that she wore primarily for appearance perched neatly on her face as she perused the material and seemed to give me half her attention. All of us had been sneaking glances at her since we walked in. While she almost never left her suite of rooms before the sun went down (our sensitivity to sunlight increased with age—while I had no problems walking around at any time of day, Madeline had been born in the fourteenth century, and her suite had been built to carefully obscure its lack of windows), she had always been precise in her personal presentation, even though her style might've mimicked Betty White on *Golden Girls*. Today, though, she was wrapped in a magnificent dressing gown of silver and pink that actually had small seed pearls sewn along the sleeves, and was swathed with blankets. She was in her pajamas.

I'd learned months ago that my mother, who was old even by vampire standards, was beginning to decline in health. But when I'd heard that, I assumed that she had decades left to live. I was starting to suspect that I was wrong. In the three days since I'd seen her last, she looked more fragile and delicate. Tinier, as if she was collapsing in on herself like an old barn. She'd been ensconced on her chaise longue when the three of us were ushered into her presence by her personal maid, Patricia. I was wondering whether she had been able to walk, or whether one of the staff members had carried her to the chair from her bed.

As if sensing my thoughts, she glanced up at me and smiled, deliberately flashing a set of long, fixed fangs that wouldn't have looked out of place on a tiger. Fragile was definitely a relative thing when thinking about my mother. Prudence and Chivalry had thin, retractable fangs that were discreet and functioned like hypodermic needles. I had a set of teeth so innocuously normal that I still kept my six-month dental checkups.

I cleared my throat loudly. "And there you have it," I said, addressing my family. "The succubi have suffered a major setback by a hostile force, but I think that they would be a good addition to this territory. Low-risk, hard workers, and willing to offer substantial tithes for the protection we can offer them. I move that we offer them immediate entry."

Prudence gave me a flat stare. "Baby brother, that assessment has more holes in it than Swiss cheese. Look at your own numbers, much as you've attempted to hide them behind pretty pictures. With their established income levels plus their adult-to-child ratio, they'll be struggling for a subsistence existence for at least the next decade."

"And what's a decade to us?" I countered quickly. "You're always telling me that vampires need to look at the long-term picture."

"Yes, the long term." Prudence flipped pages. "Let's talk about their risk level. I'm not sure I'd categorize feeding side effects that can mimic syphilis as a 'low' threat. Even if we followed your suggestion and restricted their feeding to the tourist populations in the casino towns, it's clear that careless actions on their parts could very easily leave us with the CDC breathing down our necks as they look for the source of a venereal disease outbreak hot spot."

"An even larger population lived in Las Vegas and never drew attention like that. Besides, they express themselves as very willing to abide by guidelines that we put in place." My brother was being ominously silent during Prudence's cross-examination, and now I shot him a sidelong glance. "Plus, Chivalry has kept plenty of groups toeing the line who are way more of an exposure risk than the succubi. I mean, the kobolds aren't exactly ready for prime time."

Chivalry shifted his weight carefully, and flipped some pages. "The succubi probably benefited substantially in the past from Las Vegas's reputation," he said carefully. "Their recent tourism campaigns notwithstanding, I don't think anyone hears the words *VD outbreak* and *Las Vegas* in the same sentence and exhibits much real surprise."

"They might not have legalized brothel prostitution, but let's not pretend that the Connecticut casinos have figured out a way to have blackjack coexist with Puritan ideals," I pointed out, feeling serious worry creep its way up my spine. While I hadn't expected Chivalry to embrace the succubi outright, I'd hoped for a little more support from his direction, or at the very least a little more postvacation optimism. "And the tithing rate that they were willing to sign on to for the next twenty years exceeds every other group currently in residence."

"Tithes that come out of service workers' salaries," Prudence noted immediately. "You can't tax what isn't there, and I also noticed that your little asterisk on that sentence led to some very fine print noting that our tithe could only apply to income that exceeded the poverty line."

I'd been hoping that she wouldn't read the fine print.

"That's not language that appears in any of our boilerplate contracts," Chivalry said gently. "Loren wouldn't have put it in there, and a group as desperate as this one sounds wouldn't have dared suggest it. This was you, wasn't it?"

I looked at him wordlessly. He rested a hand on my shoulder and squeezed lightly. "This can be a difficult job," he noted. "It's clear that you feel sorry for this group—"

"Yes, and maybe instead of spending the next few minutes in feeling-sharing mode, we can talk about this patently obvious sob story that they've spun for Fortitude." Prudence's voice was like acid.

My own voice raised. "You weren't there listening to them, Prudence. I was. They're all clearly traumatized after most of their community was slaughtered right in front of them—"

"Conveniently out of sight, with no evidence, and by skinwalkers," she snapped, flipping a strand of her red hair that had escaped her rigidly no-nonsense bob. "I don't doubt that skinwalkers would enjoy nothing better than to terrorize a community, but the last time I checked, practically the entire continent's population was ensconced in that cesspool we call Miami. I find it ridiculous to even conceive that the entire group suddenly relocated themselves across the country to *Nevada*—"

"Oh, my turtledove, that part is quite true." Madeline spoke for the first time in this meeting, with breezy confidence.

There was a long pause while we all turned our heads to stare at her. Prudence's jaw had even managed to slacken a bit, a sight that I tried to burn into my memory for later enjoyment. Madeline glanced up from the meeting handout, her brilliant blue eyes blinking in surprise. "I never mentioned that, dear hearts? I'm sure I did."

"Not to my recollection, Mother," Chivalry said carefully. "Would you mind perhaps . . . repeating . . . this information?"

She sighed and let her binder slip down onto her lap. "How tiresome. Well, it's quite simple, really. Maximilián closed his borders about two months ago and cleared his entire territory. That included Miami, so the skinwalkers would've been casting about for a new area to live."

We all blinked a bit. The name sounded familiar, and I asked cautiously, "Maximilián is the vampire who holds Florida and most of the Keys, right?" After spending most of my life trying to pretend that the supernatural didn't have anything to do with me, I'd been on a steep learning curve in the last few months. I'd mostly been trying to catch up with the basic knowledge of our territory, but I'd always known that my family weren't the only vampires in the New World. However, everyone had always downplayed the other vampires on our continent as being so beneath notice that I supposed that I'd absorbed their prejudice without really thinking it over. Certainly this was one of only a handful of times that I could even remember us mentioning one of the other vampires by name.

"Florida, the Keys, and a small slice of southern Alabama," Chivalry acknowledged. Then, probably because he'd gotten so used to being my walking Wikipedia over the last few months, he continued. "Maximilián came over from Europe in 1886, and Mother allowed him to establish and hold that territory."

"I felt terribly for the poor dear," Madeline put in. "Really, so unprepossessing. In his late three hundreds, but so depressingly lacking in power. His original territory was in the Slovakian area of Europe—don't even ask me what they were calling his country at the time he came begging, because the maps change so often in that area of the world that I didn't even bother to ask—but when his father died unexpectedly, there was just no way that Maximilián was going to be able to hold his borders against the Nests around him. And it is a crowded area of the world for our kind, with plenty of other vampires who were interested in helping their offspring set up territory."

"Oh. That was kind of nice of you to let him have Florida," I said.

Prudence snorted. "Mother drew a circle on the map in a spot where she had no intention of ever going to, was far enough away from us that she couldn't imagine him ever being a bother, and where she couldn't conceive of anything of real value ever emerging."

"He hasn't done too badly," Chivalry said. "I mean, that deal he made with Walt Disney certainly worked out well. Plus, air-conditioning really turned things around down there."

I held up a hand before they got started on that tangent. The delights of climate-controlled living were a favorite conversational topic with my family, challenged only by the thrills of window screens and refrigerators. I'd heard more maggoty food stories than anyone outside the range of a Ken Burns special. "Okay, with background now thoroughly established, why would this guy suddenly clear his territory?"

"Living the dream?" Prudence muttered.

"Be serious," Chivalry chided her. "Fort has actually brought up a decent point."

"It's because he Brooded his first offspring," Madeline said absently as she adjusted her blankets and reached for her cup of tea. At our expressions, she looked irritated. "Oh, stop playing with me. I must've mentioned it as some point. I put your names on the card."

"We sent a card?" Chivalry asked. Prudence just rubbed her forehead, looking flummoxed. I was equally dazed. While Madeline had often kept many subjects on a need-to-know basis, she'd usually at least known what she had and hadn't disclosed. This level of absentmindedness was new, and disturbing.

"Well, it seemed like a nice gesture," Madeline said. "He'd been trying to Brood for over seventy years. Really, it's a bit of a surprise that it even worked for him. Persistent little thing must've quite applied himself to the task. Female offspring, quite nice. Named her Amália—very pretty, I think. One has to at least pretend an interest, of course, so I asked our Patricia for a suggestion for a gift, and ended up sponsoring a tree in Israel in her name."

We stared at her.

"Patricia assured me that that would be appropriate for a *simcha*."

The expression on Prudence's face indicated that she found my mother's use of casual Yiddish just as disturbing as I did, but she recovered herself first. "Mother," she said cautiously, "how on earth do you know this? Neither Chivalry nor I had heard any of it, and I wasn't even aware that you bothered yourself with the other vampires in our part of the world."

Madeline gave a loud snort of derision as she took a precise sip of tea. "My precious dove, just because I don't often bring up such a dull topic doesn't mean that I have willfully blinded myself to our neighbors. Even those that pose no threat should at least receive the occasional check. As for our Floridian and his baby, your uncle Edmund informed me about that. He always keeps track of these things, and he moves through so many different territories that someone mentioned it to him. Of course he was quite excited—Amália is only the fourth vampire who has been successfully Brooded in the New World, after you three of course. And given that Maximilián was the child of a single-host parent—well, he rather beat the odds on that one."

"What do you mean?" Chivalry asked, leaning forward intently.

"Nothing to concern yourself with, dearling," she said with a maddening wave of her hand, the kind that indicated that this conversational topic was closed. "Just my brother's hobby. While I do very much enjoy being able to Skype with Edmund wherever he might be, I do admit that at times I miss being able to skim over the boring parts of his letters."

"How is Amália only the fourth vampire infant?" I asked, confused. "I've seen the territory map. There are a couple of other vampire-held areas. I know we're operating on a different time scale than humans, but we're not moving geologically. There should be more."

Chivalry shifted to look at me. "Not many vampires were ever interested in leaving the old territories in Europe and Western Asia," he explained. "Mother was the first to come to the Americas, and not many others followed. There's Caterina on the West Coast, of course, but she's old, and, according to Mother, was never able to Brood offspring at all. She barely concerns herself with anything outside of Napa Valley. And there's Gavril in Minnesota, but his daughter, Yelena, emigrated with him. I'm not even sure whether she's old enough to try to Brood."

"Yelena is a little older than Prudence," Madeline said. "She might start toying with the idea."

"She has already claimed her own territory beyond her father's borders." Prudence's voice had a distinct edge to it.

"In Manitoba." Madeline was dismissive. "Gavril always had interests there anyway, so he's almost certainly taking an active hand in helping her secure it. They even share a border, for heaven's sake." Then, sounding more pleased, "Though I will at least say that Gavril taught the girl some manners. I got a very polite note when she pushed into Manitoba about ten years ago, and she was careful to leave a nicely sized comfort zone between her territory and where ours ends in western Ontario."

"Good fences make good neighbors?" I asked.

"When it comes to vampires, dear heart, the fence also needs a hundred-mile buffer unless it's a Nest member on the other side of it. Close quarters always set tempers on edge—that's why those in Europe are constantly getting into fights."

Chivalry interceded, his voice sounding upbeat. "Since Yelena set up territory, she must be trying to Brood. We'll see the first Canadian-born vampire within the next few decades."

"I doubt very much that she'll have much luck with that goal," Madeline said darkly.

"What do you mean, Mother?" Prudence asked.

"Nothing that merits attention, precious." Our mother set her teacup down in its saucer with a decisive little clink of china, ignoring Prudence's frustrated scowl. "Now, I'm sorry to say that that tangent carried us quite far from the topic at hand. Tell me, then, my doves, how do you suggest I respond to the request posed by these succubi?"

"Let them in," I said immediately. "Minimal risk, shouldn't create a population explosion, big tithes down the line, and they diversify our portfolio of residents."

"You just made up that last part," my sister accused. "And even if we allow Fortitude's overly rosy assessment of their exposure likelihood to stand, everything else remains doubtful. A tithe is a percentage, and this doesn't sound like the kind of high-earning business-owning group that we have in the *metsän kunigas*. As for the potential for a population explosion, I'd say that the kitsune have certainly taught us the danger of making assumptions. As for this idea of diversification . . . I fail to see any benefit in bringing yet more potential troublemakers into our territory. Frankly I'd say that Maximilián has the right idea."

We both looked at Chivalry, catching him just as he took a sip of his coffee. There was a long pause while he held it in his mouth before slowly swallowing, then patting his mouth precisely with his napkin. We kept staring. He heaved a large sigh. "You both have good points," he said. "Fort, I agree that they could probably be a group that would be very easy to control, and at the very least they don't seem strong enough to put up any kind of resistance if we decided to expel them at a later date. But"—he saw my expression brighten, and immediately sent me a cautioning look—"I also have to agree with Prudence that there seems to be little in the way of a financial incentive for us in allowing them into the territory—if anything, it's one more group to keep tabs on."

Prudence reached across the table and, her every movement indicating her level of pique, transferred several Milano cookies from their current position on the doily-clad nibbles section of the tea tray over onto her plate. She didn't even try to hide that she was highgrading those cookies from among the less desirable sugar or Danish butter cookies on offer. "Chivalry, you remain the king of the middle ground," she grumbled. I didn't say anything, but I found myself in (extremely) reluctant agreement with my sociopathic sibling.

Thirty minutes followed where Prudence and I attempted to shift the other in their position, while Chivalry brokered uselessly from the middle.

"Can you please just pick one side or the other? Preferably mine?" I asked my brother finally. By this time I was nursing my third cup of coffee, and I was not only getting a significant buzz on, but becoming increasingly aware of my impending need for a bathroom break. However, given the very real possibility that a bathroom break would result in a decision against the succubi in my absence, I didn't dare get up. At least the sight of Prudence making the occasional subtle repositioning that nonetheless indicated bladder distress made me confident that she was in no better position than I was.

"Fort, I see the value in both positions," Chivalry repeated for the umpteenth time. "I must say that I could be equally happy with either the succubi being allowed in or in them being directed to depart."

"Then wouldn't it at least make you happy to make me happy?" I ran my hand through my hair in frustration.

"Now you're just blatantly appealing to baby brother favoritism," Prudence accused.

"Well, since no argument that either of us has made has succeeded in budging him, I might as well attempt something else."

"Both of you have very strong feelings on this," Chivalry defended. "And I just don't see the value in getting so worked up at this point. Can't we please find a compromise position here?"

Prudence made an extremely frustrated sound. "I would be more than happy to boot them out of our territory with a 'please slaughter' sign attached, while Fort would probably like nothing so much as to establish a welfare system solely to fund them for the next half century. I'm sorry, brother, but we seem to be making no progress at all now." She turned to stare at Madeline, who had been listening silently. "Mother, I don't think that there's a single facet to this decision that we have failed to punctuate. Fort, would you be in agreement?"

I hated to give up on my attempts of finding some kind of argument that would either entice or strong-arm Chivalry over to my way of thinking, but I had to reluctantly nod. We all looked at Madeline expectantly.

"I'm not going to intercede," she said quietly.

There was a long pause while that sank in. "Wait . . . ,"
I asked, "what do you mean?" My mother had always
made the final decisions on everything, and decisively.
She could periodically ask us for advice, but I'd always
had the sense that that was more like a mother cat presenting her babies with a mostly mauled bird and waiting for them to finish the poor crippled thing off, but
always ready to step in and deliver the kill stroke if the
kitten somehow managed to still lose control of the situation. And if what we advised her to do went in the face
of what she'd already planned for, she had never had a
problem with telling us that we were completely wrong,
and that she'd be doing it her own way (which, she never
failed to assert, was also the *right* way).

Madeline's voice was still soft, but implacable. "You
have presented your arguments, but I am not making a
decision. I want *you*, my three offspring, my heirs, to decide what course of action will be pursued."

Prudence broke in. "Mother, you can't—"

The gentleness was gone from my mother's face as
quickly as a cloud passing over the sun. "Can't I?" she
asked my sister, and while her voice was still just as soft,
Madeline's blue eyes were glittering dangerously.

My sister backed down. She'd had a taste of our mother's discipline very recently, and was probably still relish-
ing the ability to walk without crutches. "All right, yes,
you can. But we need a decision on this subject now."

"I don't see why." Madeline folded her hands precisely.

While Prudence sputtered, Chivalry moved in smoothly.
Looking at my brother, I saw his dark eyes assessing our
mother closely, staring at her as if he wished that he
could peel back her skin and see into her thoughts. "This
isn't how you do things," he said carefully.

"No, my darling," Madeline agreed, her voice pleasant
again. "It isn't. But let us accept and face that, very soon

now, I will no longer be here to lead you. I will be nothing but a rotting husk and you, my children, will be choosing what directions you travel in."

I could feel a hard lump in my throat. No more avoidance. There was what had been becoming increasingly, unavoidably clear for months now, and the subject now lay before us all. Our mother was old, and she was dying. And it would happen soon.

Prudence shifted, the fabric of her skirt scraping against the sofa's upholstery loudly in the silent room. Her face was hard to read—surprise at the bluntness of my mother's statement, an unmistakable sadness, but there was something else there too. A confidence. An assurance. Madeline's death would leave an empty throne, and it was clear who Prudence felt would fill it. "Mother, I will be—"

Again the danger crossed Madeline's face, and those eyes burned. Her upper lip curled back, revealing her ivory fangs, and she hissed, *"Assume nothing, daughter."* Prudence rocked back as if slapped, her face paling, and I felt Chivalry's hand suddenly on my shoulder, squeezing tightly, warning me to stay still. We all pressed back against our seats, and I wished for nothing in that moment more than a few more feet between myself and my mother. Even as weak as she was, in that moment there was no mistaking that there was enough left in her to leave all of us as nothing more than smears on the floor. For a long minute I could hear my heart pounding in my ears, and all I could focus on was the sight of a single drop of saliva slowly dripping down my mother's left fang as she stared intently at my sister. Prudence dropped her gaze, her body expressing subservience, however reluctantly given. My mother's lips slowly relaxed, and she seemed to forcefully take control. At last she spoke, and her voice contained a world of sadness and regret. "You are all so very, very young. Had things gone as they should've, this territory would've passed to Constance, had she lived, and she would've been able to protect all of you, guide you, as you grew into adults, ready to face the challenges of this newer world. But she, the sister you never even knew, my true heir, was lost to foolishness." Her eyes closed for a moment and she seemed to waver. Constance was my oldest sister, born in England during the rule of King James. But she'd died young, killed in some kind of vampire territory clash that I'd never gotten the full details on. My mother had come to America shortly after Constance's death, and Prudence had been born almost a century later.

Prudence leaned forward and spoke carefully, and the expression on her face was frankly unnerved. It was rare for my mother to talk about Constance, and I couldn't remember a single time in my entire life that Constance's name had been mentioned in this kind of context, as a loss that somehow impacted our current situation. "Mother, you lost Constance, that's true, but I'm not a child anymore. I'll be able to protect your territory and my brothers." Prudence gave a sudden, sharp laugh, almost as if she couldn't help herself. "Look at this territory that you built, Mother! We rule unchallenged, the others of our kind in this part of the world barely even worth mentioning! What dangers could you be afraid of?"

The lines in Madeline's face dug deeper, and she shook her head slightly. A heavy, gusty sigh seemed to come from the very roots of her ancient, dusty sadness. "Oh, daughter. Just that." My sister frowned, looking both pissed and confused at my mother's simple, yet firm statement. Madeline locked eyes with her, and waited until Prudence reluctantly glanced away. Then my mother swept that intense blue gaze over all of us, leaving no wiggle room or hiding places. "You will decide this amongst the three of you. That is my will." We stared.

If anything had been revealed in the last hour and change, it was that there was almost no overlap in what we thought the best solution was. I had the sudden horrible vision of all of us trapped in this room for the next century, delivered food from the kitchen and surviving from bathroom break to bathroom break, deadlocked to the end of our days. Something of that must've been reflecting in all of our eyes, because my mother said, after a long and uncomfortable silence, "If none of you have changed your mind about the fate of the succubi, then we will simply wait. Perhaps time and consideration will soften your positions."

That opened the possibility that the stalemate might at least be punctuated by Marvel movie release days, but I didn't see that as much of an improvement. I leaned forward. "Mother, time is something that the succubi don't have."

Madeline flipped her hand dismissively. "Of course they have time. The succubi sit within our borders in the Supplicant House. The skinwalkers were reminded quite recently what the punishment is for violating my territory—they won't risk it simply for the sake of prey, however tempting." That glare swept over all of us again, and her decree was like iron. "We shall wait until the three of you can reach a decision."

My brain raced through the implications of that. The succubi were safe if they didn't have to leave New Jersey. And given that a month or more could drag by while Prudence and I argued and Chivalry sat on the fence, the most important thing to do was make sure that the succubi were able to survive. That meant making sure that the skinwalkers never got close to them, even assuming the skinwalkers knew where they'd run. And that meant . . . "The succubi are having to hunt outside our borders. If we can't grant them a speedy decision, then we should grant them hunting rights within the territory, where they can be assured of safety." I forced confidence into my voice. Fake it till you make it was a better motto than nothing.

Beside me, Chivalry tipped his head and pursed his mouth, weighing my statement. After a quick glance at my mother confirmed that she wasn't going to say anything, Chivalry noted cautiously, "It would have to be limited hunting rights, but that doesn't sound unreasonable. Prudence?"

My sister's expression left no doubt about the absolute depth of her pissiness regarding this situation, but she snapped out, "City hunting only, and have them distribute it around as much as possible. If we're lucky no one will notice a few more cases of syphilis in New Jersey."

The slur (whether justified or not) to the reputation of the Garden State was the least of my concerns, and I could almost feel my brain lurch into sudden, high gear. This was the most progress I'd been able to make on behalf of Saskia and the other succubi all morning. "So we grant them subsistence hunting in the cities, and we have them submit reports on how many humans they're feeding from, and what steps they're taking to avoid repeat victims." My words tumbled out so quickly that they were slurred together, but both of my siblings nodded with varied levels of grace. I took my victory and immediately pushed forward. "That covers that—but we're asking them to stay in a holding pattern indefinitely. That's going to make it hard for them to look for the kinds of jobs that they'll need to support themselves. We need to grant them a monetary stipend to help them make ends meet."

Oh, the disgust on Prudence's face. "Good grief, Fort, you actually *are* trying to start a welfare state. We're already allowing them to live rent-free in a house that we're paying the bills on."

"They need groceries, gas for their van, seasonally appropriate clothing," I countered. "That takes money, Prudence, money that they currently don't have."

"They can get jobs. Even if they can't get the kinds of jobs they're used to, they can still mop floors." For a woman who'd never struggled for money, even during the days when the woman's place had ostensibly been in the home (with certain exceptions always made, of course, for the devastating one-two punch of the Scott family clout and wealth), Prudence seemed very confident in her assessment.

Chivalry cut in, chiding Prudence. "We're keeping them in the Supplicant House, sister. It's not exactly located in a hotbed of industry."

Finally the kind of big brotherly support that I'd been waiting for. "Exactly, which is why—"

But Chivalry, the turncoat, hadn't finished, and spoke over me. "I don't like the idea of giving cash payments. That's not exactly the direction that money should be flowing in this territory."

"Which I'm noting from page twelve, in extremely tiny print, that you've already established a precedent for, Fortitude." Acid was less corrosive than Prudence's tone.

Prudence was clearly a lost cause on this one, so I instead focused entirely on Chivalry, who at least seemed persuadable. "There are seven children in that house, Chivalry. That's a lot of mouths to feed."

He sighed, acknowledging my point, and suggested, "We could contact our agent and have him make deliveries of groceries and food. Maybe see if we can set up some kind of reimbursement agreement with the local gas station."

"That would be good," I agreed fast, hoping that the tide was turning in my favor.

"*Too* good." Prudence flicked cookie crumbs off her lap with sharp flicks of her hand and looked quickly from Chivalry, to me, and back again, clearly weighing her position here. She grimaced, then allowed, "We have groceries for ten people delivered for as long as they're kept in limbo from our lack of a decision. But they'll have to figure out gas and clothing themselves."

"That's not unreasonable." Chivalry's voice was pleased.

I hesitated, trying to run numbers in my head. The gas and the clothing were tough, but they had the thousand dollars that I'd given them, plus whatever cash they'd still kept in the hole. Even my grocery bills were showing the signs of inflation, and I'd once spent five weeks living on nothing but white rice, salt, butter, and chewable vitamins when I was in the twilight time between the end of one job and waiting until the lagged pay on the new job started up. I had no doubt that at least shifting the burden of feeding seven children would make things much more manageable for the surviving succubi adults. It wasn't everything I'd hoped for, but it was a lot more than I'd been afraid of. "Okay, agreed."

Madeline, who'd sat back silent and alert during our brief, intense conversation, now made a small, pleased noise in her throat. "See, my darlings? I was certain that you could make strides. Now," she huffed a little, exhaustion clear, "I would like us to perhaps table the larger discussion of the succubi until we can come together for a more decisive conversation. For now, I would prefer to rest my eyes for a bit." She glanced at Chivalry. "Dear, if you could send for Patricia?"

He nodded, rising to his feet with the kind of courtesy that was as ingrained as it was archaic. "Of course." Then he leaned down and touched one hand to our mother's shoulder, soft and tentative. "And Maire as well?"

Maire was a former combat medic who had received

her honorable discharge from the army after she lost one of her legs to an IED. A capable and wholly unflappable nurse, she'd been scooped up and employed by my mother to look after the medical needs of my host father, Henry. Vampires didn't conceive and bear children directly—instead, true to our parasitical roots, we made our food sources also serve as our incubators. By carefully and patiently replacing all of Henry's blood with her own, Madeline had begun a physical transformation that changed him, from his surface biology all the way down to his DNA, into a warped and twisted creature that was capable of passing on genes that were almost entirely my mother's vampiric legacy. The process had shattered his mind, leaving him homicidally insane and a permanent guest of my mother's basement containment facility, where he'd lived for the first twenty-six years of my life with his counterpart, my host mother, Grace. As my host parents, they'd shared an uncomfortable fixation and knowledge of me, which exceeded my understanding of it, but Grace had committed suicide to deliberately trigger the beginning of my transition, somehow knowing that in that moment that had been the only thing that could save my life during an altercation with a European vampire.

Henry's current need for Maire's services came from an attempt Prudence had made on his life in order to try to complete my transition to full vampire status. Before my mother stopped her, Prudence had managed to deliver punishing damage that would've killed him had he been fully human—but my mother's blood had saved him. However, the vampire blood flowing through Henry's veins wasn't his—it was my mother's. He could survive incredible injuries, was granted inhuman strength, but the blood couldn't replenish itself within Henry's body, and he couldn't heal from the injuries my sister had inflicted without more blood from my mother. And in her current state of declining health, my mother had not chosen to heal Henry. Now he spent all of his days strapped to a medical bed, monitored and attended to by Maire for his health and Conrad, his general keeper and overseer, for security.

I'd known that Maire had been hired to take care of Henry (Conrad was a big, tough former marine who was great on security and marksmanship, but was admittedly nauseated by the very thought of changing a catheter needle), but this was the first time I'd even heard a suggestion that Maire also tend to Madeline. A chill ran up my spine.

Madeline considered Chivalry's hand on her shoulder with narrow eyes, and I could see her weighing whether to strike out at him. But his dark eyes were steady, and if it hadn't been for the slight shake in the palm resting on her thin shoulder, I would've described him as perfectly calm. Then Madeline made a decision, and the dangerous moment passed. Her voice was sharp with irritation, but it was an old woman's exaggerated crankiness, not the anger of a monster that could tear through flesh and bone as easily as I could rip a piece of paper. "Very well. If it would comfort you."

A brief flurry of activity followed. We hung back and watched while Patricia bustled in, all solicitous clucking and tenderness with her charge, and my mother submitted to her attentions with an almost affectionate air. Patricia showed all of her sixty-plus years on her face, but she'd worked in this house since she was a teenager, and had been my mother's maid since she was in her twenties. She'd grown old in my mother's service, and had probably never even imagined that she could outlive my mother. Looking at her expression, of worry fighting with an almost religious fervor, I wondered if she'd let herself admit it yet, that the unthinkable would actually come to pass, and she would outlive Madeline.

Maire followed, carrying a small bag of medical supplies, and trailed by another staff member who pushed a wheeled cart that carried more, all tastefully obscured with a linen tablecloth. Her employment with my mother could only be measured in months, not years, and her expression was clinical and assessing. She hadn't been around the family long enough to face the difference in our life spans, to observe the Scott family remaining almost unchanged by the decades that passed as the humans wilted around us.

I hadn't had to see that either, of course. At twenty-seven, I remained deceptively in step with the aging processes around me. It wouldn't last much longer, my siblings had assured me multiple times. The next twenty years, the next thirty, would strip away my ability to view myself as human, as a peer to the men and women I'd gone to college with and formed friendships and ties to. It was clear that the rest of my family was eagerly awaiting the delivery of nature's harshest lesson.

Chapter Three

My siblings and I found ourselves politely showed to the door, our ears filled with Patricia's particular blend of reassurance about my mother's condition ("just a nap is all she needs to perk her up") and almost knee-jerk guilting ("it's so important not to overly burden her, though of course I understand how difficult it might be to respect one's own mother. After all, I can tell you things about my Levi that would break your heart").

Prudence headed down the hallway in the direction of her own suite, looking—from the completely neutral expression on her face down to her professional low pumps, like any Providence businesswoman heading to work. She didn't even glance at either me or Chivalry. I didn't often feel like chatting with my sister, but after what we'd all just seen, I couldn't help feeling that at least a little postmortem was in order. "Prudence—"

She glanced over her shoulder, her mouth tight and her eyes flinty. "Later, little brother. All things can be discussed at length later." Then she turned a corner and was gone.

Chivalry rested a hand on the back of my shoulder and subtly nudged me to accompany him in the other direction than our sister, away from the family suites and toward the main staircase that would take us downstairs.

Of course there were several other staircases in the house, but given that Chivalry had grown up in an age where those had been strictly for servants' use, I didn't think it ever would've even occurred to him that occasionally they offered more direct paths around the various levels of the house. "Give her a moment, Fort. This has been a shocking morning for us all." A muscle twitched hard for a second in my brother's chiseled jaw.

"But what does it mean, Chivalry? What Mother said—"

"You know, Fort. You already knew." Nothing about my brother's tone was harsh. It was gentle, and his own sadness was readily apparent. But at the same time it brooked no argument, gave me no way to wiggle around what had been stated outright in that frothily decorated room. Nothing, not even the life of a vampire, lasted forever.

I didn't want to have to think about that, or wonder what life would be like without my terrifying, and terrifyingly loving, mother sitting in the corner, manipulating the lives of her children on puppet strings. So I thought about something else, something that I hoped would push us far away from the rawness of this topic and the way that it was making me think about my mother as transitory rather than permanent, and perhaps even have to decide once and for all whether I loved or hated her. I knew that I was acting out a cliché even as I did it, but clichés come from the truth, so I got mad at my brother.

"Chivalry, why couldn't you just have sided with me on the succubi? I was the one who was actually sitting and talking to them."

"Fort, it's critical that you begin to start finding common ground with Prudence." He let me change the topic, even as I felt his dark eyes assess me.

I pushed him, welcoming the feeling of justified irritation. The plight of the succubi was real and concrete, and with my brother's vote I could've done real good for their lives. "Mother said that it was our decision—a two-to-one vote would've ended the conversation."

"Fort, you're asking me to side with you just because of your delightful personality. That's not enough for this. I don't disagree with you about the succubi, but I also don't disagree with Prudence's assessment either."

Just hearing him reexpress that was nearly enough to make my head explode. My sister's votes against me were incredibly frustrating, but at least they'd come from a particular set of deeply felt views, even if those views were far too Randian for me to ever sign on to or even respect. "But—"

"Fortitude." We were on the main staircase by then, and Chivalry stopped and grabbed my lower arm hard, his fingers digging in with just enough force to remind me how strong he was, and how easy he would find it to snap my bone like kindling. His dark brown eyes were intense, and the irises were just slightly bigger than they should've been, a reminder to me not to push his temper. We were on the upper part of the staircase, and as I stepped back slightly I could feel the cool marble of the staircase balustrade against my waist. I resolutely kept my eyes on my brother, long practice allowing me to ignore the staircase carvings behind him. My mother's home decorating whimsy combined with a great deal of discretionary income had resulted in a marble staircase with a nautical mermaid theme. The sculptor had apparently started the project innocently enough, but by the middle of the staircase had started feeling enough artistic license to drop the mermaids' tops, and by the top of the stairs the carvings were frankly pornographic.

My brother leaned close, his voice low. "Mother said it outright today. She won't be with us much longer. When she is gone, the territory falls to Prudence. If you wish to have your voice heard in the way that the territory operates, then you need to be working with her, not just trying to outvote her. Believe me, it won't be about votes once Mother is gone."

"Mother didn't say that Prudence would inherit," I pointed out. Then, emotions running high, I broached the topic that we almost never spoke of. "And she did something different with you and me than Prudence. *Made* us different." Madeline had killed my sister's host parents the day that she was born, and Prudence had gone through transition as she moved through puberty. But later, with my brother, Madeline had left his host mother alive until he was twenty, and learned that her life had held his transition back. With me she'd gone even further, and somehow this seemed to have changed us, made us different than our Prudence.

A disbelieving, incredulous smile pulled across my brother's face. "Don't fool yourself, little brother. Whatever Mother was doing with our conception and rearing, for whatever reason, it won't change the facts. I'm a century away from mature power. You're barely more than an infant. Despite what Mother might wish for, Prudence is the only candidate, and she knows it." His hand tightened painfully on my arm, and I knew that I'd carry a bruise tomorrow. "And much as you two might be different, don't forget that she is our sister, and that she knows her responsibilities." He released my arm, and continued walking down the steps. After a second's hesitation, I followed. We walked through the labyrinthine hallways of the house until we reached my brother's office, tucked well away from the public rooms of the house where guests (both human, supernatural, and politicians) were entertained. It was decorated in dark wood, with luxuriously deep carpeting and almost stereotypical paintings of dogs and horses on the walls. I'd become a regular user of this office in the last few months, enough so that my brother had even floated the idea of getting a second desk brought in for me to use. But I'd said that I was comfortable enough making use of one of the long study tables in the corner when I needed workspace, and my brother was usually generous about sharing his computer, though he'd thrown something of a fit when I installed *Minecraft* on it. Truthfully I felt more than sufficiently involved in the family business, and, like the fictional Michael Corleone before me, preferred a bit of distance, however symbolic.

Other than us, the office was empty. The family employed two accountants to process tithes and print up the bills (yes, we actually did mail out tithing statements, which looked suspiciously similar to Rhode Island property tax bills) as well as determine what everyone should be paying. They were both human, and occupied a tidy little office in what had previously been the music room. Loren Noka also had a desk in that room, though she was just as likely to be found in this room, researching pieces of information in the extensive files that we still maintained in print. The file cabinets Chivalry owned were modern and top-of-the-line, but it wasn't uncommon to open up a manila folder and find that the documents within it had been written on vellum centuries ago.

"Ah, excellent," Chivalry said with forced heartiness as we came into the empty room. "Given how early Loren showed up this morning, I asked her to take the rest of the morning off and go have a nice brunch on us. Now"—he eyed me cautiously—"since I have you to myself for a moment, there are some line items in Ms. Hollis's reimbursement sheets that I'd like to discuss with you."

I immediately dropped into one of the comfortable leather armchairs in front of Chivalry's desk and settled in for the long haul. Suzume was paid well by my family to accompany me around the territory and assist in the investigation of any issues or the enforcement of the Scotts' rules, but she was not above submitting reimbursement sheets for any expenses that she felt that she had in some way incurred while on Scott time. After I'd gotten mud from my shoes on the inside of her Audi, I got an earful from Chivalry about receiving the bill for her car's detailing. And the argument over whether or not she could send dry-cleaning bills to the family was a long and ongoing one—probably not assisted by my comment at the time about how she only seemed to wear clothing on fifty percent of our excursions anyway. That had resulted in several faxed documents breaking down standard dog grooming costs, and suggesting that a similarly priced scale be applied to her own cleaning and upkeep. My brother had been less than amused on that day.

I was waiting for something like that, so I was very surprised when Chivalry looked at me extremely seriously and asked, "Fort, are you in any trouble?"

I blinked at him, confused. "No—not more than usual."

"I wish you'd be honest with me," Chivalry said sadly. "Surely the last few months have shown you that the family is willing to support your actions and interests, or at least have a reasonable discussion about them." He reached onto his desk and slid a file out of his stack, which he tapped with one finger but didn't open. He stared at me, clearly waiting for a confession. When none was forthcoming, because of the sheer level of flummox that I was feeling, he gave a heavy sigh and flipped the folder open, then handed it to me. "You're having the kitsune stay on duty four nights out of seven for body-guarding duties. There's clearly something going on."

Horror filled me. I desperately tried to convince myself that it wasn't the case, that she wouldn't go that far, but there it was in black-and-white itemized charges. ". . .

she's charging for overnights?" And double for the weekends. I felt like I'd been punched in the stomach, with the air shoved outward and leaving me gasping and lost. I'd been a job for Suzume when we first met—the helpless baby vampire that she was hired to keep an eye on. But that had been a long time ago, and things had changed—or I'd thought they had. A nasty thought intruded into my head—was I still a job to her?

I mentally shook myself hard. That couldn't be the case, and it *wasn't*.

But that's the horrible, insidious thing about doubt. Doubt lingers, undermines. Doubt is like the salt that was put down on all the New England roads every winter. It kept our cars from sliding on the ice, but it was corrosive. It devoured the metal of our cars, spreading rust through them like cancer. It weakened the roads, creating fissures in the asphalt. It washed off the roads and into the rivers, poisoning our waterways.

"Yes—" Chivalry was confirming.

"I'll handle this," I snapped. That airless feeling was going away, but I could feel my neck and cheeks getting hot as the shock faded and was replaced by anger. In what alternative universe, even a kitsune universe, was putting together an invoice for the time we spent together socially okay? My body felt numb, and I had a brief moment of gratitude that I had already been sitting down before my brother had unwittingly sprung this emotional can of snakes on me.

"But—"

"It's a miscommunication, Chivalry, and *I'll handle it.*"

Chivalry's jaw firmed, and I saw a familiar, and wholly inconvenient, stubbornness as he refused to heed what I could only hope was a truly gimlet look in my eyes. "I know that you've done things on your own before, Fort, but given everything that's currently going on here, I really don't want you to be—"

I couldn't take it anymore, and I blurted out, much louder than I'd intended, "I'm *dating* her."

There was a long pause, and I could see the wheels turn in my brother's head. "Oh. *Oh*." He looked hideously embarrassed, which seemed only fair given the level of personal humiliation I was currently experiencing in realizing that my girlfriend had been logging her overnights as a business expense. The file was yanked out of my hands and shoved under his blotter, as if by immediately excising it from our sight we could pretend that the conversation had never even come up. "Well, then . . . yes, good chat." He smoothed out his already immaculately pressed sweater, then made a show of checking his watch. "I'm going to see if Simone needs anything. Like . . . lunch."

I turned to stare out the window. Just looking at him felt like too much right now—a million times worse than if I'd just found the numbers myself. It was like a mirror reflecting light, exacerbating the whole wretched moment. "Yes. Super. Do that."

Chivalry made a hasty exit out the door, ostensibly off to go see my newest sister-in-law. I sat in the chair for a long minute, the blinding feeling of my wholly justifiable pissed-ness rolling over me in a wave, letting my fingers clench into the leather of the armchair until my knuckles ached.

I knew she cared about me, I reminded myself. She'd risked her life for me (even though she'd later put a dollar amount and an invoice on that too, if memory served me). She'd comforted me when the truth about vampire feeding almost broke me apart and turned me to desperate actions. She'd teased me, taunted me, slept beside me.

An image of her from that morning forced itself into my head—not of her smiling face or the sight of her bare skin in the morning light, but a furry ball on my pillow, white tail tip tucked over her nose.

She'd never stayed in her human shape all night with me. She always became a fox again. That had been bothering me for weeks, scraping at the back of my mind. Was that significant? Had that refusal actually been her true feelings coming through?

I tried to pull myself back. I needed to be reasonable, to try to force myself to look at this from her point of view, see things through her eyes.

At least she hadn't included condoms on her last list of reimbursement charges.

That I knew of.

Shit. I pulled my phone out of my pocket and sent Suze what I felt was a rather remarkably restrained text mentioning that we had something that we needed to talk about when we saw each other tonight.

My phone immediately rang, filling the room with the Imperial March, her customized ringtone.

"Oh no," I muttered to myself as I hit the ignore button. "I'm too clever for that." This was *not* a discussion that we were going to have over the phone.

Not that it really gave me something to look forward to later, of course. And, just my luck, she'd already mentioned that she and her cousins would be swinging over to my workplace later. Fantastic.

If I'd been at home, there would've been no solution to my situation except to break out *The Lord of the Rings*, extended cuts, and mainline nine hours. Lacking that, I gave serious consideration to going over to the mansion's home gym and exhausting myself with one of the punching bags. But instead, I spent the next few hours in my brother's office, poking through the older immigration records in the hopes of finding a useful parallel to the current situation of the succubi. At least, I reminded myself, the succubi were actually sincere in their need for me. I was hoping that the records would hold something that I could use to help strengthen my current case—and while I had no real hopes of convincing Prudence, a little bit of precedent seemed like a useful way to leverage my brother out of his current state of Swiss neutrality. Loren came in when I'd been at it for about forty minutes, and after a quick assessment helped me out by checking the reference catalogue for me. While my family did follow trends in such areas as plumbing and fashion, in other ways they could remain frustratingly old-fashioned, such as my brother's dislike of the Boolean method of searching. So far he had refused to allow Loren to make our records searchable with an online system, and instead we were stuck with a neatly typed and maintained card catalogue. I'd attended college at Brown, and was no stranger to researching my way through the periodical stacks, thanks to a number of my professors who were fanatical about the value of primary sources when putting together research papers, so going through the old family records at least brought back a few moderately pleasant associations to offset the flavor of dust and old paper. Chivalry had even undertaken the practice of using bound books for record-keeping, which were numbered and ordered, so once I had Loren working the card catalogue, the process went fairly smoothly.

The problem wasn't in the methodology—it was in the result. Over the next few hours, a clear picture emerged about the Scott approach to supernaturals hoping to reside in the territory and benefit from staying in my mother's long shadow. Most who were allowed to enter were large and established groups who could promise quick prosperity and had notable cash incentives that they were willing to offer, like the ghouls or the bears. Others were small, such as when Atsuko Hollis had entered the territory after the end of World War II—but she had offered the potential for a powerful future ally. The witches who came in were the best parallel to the succubi—a troublesome possibility of exposure, and they had never petitioned for entry in groups any larger than individuals or immediate family units, but their offers of crippling fees and painfully high tithes had been balanced with the fact that most witches worked as some kind of doctor or medical professional, and their earning potentials were almost universally high. The succubi had no cash reserves to smooth their passage, and frankly, my sister's dislike of the witches was strong enough that even mentioning them in conjunction with this current situation would only hurt the succubi by mere association. Prudence had done her best to shut down any witch immigration completely, and had made no secret that her preference would've been to kick all the other witches out of the territory completely. Her hatred for the witches was as pure a passion as any I'd ever seen her exhibit, yet one that no one in my family had ever explained the history of, making me wonder if she had experienced some strange inversion of love at first sight. It was probably as good an explanation as I'd ever get—my family excelled at keeping secrets.

By three in the afternoon, I had a solid coating of dust from pulling down and looking into records that hadn't been touched in decades and a splitting headache from deciphering the handwriting of generations of Chivalry's secretaries, which ranged from perfect copperplate to downright cramped. I vowed that if I ever ended up the boss of Chivalry for a day, my first decree would be that we hire a fleet of temp workers and have all the records transcribed to digital files. I was nursing a very new but passionate appreciation for standard font styles.

What I didn't have, unfortunately, was anything that would help the succubi.

At least I'd been able to give Loren the ability to carry out the grocery directive. Given my new knowledge of her firsthand experience with the feeding and maintenance of teenagers, I'd put the entire task in her capable hands. My own lunch had been provided by Madeline's cook and served to me, unrequested, on a tray. The remnants of an excellent grilled cheese sandwich with an accompanying bowl of applesauce and a slice of pecan pie rested on a side table. While I'd lived on my own since college, and had never regretted it for even a single moment, I had to admit that there were huge perks to having a dedicated kitchen staff who not only knew all of my favorite foods, but were more than willing to make it almost magically appear along with a dessert. It was kind of like having Potter-esque house elves.

Another check at my watch, though, had me heading for the door. I could make a check-in call to Saskia during my break, but it was time to head to work. In my current financial situation, quitting this job was not exactly an option, however tempted I might be to deliver my resignation over the phone and continue scraping through the Scott archives in the hope that a scrap of paper could solve all of the succubi's problems.

The drive from my mother's mansion in Newport to my apartment in Providence generally took anywhere from forty minutes to an hour, depending on the season, the traffic patterns, and whether I had the misfortune to become trapped behind an elderly driver on one of the one-lane roads. Today, with the bitter cold keeping the tourists and the pleasure drivers safely tucked in their houses, and an overcast gray sky that, while not overtly threatening snow, was certainly keeping it a possibility, I was able to make the drive quickly. After tucking the Scirocco safely in the parking lot, with its solitary windshield wiper lifted up just in case a few inches came down before I got home, I made a brief stop upstairs to change into my work clothes. Knowing that a possible relationship-shattering fight in my future added a strange dimension to getting dressed. I put on my third-favorite set of jeans. If a pair of pants had to forever be sullied as the pants I was wearing when Suzume and I broke up, then it was better that it be a pair that I could throw away without regrets.

The hours of research into historical records, and lunch, and the drive back might've given me some welcome distance from my anger at Suzume, but I was under no illusions that it had smoothed things out. That anger was still there, and the mere thought of "billable hours" was more than enough to bring it surging back to the forefront of my brain.

There were a lot of things I didn't enjoy about my current job, but at least the uniform wasn't one of them. It was a fairly minimal dress code—just a company T-shirt and a small waist apron to stash crucial items like my order pad and a few dozen extra pens. I also appreciated that my workplace was in my own neighborhood of College Hill, just a quick bus ride away from the apartment. In better weather, it would even be within a possible walking distance if I wanted to save on the bus fare—not that I really expected to still be working there by the time summer rolled around again.

Waiting tables at a karaoke bar was not something I particularly wanted to make a long-term career choice.

I'd been to good karaoke bars before—the ones that did karaoke in the Japanese style, with fancy private rooms and sake cocktails, with incredible decor. Redbones was not a good karaoke bar. The owner, Orlando Bouchard, made no secret of the fact that transforming Redbones from a local dive bar into a local dive bar that centered on karaoke had stemmed entirely on his desire to find a way to get more people through the door without having to do any kind of major upscaling of the bar, which would probably have necessitated getting a real kitchen going. I personally felt that he'd also realized that if he could find something to appeal to the female college student population, the local male population would invariably follow. In that, Orlando wasn't exactly wrong.

My employment at Redbones was actually even flakier than my usual fly-by-night minimum-wage drudgery. The waitstaff position that I currently occupied was one that had been vacated by Orlando's niece when she went on maternity leave (an event that Orlando cursed daily), and it had been made extremely clear to me that as soon as the niece felt ready to come back to work, I was out on my ass. Not that I was making any arguments. I'd done more than my share of waitstaff jobs before, and nothing at Redbones was particularly difficult. There was no kitchen, and the only food that could be ordered was table baskets of popcorn, pretzels, cookies, and things like that, which were the simple matter of going into the back room, dumping the requested foodstuff into the basket, and carrying out again. The fanciest anything got was when people ordered off of the "celebration specials" page, which involved cupcakes. That meant that I went into the back room, took down the requisite number of cupcakes, put them on a plate, and stuck in the appropriate party toppers. Those came in birthday, bachelorette party (Orlando had tried stocking bachelor party, but no one had ever ordered those), and breakup. Breakup had sad kittens.

Ninety percent of the menu focused on what we did best—alcohol. Orlando was the man behind the bar, both literally and figuratively, and I had to admit that he was pretty good at mixing drinks. Another big part of my job was that whenever he was busy mixing particularly fancy drinks, I was empowered to fill up basic beer requests or simple drinks myself. That kept the system moving, continued to lubricate the customers, and saved Orlando from having to hire a second barman on busy nights. Not that I worked the busy nights. The bar was open five nights a week, Wednesdays to Sundays, and I was invariably awarded shifts on the slower nights (generally Wednesdays, Thursdays, and Sundays), when Orlando could get away with just having one waiter on duty. Working at a bar was one of those rare jobs where people fought for the weekend shifts, which usually brought much higher tips. I was okay getting the unwanted weeknights, as it was actually better for my schedule. But Thursday night at a karaoke bar could be a very grim vista.

Which of course brought me to the major crux of the issue—it was a karaoke bar. Most people attended in groups, usually after they'd started the evening with dinner at a restaurant. Sometimes people came in groups from particularly friendly workplaces as a way to have a fun night out, but not usually. We had about two dozen small tables, which could be reserved in advance but almost never were except with bachelorette parties. I met groups at the door, escorted them to a free table (and with the nights I worked, there was always a free table), and handed them menus and a laminated songbook. When I swung over to take their drink or snack orders, I also collected their song requests, which they wrote on pads of paper that were kept at each table. I would then deliver those song requests to the karaoke DJ, who put together the song list. There were two large screens on the walls of the bar—one that displayed the lyrics of the song currently being sung, and one that had the arranged song order on it so that people could know if their song was coming up. Redbones had almost four thousand songs in the karaoke catalogue. But most nights it seemed like all people wanted to sing was Journey or Bon Jovi.

Work began as it usually did. We opened at four, but not even the most committed karaoke buff showed up that early, so we spent the first hour prepping. I turned on the popcorn machine in the back room (Orlando had gotten it when the movie theater down the street closed down) and made sure that there were plenty of cookies. We had a deal with a local bakery that I strongly suspected involved taking the cookies that normally would've been disposed at the end of their workday and giving them a few more hours of shelf life. I also pushed a broom around the floor—not that that really was going to help the situation, but it at least removed the visual issues. Sometimes I had to push really hard at stuff that was slightly adhered in a gummy mixture of ancient spilled drinks, dirt from shoes, and crumbled food, with just a slight veneer of vomit. What the floor really needed was an exorcism, or at least a few buckets of bleach, but my broom helped cover up its sins for another evening.

At the bar, Orlando furrowed his brow and began the first of several hundred rubdowns with a soft rag. Before the bar was Redbones, it had been various other liquor-dispensing establishments all the way back and through Prohibition, and the bar was as original as the bricks that made up the walls. Unfortunately, like the bricks, the bar really needed some serious rehab. While Orlando argued history as his reason for avoiding an upgrade, I suspected penny-pinching. Pratibha Vhora was the DJ, and she played with her sound checks, cross-examined her equipment, and when all else was done, she just popped on a preset song list and did a few crossword puzzles.

"Hey, Fort," Pratibha said as I passed her. "'Actor Guinness.' Four letters, third one *e*."

"Alec," I answered.

She nodded, looking pleased. "Nice." Once she'd realized my level of film trivia, Pratibha warmed up to me significantly. Supposedly Orlando's niece had only been able to help out with gardening questions, which didn't come up as often. Pratibha glanced up from her puzzle, and frowned. "Hey, are you okay tonight?"

Apparently my poker face was not as perfectly in place as I'd thought. "I've been better," I hedged. A lot better, actually, this morning when I had a snuggly, sexy, happy girlfriend who I *hadn't* been aware wasn't punching out on the clock until she walked out my door.

"Stop distracting the talent, Fort!" Orlando bellowed from the bar. I sighed and kept sweeping as Pratibha gave me a sympathetic grin, put up her feet, and winked at me. Orlando was in his late fifties, built like a keg of beer, and seemed to feel emotionally bereft if he didn't have something to complain about. Given that Pratibha had, presumably, more career options than I did (though she'd come to this job after fifteen years of DJing weddings, proms, and bar mitzvahs left her completely burned out on all formal-wear occasions), that often left me as the eternal target of Orlando's grousing.

He eyed me when my sweeping brought me closer. While Orlando's days of tight jeans were several decades in his rearview mirror, even a quick glance at the musculature in his dark brown arms generally was enough to disperse even the most assy of drunks. Orlando was also a possessor of a set of crazy eyes that would've made Christopher Lloyd jealous. He wasn't the worst boss I'd ever had, and he'd mellowed after the first month made it clear that I wasn't a slacker on the job, but even though I had some confidence that Orlando's bark was rarely followed by an actual bite, he wasn't exactly my favorite conversational companion.

"Is that girlfriend of yours coming by tonight?" he snapped out.

I answered in the affirmative, and was immediately rewarded with a string of expletives, which for once I at least partially agreed with. "She said that she's bringing some of her cousins too," I added, which triggered another explosion of curse words. Orlando had spent a few years in the navy, and it showed.

"You remind those jackals that only your girlfriend gets to drink for free," Orlando snapped, scrubbing aggressively with his rag cloth. "And you tell them that if they try that polygamy story on me again, I'm watering every drink I hand them."

Orlando's relationship with the kitsune was fraught. On the one hand, he'd tended bar long enough to have a well-defined radar for trouble, and the kitsune were capable of so much mayhem that they probably should've been banned under international accords. On the other hand, the revelation that I was dating Suzume seemed to have garnered me a certain reluctant respect, if only in the sense that he admired my complete disregard for basic survival instinct. He also was a reasonable enough man to let Suze drink for free, since he knew that she'd probably wrangle free drinks out of me anyway, so it was for the best to just streamline the process. And as a business owner, he did acknowledge that having attractive single women in a bar was never a bad thing, and the kitsune certainly tended toward the attractive. Even the ones who weren't hot had charisma to spare, which was usually pretty much the same thing in person. The male population of College Hill was essentially subsidizing the drink orders of the Hollis women, and was apparently grateful for the privilege.

Most of the problems stemmed from the fact that Suze and her cousins *loved* my new job. Suze had even told me that it had practically been my Christmas present to her. They tried to push people into poor song choices—awkward and painfully too-soon expressions of devotion or encouraging angry breakup songs. Those too drunk to know better often found themselves onstage trapped at the halfway point through "Bohemian

Rhapsody" with no way out and nothing but a group of high-fiving women in the audience to explain their predicament. The kitsune also had an ongoing game where each picked an individual song, then tried to convince as many different people as possible to sing it over the course of an evening. Each time one of them got someone to sing her song, she won a point. High score won. Sometimes, to add an extra challenge, they'd all choose songs by the same artist.

I still had horrible flashbacks to Kelly Clarkson night.

A slow trickle of customers began just after five, and I was able to put the ineffective broom to one side and get to work taking drink orders and ferrying around baskets of snacks. I even tried to cheer up Orlando by reminding everyone that singing a song by Redbone would get them a free beer. An hour and a half in, one of the frat guys managed to give a halfway decent rendition of "Come and Get Your Love," making Orlando's perpetual scowl lighten.

The kitsune hit the bar at just past eight, strolling in like predators assessing a herd of sheep. Suze was in the lead, of course, but at this point I could recognize all of her six companions. The roster of kitsune had fluctuated wildly in my first few weeks of employment, but at this point it had settled into a more regular group. Suze's younger cousin Takara aimed herself directly at the bar, right where the concentration of potential mayhem was the thickest. I'd seen the blue-haired and freckled kitsune dressed for work the first time I met her, but Takara dressed for fun was always a terrifying prospect. Tonight she'd pulled out all the stops with a tiny flared skirt, corset top, and, worst of all, a faux fox-ear headband. One of the favored Hollis games was the over-under on how many different guys would try to pick her up if she sat alone at the bar with a gin and tonic. I'd lost money at this game.

Despite hours spent thinking of exactly how I would begin the conversation with Suzume (screaming *"J'accuse"* at her across the room seemed too extreme, but kind of captured where I was at the moment), I was still without a plan and was therefore grateful when my attention was co-opted by the occupants of table five, who were protesting that they hadn't been given any pens to write their song selections down with. I lifted up one of their discarded menus, revealing half a dozen pens. My excellent waitership was rewarded with sulky looks that suggested that I'd somehow deliberately hidden their pens to make them feel foolish.

My particular vocation of the moment preventing me from approaching Suzume immediately, I moved on to the next table, which was occupied by a post-breakup solidarity group that had already put in several requests for Fiona Apple songs, which I was not looking forward to. I cleared away a few of the empty cosmo glasses and tried not to take any of their irritated glares to heart. After all, from the snippets that I'd overheard, he *did* sound like a jerk.

As I carried the glasses back to the plastic box that I'd stashed just outside the back room, I felt a sharp tap on my arm. I looked over to see Suze's cousin Hoshi keeping pace with me. The Asian lines of her cheekbones and jaw were a strange contrast to a nose that would've done any Hassidic woman proud, and exuberantly curled hair that was acutely sensitive to the slightest humidity in the air. Hoshi was one of those women who, going by facial symmetry alone, should have been unattractive, even discounting an impressive knife scar that ran halfway across her throat and then shot abruptly up her chin. Yet, like the rest of the kitsune, she presented herself with such an air of "I'm doing you a favor by letting you buy me a drink" that the average brain simply accepted that she had to be hot. Plus, her usual cover story for her scar was that she was a CIA agent, and frankly, it was no surprise that men fell before her in droves.

"Heya," Hoshi said, giving me an affectionate nudge with her elbow. "Any potential targets identified?"

"Hoshi, I'm really not sure that I'm comfortable with getting involved in this, and frankly, I am not in even remotely the right headspace right now to even be contemplating your particular subset of needs." Hoshi was apparently the latest of the White Fox's granddaughters to feel a desire to hear the pitter-patting sounds of little kit paws in her home. The traditional reproductive approach in the kitsune was to find an appropriate man, get laid as many times as necessary until she was pregnant, then cut all ties with him and raise the resultant kits within the family. I didn't particularly argue with the merits of this approach, particularly given the havoc Suze's twin sister, Keiko, was currently creating by trying to have a relationship on the down-low, but I did object to Hoshi's belief that I should help in the screening process of potential baby daddies. Also, given my current bone to pick with her cousin, my interest level in Hoshi's family planning was in the negative zone.

"You've been awarded a partial vote, Fort. That is an honor that has never before been extended beyond the family, and you need to take this seriously."

"How much is this vote worth?"

"One-eighth of a fox vote," she said solemnly.

I dumped the glasses into the bin. "Well, I definitely feel honored now."

Hoshi completely ignored the edge in my voice, and smiled happily. "Suzu-san said that you'd say that." Her expression shifted, and playtime was clearly over. "Now, prospects?"

I knew from previous evenings that if I didn't throw one of my fellow men under the reproductive bus, Hoshi would continue to pester me all night with my opinions on various men and the traits that they might or might not have to offer to her future offspring, with all the tenacity of a small terrier with a rawhide bone. And the only thing worse than the conversation I was about to have with Suzume was to have it in front of one of her cousins. "You're into blonds, right? The tall blond at table seven has been bugging Pratibha for the last hour, so I think he's single. And judging by the chatter when I've been taking drinks, I think he's in a STEM field. He's got kind of a honking laugh, but I don't think that that's genetic."

Her eyes shot over to acquire the target, and she brightened. "Excellent start." Never glancing away from her unsuspecting victim, who continued drinking blissfully, with no awareness of the one-woman mobile unit of Ancestry.com that was about to swoop down upon him, Hoshi slipped a folded dollar into the front of my apron. "Buy yourself something pretty."

Normally I would've let her go at that, but I stopped her as she started moving in on the blond. "Hey, where's Suze?"

She frowned and gave the room a quick glance. "Um . . . not sure." Then a diabolical grin spread across her face, and she leaned toward me and whispered loudly, "Tonight's theme is *Cher*."

"Well, isn't that just the cherry on top of the shit sundae that my day has become." At the tables, people were signaling me, in dire need of snacks, drinks, or the need to complain uselessly about particular songs that were not included in our catalogue. "Hey, I've got to get back to my tables, but tell Suze to follow me into the kitchen next time I go back."

"Hell yeah, I will," Hoshi said, lasciviousness dripping from her voice.

I glared. "No, I need to talk to her."

Hoshi's expression didn't change. "*Suuure* you do. In

the *kitchen*." Her eyebrows were doing an impression of Groucho Marx. One hand whipped out and delivered a sharp slap across my ass, which, as I gritted my teeth and reminded myself, was probably some kind of attempt at affection. *"Talking."*

"Hoshi, do you mind?" Suzume's cousins seemed determined to give me excellent anecdotes to share whenever my female colleagues began chatting about on-the-job sexual harassment.

"Nope!" Hoshi assured me with a chipper lilt, then sauntered off in the direction of the blond.

Thirty minutes later, with the tables momentarily appeased with orders taken and drinks delivered, I ducked into the kitchen to fill up more popcorn baskets and avoid a particularly strangled take on "If I Could Turn Back Time." Apparently the kitsune Cher plan was already being executed.

A quick movement next to me revealed Suze, hopping up with vulpine ease to sit on the counter beside where I was working. Her dark eyes were gleaming with amusement, and she swung her legs casually. "Hey, did Hoshi tell you that tonight's theme is Cher? I already got a guy to request 'Half-Breed.'" She bumped me lightly with her knee. "Oh, and she also said that you had plans to slip me the salami, but I gotta say, I have concerns about the cleanliness of the surfaces in this kitchen already. Can you get a yeast infection from common food mold? Anyway, you'll understand why I would prefer to be on top for this endeavor."

I ignored her comment and, still lacking any plan on how to raise the subject, just spit it out. "Suze, you're charging my family for the nights you stay over?"

She blinked. "Of course."

This was not the response that I had expected, and my carefully planned response to what I had *thought* she would say was lost in my own incoherent sputtering.

Suze looked completely surprised. "You are *exponentially* safer with me around," she said firmly.

"Suze—"

"Remember last week when I killed a mouse? I probably saved you from Lyme disease!"

"Suze—"

"And when I told you on Tuesday that the milk had gone sour?"

"Suze."

"And how about when I warned you about the broken glass on the floor?"

"You broke that bowl!"

"And *warned* you about it!"

Our shouts fortunately coincided with a particularly up-tempo moment in the current song roster, but we spent a long moment glaring at each other as we reassessed our positions.

I took a deep breath. "Suze, this was a big fucking betrayal of trust, so I need you to actually take this seriously for one goddamn moment."

For one second, she looked completely stunned. Then her upper lip curled just a fraction. "Correct me if I'm wrong," she bit out, "but every cent I'm paid comes from your mother, and not you. And given how often I've listened to you explain and justify your reasons for trying to keep yourself as far from that dragon's horde of questionably acquired cash as possible, does it strike you as slightly hypocritical at this stage for you to suddenly clutch your pearls at the thought that I'm exploiting a few loopholes and stretching some justification to get my hands on a bit more of that wealth that—and, again, do correct me if I'm wrong—*you want absolutely nothing to do with*?"

"This isn't about money and it's not about family," I snapped. "Our personal time is *personal*—you and me, without you glancing at the clock and thinking about rounding up the damn quarter hour!"

"Nothing about you can ever *be* just personal, Fortitude Scott." Suzume's voice had dropped, and she wasn't loud, but low and almost snarling out the words. "Your mother holds the life of every person in her territory in her hands, and you think you can pretend that you're just another guy? Yes, I skimmed the top. No, I'm not even the least bit sorry. But if you think that me writing out those invoices had anything to do with what I feel about *you*, that it was nothing except the bottom line, then you are the biggest goddamn idiot I've ever met."

We broke apart at the same time, pacing away, as if too much had been said in those heated moments and we'd been shoved apart by magnetic forces. My chest was heaving as if I had run a mile, and I could actually feel a bead of sweat trickling between my shoulder blades. I turned and pressed my hands hard against the metal countertop, the cold shocking against my skin. Out of the corner of my eye I could see Suze pacing, stalking from one wall to another, and I could see the moment that she visibly restrained herself from giving a kick to my mop bucket, and instead nudged it aside with almost exquisite control.

I turned my head, just enough to see her fully, and said, softly, but with no softness, "No more charging for personal time."

Suzume's eyes were slits of discontent as she spun on her heel and marched away. She paused just at the doorway and, without turning, said, "My cousins and I considered making this a Bieber night, Fort. I can still make that happen." No mobster could've delivered a threat with such tightly leashed menace.

"I'm going to be checking your reimbursement requests in the future, and your overtime requests. Not Loren Noka, not my brother. Me."

At my words, she turned completely to face me, and had she been in fox form, there was no doubt that her ears would've been tightly pinned against her head. While her body language in human form was hobbled slightly by the lack of a luxurious tail and mobile ears, there was no mistaking that she was deeply and profoundly pissed off. Without breaking eye contact she swiped out one hand to snag a cookie from one of the snack baskets, and brought it up to take a rather vicious bite out of it. Chewing with deliberate slowness, she let the silence hang between us while she masticated, then swallowed. I glared right back at her, refusing to give an inch. After a long minute of assessment, she snarled, "Prepare for retribution. Shock *and* awe." She shoved herself away from the counter and was through the kitchen door with kitsune swiftness.

Fourteen renditions of "Baby" later, Orlando snagged my elbow while I was filling up a beer order.

"What did you do to piss those women off this badly?" he bellowed into my ear. The shouting was completely unnecessary, but I'm sure that it made him feel better. Frankly, I would've welcomed some temporary deafness, so I wasn't even going to complain about his manner of delivery.

"Suzume and I are negotiating relationship boundaries," I gritted out. The architect of my current misery and the still-churning outrage in my gut was perched on a bar stool five feet away, nursing her way through a Dogfish Head and refusing to meet my eyes, though every time my back was turned I could feel her glare of death burning into me.

Orlando shook his head. "Best work on your negotiation skills, boy."

It was a long night.

Last call came at a quarter to one. The bar had slowed down long before, with only a few people remaining. Pratibha was playing dance music, which Suze's cousins were enthusiastically hurling themselves around to. Unexpected Bieber frenzy aside, it had been a fairly normal Thursday night, and I'd been able to get a lot of the tables cleaned up as most people filtered out. Suzume was still at the bar, her back to Orlando, ostensibly watching her cousins.

I handed the last of the drink orders to Orlando, then snagged a bottle of Sapporo from the small below-bar fridge where we kept the good stuff and poured it into a glass. My boss lifted an eyebrow—apparently this was taking things slightly too far. I fished my tip money out of my apron, counted off the dollars, and handed it over. He gave a satisfied nod and returned to constructing the last set of drinks.

I walked over to stand next to Suze, and silently passed her the drink. She took one long sip, then tilted her head to give me a look that was half banked anger, half begrudging sheepishness.

"You know, I wasn't dating you because of the money," she said, her voice low and reluctant.

I didn't say anything, just accepted the glass when she handed it to me and drank. It had been hours since we sliced each other with words as sharp as glass, long enough for exhaustion to balance out the anger. Long enough for me to acknowledge that, as angry as we'd been (and still were) with each other, it meant something that she'd stayed. She could've walked right out the front door, but instead she'd stayed. Fumed, but stayed.

Even quieter, she said, "I didn't know it would hurt you. It was mostly a joke—I could do it, so I did."

I swallowed a second time, then passed it back to her. I could hear the honesty in her voice, and I recognized that ultimate truth about her nature in what she'd said. She could do it, so she did. *Nogitsune*, her grandmother had once said to me about Suzume. Forest fox. Trickster.

It should've made it hurt less, but it didn't.

She was watching me, those dark clever eyes flicking

over my face, picking up on who knows how much. After another long silence, she nodded to where her cousins were still dancing. "You gave a good tip to Hoshi. She moved the blond into the Reconnaissance stage."

"That's fantastic," I lied. What I had rather unwillingly learned was that this meant that Hoshi hadn't found anything to remove him from the genetic running tonight, and so the kitsune were going to now research him online, snoop into his financial records, and probably also break into his house at least once. It was also likely that they'd be obtaining some kind of genetic sample to send to those companies that offer a full DNA workup and print up a report about any dodgy genes or predispositions. If all that worked out, then she'd probably call him up for a date. The whole thing sounded pretty exhausting to me, and I had my moments when I wondered whether it was just another example of the kitsune's propensity to make a game out of everything.

Suzume finished off the beer, then handed the empty back to me. "I should probably move the herd home." There was the ghost of a smile at the corner of her mouth for a second, but it faded as she looked at me. "I'm the designated driver."

I nodded. I was glad that the night was at least over.

"Fort," she said, and there was just the slightest furrow in her forehead, the hint of worry in her eyes. "We're okay, aren't we?"

That worry loosened something in me, along with the question. Of anything I might ever have doubted about Suze, I could never doubt her intrinsic predator's hatred of expressing vulnerability. I could feel my shoulders unkink just slightly, and I moved my left hand over, sliding it along her shoulder, around the back of her neck to stroke that soft place just below her hairline. I felt her relax into my touch, saw that furrow smooth and disappear from her forehead. "We're okay for tonight," I said, unable to truthfully say anything beyond that, but feeling my own intense gratitude for the words.

Surprise flitted briefly across her face, replaced almost immediately by careful assessment. She hadn't expected my response to be conditional. But, then again, she hadn't expected me to be hurt.

Suze gave a slow, thoughtful nod. "Well, then don't forget to make sure you've got a clean shirt for tomorrow."

I blinked at her.

She stared at me for a second, and then a smile tugged at her lips. "You forgot, didn't you?"

"Forgot about wha— Oh, fuck that shit." I mentally kicked myself. Tomorrow was the *karhu* crowning ceremony for the *metsän kunigas*. It had been on the calendar for over a month, and I'd been tapped to go to represent the family as a fairly obvious punishment for my actions regarding the elevation of the newest *karhu*. With the recent kerfuffle over the succubi, I'd honestly forgotten. "When does this thing start again?"

Her smile widened. "Sunrise. Seven thirteen a.m. Didn't you read the e-vite?"

I cursed inventively.

A burble of a laugh escaped her, and she leaned over and into me, her right hand squeezing my knee as from shoulder to hip we fit against each other in that way that was still so new for us, yet was now so wonderfully familiar and natural. "For the bear-only part of the ceremony, Fort. We show up for the rest of it at nine." She slid off the stool with that easy vulpine grace of a creature who always knew where her body was in space, and tugged on her jacket. "Formal dress." She looked at me with fathomless dark eyes as she slowly fastened all her buttons. "I'll be at your place at eight thirty."

I nodded, acknowledging. But then she slid forward, her hips easing smoothly between my knees, her hands sliding up until her wrists were dangling loosely down my back, and she pressed one soft cheek against mine so that the smell of her hair filled my nose. "Do you see how much I like you, Fort?" she breathed into my ear. "I could've let you think that you had to attend the sunrise portion. And that part, BTW, is in fur. I think they're doing a formal investiture of shitting in the woods."

I knew there was no way that she could see the way that my mouth involuntarily curled into a smile, but I knew that she could feel the beat of my heart, and the way that my hands almost unconsciously wound around to rest at her waist. We stayed like that for a long moment, and all my anger from before couldn't hide just how good it felt.

When she finally moved out of the embrace, it was slow, her cheek dragging against mine just enough to rasp the beginnings of my one a.m. stubble. Every cell in my body knew exactly how many micrometers her mouth was from mine, but she didn't push for a kiss and I wasn't ready yet to turn and take one. But I didn't hurry to take my hands from her, letting them slide down from her waist and rest on her hips, my fingers pressing just harder than gentle into her flesh before I finally let them drop.

Whatever she read in my face, that signature strut was back in Suze's step as she walked out the door, the rest of her cousins falling in behind her as if by some unspoken signal.

"Bunch of jackals," Orlando muttered loudly behind me.

"Right genus, wrong species," I replied.

Chapter Four

I didn't mind working late-night hours, and in fact far preferred it to insanely early morning hours, but I wasn't exactly at my most bright-eyed and bushy-tailed when I rolled out of bed the next morning after a mere five hours of sleep. A hot shower helped dispel some of the cobwebs from my brain and the steam removed wrinkles from my shirt. Typical for me, I had arrived home so tired from work that I'd completely forgotten Suze's clothing advice, and wasn't able to find any appropriately clean button-downs in my closet. After a quick pawing through several of the clothing piles that seemed to spring up around my room like mushrooms following a rainstorm, I finally managed to extract a nice white oxford that had only a minor sweat funk, easily cured by some strategic Febreze-ing. It did have a small tomato-sauce stain, but thankfully only where I was confident that my tie could cover it.

I spent extra time shellacking my hair down with extra-hold gel. I knew it made me look like I was trying to audition for a bit role in *The Godfather*, but my hair had two settings—gelled into submission or Rorschach test. The latter didn't exactly seem suitable for today.

Dan was sitting at the table when I came into the main room, snacking on the leftover Redbones cookies that I'd brought home the previous night and quizzing himself with his ubiquitous stack of flash cards. He must've just gotten back from his morning jog, since he was dressed in sweatpants and a long-sleeved shirt, and bless the man, he must've started the coffeepot before he left. He had a steaming mug in front of him, and there was just enough in the pot for a second cup.

"Hey, did Jaison stay over last night?" I asked, pondering the coffee.

"Nah, the rest is for you."

Reassured, I poured out the rest, then dug around in the fridge for the creamer. During my leaner financial times, I'd gotten to the point of stuffing my pockets with extra nondairy creamers when I was at restaurants and just keeping them at home, and even with decent paychecks I'd kept the habit going. During our first week of living together, Dan had watched my preparation with silent horror. For his coffee he bought pint containers of heavy cream from the grocery store, and had finally broken and staged a coffee intervention on me. Jaison, who simply drank his coffee black, had watched the entire fracas with great amusement.

I sipped at my cup while I pondered my breakfast options. Already being dressed was leaving me leery about eating anything that could leave a stain, since with my luck this *would* be the day that I dropped breakfast all over myself. Wherever things had been left between me and Suzume, I knew for certain that I didn't want to pick them up with a butter smear down my shirt. At last I dug out a half-petrified container of s'mores Pop-Tarts and set in on them.

"Big day today?" Dan asked as I settled myself and my breakfast at the table. He gestured at my suit, which was definitely not daily attire.

I nodded. "For the *metsän kunigas*, yeah. I have to go and be the Scott rep." I tugged open one of the foil packets. "Hey, I look okay, right? Like, no holes in the back of my pants?" Suze was due over soon, but I'd learned the hard way that expecting her to point out holes in my pants was asking her to compromise her future hilarity at the expense of pointing out things that I should've caught myself, and that really wasn't a fair position to put her into.

Yes, we'd had that conversation.

Dan shook his head. "I didn't see any. But, Fort, the four-in-hand knot really doesn't look good when you have a suit jacket on." His expression was pained. Dan took personal presentation very seriously, and seemed eternally put upon that both Jaison and I completely failed to keep up.

"It's the only one I know how to tie, Dan." I knew that I sounded grumpy, but it matched how I felt.

Immediately Dan set down his flash cards and started tugging at my tie. "Gimme that."

I let him, frankly somewhat relieved. I didn't like showing up and knowing that people thought that I hadn't made enough of a clothing effort, but at the same time I frankly just sucked at putting myself together and it was hard not to just feel irritated that we hadn't reached the promised future of sci-fi fiction that consisted of easy-to-wear zip-up jumpsuits for every occasion. That, at least, I figured I could handle. I mean, assuming that the fabric also self-cleaned.

"Fort, your shirt has a stain." From Dan's expression I might as well have burned down an orphanage.

"The tie was covering it," I defended.

He shuddered. This was why I preferred it when Jaison stayed over—yes, it put a strain on our tiny coffeemaker and required the drinker of the second cup to start a second batch, but at the same time it also gave me some backup whenever Dan gave me that look that suggested that I was practically a caveman, barely able to wrap animal skin around my nakedness as I gnawed at mastodon with my teeth.

"I'll loan you a tie tack," Dan offered. He quickly removed the last traces of my apparently substandard knot, then with a few quick passes around his own neck put together a frankly really impressive knot. He left it loose enough that he could take it off himself and hand it over to me. Maybe I should've had more pride to reject his mommy-bird-feeding-baby approach to formal wear, but I certainly wasn't going to argue with results. I slid it over my own head, then tucked it under my collar and tightened it up. A quick look in the reflective surface of the microwave confirmed that it actually looked pretty damn good. Good enough that I had to restrain the urge to take a selfie and send it to Chivalry. The only thing that held me back was the knowledge that he would probably print it out and keep it in his wallet like a baby picture.

"That's really cool, Dan. Where'd you learn how to do that one?"

"Ghouls are great at tying knots," my roommate said. "It's a cultural point of pride, since we spent so many years having to tie our human victims on spits to roast over the fire."

I stared as he took another sanguine bite out of his chocolate-chip cookie.

Dan laughed. "You're too easy, Fort. The knot is called a Euclid, and I learned it by watching a video on YouTube."

"Oh, well, thanks." I pondered the awesomeness of the tie for another minute, then asked, "Hey, do you know any of the bears?" I'd spent my early childhood living with my human foster parents, with no real contact with any of the supernatural elements beyond a monthly dinner with my mother and siblings. After my foster parents were murdered by my sister, I'd been brought down to live in the mansion, but even then I'd seen very few supernaturals beyond my family. Firstly, I'd tried as hard as I could to reject everything that wasn't a strictly human life—as much as I could, of course, while at the same time living with three other vampires. But also there really weren't that many to see, even had I wanted to.

There were two kinds of nonhumans who lived under my mother's rule—the ones who could pass for human, and who spent much of their lives hiding right in plain sight, and the ones who would never be able to pass for human, and had to stay far away from humans. Newport was one of three towns on Aquidneck Island, which made up just under forty square miles in the mighty state of Rhode Island, and its entire supernatural population consisted of my family, plus a small colony of Norwegian-extract trolls that lived under the Claiborne Pell Bridge and did a better job of passing as boulders than as humans. So during my entire career in elementary, middle, and high school, I'd been the only nonhuman in the building. Which had not done my sense of isolation any great favors. When I left home for college, I'd played human with such an intent focus that I probably would've run in the other direction if I'd seen another nonhuman.

Dan was my first nonhuman roommate, and there was still a strangeness in being able to talk with him about all the things that I'd spent so many years never daring to talk about with anyone other than my family, who I'd been spending all my efforts to avoid seeing anyway. And despite my recent crash course in the running of the territory and the races who owed my mother fealty, it occurred to me suddenly that I actually didn't know too much about how they functioned between their own separate groups. I mean, maybe they'd had their own Cub Scout troops.

"I went to high school with a few," Dan said, giving a

small shrug. "Never had much to do with them, of course."

It was the "of course" that piqued my curiosity. Apparently that was a no to the Cub Scout question. "Why is that? I remember from when I was talking to Lilah Dwyer that she said that the Neighbors didn't socialize with the bears, but I figured that that was a bear/elf thing. Is it actually normal?"

A cynical smile spread across Dan's face and he shook his head slightly, as if my naïveté in this situation was something that he was trying to decide was infuriating or cute. "Fraternization isn't exactly something your family encourages, Fort, so most of us keep to within our own kind." He took a deep drink of his coffee. "I think one of my biggest teenage rebellion moments was when I was friends with a changeling kid for a while. Drove my father crazy, which was really half the reason I did it. I mean, Nate wasn't a bad guy by any stretch of the imagination, but I'm not sure I ever really liked him. Felt sorry for him, mostly. One minute he was living with a normal family in Connecticut, and the next minute his death gets faked and he gets told that he's actually part elf. We still do Christmas cards, but we drifted after graduation. Poor guy got an arranged marriage with another changeling girl who is even more screwed up than he is, so now he's got a wife with a drinking problem and four kids under the age of five. Talking with him is like dipping a toe in the Swamps of Sadness."

"Huh." I considered that for a second, adding it to the puzzle of what I'd already observed or been told. "But, depressing high school friends aside, I mean, even if my family isn't big on different groups socializing, there's no rule against it that I've seen. Besides, you outnumber us by a lot. Why not try to get some strength in numbers, use other groups to shore up your own weaknesses, or at least form some bonds and support?"

I said that last part while Dan was taking a swig of his coffee, and the ghoul laughed so hard that he ended up spitting liquid. Even then he continued to laugh until he was doubled over, tears coming out of his eyes, and he was slapping the top of the table with one open hand, as if his mirth was so great that mere laughter alone was insufficient to express it.

I tried not to feel insulted.

Finally, when he'd managed to calm himself sufficiently so that he was only making the occasional small snorting noise, Dan pulled himself together enough to answer, "Fort, if I didn't know you by now, I'd wonder whether your family was using you to encourage every fringe wannabe Thomas Paine in this territory so that they could eventually just get them all in one place and kill them."

There was a long pause between the two of us while I stared at him and tried to process what he'd just said. It took me a minute to realize that there had been nothing really amused about the way he'd laughed earlier, and that he was actually deadly serious in what he'd just said.

"Shit," I said, stunned. "You actually thought that for a while, didn't you?"

"Yeah, I did," Dan replied honestly. "For, like, the first two weeks. But if that's the plan, you sure as hell don't know it. You're the real deal, a vampire bleeding heart."

"Ooh, blood joke for the vampire. Funny, Dan. Real funny." I was grumping mostly because it was hard to fully respond to what he was saying while at the same time dealing with the dissonance of being handed an entirely new lens to view our first month of cohabitation through. No wonder he'd seemed so cranky and close-mouthed at first.

"Okay, that one was a little bad," Dan admitted. "But seriously. No one wants to be the one to stick their neck out. And if the elves go down, or the bears, or whoever, no group wants to get pulled down with them. So the ghouls worry about ghoul business, and everyone else can go get burned."

"That can't be what everyone thinks," I insisted.

"But enough of them do." He pulled the last cookie out of the bag and gestured at me with it. "That's what you don't get, Fort, and it's why the Occupy movement fizzled. Most people are getting along okay with the status quo, and they aren't going to rock the boat."

I thought about what my mother had openly discussed the day before, and wondered how much longer that status quo was going to continue to exist. Prudence's idea of a great territory, which I'd been subjected to at length during my mother's New Year's State of the Territory financial review, was one where instead of it being vampire-only on Aquidneck Island, it was vampire-only for the entirety of my mother's territory. I couldn't help wondering how well avoiding fraternization would reward the races in the territory at that point. "Yeah . . . but what happens if the water suddenly gets choppy and the boat flips over anyway?"

Dan's dark eyes were serious. "I guess that's the question that would come up if a rogue wave came along," he said quietly, and I knew that, beyond our tortured metaphor, we were both thinking about the same thing, but that neither of us was going to say it.

A loud knocking on the door broke the moment, and Suzume strolled in. I'd never given her a key, yet she had somehow acquired one on her own. I'd decided that it was in my own best interest not to investigate her sources too closely, so I hadn't commented on it. Dan had very seriously proposed having the locks changed, but I'd pointed out that that would simply make it a fun challenge for her, and we'd be completely out the cost of getting the locks switched the moment that she successfully acquired a new key.

Unlike me, Suze had the uncanny ability to look as good after five hours of sleep as most people could only dream to look after eight. If I hadn't been looking for it, I would've missed that slight hint of caution around her eyes, the forced brightness in the smile that she flashed as she said, "Looking good, Fort!" I wondered whether she was maintaining a facade to attempt to gaslight Dan, or whether she was testing the waters to see whether last night's argument might've blown over like a midsummer squall. "Dan tied your tie, didn't he?"

"I might've outsourced some aspects of my appearance, yes," I acknowledged loftily, letting her set the tone for now. "But in an entirely managerial sense."

"He made use of local artisanal talent," Dan added.

I nodded. "This is an organic, farm-to-table tie knot."

She laughed. "C'mon, we need to hit the road. We only got half an inch of powder last night, so the Scirocco will be fine."

"You've got studded winter tires on your Audi, Suze. Why can't we just take that?" I didn't bother to hide how irked I felt. While it was my own financial choices that had resulted in the same all-season tires that had been on the Scirocco when I bought it, I wasn't above coveting the awesome tires on Suze's car. And as unreasonable as it might've been at the moment, I also wasn't above taking some of the residual hurt over last night's fight out onto exposing her Audi's underbody to the rock salt undoubtedly coating the Providence roads.

Suze made a show of running a hand along her temple to carefully adjust any strands of hair that had escaped from her perfectly constructed braided bun—though of course there weren't any. "My Audi is sitting where it belongs—in my garage. Taka gave me a ride over this morning so that the road scuz can go where *it* belongs—on your car." There was a slight narrowing of her eyes, a hint of a warning that she might not be happy with where we were right now, but that I shouldn't expect any undue favors.

"And on Taka's car, apparently," I said wryly, privately accepting the message.

"Taka leases, so she doesn't give a shit about what happens to that car, short of it being hit by a meteor." Suze paused to consider. "Okay, actually a meteor would probably be okay as well, since I think that counts with the insurance as an act of God. Plus, as long as she wasn't in the car at the time, that would just be awesome."

Dan shook his head and picked his stack of flash cards back up. "Have a great day, guys."

My one good formal coat was not meant for Rhode Island in January, so I did what guys almost always do in the winter, which was to pull on my regular winter coat, a battered yet exceptionally toasty parka. Once we got to the venue, my plan was to leave my coat in the car and just run the gauntlet inside, trusting in my suit jacket to keep me from getting hypothermia on the way. Once inside, I knew, things would probably swing in my favor as the men walked around in comfort in suit jackets and the women shivered in their dresses and thin cardigans. Game, set, and match to the patriarchy.

As I pulled the door shut behind us, Suze looked up at me, the mask of normality that she'd put on in front of Dan dropping. There was worry there, and a lot of unhappiness—probably that I'd made her worry, but I didn't think that that was all of it. Some of it, I thought, was for me.

"I'm sorry that it hurt you," she said, so quickly that her words almost ran over one another. She spoke as if the words were an unpleasant medicine, and she twisted her face away for a moment, a hard frown pressing her dark eyebrows together, before focusing her eyes on me again.

I heard what she said, and I could feel what she hadn't.

"But you don't understand why it hurt me," I said, filling in the blank.

There was a pause, and her mouth twisted, real anxiety curling the sides of her mouth down, her eyes darting away from me. A long silence passed. "Can't it be enough that I'm sorry?" she said finally, quietly, her shoulders slumping almost in despair.

I looked at her, weighing it—that brutally honest apology, with all its flaws and gaps, almost beautiful in its truthful insufficiency. She didn't understand—and she was admitting that she couldn't.

When I'd told her that I wanted to date her, she warned me that she couldn't, and wouldn't, change who she was. I'd told her that I'd known that, but still wanted her. For the first time I was really faced with those words—had I been honest? Had I meant it? Or had I meant it, but been wrong?

Everything felt balanced for a moment, and I don't think either of us breathed. I considered those questions.

"I don't know if it'll always be enough," I said, trying to give her the same painful honesty she'd offered me. "But it's enough now. It's enough for today, and for tomorrow."

A small smile curled at her mouth, and her dark eyes brightened. And then she was leaning up and I was leaning down, and that kiss was a relief like a sip of water in the middle of a heat wave in July.

On the way down, we passed Mrs. Bandyopadyay, who was bundled up with the kinds of layers normally associated with treks in the Yukon. Her bichon frise, Buttons, was snapped into his own insulated Lands' End doggie coat, with matching booties on all four paws and a rather jaunty hat. They were beginning a slow promenade down the stairs, and I immediately stopped. Mrs. Bandyopadyay was somewhere in her upper eighties and increasingly delicate, and even the sight of her navigating the hall steps during the winter was enough to make anyone cringe, and taking Buttons for walks seemed like an invitation for breaking a hip and dying of exposure. I knew for a fact that she'd promised her adult children that she'd have Buttons do his business on pee pads during the winter—mostly because at some point all three of them had cornered me in the hallway to beg me about trying to prevent their mother from walking Buttons when the weather was bad. And by bad, they really meant "before May."

"Mrs. Bandyopadyay," I said, and at the sound of my voice she gave me a guilty look—she hadn't seen me earlier because of the size of her hat's wool earflaps, which restricted any periphery vision, "if Buttons needs to be walked, you know that Dan or I are always happy to do it."

"I know," she replied, sounding fretful, "but I hate imposing. And I saw Daniel coming back from his run and considered asking, but you know how Buttons gives him trouble."

I did, actually. For a ten-pound dog that seemed composed primarily of white and apricot fluff, Buttons had a very definite idea about who was in charge—and that was Buttons. Even now, dressed in his ridiculous getup, he was emitting a very seriously pissed-off growl at Suzume, who was responding by completely refusing to acknowledge his existence and exhibiting a demeanor of icy disdain. If Mrs. Bandyopadyay hadn't been around, though, I wouldn't have put it past Suze to change forms and throw down with Buttons to prove, once and for all, who was the top canid in this building. Buttons was probably the one area that Suze and Dan could agree on.

I knew for a fact that Suze had, in fox form, peed in every one of Buttons's favorite spots, just to piss him off. It was kind of hard to figure out how I was supposed to respond to that one. Discussions of relationship boundaries, after all, so rarely involved actual urination boundaries.

"I don't mind walking him," I said. "And I used to walk dogs for a living—Buttons is no comparison to walking a Great Dane."

That seemed to reassure her, and she handed over the leash and went back inside, presumably to start what had to be a half-hour process of delayering herself.

"No comparison, huh?" Suze asked as we continued downstairs, Buttons alternating between hauling on the leash so hard that he nearly choked himself and wheeling around to run at my ankles threateningly, mouth open to reveal his sharp little teeth.

"None at all," I agreed. Paprika the Great Dane might've been a hundred and eighty pounds, but he'd been a dream to walk, with the only challenge coming when the fierce desire to be cuddled became too much for him, and he would attempt to rub his massive head against me, occasionally with enough enthusiasm to almost knock me over. "I would take ten Paprikas over one Buttons."

Suze took the keys over to warm up the Scirocco and get the de-icing process going while I gave Buttons a quick morning constitutional. The little demon showed his gratitude for his successfully empty bladder by giving the leash a hard and unexpected yank just as we walked over a section of black ice, and I slipped and went down hard on my left knee. Then, while I was still cursing the heavens over that, Buttons took the opportunity to nip my right hand, hard enough to draw blood.

I used the first aid kit in the car to patch up my hand while Suze carried Buttons back to his owner by the scruff of his neck. When she arrived back at the car, I was examining the damage to my knee—I had a hell of a bruise and it was throbbing, but at least I'd somehow managed to avoid tearing my best pair of formal slacks—which was very lucky, since my second-best pair was my last pair, and those had a huge hole ripped in the right cuff that needed a tailor's attention before they could be worn out in public again.

Suze shook her head at me. "Fort, why don't you leave the good deeds to Jaison? He's the only one apart from Mrs. Bandyopadyay who even likes that little shit of a dog."

"That's because Buttons likes him," I muttered. It was typical—everyone liked Jaison, even Satan's own bichon frise. "Besides, better me than Mrs. Bandyopadyay. Can you imagine that poor woman stepping on that ice? It would be like you and my best mixing bowl all over again. Nothing but wreckage."

Suze snorted in amusement as I turned the engine over to start the car, patiently waiting through its initial sluggishness. Mechanically fuel-injected engines didn't like the cold. "Mrs. Bandyopadyay apologizes for Buttons, by the way. She says that using the pee pads makes him cranky."

"Breathing oxygen makes that dog cranky."

She ignored me. "I told her about all the black ice, and said that maybe she should just try walking Buttons in the hallway."

I paused in the act of merging into traffic and stared at her. "You what?"

"She was a little hesitant at first, but then I reminded her about what a dick your landlord was about fixing her stove that time she had a gas leak, and she seemed to warm up to the idea. She agreed that karma might need a little assistance in this situation."

"Suze, I really don't want to have to be walking through dog piss and shit every time I go home. Tell me that she's not actually convinced."

"Oh, stop worrying so much," Suze said. "Besides,

your landlord hasn't cleaned that hallway any time this decade. I doubt you'll even notice the dog piss, and Mrs. Bandyopadyay is pretty confident that she can use the pooper scooper to get his crap off the carpet without having to bend over too much. You know, 'cause of her back problems."

"Suze, I say this from a place of deep and abiding affection: I'd rather think about the odds that the dog bite on my hand gets infected and gangrenous than about the ways that you're trying to help out right now."

Silence reigned for half the drive over to the *metsän kunigas* ceremony, at which point I stopped at Dunkin' Donuts to get her a salted caramel hot chocolate—a beverage that to me made my taste buds attempt ritualized suicide, yet always seemed to entirely satiate that portion of Suzume that was basically a hummingbird. It was apparently judged to be a worthy peace offering, and Suze was back to peppiness as we arrived at the East Providence Elks Lodge. I was almost entirely certain that the *metsän kunigas* had lied in some way on their rental application for today's ceremony. Or this was a much looser fraternal order than I had previously been led to believe.

I mentioned this observation to Suze as I cruised through the overfull parking lot. She smiled beatifically in response. "The bears had a sixty-thousand-dollar bill to pay to my family for disguising the bodies of Matias Kivela and Peter Utrio from the police. Then we hit them with another thirty thousand to fake a suicide for their murdering psychopath of a cousin. My understanding is that Gil and Dahlia were practicing some austerity measures with this place."

"That's terrible, Suze. Why are you so happy about that?"

"Because, unlike you, I believe in the beauty of capitalism. I am proud to be an American, while you are showing suspiciously Canadian elements of socialistic inclination."

I couldn't restrain my laugh, and she gave a satisfied smile, then leaned over to give me a salt, caramel, and chocolate-flavored kiss, which managed to taste better than I would've expected. "Don't get so worried, Fort. You have the financial paperwork on the Kivela family— their company is in great shape, and after we set up that suicide front for Carmen, Matias's assets were able to get through probate and end up with his sister. They're selling the house to another of the *metsän kunigas*, and once it goes through, they'll be able to pay off those lines of home interest credit that both of them pulled to cover our bill."

"Dan says that groups in this territory avoid fraternization. But you always seem to know plenty about what people outside the kitsune are up to. Why is that?"

Suze leaned over to tap the tip of my nose affectionately. But despite the playfulness of her gesture, her voice was completely serious. "Because this isn't fraternization, Fort. It's keeping a cautious eye on all the idiots around us who suffer under the weighty burden of not being foxes, and who therefore cannot be trusted to act in a rational manner." She looked around the lot that we were currently taking a third circuit around—while I was sure that it was large enough to comfortably fit all of its fraternal member automobiles during the summer, it was suffering from the typical winter issue of snow removal. Their plow service had been pushing all the snow to the back third of the lot, which at this point had consolidated into an unmovable edifice of icy and very grimy snow, looking solid enough that I probably could've ascended it with an ice hammer and some pitons. It definitely wasn't going anywhere until at least late spring, and in the meantime had severely reduced the parking options. And given that we'd arrived after all the *metsän kunigas*, there was simply nowhere for me to stick the Scirocco. Even the handicapped spots and the fire lane had already been filled with cars. Suze gave a decisive gesture. "Now I think it's time to stop dillydallying here and abuse your power the way it was meant to be abused—park one of these fuckers in. Preferably by the door. It's as cold as Frosty the Snowman's scrotum out there."

There was no other way around it, so I ended up parking in a trio of Saabs. The bears were of Finnish extract, and clearly had a preference for Nordic cars. "I'm pretty sure that Frosty the Snowman was never constructed for anatomical correctness, Suze."

"He was when my cousins and I used to make him."

My introduction to the *metsän kunigas* had begun under extremely poor circumstances, when Suze and I got called in to investigate the murder of the then-*karhu*, Matias. Today's ceremony was to formalize the passing of the title to his nephew, Gil. Gil hadn't been a popular choice in my family—he was a hot-blooded guy, intensely devoted to his family and the well-being of the bears in the territory, and wasn't afraid to be critical of what he saw as flaws in the way that the Scotts controlled and ruled the *metsän kunigas*. But his older sister, Dahlia, who'd been my brother's pick to inherit, had supported her brother over herself.

When they greeted me at the door, I was struck once again by what a contrast the siblings presented. Dahlia was all poised, smooth control, her bobbed hair sleek and carefully presented, and her expressions so tightly tamped down that Vegas card champions would've envied her poker face. Gil, however, was an inch shorter than his sister and built like a wrestler, all boxy muscle, with a face that showed every emotion that went through his head. When Gil was pissed at you, you knew it—

usually because he was bellowing at you. And when he liked you, there was no guessing at it.

Since Suze and I had helped him save the lives of both his sister and his husband, in addition to supporting his bid for the title of *karhu*, we were apparently in his good books right now. And I learned that when he greeted me with a hug that strained the integrity of my rib cage and lifted me several inches off the ground. Since I hadn't realized before this that we were on hugging terms (and the term "bear hug" had never been more appropriate), it was somewhat of a surprise. I was feeling distinctly rumpled when I was finally released from his embrace.

"I feel incredibly welcomed," I said honestly. The wide smile across Gil's face was infectious, and I couldn't help returning it. Beside him, Dahlia settled for a more sedate handshake.

"Don't even think about it, teddy bear," Suze warned Gil as he turned to her.

"You don't have to worry, Suzume," Gil replied, leaning in to give her a quick kiss on the cheek. "I don't like you as much as Fortitude."

"For which you have my eternal gratitude."

I shook my head and greeted Gil's husband, Kevin. The Kivela siblings had inherited their Mexican father's coloration, and it was kind of funny how the blond, pale Kevin matched their mother's Finnish looks so closely and in fact blended right into the majority of the group. There were two groups of werebears in my mother's territory, the Providence group and another in northern Maine. Both traced their roots back to an original community of Finnish bears who had petitioned my mother for entry over a century ago.

Among the group of conservatively dressed people standing around the open area of the Elks Lodge interior, a blend of the werebears and several human spouses, which I found impossible to differentiate just from a glance, were two bear cubs, incongruously rolling around with each other in the pursuit of a bright green rubber ball. All the people standing around them, nursing cups of coffee and the occasional portion of bagel, simply ignored the spectacle of the two cubs, stepping aside when the two and their ball barreled past them, and at most giving them slightly amused glances.

"Anni and Linnea," Gil supplied, following my glance. "My nieces."

"I'd never seen them in their other forms before," I said politely, hoping that the bears used similar terminology to the foxes.

"It's not usual," Dahlia said quickly, surprising me in her emphasis. After all, whenever I'd seen the younger kitsune, Yuzumi's three-year-old triplets, they spent more time in fur than skin. I'd spent more than my fair share of time trying to discourage Riko from gnawing her sharp white canines into my shoes.

Gil must've seen something in my face, because he explained, "To become a bear is a gift that comes with our blood, but it is a learned skill. The part of the ceremony that is private is conducted as bears. As members of the bloodline of the ruling house, Anni and Linnea needed to be there, but changing is more difficult for them, and it will be a few more hours before they can return to their natural forms."

"They look like they're having a fantastic time," I said, while beside me Suze gave a small, smug sniff. It never took much to reassert a kitsune's belief in her inherent superiority to other species, and apparently this more than qualified.

The ceremony started soon after that, with everyone pitching in to set up an array of folding chairs. I quickly realized why this assignment had been characterized by my family as a punishment for my choice in supporting Gil as *karhu*—and it hadn't been because of the early start time. The ceremony was a long series of blessings being read, then protracted periods of solemn reflection by all participants. Worse yet, the blessings were all in Finnish—which, unfortunately, none of the current crop of *metsän kunigas* actually spoke. Apparently the last person who had a working grasp of the language had been one elderly bear in his nineties who had recently passed away. Much of the ceremony was actually achieved thanks to the forethought of Gil and Dahlia's grandfather, who had, at some point in the nineteen sixties, committed the ceremony text to a series of slide projections with accompanying audiotape. While I gave him points for the preservation of historical tradition, I also could've lived without three hours of staticky droning in a completely incomprehensible language, punctuated with barked orders of "Advance slide!" The slides themselves were simply the text of what he was reading, which was useful only in the sense that I could visually identify that I had no idea where each word began or ended.

As the visiting dignitary, I was seated in the front, beside the Kivela family, so there was no escape. Suzume was no help at all, since after the initial ten minutes she excused herself to take a bathroom break. She never returned from that break, which might have concerned me, except Anni and Linnea were suddenly joined in their ball-chasing fun by a black fox.

When the final tape of the recording was finally at its end, everyone roused themselves from their glazed-eyed stupor long enough to make polite golf claps. While I was shaking hands with Ilona and several of the other older bears, Suzume appeared at my side, again neatly put together in her navy wool dress and smiling politely, giving no indication at all that we'd all seen her pass the time during the ceremony by, at one point, stealing the ball from the little girls, jumping to the top of the stack of still-folded metal chairs, and taunting them into climbing for it, with entirely predictable results.

Gil made his way over to us. "I'm actually thinking that one of my first proposals will be to translate the ceremony into English."

"That is so Vatican Two of you, Gil," Suze said.

"Well, it's either that or have the film converted to DVD, and I'm not sure that that's something I can do in good conscience. After all, someday Anni or Linnea will become *karhu*. Having to sit through Grandpa's presentation is not exactly the legacy I'd like to pass forward."

"You're a good uncle." I hoped that my level of fervency wasn't rude, but just the thought of anyone having to sit through that again was horrifying.

With perfect timing, lunch was announced. It was a huge potluck affair, and I was able to fill my plastic plate multiple times and I still hadn't even managed to taste half of the dishes. The bears were apparently very serious about food. As I swallowed my third smoked salmon hors d'oeuvre, I noted to Suze that, as terrible as the ceremony had been, the food was almost good enough to make up for it.

She gave me a sly smile. "I see that you enjoy eating like a bear, then." I frowned, then looked back at the tables of food and realized what she was referring to — every dish contained either fish or berries. I shushed her as she snickered.

Toward the end of the afternoon I was sitting off to the side of the group, making conversation with Kevin about his Web design business while Suze applied herself to working the room, probably collecting scraps of noteworthy information to bring back to her grandmother, the White Fox. Gil made his way over to me, accepting congratulations from a few other bears with polite nods, but homing in on me with all the subtlety of Bullet Bill in *Super Mario Brothers*.

"Let me guess," I said when Gil parked himself in the chair next to me. "You'd like to have a chat about some territory issues."

"I promise to at least keep it a friendly chat," he said, with a little "what can you do?" shrug. Kevin gave a smothered laugh and headed back to the crowd. Suzume caught my eye from where she was chatting with a few other women in their early thirties, and lifted an inquiring eyebrow, clearly wanting to know whether I wanted her to come over. I gave a quick shake of my head, and she returned to her conversation.

"So this conversation is going to be fox free," Gil noted. "I'm flattered."

"Gil, you really should ask your sister for some pointers on diplomacy. And I'm not even someone who usually wants all the fluffy language and talking around a subject."

"That's why Dahlia runs the business and I just go out to check out claims," Gil said. "We each have our strengths. And you know that I'll never stop being grateful that you and Suzume helped me save Kevin and my sister, but I think that maybe it's time for a little more plain dealing between the *metsän kunigas* and the Scotts." He held up a hand when I initially began to respond, saying, "I'm not pushing today, Fort, I'm really not."

"I notice that emphasis on 'today,'" I replied. "But I have to tell you that my sister wasn't happy when I supported you as *karhu*. None of my family was. So you need to be really careful, and really cautious. Please"—I dropped my voice almost to a mutter—"please don't give them a reason to want you dead."

Gil's dark eyes were steady. "We both know that they already want me dead. Not actively, but enough that I'm certainly not going to let myself cross paths with Prudence Scott any time soon." He shifted. "But you were on the front lines with what happened—you saw the way that Carmen planned to exploit Scott control to get what she wanted. If the bears had more self-governance—"

"*Gil,*" I cautioned.

He frowned, irritated. "Fine, okay, we'll use different words. After what happened with Carmen, I think it would be in *everyone's* best interest if the bears had more of an ability to handle and investigate more problems internally."

"My sister is not happy that even the kitsune have those rights right now. I'm not sure that either she, or even my brother, will be overly enthused at the bears requesting them." I sighed and rubbed my hand hard over my head, forgetting for a second how much gel I'd applied that morning. The result was a disturbing crunchiness under my palm, and a very real feeling that I probably didn't want to know what I looked like right now. However, my hair was very much the least of my problems at the moment. After the issue with the succubi, the last thing I wanted was to have to get into another discussion with Prudence and Chivalry—yet from the increasingly stubborn look on Gil's face, that was exactly what I was heading toward. And even worse, I agreed with Gil. Carmen had been relying on having a vampire roll in to investigate her father's death who had no interest in finding anything other than a quick and easy target for blame, and had come closer to getting exactly that than any of us really wanted to think about right now, given that her plan would've resulted in Dahlia's death, and quite probably Gil's as well.

"Listen," I said, "what about this—I go to my family and suggest that a specific member of the *metsän kunigas* is assigned to be an assistant or an attaché, or whatever, whenever the Scotts are dealing with bear affairs. That person not only advises us about what's going on inside the community, and gives us feedback about what might work or not work, but also keeps you informed about what's going on. Now, I can't make any promises, because I have to sell this to my family. But this way you're not in the dark on what we're doing, and you know that at least you guys have a voice in the room, even if right now it's just in an advisory capacity."

It clearly wasn't what Gil had been hoping for, but at the same time I could see that he was weighing that against his likelihood of getting anything better, and realizing that that was pretty much nil. Which obviously didn't make him any happier about it, but with a small grimace he nodded. "Okay, that's okay as a first step."

I heard his emphasis on the last two words, and couldn't help sighing internally. Standing between my family and Gil was like being in King's Quest VI during the crushing ceiling trap scene. Two unyielding surfaces and one squishy person in the middle.

There was a brief pause, and then the unhappiness on Gil's face was replaced by worry. I could feel the hair stand up on the back of my neck, and I knew even before he started talking what Gil was going to ask about. "Fort, I'm sure you know that there are a lot of rumors right now. Rumors about your mother . . . and her health."

He looked at me, and I could see, for just a second, just how terrified he was.

I paused. Maybe the smart thing was to keep quiet, to keep family business to the family, but we'd been through some stuff together. Maybe Gil would never be the kind of person who I could really feel comfortable around, or have a real friendship with, but I owed him something.

I leaned closer to Gil, and, very quietly, so quietly that even he would have to strain to hear, I whispered, "I don't know what the rumors are, Gil, not for sure. But things are changing. I think things are going to change fast."

Gil shuddered, just once, and his mouth pressed into a thin, pained line. He nodded quickly, then clapped me hard on the shoulder with one broad palm.

Back in the car, Suze immediately cranked up the heat to full, threw her heels into the backseat, and started wiggling out of her panty hose. Given that she was sitting in the passenger seat of a German compact car, that required near-contortion levels of wiggling.

"You know, we're going to be at your sister's place in less than twenty minutes," I noted. "I'm sure they'd let you change in their bathroom."

Completely ignoring all rules of safe driving, Suze threw her balled-up panty hose at my head. Since panty hose doesn't exactly throw well, it mostly ended up draped around my shoulders. "Women's formal wear should be classified as cruel and inhumane between the dates of November first and April thirtieth." She pulled a pair of wool socks out of her purse and yanked them on, then took off her seat belt and started rummaging in the backseat for her bag of spare clothing.

After a quick glance to make sure that I wasn't in danger of hitting any other cars if I took my eyes off the road, I glanced to my right to contemplate the sight of Suze's rear draped over the center console, her wool dress still rucked up to her waist after the removal of the panty hose. Her dress must've been thick enough that she didn't have panty-line concerns, because her underpants today were cotton hip-huggers, decorated liberally with daisies. I wondered whether she fully appreciated the extent to which the sight of her underpants consistently improved my day. Perhaps that effect would eventually begin to fade with familiarity, but I was willing to continue my exposure to her underpants to test that theory.

"You could always have worn dress slacks, you know," I said mildly.

Her immediate response was both pithy, foul, and anatomically unlikely. She wiggled back into her seat, now in possession of her duffel bag, which she began rummaging through for clothing as she continued her retort to my suggestion. "Have you *seen* how good my legs look in this dress? Wearing slacks would've been a crime against humanity."

I knew I was grinning like an idiot at her smug self-confidence, yet I couldn't help it. "You do love your contradictions, Suze."

"And don't you forget it, man friend," she said as she tugged on the fleece-lined pants that were apparently her reward for the thermal sacrifice her legs had made for the sake of the human race.

Twenty minutes later we were parked in the driveway of the compact town house that her twin sister, Keiko, shared with her boyfriend, Farid. Suze had completed her outfit change in the car and, now comfortably ensconced in pants and a sweater, began hassling me about the moments I was spending trying to attain a modicum of her own clothing comfort.

"Come on, Fort, get the lead out," she grumbled.

Ignoring her, I continued loosening my tie gently, doing as little damage to the knot as possible, until there was enough slack for me to ease it over my head.

"Oh, you're not serious." Suze's expression made it clear that she already knew the answer but felt the need to make the statement anyway.

"Completely," I assured her. "I'm going to get as many uses out of this knot as I can." Technically I supposed that I could track down the same YouTube video that Dan had learned it from, but despite all the aphorisms about teaching a man to fish, I had no intention of leaving the frozen fish aisle. "Also, I'm visiting *your* sister for the umpteenth Friday night in a row. I'd expect a little more buttering up." I knew that I could've made an allusion to the complete lack of make-up sex that had occurred since our fight, but things felt too delicate to go there.

"I *am* buttering you up," she insisted. "That's why I'm not pointing out the stain on your shirt."

"Shit." I'd forgotten about what the tie had been covering up. I pondered it for a second, then shrugged. This would certainly not be the first time that I'd shown up somewhere in less than adequate attire. If I listened to Chivalry, that would basically be the story of my life.

With a long-suffering sigh, Suze dug again into her duffel, then fished out a rumpled wad of dark green cotton. I stared.

"Is that one of my sweaters?" I asked. She nodded, pleased. "Not that I'm not grateful, Suze, but . . . when did you stick my sweater into your duffel? You weren't even in my bedroom today."

Her dark eyes gleamed as she preened. "My ways are mysterious."

I pulled off my stained button-down and exchanged it gratefully for the sweater, which was significantly warmer. As I tugged it all the way down, though, I gave Suze's pleased expression a sidelong look. "You climbed the tree and broke into my room this morning, didn't you?"

Her smile widened.

"You climbed a tree, broke into my room, kidnapped one of my sweaters . . . all to surprise me with—oh, shit, what else did you do?" I couldn't help feeling impressed— some girlfriends would've responded to a fight like that by bringing over baked goods or suggesting kinkier-than-usual sex. Mine engaged in third-floor burglary.

"I hate to ruin a surprise." She leaned closer to me. "But you hadn't logged off of your computer, so I might've spent a little time doing some research. Your Amazon account might have some confusion about your preferences for a while." A quick kiss, then that foxy grin. "Now let's go in. Farid is sure to have the heat cranked."

"At least he's got that much going for him," I muttered. Unlike my own apartment, with my landlord's Professor Coldheart approach to interior heating, Farid took a very heavy hand on the thermostat whenever guests were coming over. Apparently his mother had emphasized hospitality pretty heavily when he was a kid, because the inside of that town house was never less than seventy-two degrees whenever we went over for dinner. It was pretty nice, actually, though when I'd mentioned it once to Suze she just gave a little sniff and said that, since they had natural gas heat rather than oil, it wasn't a big sacrifice.

When Suze first addressed the idea of a weekly visit to her sister's place, I'd been pretty surprised. Firstly, Keiko didn't really like me. Secondly, Suze didn't approve of Farid—the kitsune had pretty strict rules when it came to romantic relationships with humans. Casual dating was okay, but live-in relationships were completely forbidden. When it came to starting a family, the approved methodology was the one that led to Hoshi's genetic screening process at Redbones. Keiko was her grandmother's chosen heir to lead the kitsune someday down the line, yet she was in the midst of breaking some of the biggest rules by not just living with Farid, but also making him aware of her pregnancy with their baby.

For now, Suzume had been convinced, albeit very reluctantly, to stay quiet about Keiko's master plan of keeping Farid in the dark about both his wife and daughter's true natures indefinitely. Operating under the theory that it was better to ask forgiveness than permission, she was keeping their grandmother out of the loop, planning only to make her big reveal once she had a few years of success to show for herself. The modern kitsune woman, Keiko was trying to have it all—and a big part of that meant lying to Farid.

Which was where these weekly visits came in. During one dinner party of the damned, I'd actually ended up on Keiko's side in convincing Suzume that the best thing she could do, despite her very sizable reservations regarding her sister's plan, was to help keep the situation stable. So, in Suzume's eyes, this meant that the whole situation was my fault. Having a good sense of timing, Suzume had informed me about both my culpability and the proposed weekly visits during the first month that we were having sex, right after she'd dropped her pants. No surprise, I'd agreed to everything she proposed.

Also—still worth it.

The dinner visits were to give Farid the mistaken impression that he was seeing a lot of Keiko's family. She'd met Farid's parents and extended family, and was apparently a regular guest at Amini family events, so it was necessary for her to fool him into thinking that there was an equal exchange. Both sisters had heavily downplayed exactly how extensive and local their family group was, and by the institution of weekly double date nights with me and Suze, poor Farid probably never really got the chance to realize that he'd never met any member of Keiko's family beyond her twin sister.

I also knew that Suze was considering the possibility of hiring paid actors to pose as extended family at big events in the baby's life, when it would be necessary to have a presence beyond just a sister, and using their fox tricks to smooth over any rough edges. I'd thought that it was a terrible, terrible idea, but I'd acknowledged that it at least showed that Suze was committing more to helping out her sister.

My own sacrifice of two months of Friday evenings had, I felt, been somewhat undervalued by the Hollis women. In some ways it hadn't been too bad—for the first month, we'd gotten into a regular habit of eating out and then going bowling. Why Suze and Keiko had decided that bowling was the key to establishing a working cover of family togetherness I'd never entirely figured out—Farid and I mostly found ourselves in the position of talking the twins out of hurling the bowling balls at each other. There had been a certain excitement to those evenings—as much as any evening in rented shoes can really be called exciting—but we'd had to scrap those outings after Keiko's pregnancy advanced sufficiently that her center of gravity started shifting, leading to just a weekly dinner and board game evening.

There was a brief flurry of greetings, as well as the near-ritualized feeling of Keiko's belly to see if the baby would grace us with a kick, as we entered into the town house, already smelling mouthwateringly like pork cooking in the oven. At six and a half months along, Keiko was definitely visibly pregnant now, though not quite at the waddling stage. As I put my right hand on her belly, wishing that this weird temporary time-out of usual personal space and boundary rules would feel somewhat less like I was just standing there with my hand on the protruding stomach of a woman who, frankly, I didn't know particularly well, Farid noticed the Band-Aid on my hand. It was only partially covering the bite that Buttons had given me that morning, but I still wondered if his hawklike vision for injuries was a result of being a surgical resident, or some intrinsic sharpening of the skill in preparation for fatherhood.

Either way, no sooner had I said the words *dog bite* than I found myself dragged into the downstairs bathroom and subjected to a full antibacterial scrub.

"Honey, can you watch the ham?" he called out the door.

I was gritting my teeth against the distinct agony of having a hospital-grade sponge-brush covered in iodine ground enthusiastically against a raw wound. "You realize," I gritted out as he scrubbed, "that they're probably just standing there staring at the ham, right? I mean, neither of them really does much cooking."

"You've got such a good sense of humor, Fort," Farid said with a grin.

Keiko appeared in the doorway. From the expression of her face, she not only had heard my comment and correctly identified that it had not been meant as a joke, but was now pissed off because she'd been coming over to ask Farid about what exactly he meant by watching the ham. Unfortunately for me, her vengeance was close at hand. "Dog bites can get infected so easily," she said, her voice making a good approximation of real sympathy as long as you ignored the gleam in her eyes. "I sure hope you're being thorough, sweetie."

"Absolutely," Farid said enthusiastically. "I'll do a second scrub, just to be sure."

"That's great. Absolutely fabulous." I dug my free fist into my leg to try to distract myself from that second sponge-brush coming toward my hand. I knew that Farid was being careful about my health, and I couldn't bear to try to brush him off—even though my odds of getting an infection were pretty low. Since the beginning of my transition, I'd healed faster than I ever had before, and for the first time in years had managed to remain unaffected by flu season.

Suze poked her head over her sister's shoulder. "Farid, how much of the hospital has ended up in your medicine cabinet?"

"Just getting prepared for the baby," he assured her. Then, looking over at what had probably started as a linen closet, and now consisted entirely of various bottles, ointments, bandage wrappings, and even a couple of bags of saline that had to have started their lives on the shelves of a supply closet in his workplace, he gave a sheepish grin. It was a grin that transformed looks that even I had to admit were damn attractive into the Middle Eastern version of Ryan Gosling. "Maybe a few things found their way home," he admitted.

After he'd finally judged my wound to be fully sterilized, and had been talked out of putting in just one or two stitches to help things heal faster, Farid gave me a wrap with gauze and medical tape that did turn out to be a significant improvement on my Band-Aid approach. Not that it in any way was worth the throbbing in my much-abused hand, but I was trying to focus on silver linings. Particularly since the ham had ended up over-cooking while Farid was distracted.

"The timer went off," I muttered to Suze over dinner. "Why the hell didn't you take the ham out?"

"That timer could've been indicating many things," she replied with a sniff.

I just shook my head. "Hey, Farid, what game are we playing tonight?"

Across the table, where he'd been surreptitiously trying to sneak more kale onto Keiko's plate, Farid perked up. "I actually have one that you guys haven't played yet."

"You mean we're not going for a repeat of last week's game of Settlers of Cataan?" I asked.

"Those dice had it coming," Keiko said darkly, her eyes narrowing. "It flies in the face of basic probability for the number eleven to be rolled that often."

Suze nodded and set her wineglass down decisively. "And nine didn't come up at all. Keiko was completely justified."

Farid rubbed his partner's back soothingly. "Those were a lot of obscenities that ended up getting screamed at the dice," he noted. "Maybe that was kind of a peek at how things are going to be in the delivery room, but one look was enough." I nodded in agreement. The Cataan Incident, as I'd referred to it to Dan and Jaison, had definitely been interesting to witness, but wasn't exactly something that I wanted to sign up for a second round of. Farid continued blithely. "So tonight's competitive delight will be Small World." Keiko began a query, and Farid, clearly anticipating her question, said, "Yes, you can attack each other. And no, the dice involvement is minimal." Both sisters looked pleased.

"Good plan," I complimented him, and meant it. I'd played the game before—Small World was what the result would be if Risk was put in a blender with Tolkien, and then a few adjustments made to avoid infringement lawsuits.

Suze and I cleared the plates and acted like good dinner guests by cleaning up while Farid began setting up the game on the coffee table in the living room. Keiko, feeling the pressure of her gestating offspring on her bladder, took what was easily her twentieth bathroom break of the evening. I was rinsing the dishes when Suze nudged me lightly with her shoulder and, as the sound of the running water prevented anyone from overhearing us, muttered to me, "Try not to get too attached, Fort."

"To dirty dishes?" I asked, deliberately misunderstanding her. "Well, I admit that it does take me back to more than a few line items on my résumé."

This time her nudge had significantly more force to it. I was reminded of those first-person accounts of shark attacks, where first the shark deliberately bumps into the person to see if he can fight back. "You know what I'm talking about," she said, drying the dish that I'd handed her with extra vigor. "Nice dinners and board games aren't going to make Keiko's plan work. This is going to end badly, and Farid is going to be the one to pay the price."

I pushed the faucet, increasing the amount of water coming out, then glared at Suze. "Don't talk to me like I haven't seen consequences," I warned. "I've lost people because of the truth."

"Then you should be on my side here," she insisted. "Convince Keiko to pack her shit up and leave when Farid is at work. Denial of paternity, maybe slipping a few dollars to someone to fake a DNA test if he keeps pushing it, and Farid ends up with a broken heart and possibly some trust issues, but he gets away without physical damage."

The anger that had been building up within me disappeared when I looked at Suze, really looked at her for a second, and realized what was going on. She'd been against Keiko's plan from the beginning, but that had been because she'd been defending the rules her grandmother had laid down, and because she'd been trying to protect her sister.

"You're starting to like him," I said softly, and she turned her face away, a few strands of hair that had managed to work their way loose after a day of being tucked away in her braided bun flicking over her shoulder. And, because it was the truth, I said, "I like him too, Suze. I didn't really want to, but I do."

"Then help me convince Keiko." Suze's expression was deliberately blank, covering up what she was thinking.

I finished rinsing the last of the plates and handed it to her. As I wiped my hands with the spare dish towel, I turned around and leaned against the countertop. The small eat-in kitchen had been designed to feel less restrictive by cutting an overlarge entryway arch instead of a standard doorway, and through that opening I had a great view of the rest of the claustrophobically tight first floor. Farid had the game already set up, a small, pleased smile on his face as he made sure that the brightly colored board was perfectly arranged so that everyone had the best possible view of the action, and there were little piles of point tokens at each separate place. Keiko had emerged from the bathroom, and was sitting on the couch across from where he knelt on the floor, having taken the most awkward playing position without making any kind of fuss about it. She was smiling at him, listening as he spoke and pointed to various portions of the board, probably explaining the rules.

"She loves him," I said softly to Suze. "You know that. And she loves him so much that she's going to risk everything to try to be with him."

"You're usually a lot more conservative than I am about risk," she noted, making a show of moistening a sponge and running it lightly over the counter. "At least, about nonpersonal risk."

"But isn't what she's trying for worth it? She wants to be with him, to give her daughter a father. And if we help her, if she can make it work—"

"Fort." Her simple, calm tone cut me off. Once she was sure that she had my full attention, she placed her hands on my shoulders and pushed herself up onto her toes, looking me as full in the eyes as she could. After a second she leaned in and brushed a kiss against my mouth, then pulled back, her expression unreadable. When she spoke, her voice sounded regretful—a rare emotion from her. "When this ends the way I know that it will, I'll be sorry. But you'll be hurt. And I'm sorry about that." She relaxed back to the flats of her feet, then reached over and turned the faucet off decisively. With a quick roll of her shoulders she pivoted around and sauntered into the living room, her voice and demeanor changing smoothly, perfectly, to fit the persona she was presenting for Farid's benefit: a friendly, bubbly sister of his girlfriend, with no dangerous undercurrents or hidden knowledge. "Now, how do I win this game?" she demanded.

The temperature was plummeting when we said our good-byes and left the town house. A light coating of frost was already covering the windows of the Scirocco, and I paused for a moment to look up at the sky. It was cold enough to make the exposed skin of my face hurt, but the sky was still clear of snow. I pulled my keys out of my pocket, the fabric of my gloves making my movements clumsy as I sorted to find the one I needed; then I suddenly paused. There was something in the silent night air, something that I wasn't hearing or feeling . . . something that I was smelling.

"Hey, Fort, any plans on opening the car door before I die of hypothermia?" Suze groused, but I waved a hand at her to be quiet. I closed my eyes and inhaled as deeply as I could through my nose, trying to figure out what that was. It was like a wisp of perfume in the air, tugging at me, almost daring me to identify it.

"Fort, what's going on?" Suze's voice was softer, and I heard the rustle of her coat and the crunch of old snow beneath her boots as she came around to stand beside me. My eyes were still closed as I tried to tease out that smell, but I felt her press her elbow against my side—not in a jabbing or demanding way, but in a way that reminded me that she was there, and grounded me.

Acting on instinct, I opened my mouth and inhaled, as if I could taste the smell. And I could—it was there, again, flirting against my senses, playing over my tongue. I could hear Suze begin sniffing, applying her own kitsune senses to the task—though her nose on two legs was no comparison to what it was on four legs, she still had a better sense of smell than any human, or even any vampire. There was only one thing that I'd ever been able to smell better than her, and the knowledge pinged into my brain and finally identified that drifting, perfumed aroma.

"Blood," I said, opening my eyes and looking at Suze. "I smell human blood."

She gave a small shake of her own head. "It's too faint for me." She nudged me lightly. "Follow it. Let's see if you can track."

I gave a small, startled snort. "I can't track, Suze. I'm—"

"Let's find out," she repeated. Her voice was low and rich. "Just close your eyes and focus on the smell. I'll make sure that you don't bump into anything." Her arm wrapped around my waist, a warm, comforting band. "See what you can find," she urged, and I looked at her again for a long second, then closed my eyes.

The scent was still there, waiting for me. Trusting in Suze to keep me from falling on my ass, I began walking. It took me a few false starts to figure out how to follow it—I had to keep sampling the air over my tongue and using that to orient myself. I was lucky that it was a still night, with almost no breeze. We were away from student areas, and it was late enough that even on a Friday night, most of the residents of these brick town houses and apartments were tucked away in their beds. Once or twice Suze's arm tightened around my waist, forcing me to stop and wait while a car passed by, and other times she used her body to nudge me around obstacles, but she stayed quiet and let me focus on the smell.

The blood smell was like warm cinnamon rolls from a bakery, or a steak searing away in a bed of chopped onions. It was a pot of warm stew bubbling on the stove on a cold day, or a fresh-cut slice of watermelon in the summer. The farther I walked, the more it urged me forward, every instinct in my body switching on and adding to my desire to follow it.

We'd walked a block before Suze tugged me to a stop and spoke for the first time. "There it is," she said quietly. I opened my eyes to see her pointing down at the sidewalk we were standing on. Slowly I crouched down, my eyes picking out what she was gesturing to far better than they should've in the darkness, even with the improvements my vision had undergone since my transition began.

It was a little splash of blood, smaller than a dime, fresh and unnaturally bright against the cement. It drew my eyes and the smell, more delightful than a pan of frying bacon, filled my head. I had to shove my hands into my pockets hard to resist the urge to reach down and touch that little spot with my finger, because I knew that touching it would never be enough. I'd want to put it against my tongue, rub it against my gums and the inside of my cheeks. I'd want to roll in it. I pressed my hands into my pockets harder, and felt a seam rip.

"This is fucked up," I said, louder than I needed to, but wanting to hear my own voice again, to force myself back into normal, back to the real me, not the tracking-a-drop-of-blood version of myself. "Is this what it's going to be now? We just walked a block because of a dot of blood. Someone probably just slipped on the ice and skinned their knee. God help me if Jaison nicks himself shaving, or if Mrs. Bandyopadyay pokes herself with a needle while she's quilting."

"Hold off on the emo for a second there," Suze said, then got down on her hands and knees. She pressed herself right down to the cement itself, brushing her face against the ground.

"I know what just happened here, Suze," I snapped. "Someone lost a few drops of blood and I went haywire."

She sat up fast, and with fox speed she smacked me in the shoulder, hard. "You dope," she said affectionately, even as my shoulder throbbed. "You don't even know what you're smelling." Suze hopped agilely to her feet, then extended a hand. "Come on, I've got the scent now, so we can move a little faster."

"What do you mean?" I asked, linking my arm with hers as we resumed walking, though at a much different pace. We weren't jogging, but we were at the speed just below that. Anyone looking at us would think that we were late for something.

"You humanoids have no idea how your own noses work," Suze said as we sped along. "Even the werebears are barely better than our kits. You aren't following blood because it's blood. You're following it because of what was going in it when it came out."

"That made zero sense."

She grinned at me, and the shape of Suze's face in the darkness was suddenly longer, more vulpine. She could still pass for human, barely, but there was no hiding the gleam in eyes that seemed subtly different. "You're a predator, Fort," she reminded me. "Whoever the owner of that blood is, they were scared when they bled. And not just startled, but terrified. There was extra adrenaline flowing, the heart rate was kicked up to the max, and"— she sniffed again, harder, as we walked, then nodded, more to herself than to me—"*her* body was terrified."

I frowned. "I didn't respond to the blood on its own—I responded to its circumstance?"

"A predator responding to weak prey." She nodded, then lifted an eyebrow. "And guess what smell I just picked up on?"

"Another predator?" I guessed.

She grinned. "I'm smelling kobold. Multiple kobolds, in fact. And they're right"—Suze sped us up, then turned a quick corner down an alley—"here."

The smell of the blood was thick here, but it was actually easier to ignore because of everything else that demanded my attention. An old woman wrapped in layers of old coats, loose shirts, and part of what looked like a quilt tied around her waist was huddling against the wall of the alley. Her eyes were huge in the darkness, and her hands, covered in old grime and dirt, were pressed over her mouth. She was trying to stay quiet, to make herself as small as possible, but little whimpers of raw terror kept creeping out. There was blood on her wrists, and I could see a little on her ankles as well.

Surrounding her were three kobolds, and as we watched, one darted forward and nipped her hand, just hard enough to break the skin and make a few droplets of blood bead on the surface of her skin. "It doesn't make a sound," one of the others crooned in that high, child's voice that made the hair on the back of my neck stand up. "It wants to live to see the dawn, so it doesn't cry out."

Imagine the body of a hyena, with that sloped back and hunched shoulders, the thick torso and the awkwardly long legs. But instead of a hyena's head there's a human face, long and sallow, the skin almost gray in a way that blends into the shadows. The jaw struggles to contain a mouth full of animal teeth, jagged and yellow, built for ripping flesh and gnawing at bones, and they poke out and rest against lips that are black like a hyena's, not like a person's. Each of the front two legs ends not in a paw, but in a human hand, the backs still bristling with fur all the way down to the fingers, where each digit ends in a blunt claw. The fur on the body is charcoal gray, with lighter spots that should make them stick out, but actually just add to their camouflage. These were the kobolds, who could never pass for human, but whose minds were too keen to ever be mistaken for an animal.

They were city dwellers, scavengers who hung at the edges. They lived in abandoned buildings, darkened alleys, and of course the sewers. Anyone who had ever feared alligators in the sewers had no idea what they really needed to be afraid of. In my mother's territory they were permitted to eat the wildlife of the city—stray dogs and cats who would never have owners looking for them, pigeons and rats, and whatever treasures they found in Dumpsters. Months ago Chivalry and I had had to discipline a small group that had gotten tired of the lean denizens of the street and had started snatching plump pets from out of yards and off leashes. But this was something else altogether.

They were too focused on their prey and didn't realize

that we'd entered the alley. A second kobold darted forward to nip the woman again, but I was already moving, and moving faster than a human could've.

I got a hand on the back of the moving kobold's neck, right at the scruff, and hauled it backward and away from its target. It snarled in surprise, but the forearms on a kobold were built like a hyena's, not a person's, and it didn't have the joints or movement to bend its forearms up or around to get at me. It threw its heavy weight around desperately, but I dug my hand in harder and refused to let go. Months of working out, plus the onset of my transition, had given me enough arm muscles that it couldn't break my grip and get away.

The kobold beside it gave a guttural cry that was somewhere on that midpoint between human and animal, and it charged me. I punted it hard in the chest with my foot, and it slammed backward and into the wall with a yelp of surprise and indignation. I looked around to see whether the third kobold was coming up behind me, but I didn't need to worry. It was flat to the ground, with Suze's knee keeping it pressed firmly in the position she wanted it, and it wasn't making so much as a sound, given that she had her best switchblade fully extended and the point positioned less than an inch from one of the kobold's large eyes.

"Not a cry, not a whimper," Suze said to the kobold in a deliberate echo to what they had said to their victim. "Or you truly will never see another dawn."

"Ma'am?" I called to the woman, who was still frozen in place against the wall. "Ma'am, are you hurt?"

She stared at me, her mouth an *o* of surprise, and her rheumy old eyes still blank with fear. Beside her I could see one of those sleeping bags that's made from sewing layers of old blankets together, the kind that I had seen other homeless people on the streets of Providence wrap around themselves and sleep in. She didn't say anything to me, and I wondered if she'd really heard me, or if she was even able to respond.

"Ma'am," I said again, making my voice as gentle as I could. "Ma'am, it's going to be very cold tonight. Is there a shelter that you can go to tonight? I promise you, ma'am, that these things aren't real." And I ground my fingers farther into the neck of the kobold I was holding, and gave it a shake that even I knew was vicious. "These things aren't real," I repeated, "but even if they were, you'd never have to worry about them again, because I won't let them harm you."

She nodded slowly, to what part of my statement I wasn't sure, and then, holding my gaze, reached down with shaking hands to collect her sleeping bag and a grimy backpack. She pulled those things to her and stood up, then hurried away on shuffling feet, whispering to herself, "Not real, not real," even as she stepped over the gray tail of the one that Suze kept pinned to the ground. We all listened as her footsteps in the snow moved farther away and finally were gone in the night.

The kobold that I had kicked kept its distance, but its gleaming dark eyes watched me. "Young prince," it said, and its voice was a little girl's, hurt and betrayed. "Why does the prince attack us?"

"You live in Madeline Scott's territory," I ground out, my temper spiking as the kobold tried to pretend innocence. "You live by Madeline Scott's rules. And those rules are clear—you don't hunt the humans."

The kobold snickered, its black lips parting. "Just amusement," it said. "Just a game with one whose mind is already lost. If we hunted in earnest, you would know." The black lips widened farther, showing every sharp tooth.

"Or would he?" interjected the kobold that I still held by its scruff. It had gone limp when the first kobold spoke, and now it hung from my hand with every appear-

ance of relaxation. Its voice was a young boy's, the kind
you'd hear from a five-year-old, and then it laughed, a
high titter that raked against the ear. "So many secrets
are known only to the queen. And when she fades to
nothing, who is left to speak the secrets?"

A chill ran up my spine that had nothing to do with
the ambient temperature. As hard as it was to imagine
when you looked at them, the kobolds were where the
myth of the sphinx had developed. They spoke in riddles
and confusion, and there were those who believed that
they also spoke prophesy.

The third kobold spoke then, another little girl, but
this one was sly and gleeful, though still eyeing Suzume's
knife warily. "Perhaps then a value would be placed on
those who give tongue to the dead."

Suze's lip curled. "Well, that's an insight into the kobold dating scene that I didn't need."

The first kobold by the wall hissed in rage at Suze's
words, and the fur along the ridge of its back lifted. "The
little fox laughs, but soon she'll be in tears," it snarled,
that little girl voice raging. "The offspring of the White
Fox harbor their own poison." Then she turned coy, turning her head to one side and watching both of us from
the corner of her eye. "Or don't you wish to know what
the future holds?"

Suze gave her own snarl, and in one quick movement
had turned the knife in her hand away from the kobold's
eye to slice down against its leg, one fast cut into the
flesh that for a second exposed the whiteness of bone
before the blood began to flow. The sound the kobold
made wasn't an animal yelp, but a disturbing child's
scream of pain, and then Suze was off its back and had
hurled it, one-handed, to where the first kobold stood.
They went down in a pile of yelps, but when they came
up neither made a move against her, just pressed backward. The wounded kobold leaned down to lick its leg,

but the one that had spoken smiled tauntingly, proud that it had clearly struck a nerve.

I cut in, dropping the kobold that I'd been holding after one last brutal shake. "Save it for the tourists, guys. There's no prophecy, just good background and guesses. Now keep your attention on stray animals, because you remember what happens when you break the rules, don't you? My brother and I left your kind bleeding into the gutters last summer." I looked at all of them, not hiding just how much I wanted to make them feel just a hint of the terror that they'd inflicted on that homeless woman, so breakable in her obvious madness.

"The prince denies prophesy, but we are the speakers of truth, the seers of hearts," was the sibilant response hissed from the shadows. "And your own heart is so obvious, so soft." A high laugh. "You hunger to break our bones, wreak your vengeance, though you might dress it up in the clothing of justice. But you fear to be like your sister, fear to glory in violence as she does, so you will let us go with no harm."

I hated how right they were, but I looked at those too-intelligent, mocking eyes, and refused to be taunted into an action I'd already decided against. "You like talking about my sister's violence," I said coldly. "That's good, because I'm going to be talking with my sister about what I saw tonight. She'll probably want to have a chat with you guys. You remember Prudence's chats, don't you? The kind that end with her ripping out organs. She's not like me—she won't stick to the things that grow back." I might disagree with almost everything that Prudence stood for and believed in, but when it came to the kobolds I had no problem with using her as the bogeyman to prevent the kind of behavior that I'd seen tonight.

The kobolds made shows of sneering and flicking their tails to show disdain, but the one that Suze had cut faded quickly away, followed by the second. The third also began to slink off, but stopped at the entrance of the alley to get one last taunt in. "And what will happen when the hand that holds the dog's leash is gone, and the master's voice is silenced?" it asked, with that lisp on its consonants that so many little children possess as they shape their soft palates around words made for adult mouths. "The dog will bite then, and no one can tell it not to." Then it was gone in the night.

"I hate those creepy little bastards," Suze bit out grimly. She hunkered down to wipe the blade of her knife clean on the snow, and shot me a sideways look. "We could've just killed all three, you know."

I knew, of course. I was a Scott vampire, and no one liked the kobolds, even other kobolds. It was because I'd wanted to kill them so badly that I hadn't. "I'll talk with my mother about this. They were right—they hadn't engaged in a real hunt, not the way they or my family would see it."

"So, nothing?" Suze asked, her eyebrows shooting up in surprise.

"Definitely not nothing. I don't think that was the first time they tormented someone like that—they were too quick with their defense, too sure that the woman was mentally ill." My hands clenched again as the memory of the woman's vulnerability flashed through my mind, overlaid with my own shame at the part of myself that had assessed and been fascinated by it. For the millionth time, I wished that I could've been born something other than what I was. I forced my mind to focus on an active solution to what was going on. "I'm going to call my brother tomorrow morning. Prudence is sitting on top of some major aggravation right now—if she agrees that they're too far over the line of behavior, then I'm sure she'd love to make a trip to the city to reinforce some manners."

"And if she agrees with the kobolds, or just doesn't give a shit about the homeless?" Suze put her knife away and, linking her arm in mine, began the walk back to the car.

"Then tomorrow night you and I will go around and have some chats with kobold groups," I said, deadly serious. I could avoid feeding my own violent urges when it was possible, but I wasn't the guy I'd been a year ago. I couldn't look away entirely from something when I had the means to correct it, even though that correction meant embracing the part of myself that terrified me.

We walked in silence for another few steps, our feet landing on a mixture of bare sidewalk, rock-salt-covered ice, and old snow. I felt Suze's arm slide through mine, feeling utterly right and comfortable. "So," she asked, watching me from the corner of her eye, "am I go for an overnight?"

I couldn't help the smile that stretched across my face at her bluntness. No delicate hanging around in the living room for her, ticking down the hours until one could believably claim to be too tired to drive home. I snuggled our linked arms tighter and slipped my bare hand from my coat pocket to hers. There was a lot left unresolved, and as our first major fight in the relationship, it was still as open and delicate as the dog bite on my hand.

But the kobolds were liars and charlatans, and there was no such thing as fate.

"I'd like that," I said, and even in a night so cold that the skin of my face was aching, the sight of her smile made me warm.

I'm not sure which of us started walking faster, or maybe we both did, but soon we were back in the car and making our way to my apartment at a good pace. After all, there was something to look forward to now.

"Succubi refugees, werebear attachés, and now kobold corralling," Suze noted. "You have a few plates in the air, don't you?"

"Yeah. And if they'd ever seen me wait tables, they'd know that I'm the last person in the world who should be trusted with delicate china."

Chapter Five

I woke up to a jabbing in my side. The room was dark, illuminated slightly by the light from the streetlight seeping through my cheap curtains. I could feel the cold of the room on my face, but the rest of my body, tucked beneath flannel sheets, heavy comforter, and augmented by the toasty heat of the woman snuggled next to me, was warm. I was aware that my skin was damp with sweat, not just on what was beneath the covers, but also my face and head. My heart was racing so hard that I could almost imagine that I could feel it thudding against the inside of my chest. That, apart from the jabbing, was my first hint.

The jabbing, courtesy of a surprisingly bony kitsune elbow, stopped, and I felt her snuggle closer. "You were having a nightmare, Fort."

I ran my hand over the back of my head, feeling that my hair was actually wet from the sweat. There was an almost metallic taste in my mouth. The cobwebby feeling finally left my brain, and I remembered my dream. It was an old one, mostly.

"I'm sorry," I said. "I didn't mean to wake you up. Was I making noise?"

"A little. Mostly you kept tensing up, though. And when I tried to wake you up at first, you flinched so hard that you almost fell out of bed." She paused, and then I felt her hand lightly touch my face. "Do you want to talk about it?" Suze was tentative, uncertain. It was oddly comforting to know that she trusted me enough to show that vulnerability—that she didn't have all the answers, or all the know-how. Apparently even ass-kicking kitsune could be flummoxed about the protocol of dealing with the nightmares of a significant other.

"Not really," I said honestly. And I didn't. It was the old dream, more of a memory, really, of the day that my foster parents, Brian and Jill, had been murdered. My sister had painted the floors and walls with their blood because I'd told them the truth about what we were, and they'd believed me. They'd loved me, they'd believed me, and they'd died for it.

It was a dream that I'd had for almost two decades, but tonight's rendition had been worse, and a recurring nightmare that had begun around the time that my transition started. The events of the dream were the same as ever, but this time my reaction had been different. I hadn't cared when Brian came home to see Jill's broken body, and I hadn't even reacted when Prudence had torn open his throat. All I'd cared about was that arterial spray, and all the fear and terror and anger that had made his blood smell so good.

I really, really didn't want to talk about that dream. Not even with Suze.

Her voice pulled me back to myself, and helped push the nightmare down. Not away—it could never really go away. But down was at least an improvement. "Do you need anything?" she asked.

"Just you." I wrapped my arms around her, pressing my cheek against hers, smelling her hair, feeling her bare skin against mine. "Just stay with me."

"Oh, that. That I've got covered. That I can *rock out with*." Then her lips were pressing against mine, and I didn't have to think at all.

*   *   *

The next time I woke up, the sun had risen and was shining through my wholly inadequate curtains. The woman I'd fallen asleep entwined with was gone, but there was a warm, fluffy lump between my knees. I pulled the covers up and peered down. A long, dark snout lifted up from where it was resting on my left thigh, and Suze gave me an annoyed glare and a small *grf* noise, though whether she was objecting to the influx of cold air from me lifting the covers or simply that I'd woken her up, I wasn't sure.

I dropped the covers and began the task of awkwardly wiggling out of bed. Suze made no move to leave her warm little den, and I had to tug my legs out while trying not to accidentally knock her or squish one of her little limbs. One of my previous roommates had had an elderly Siamese cat named Rousseau. Among his many other accomplishments, Rousseau was able to use his long, monkeylike paws to open doors, and I'd woken up on a number of mornings to discover that Rousseau had entered my room and slid under the covers at some point in the night to snuggle himself comfortably right in the *v* of my crotch. Having an unexpected furry guest that close to my testicles was never a comfortable discovery, particularly given Rousseau's notably cranky and volatile temperament. So my history with furry bodies under the covers was a decidedly mixed one. As I finally extricated myself from the bed and began pulling on an assortment of warm clothes, the cold air of the apartment hitting me like a full-body slap, I also couldn't deny that it nudged against the sore spot of our fight. As much as Suze clearly didn't see a problem with having sex with me in human form, then spending the night cuddled against me as a fox, it was doing a pretty good job of weirding me out. Going to sleep next to a woman, I expected to wake up beside her as well.

Standing under a stream of hot water in the shower, I acknowledged that this was probably going to have to require another relationship discussion. *Ugh*, was my immediate response. After the last two days, that was the last thing I wanted to do. I racked my brain for any way to avoid that particular branch of the decision tree. Maybe I could get her a little doggie bed for those times when she preferred being in fox form. I pondered that for barely half a second before shuddering. Somehow I'd managed to come up with a way to make the whole situation even weirder.

Suze was slowly emerging from the bed when I went back into the room. Still in fox form, she'd gotten out from under the covers and was stretched out lazily. At the sight of me she gave a large yawn, exposing her sharp white teeth, then thumped her tail enthusiastically. I'd brought underwear, jeans, and a long-sleeved tee into the bathroom with me, so as she bounced playfully around the room, stealing a pair of clean socks from me before I could put them on, making happy little fox noises, and generally acting in a way that would've guaranteed viral video success, I pulled on a heavy cable sweater and finished getting ready.

Wondering if she was just reluctant to make the shift to human form because it meant the loss of her fluffy winter coat, I collected her scattered clothing from around the room and put it in one convenient pile on the bed. She responded by rolling on her back and presenting her belly for rubs.

"C'mon, Suze," I said, unable to fully keep the irritation out of my voice. "I'd like to be able to get a response in human words."

She narrowed her eyes, and shifted. Between one moment and the next, the dark-furred fox was replaced by Suze, though the expression of annoyance in those eyes remained even as they changed from gold to dark brown.

"Someone woke up on the wrong side of the bed this morning," she noted.

I bit my tongue to avoid mentioning which part of the bed she'd woken up in.

She continued looking at me steadily, tilting her head to one side as she assessed me.

"Want to go out for breakfast?" I asked, shaking off the creeping discomfort of being examined so closely. "You'd be able to get real bacon."

"Is something bothering you?"

She wasn't really psychic, I reminded myself. She just had the unfair advantage of having increased senses that probably could pick up on my increased heart rate and the prickling of sweat. "I didn't sleep too well," I said, which was actually at least halfway true.

After another assessing pause, she seemed to accept my justification, and nodded. She started getting dressed. "Hey, let's go to that little diner we went to a while back. The one with the silver-dollar pancakes."

"That's a good idea," I agreed. "Want me to check if Dan and Jaison want to come?"

Suze's head popped out of the top of her turtleneck, and she made a face. "Are you sure we can't just take Jaison and leave Dan behind?"

"Ha-ha." I had started to head out the door when my phone rang. I took it out of the charger and checked the caller ID—Chivalry. I cursed a little, remembering that I'd forgotten to give him a call after the *metsän kunigas* ceremony. Between that, checking in to see if he'd changed his mind about the succubi situation, and needing to update him about what Suze and I had seen the kobolds doing last night, I definitely owed him more than a prebreakfast text.

"Go knock on Dan's door," I asked Suze as I hit the answer button. "Hey, Chivalry, listen—"

My brother cut me off, his voice low. "You need to

come home," he said softly, and something about the way he spoke made me freeze and listen, and even as I did I realized that I'd been waiting for this call for a while now, and that part of me had known that this moment was coming without even realizing it.

"It's Mother," I said—not asking, because I knew it wasn't a question. I had a sense of unreality, of cliché. All of Madeline's hundreds of years of life, and it came down to this—a call on a phone that interrupted plans for Saturday brunch. I was holding the phone with my right hand, but I was suddenly unsure about what to do with my left. If I reached up to touch my face, was I doing it because I needed to, or because I was acting out this moment? I shoved my free hand in my pocket.

"It's Mother," Chivalry agreed. He cleared his throat loudly, and seemed to force himself to speak more regularly. His voice came out clipped, strained. "She's very weak today, Fort. Prudence." He coughed, cleared his throat again. "Prudence thinks that it isn't going to be much longer. You need to be here."

"Should I—"

"Pack a bag."

"Okay." I accepted it, feeling the weight. I'd known yesterday that my mother was dying, but now it was different. I was a son whose mother was dying, and I needed to go home and wait until she was dead. I rubbed my hand hard against the back of my neck, and I realized that I didn't even remember taking it out of my pocket. "Okay, I'll be there soon."

"Thank you." We both paused; then Chivalry was the one who said, "Good-bye," and hung up.

I just held the phone for a second, then put it back down beside its charger. I was going to pack that, I thought to myself. That was easier to think about. I'd have to call in to work, let Orlando know that I wouldn't be coming in tomorrow, so that he'd have time to find someone else to fill in. I had to pack toothpaste and a toothbrush, or else I'd have to buy some down in Newport, at the grocery store. I knew that if I really wanted to I could just get in the car and drive down, and ask my mother's staff to stock me with a complete wardrobe and toiletries set, but it felt better to be thinking about packing up my duffel and choosing what I'd need. It felt substantial, the only substantial thing in the world at this moment.

I didn't want to look at Suzume, because I didn't really want to say the words yet. But she was right there, sitting on my bed, and there was only so long that I could avoid looking at her.

She was looking at me, with that patience that she was wholly capable of but was always a surprise to be reminded about. It was the patience of a fox waiting for a mouse to move, to reveal its presence, and it was endless.

"Do you want me to drive you down?" she asked. Of course she would've heard the whole conversation—even in her human form her hearing was excellent. But there she sat on my bed, in a turtleneck and a pair of underpants, her legs and feet still bare in the morning cold. She hadn't even combed her hair yet, and the midnight strands were fluffy and tangled on one side of her head and completely flat on the other. Her dark eyes were focused on me, and there was nothing but patience from her.

If I hadn't loved her before that moment, I would've loved her then.

"No," I said, focusing on those clear options in front of me, grateful for the choice she'd given me. I wouldn't have to talk about feelings or the future yet, just the mechanics of what to pack, how to travel. "No, if you drove me down, then you'd have to get someone to pick you up. I can drive myself."

After that, I just focused on getting out the door. My

duffel bag came out from under the bed, and I stuffed it with clothes and toiletries. It was my family, so I stuffed in my Colt .45, along with some boxes of ammunition. I called Orlando to let him know that I wouldn't be coming to work at Redbones, and I didn't know for how long. I said that it was a family crisis, but didn't bother to explain the details. I heard the irritation under his sympathy, and it didn't really matter to me. He started to warn me not to stay away too long, or he might like the coverage person better than me, and I hung up.

Suze told Dan what was going on, and he put coffee in one of his travel mugs for me and made a grilled cheese sandwich so that I could eat while I drove. Jaison said something to me that I registered as being heartfelt and meaningful, but a second later I couldn't remember what he'd said at all.

I got into the Scirocco, which Suze had started up while I was packing, so the air coming out of the vents was warm enough to dry out my eyes, and the steering wheel wasn't so cold that I had to wrap my sleeve over my palm to touch it comfortably. Once I was in the driver's seat, she leaned down to me.

"If you need some company, give me a call," she said. I nodded, and she kissed me. Then she backed up so that I could close the car door, and we waved to each other. As I was pulling out of the apartment's lot, I looked in my rearview mirror and saw that she was still standing there, watching me as I went. I raised my hand to wave one last time, and she returned the gesture. Then I turned onto the road, and she was gone.

I drove almost in a fugue state, taking every turn by habit and memory, both thankfully distracted by the minutiae of driving and all too much in my own head. And then, almost too quickly, I was pulling into the driveway of my mother's mansion, where my brother was standing in the doorway, waiting for me.

*   *   *

Days went by.

Madeline spent most of her time sleeping. We sat around her bed, talking quietly, or sometimes just reading. Chivalry's new wife, Simone, was constantly at his side, and it was clear that he was leaning heavily on her. That left me and Prudence as a very uncomfortable pairing. When Madeline was awake, she would talk a little to us, but sometimes she was confused. She asked for people who had been dead for years, and then when she was reminded of that, she'd nod, then ask for them again. Other times she would wake up and be the same Madeline she'd been before her decline, but it was impossible to know when that would be the case, so we were always on edge when she first began talking, as we tried to figure out which Madeline we were speaking to. When she was fully cognizant, that tended to annoy her, and that tired her out faster, so even when we could really talk with her, it never lasted long.

When she did sleep, it was restless, tossing back and forth. She muttered a lot, sometimes too low for me to understand, and other times in languages that I didn't know. Whenever I did understand something, it was always fragmented, disjointed.

Once, I was sitting next to Prudence when the muttering started, and I asked her if she knew what Madeline was talking about.

"I wish I did," my sister said, her blue eyes never shifting from our mother's face. There was an angry edge to her voice, under the sadness that lay over all of us like a stifling winter quilt, pressing us down and making it hard to think or even register the passing of time. "She always kept so much back, always said that I wasn't ready to know things, or that she'd tell me later. And now there's no later left, and I still don't understand." Prudence's mouth twisted, angry and sad in equal measures now, and I remembered the words that the kobold had taunted me with. I reminded myself forcibly that they were history's best publicized con artists, but somehow it was harder to believe while sitting beside my mother's deathbed than it had been in the alley.

Maire was often present, checking my mother's condition, giving her small shots of painkillers to try to make her more comfortable. Madeline's staff flocked around her—on some days it felt as if every person my mother employed was finding a reason to come into the room. They brought flowers and get-well cards, and even a little teddy bear with GET WELL SOON embroidered in pink thread found its way into the room. Patricia agonized over arranging my mother's pillows just so, and even though my mother hadn't been able to eat solid food in a century, the cook kept putting together the most beautiful tiny sampling plates and sending them up, claiming that just smelling something delicious would perk my mother up.

The hours ticked past. It felt like we'd been there forever, and at the same time everything going on outside of the mansion seemed to fade away.

On the morning of the fourth day, I put on my last pair of clean underpants and realized that I would have to do my laundry, or go home and get more clothing, or go out and buy more clothes here. I sat next to Madeline's bed and read articles from the *New York Times* to her, on the assumption that, even mostly unconscious and slipping into death, she'd probably still want to know what was going on with politics, and tried to decide what I was going to do about my underwear situation. It was the most basic decision, and one that was pretty easy to resolve, yet I found myself dithering. In the strange twilight world that I currently resided in, one where my mother was dying neither quickly nor slowly yet very, very immediately, I couldn't even figure out how to provide myself with clean underwear. In a strange way, it almost began to seem to me that if I made a decision, then the situation would finally end and my mother would die, at which point I realized that I'd slid fully into magical thinking. Yet even identifying my own brand of temporary madness didn't resolve the problem.

What resolved the problem was when Suzume showed up just after lunch with a second duffel bag of clean clothing.

"I was pretty sure that the kitsune weren't psychic," I said to her in the front hall of the mansion. It was the first thing I could think to say, given the completely unexpected sight before me.

"We aren't," she assured me. "But I counted how many sets of clothing you packed before you left, and when I knew that you'd be running out I asked Dan to pack some more for you."

She stayed with me for the rest of the afternoon, but in fox form. It was comforting to have her with me, because she was soft and nice to pet as she sat in my lap, but I would've significantly preferred to have her in human form. When she was getting ready to leave, just before dinner was going to be served, and had finally resumed her human form, I asked her why she'd stayed fox.

"Low profile, Fort," she said, sitting on my bed as she pulled on her shoes. "While I'm happy to be there emotionally for you, my grandmother was pretty specific about me staying under Prudence's radar."

"What's Atsuko worried about?"

Suze's feathery black eyebrows arched. "Your sister—who by the way was not exactly thrilled when your mother granted my grandmother and all her kick-ass unborn progeny, i.e., me, unprecedented levels of self-governance—is about to become head of the territory. Man friend, I know that you're in a difficult emotional place right now, but think this one through." She paused, then looked around. "Also, I'd consider trying to brighten your day by jumping you and defiling what is undoubtedly your virgin childhood bedroom, but I'm not sure that I can work up enthusiasm while surrounded by this many stereotypical teenage boy movie posters. What's up with this?"

"Summer blockbusters with copious explosions were my gateway drug to film theory," I acknowledged. Then, refocusing on the important part of her statement, I asked, "Atsuko is worried?"

"Everyone is worried," she said. "But I can stay longer if you need me to."

I appreciated her offer, but turned it down, to her obvious relief.

As I walked her to her car, a thought occurred to me. "Have I been fired yet?"

"Do you want me to find out?"

I thought about it for a second. "No. No, I think that I really don't even give a shit."

She hugged me, and I leaned into her, linking my arms behind her back and pressing my face into her neck. "I just want this to be over," I said, quietly enough that I could barely hear it myself. "But if it's over, it means that she's dead, and I don't want that either."

Suze didn't try to say anything. She just stood there holding me as the sky darkened around us from the violet and orange tones of sunset to a soft gray, and finally blackness. We could hear the distant sounds of crashing waves from where we stood, and the occasional lonely cries from seagulls. She didn't complain that it was too cold, or that she had places to be—she simply waited until I was ready to let go.

Another week passed with no change. Then one morning I was walking along the hallway to my mother's suite, and I saw Chivalry and Prudence standing outside her door, clearly waiting for something.

"What's going on?" I asked.

Chivalry just shook his head. He stretched out one arm and put a hand on my shoulder. I could feel the strength in that hand, and was reminded how much stronger he was than me, how he could probably crush my shoulder without much effort.

"Wait with us, brother," Prudence said quietly. Her pupils were larger than they should've been, so wide that there was only the faintest hint of the blue of her iris present.

We stood in the hallway for long minutes; then I felt a sudden yank of the bond inside me that linked me to my mother. Beside me I could feel my siblings flinch at the same moment, and knew that they had felt it as well. There was an electricity in the air, like before a storm rolls in from the ocean, and I could feel every hair on my body stand on end.

"She's ready for us now," said Prudence, and opened the door.

My mother's sitting room was the same as ever, innocuous. My hands began to shake as we walked to the closed door of her bedroom. Chivalry and Prudence looked grim, though not as affected as me.

The first thing that I saw when the bedroom door opened was that my mother was sitting up in bed. Her expression was lucid, alive, and her blue eyes glowed. Power radiated out of her, strong enough that I felt it not just in the bond between us, but along my skin and even in the air that I sucked into my lungs. For a second my heart skipped a beat, and I thought, *She's better.*

Then I saw what was lined up against the wall of the room. The bodies of eight of her oldest, most loyal staff members, lying against the wall like broken dolls. Patricia was there, seated on the floor, a euphoric expression still frozen on her dead face. Her sensible slacks were tan, and her sweater was cream. And her face and skin were paler than they'd ever been, as pale as wax paper, except for the long, ripped wound on the side of her neck that still oozed blood. Beside Patricia was James, who had served my mother since he was a young boy, even after I'd attacked him in a fit of bloodlust a few months ago. The wrinkled skin of his face was smoothed out now, relaxed. And six more beside them, all of whom I knew, had known since I was a child. The ones most devoted to my mother, the ones who had served her longest. The ones who'd been the most distraught over the past week, visited her the most frequently.

"Are you a pharaoh, Mother?" My throat was almost too tight to force words through, but I managed it. "Demanding that your retainers follow you into the afterlife?"

"My poor Fortitude," Madeline crooned. "You still do not understand. They volunteered for this, my darling. Gave up those last few years of their lives for a greater purpose."

"I don't understand either, Mother," Prudence said, surprising me.

"Come." Madeline crooked a finger at us, urging us closer. "Time is short, my dearest ones, my babies. This gift will not last long, and must not be squandered."

We shuffled forward, almost pulled, though whether it was by the power that rolled off her or by those old instincts to obey our mother, I didn't know. Maybe it was both. We lined up beside her, with Prudence the first in the line, standing by Madeline's pillow, and me third, by her hand.

"Our lives are long," Madeline said. "So long that humans think us immortal. And when our bodies begin to fail, many of us fall into a sleep that can last decades, as we struggle to maintain ourselves, to hold on to life. There are periods of waking—hours, then minutes. Eventually moments so brief that the eyes cannot even open before consciousness falls back into slumber. There are those who cling to this, who refuse to pass until they have wrung every droplet of life. But I have tasted that these last days, and it's not what I choose."

"No, Mother," Chivalry whispered.

"Hush, my dearest." She was so gentle in that moment, and so terrible. Like a mother crocodile lifting its hatchling with its mouth. "I have lived long, seen much, and done great things. I am content that this is the end." Madeline looked at all of us in turn, those bluer-than-blue eyes lingering, drinking us in. "This is my will, my final order, my final wish. It is the last thing I will ever ask of you, and my hope for your future." She paused, drew a deep breath. "I have no sole heir."

We stared at her. Then we stared at each other. Prudence began to open her mouth, and Madeline cut her off.

"No, listen to me, because there is no time left. I have left the paperwork behind, for the banks and the property, but this is more than that. Each of you will receive a third of my estate, of my interests, and also of my authority. You must remain together, act not as a Nest with a single ruler, but as siblings and equals. We vampires have thought that we are stone, unchanging as the winds of time and humanity swirl around us. But change has worn us down, diminished us. Few see the changes that have already been wrought, even though to an outside eye the damage is clear. I will be gone, my doves, and will not live through the times ahead. You will, and you must work together to see them through. With one of you left to rule, the other two would flounder and move away, regardless of which I chose. Only with this is there a chance that you would stay together, to gain strength through each other, to advise and guide. Swear this, my children."

Chivalry was first, speaking without hesitation, even as tears ran down his cheeks. "When have I ever doubted or turned away? You know that I'll do whatever you ask. I swear."

Madeline looked at Prudence. Rage and anguish fought each other on my sister's face, and then she slid down to her knees and pressed her forehead against my mother's. "I could've done it, Mother," she whispered, and now the tears were coming for her, the sorrow winning out. "I could've protected them."

"Whatever waits for me on the other side of death," Madeline said, one hand reaching up to stroke my sister's red hair, "it cannot change that I will miss you, my daughter. You were the gift that filled my arms after your sister died, and how I have loved you. Now promise, darling. Promise me this last thing."

A long minute passed. Then, muffled, but unmistakable, Prudence whispered, "This last thing, Mother, this hardest thing, I promise."

Madeline's eyes turned to me, and she stretched out her left hand. I caught it, feeling the veins, the dry, thin skin, the chill of the flesh. "And you, my last born, my rebel, fool and foreseer both. Swear."

"I don't understand why you're doing this, Mother," I said, my voice breaking. "None of this makes sense."

"Trust me, my son, my creation. All your terror, all your love—trust me now."

Her hand moved up and cupped my face. How many times, I wondered, had she done this one action since the moment that I was born? And now here was the last time. There were centuries of life stretching in front of me, yet my mother was dying when I wasn't even thirty. My tears were hot on my face, and I nodded. "Fine," I said. "I promise. I swear."

"Thank you, my little virtues, my greatest loves. Now . . ." She relaxed back against the cushions of her bed, spreading out her arms. "My final gift to you: drink. Drink until nothing remains. Whatever strength, whatever power is still flickering in me, better that it be yours, my children, then be cast aside or preserve a useless half-life." She smiled at the expressions on our faces, her long ivory fangs flashing. "Yes, I know that this is difficult, dears. But this is the death I choose, rather than lingering and dwindling down to nothingness. This is what I want, and I've already given Loren and the staff their other orders." Her hands stretched out, touching each of us on our heads, our cheeks. "All has been arranged."

We arranged ourselves the way that our mother directed us—Chivalry gently carried her over to her chaise longue, then knelt at her left side. I was at her right, and Prudence was at her neck. As my sister turned down the collar of Madeline's dressing gown, I rolled up her long sleeve, exposing the soft bend of her elbow. Chivalry was echoing my movements, or maybe I was echoing his— this was nothing that I could've ever imagined doing, and yet somehow, as we all acted together, there was almost a familiarity to what we were doing. A strange, disturbing, wholly unwelcome sense of rightness.

Prudence and Chivalry's needlelike fangs slid out, delicate and precise. I had nothing like that, so it was my mother who did what she'd always done for me—drew one of her sharp nails across the inside of her elbow to split the skin for me. I cupped her elbow in my hands and started to lean down, and I paused for a moment to look at her. Her eyes were focused on mine, and, even as my sister leaned down and bit her neck, my mother's lips widened into a smile as she looked at me. Across from me, Chivalry was already feeding.

I leaned down and began to drink at the wound.

I'd been dependent on my mother's blood for my entire life, but her blood tasted different this time. It was thinner, for one thing—instead of it being so thick that I had to suck hard to get any into my mouth, today it flowed freely, easily into me. The taste was saltier, and there was a faint hint to it that reminded me, very strangely, of roses—of the smell that cut roses have just before they begin wilting. That bond, the tie between me and my mother was winding tighter as I drank, and it felt like my whole chest was compressing, and that awareness of my parent was a throbbing certainty that blacked out my vision, my hearing, and anything that existed beyond the blood that I was swallowing.

The blood began to thin, and I drank harder, not letting go. Then it was one last droplet on my tongue, and as it slid down my throat, I felt the bond shatter, like a fluted sugar sculpture that has been spun out like stained glass and is dropped to the floor. The death of the bond, and the death of my mother, cut through me, and the pain was unimaginable, as if a heated knife had been drawn across every nerve ending in my body. I opened my mouth to scream, and it was gone, leaving only an empty well of loss.

Inside me, somewhere in my head or my soul, whichever I was more inclined to believe in that day, there had been three strings that tied me to my family, that let me know that they were around. Chivalry had once told me that those had existed before I had even been born—that from the moment I'd quickened in my host mother's womb, he'd felt the beat of my heart, and the bond between us.

Now my mother was gone, and only two ties remained. They felt fainter, more delicate, as if the loss of my bond to my mother had changed them from the heavy ropes on a ship to strands of a spider's web.

She was really dead, really gone.

Madeline had left her orders, and they were carried out.

A funeral pyre had already been built on the back lawn, in full view of the ocean. There were large logs, and hundreds of pinecones of many different varieties, from the tiny ones that littered the forest floors around us to huge ones that must've come from the sequoias in California. There were braided wreaths of pine boughs, rosemary, sage, and things that I couldn't identify by scent or sight, beautifully woven together. The pyre had been built within a frame of black wrought iron, the design showing birds, and flowers, and the ocean waves. Beneath the pyre was a flooring of bone-white tiles, something that I knew hadn't been there yesterday, sitting on top of the recent snowfall. Strings of delicate white lights in the shape of lilies had been strung around the backyard between recently erected posts swathed in white silk.

My mother's body had been wrapped in a red shroud of some heavy fabric and was now carried on a board of polished rosewood, covered all over in more carvings, and around the edges ran the inscription—Madeline, mother of Constance, Prudence, Chivalry, and Fortitude, sister of Edmund, daughter of Blanche. It repeated a dozen or more times, each time the lettering subtly different, the spelling and presentation shifting from the modern all the way back to what the carving might've looked like on my mother's own cradle, back in 1387.

We followed behind the body, the chief mourners in a procession that consisted of us and the staff of the house. There were no representatives from any of the races that my mother had ruled—perhaps it was tradition, or maybe she just hadn't cared to include them in her plans. She was no longer there to give us an answer, if she'd felt inclined to do so.

There were no clouds in the night sky, and the moon was barely a sliver, leaving the stars to gleam perfectly and coldly above us in all their winter glory. The board that carried my mother was placed gently on top of the pyre, her feet facing the ocean.

Three torches were produced, and lit, each a masterpiece of wood carving, each with our name set into the sides, entwined with delicately rendered leaves and berries. The tops were dipped into a small container of kerosene, then lit and handed to each of us in turn. We stood at three corners of the pyre and waited for our cue, as one final item was produced. This was a carved wooden candle, this one marked for my dead sister, Constance. It was lit, then gently placed just above my mother's head, the flame flickering and building in strength.

Then Loren Noka gave us a subtle nod, and we each brought the flaming tips of our torches down onto the wreaths, letting them catch and the fire spread. Then we slid our torches farther down, completely inside the intricately built nest of wooden logs, the fuel that would allow the pyre to burn long enough to break down bone to ash. The flame built greedily, catching in a fierce and immediate blaze on the pine and the herbs, more sluggishly on smaller pieces of kindling, until finally it built into an inferno that caught even the thickest pieces of wood and wouldn't go out until everything was consumed. There must have been little pockets of chemicals tucked into the pyre, because the fire was many colors—brilliant scarlet red, a rich purple, sullen green, and even a sapphire blue. The smell was a cacophony—some pleasant and deliberately aromatic, some undeniable as the scent of burning flesh.

As we stood in the darkness, the heat of the pyre enveloping us and melting the surrounding snow, music began to play. Somewhere, probably back on the patio, a string quartet played for hours—everything from modern pop to old chamber music that had been played for kings and queens.

The fire burned all night, and we all stood beside it. Once, out of the corner of my eye, I thought I saw a white fox and the glitter of many eyes behind her, but when I turned to look there was nothing. Eventually, as the sky began lightening to a pale gray, the pyre began to gutter, even the thickest logs consumed, and the shape of my mother's body had long since disappeared. And when the lines of delicate pink and orange appeared above us, reflected down onto the churning waves, it was finally over. The coals still winked with ruby lights, the mixed gray and white of the ashes still hot enough that a second fire could've started just by placing a sheet of paper or a few pieces of kindling down. I saw now that a few people stood off to the side with what looked like overlarge fireplace tools.

We hadn't touched or spoken since our mother died, but we'd stood together, watching her burn. Now Chivalry's hand closed around my arm, and he said, softly, "It's over, Fort."

"What do we do now?" I asked. Madeline was dead. She was gone, and we were left without her, to somehow move forward on our own.

There was no answer, just Chivalry tugging me around, walking back toward the house. Simone, his wife, had appeared on his other side, and Prudence walked ahead of us. The string quartet was packing up their instruments. Staff members had begun taking down the strands of white flower lights, as well as the posts. White silk was being folded, tucked away. Behind us I could hear the wrought-iron frame being disassembled. The new day, the first of my life without my mother, was beginning.

She was gone, but nothing had stopped, and nothing would stand still.

Chapter Six

The next day, I sat and ate breakfast with Chivalry and Prudence. The cook had been one of the fatalities in my mother's bedroom, and the new cook was her niece, who had been her aunt's assistant for almost twenty years. I was disturbed to realize, as I ate, that I could discern no difference in the taste of the food whatsoever. Had I not been told about the change, then my only hint that a new administration was in place in the mansion's kitchen would've been that a vegetarian quiche had been served alongside the rest of the dishes, with zero fanfare, something that never would've occurred while my mother was writing the menus and waiting for my "experiment" in vegetarianism to come to an end.

"Stop pouting, Fortitude," Prudence snapped at me.

"I'm not pouting," I defended.

My sister pointed her parfait spoon at me. "You're definitely pouting."

"You're sulking a bit," Chivalry, the traitor, noted. "Just admit that Mother knew what she was doing when she put together her will. If you'd been given immediate access to your inheritance, you would've given the whole thing to Doctors Without Borders or something like that just to make a point."

"And what a tragedy that would've been, if a worthy

and selfless cause suddenly benefited from millions of dollars," I said. My siblings shook their heads, horrified at the thought. Across the table, Simone gave me a sympathetic smile. Slightly bolstered, I continued. "Don't think that I'm going to feel any differently when the trust finally matures."

"I trust in Mother's wisdom, little brother," Chivalry said, putting another forkful of omelet in his mouth and eyeing the plate of bacon assessingly, clearly wondering if he was up for a second helping. Wordlessly, Simone reached out and put two more pieces on each of their plates, and they shared a smile. Chivalry turned his attention back to me. "Holding the trust back until you're fifty will give you time to mature, to attain new thoughtfulness—"

"To conform to your values rather than mine?"

Prudence snorted heavily. "Mother knew what she was doing. You can play human all you want now, when you see no visible differences between yourself and your peers. Just wait until you're fifty, brother, and all the people you went to college with are now checking in with their doctors about their cholesterol and worrying about how they're going to pay for their children's educations, and you still look exactly as you do today." A somewhat smug look slid across her face. "Perhaps then you'll be a bit more willing to embrace who, and what, you are."

"And in the meantime," Chivalry pointed out, "you are being given a perfectly appropriate allowance, which you are more than free to hand over to worthy causes at the beginning of every month, if that's what you feel is best."

"A monthly allowance that just happens to be in the exact amount as my half of the apartment rent," I noted. "How amazingly convenient."

"The amount will go up when you turn thirty." My brother chomped down on a perfectly prepared slice of bacon with every indication of enjoyment. I nudged my glass of orange juice over to block my view of the serving plate. "And then continue to go up, a little bit every year, until you turn fifty and can touch the bulk of the capital."

"Mother decided all this on her own?" I asked. Both of my siblings looked at me blandly. "Of course not."

"Don't fuss, Fort. There's too much going on at the moment." Prudence deliberately leaned forward and nudged the serving platter of bacon back into my eye line. "The faction heads are all being informed about Mother's death today, though heaven knows that they probably know about it already. They've been twittering about nothing else for the last two weeks."

I moved the mimosa jug a strategic two inches to the left to block my view again. "Twittering as in your old-fashioned fancy-pants term for gossip, or actually tweeting, on Twitter?"

Prudence gave me an icy glare. "Loren Noka can show you the screenshots, I'm sure."

"The cards are being delivered today by personal messenger," Chivalry broke in calmly, giving his mouth a delicate dab with his napkin, "so we need to start having discussions about how we want to proceed. Mother was clear that these decisions needed to be made together." He turned to Simone and gave her a melting smile. The worst part of the sudden radiation of charm that was emerging from him—as if clouds had suddenly parted to reveal the sun—was that he wasn't even doing it on purpose. It was patently obvious that just being around Simone made him happy—of course, that had been the case with all his wives, before he'd eventually killed them. "My darling, I have the unfortunate inkling that this is not going to be a swift conversation, so would you mind terribly if I . . . ?"

Simone leaned over to give him a solid kiss. "I need to do some endurance training anyway, honey, and I know that jogging around Newport with sixty-pound weights strapped to you is something of an acquired taste. I'll catch up with you at dinner." She got up from the table with a cheery wave, more enthusiastic than any person should be at the prospect of hours of jogging while weighted down with the equivalent of a baby harp seal strapped to her back. Simone was a professional mountain climber and guide, though, currently training in the hopes of being included in a May expedition to attempt an Annapurna ascent in the Himalayas. I liked her, but I wasn't sure that we really understood each other, given that my ideal day involved being wrapped in blankets and watching a *Doctor Who* marathon, while hers involved using nothing but an ice ax and belaying pitons to inch her way up a mountain while icy winds attempted to rip her off to her death. I waved back as she left. Prudence lifted one hand and gave a small wiggling of her fingers that managed to effectively convey her sarcasm.

"So, it's just the cards going out?" I asked. "We don't have to do a memorial service or something?"

"Mother didn't see the point, I suppose," Prudence replied, toying with the last drops of her parfait. "She set the pyre details herself in advance, and Loren Noka let me know this morning that her ashes were collected into the appointed box, but that Mother's directions indicated that the spreading of the ashes should wait until Edmund arrives."

"He's coming?" I felt shocked, and more than a little disturbed. None of us had ever met our uncle, or even spoken with him. And after the last visit we'd had from a European vampire . . . well, it wasn't something that was necessarily a good surprise.

Prudence shrugged carelessly. "Mother apparently thought so. As for when, who knows? A month? A year? Ten years? He dates back to the Battle of Bosworth, Fort. Time has a different meaning for the old ones. And his tie was to Mother, not to us. I'd be surprised if he shows up before the colonization of Mars."

Chivalry gave a small snort. "Is that estimate including the defunding of NASA?" The space program was a sore subject with Chivalry. For all my own disappointments about the lack of emphasis given to exploration, he'd actually been present at President Kennedy's speech at Rice University, and felt a personal affront whenever the NASA budget was cut. With a visible effort my brother pulled himself away from his usual diatribe and focused on issues closer to terra firma. "Well, this is my proposal—we need to start things off right, and move forward in the spirit of cooperation that Mother intended. Therefore, I believe that we should not move from this table"—Chivalry rapped the tabletop decisively with his knuckles—"until we can come to a unanimous consensus on one issue."

There was one piece of immediate consensus, and that was the clear horror that both Prudence and I felt at the thought of that proposal. Clearly we had much clearer memories of the miserable afternoon spent debating the succubi petition than Chivalry did.

"Now, don't look at me like that," Chivalry chided, his voice laden with deliberate enthusiasm. "We can do this if we just work together. Now, what are some of the items on our agenda? The succubi? The request from the new *karhu* that was conveyed at the coronation? The kobold activities that Fort observed?"

If Julie Andrews had been male and a vampire who dated back to the Civil War, this was what sitting at the table with her would've been like. I could only count my blessings that Chivalry had always considered spontaneous singing outside an opera house to be incredibly vulgar; otherwise I could quite easily see him try to motivate togetherness through a Disney-style song and dance number.

After a long, horrible pause, where I mulled over the fact that the grieving process was clearly being expressed differently by all of us, I asked, "Are we going to be able to take bathroom breaks?"

Chivalry frowned at me. Apparently this was not the response that he'd expected. "What? Fine, fine."

"Oh, good," Prudence cut in. "I was worried that we'd end up resorting to the flower vase, and if there's one thing I don't miss about older and grander ages, it's the chamber pots."

As ever, the realization that I was actually in agreement with my sister was a terrifying one, and something that made me wonder if a reappraisal of my life choices and value systems was in order.

Over the following four hours, I was at least reminded about all the ways that Prudence and I disagreed, as we moved through every prominent item on our collective agenda and managed to fundamentally deadlock on every single one. Our progress on the succubi was nonexistent, with forty minutes spent just disagreeing on whether or not we should even continue to support them as they hovered at the edge of the territory in red tape limbo. The only reason the food funding was still in place at the end of that conversation was simply that we couldn't even agree to cut it—and any greater issue remained almost congressionally untouchable. Prudence absolutely hated the idea of agreeing to a *metsän kunigas* adviser on bear issues, which killed the whole thing, even when I pointed out that Gil Kivela had made significant compromises on what he'd actually wanted. The only result of that had been Prudence's suggestion that we kill Gil, along with Dahlia for good measure, and institute a puppet regency for Anni Kivela. That, thankfully, died quickly, as even Chivalry agreed that that seemed like a bit of an overreaction (though his use of the term "a bit" had me more than a bit worried). Even the kobold issue was something that we couldn't agree on—my sister actually liked the idea of allowing the kobolds to hunt the homeless population, provided that they were discreet about it and left no survivors.

"Can we at least agree to expel all the witches from the territory?" Prudence asked plaintively.

"Absolutely not," I said, my forehead pressed against the tablecloth in despair.

"Maybe just some additional regulations?" Chivalry suggested. Prudence and I both disagreed in unison—though of course for entirely different reasons.

There was a long silence, born of exhaustion, fruitless arguing, and the sad realization that we'd all used our allowed bathroom breaks.

"Okay," I finally said, breaking the silence. "This has been a complete bust. And if we stay here any longer, then we're going to have to eat lunch, which is a depressing thought. So now we've also managed to ruin lunch, which I didn't think was possible."

Prudence nodded. "On this sole subject, Fortitude is right. Chivalry, my brother"—her voice became coaxing—"perhaps we need to adjourn this for another time."

Chivalry's expression was dogged. "Absolutely not. I refuse to believe that we are incapable of all agreeing on just *one* subject."

"Despite all available evidence?" Prudence furrowed her brow, perplexed. "Really, I would think that you've been given a more than adequate sample set to draw conclusions from."

I finally lifted my head off the table and really looked at my brother, at the grim set of his jaw and the strain showing on his movie-star-perfect features. He'd driven the conversation for hours, ignoring every completely predictable deadlock, and now he sat there looking incredibly disappointed in us. We were all grieving for Madeline, even as much as none of us wanted to show it, and this fixation of my brother's to act out our mother's last directive to us was clearly how he was trying to deal with the situation. I racked my brain for a long minute, trying to come up with something that could give Chivalry the unanimous agreement that he needed right now. After considering and rejecting half a dozen ideas, I finally just spit something out. "How about we change the staircase?"

Both Chivalry and Prudence turned to look at me, nearly identical quizzical frowns stretching across their faces. ". . . the staircase?" Prudence asked, clearly wondering if she could have possibly heard me correctly.

I was committed to this now. "Yes. Our sexually explicit staircase. I'm just going to say it—I find it kind of embarrassing whenever I pass by a female staff member when I'm walking up it. Between the toplessness and the bottomlessness, I'm kind of sure that we're creating a hostile work environment. Also, it's really weird."

There was another long pause while we all took a second to picture our grand staircase, with its extravagant upward sweep of solid marble, and its depictions of human-mermaid sexual congress engraved with such clear detail that one was practically forced to entertain disturbing insinuations about the personal life and inclinations of the sculptor responsible. Especially when one also considered the clear voyeurism expressed on the parts of the carved porpoises. It was a staircase that had prompted hundreds of visitors to say, "Oh, how *interesting*," in tones that left no doubt that "interesting" did not in any way indicate "good."

"I . . . actually agree with that," Prudence said, practically tasting the words as they came out of her mouth, her amazement clear. She paused, considered, then gave a decisive nod and returned to her usual clipped and confident delivery. "Yes, I agree. It makes for a very awkward moment when giving someone the full tour. Let's replace the staircase stonework. Chivalry?"

I felt the kind of internal triumph that should probably only be reserved for discovering radium or teaching a cat to use a toilet. Chivalry was staring at us, his jaw hanging. "Look, Chivalry, it's happened!" I said happily. "We're all in agreement, and it didn't even break the seventh seal and bring about the end of the world. Go Team Scott!" I extended a hand in perfect high-five position to my sister, which she met with withering scorn. I attempted to pretend that I'd actually meant to scratch my ear.

Chivalry was still just staring at us.

It was starting to feel a little ominous, and it was Prudence who leaned forward and asked, very cautiously, "Chivalry? You *do* agree with us, don't you?"

My brother, that final beacon of good manners and fine breeding, hit his breaking point at last and absolutely exploded. "Of course I don't," he yelled. "That stonework is a one-of-a-kind work of art from a master craftsman! We've been featured in architectural magazines that have taken and displayed close-up photos of that staircase, and I know for a fact that there are at least four professors of well-regarded private universities that include pictures of it in their PowerPoint presentations. We are not going to destroy an amazing piece of artistic expression simply because the two of you find the sight of a naked breast distressing to your sensibilities!"

"Chivalry . . ." I blinked, trying to process what was actually going on. "You covered up the pornographic portions with newspaper when I was little."

My brother adjusted his shirt collar fussily and smoothed back his still perfectly coiffed hair, pulling himself together. He slanted an annoyed look at me. "I also put our copies of D. H. Lawrence on upper shelves and locked up the rolling ladders. As I assume that you are not also proposing the censorship of *Lady Chatterley's Lover*, I fail to see your point."

"Oh, for heaven's sake, Chivalry," Prudence snapped, "this is not about defending artistic liberty. This is about how Mother hired an artist, gave him too much leeway, and then kept the result because she enjoyed how uncomfortable it made guests. It is the Egyptian Room all over again, and you are just being stubborn."

"The Egyptian Room?" Clearly this reference predated me.

My sister gave her most superior sniff, one that usually came out whenever we got trapped in a family game of Trivial Pursuit and I'd missed what she considered to be an obvious question. Snobbery established, she finally gave me the background. "There have been several waves of Egyptomania in the United States. Mother decided that it would be amusing to jump aboard a brief one that rolled through in the eighteen eighties. She bankrolled an archaeologist for an expedition to Egypt that lasted three years, with the only stipulations being that he could go wherever and do whatever, as long as he brought back enough authentic items for her to decorate the main drawing room."

I considered what I'd just heard, then ventured, "So she hired Indiana Jones?"

Prudence glared. Apparently pop culture references were not an appropriate frame for this conversation. "If Indiana Jones had ever returned with a local wife, two local mistresses, a depressing assortment of small children, and what I can only imagine to be a raging case of herpes, then yes, just like that."

I pondered that particular mental image of Harrison Ford. Parts of it, I had to admit, seemed plausible, particularly when one considered the events of *Temple of Doom*.

Chivalry looked affronted. "Dr. Shearer did bring back the artifacts that he promised."

"Yes, he certainly did." Prudence leaned forward and fixed that gimlet gaze on me. "Fortitude, you may not know this, but there are whole basements in museums around the world that consist of nothing but Egyptian art and relics that they absolutely cannot put on display because of the explicitly sexual nature of the pieces. Dr. Shearer brought back seemingly nothing but that type of work, and Mother thought that it was utterly hilarious, and promptly decorated with it anyway. We'd be sitting in that room trying to have tea with callers, and none of those poor women could take their eyes off the wall mural of a fully erect pharaoh about to sodomize some poor handmaid. And do not even get me started on just how many individual pieces seemed to focus on male masturbation."

Well, that certainly put our staircase into historical context.

Chivalry shifted uncomfortably, clearly not welcoming the vividness of Prudence's references to the full frontal memory lane. "It was a very rich culture, with a fascinating series of creation mythos, some of which apparently involved masturbation. Though I'll grant you that over cake and coffee it was a bit much."

On a roll now, Prudence continued. "And we had to live with that for almost forty years. I cannot even tell you how grateful I was when she decided to have the interior of the house gutted and rewired in 1927. I donated the whole of the Egyptian Room to the Peabody Museum, and Mother didn't find out until it was too late for her to do anything about it."

"The museum actually took them?" I asked. "I thought you said that they had basements full of that kind of stuff."

"I included a very sizable check, and the Peabody managed to find more room in one of their storage areas." Ah, wealth. Prudence's answer to every problem.

"I'm really not sure that the staircase is on that kind of level," Chivalry insisted, but I could see that he was starting to waver.

Seeing my opportunity to deliver the unanimous decision that my brother craved, regardless of his own feelings on this particular manner, I saw my opening and took it. "Listen, Chivalry, you've said yourself that the staircase is a work of art. Let's give it to an institution that will really appreciate it. I'm sure that we can find a museum that would love to incorporate it, or maybe we could donate it to RISD."

"Christ, I'm going to have to endow a whole college to get that thing out the door," Prudence muttered.

I ignored her, keeping my focus on my brother as I delivered the biggest carrot I could come up with. "And then, Chivalry, we'd need a new staircase, so you could support some up-and-coming architect who would love to design a showpiece."

Chivalry visibly brightened. "That would be nice. Simone and I stopped by the Boston MFA on our last drive down from New Hampshire, and she really enjoyed the art deco exhibits. Maybe she'd be interested in taking an active hand in deciding on a new staircase." The moment he mentioned his wife, I knew that I had him. Whether he was fully aware of it or not, Chivalry loved offering his wives the opportunity to put their own stamps on the mansion. Perhaps it comforted him on some level to walk past Bhumika's elaborate rose garden, or Linda's framed watercolors. There were hundreds of tiny little touches that everyone but him had either forgotten or never even been aware of. I remembered one moment when I was about seven, Chivalry had been hanging a swing from one of the huge, ancient, gnarled trees on the property, and he'd told me quietly that it had been one that his wife Irené had planted in 1902.

Prudence clearly also knew victory when she saw it, because she said pointedly, "And who exactly is paying for all this new work, Fort?" Apparently art deco–inspired architectural showpieces by up-and-coming artists were unlikely to come on the cheap.

I gave my sister my sweetest smile. "Well, I'd love to chip in, Prudence, but I apparently can't touch the capital on my third of the inheritance until I'm fifty."

Her upper lip curled slightly. "Oh, how joyous, an unfunded mandate." She reached over and poured a glass from the mimosa pitcher, which had been refreshed discreetly by one of the staff members over the course of the long morning. "Well, however it was achieved, let's at least have a toast to our first successful and unanimous group decision." We all poured and joined in the toast.

I stood up and stretched, my spine giving a relieved crack. "Well, if that's everything, then—" At the suddenly deadly serious expressions on my siblings' faces, and a definite exchange of significant looks, I stopped. "Apparently not." I dropped back into my chair dejectedly. "What is it?"

Chivalry leaned over to me and said, in the gentlest possible tones, "It's about your feeding, Fort."

I froze. With everything else that had been happening, I had, either consciously or unconsciously, overlooked this. "Mother's gone, so I have no one to feed on anymore." The words felt like a death knell. And they were, really. After a lifetime of being able to subsist on my mother, I was going to have to become what my siblings were—hunters, parasites, leeches. There was nothing benevolent about our feeding process, just corrosive and harmful to the humans involved.

There was no gentleness in my sister, just unyielding

steel. "Your transition has been delayed too long already, brother. And now we have a timeline—you'll need to feed again in two weeks. At your point in transition, any longer than that would be asking for an accident. This needs to be completed. Now."

Desperation shot through me, and denial. This was what I'd feared and avoided ever since I was old enough to learn about my own biological inevitability, but if the time was now, then it was too soon. Anytime was too soon, actually, but I still struggled against it. "No, no, I don't want it to be completed, not yet. Isn't there some other way?" I turned to my brother, knowing that I was begging but unable to stop myself, wanting and needing him to give me a way out—an escape hatch, a magic wand, *anything*. "Chivalry, you're over a hundred years older than me. Couldn't I feed on you?"

My brother took both of my hands in his and looked me in the eye. He was regretful, Chivalry—always so full of regrets, I realized suddenly. Regrets over every dead wife, even as he married the next. And here I was, the little brother trying to fight nature itself, and he felt regret for me. "Prudence and I asked Mother that same question three years ago," he said. "She told us then that we're not old enough to maintain you, and that feeding from any vampire but her, even someone as close as a sibling, just wouldn't be safe for you, even if we had been old enough."

I struggled to process what he was telling me—not just that it wasn't possible, but that he'd approached the question himself, and long before it had even occurred to me to ask. "You asked her this three years ago? So—"

A muscle in his cheek spasmed, just once. "Fort, having you at her age, maintaining you for so long after you normally would've transitioned, *plus* keeping two hosts for so long . . . it was a lot, Fort. It put a strain on her, and it wore her down. We both wanted to help, but she wouldn't let us—not a single drop of blood to either of the hosts, even just to maintain them. She was absolutely adamant."

I stared, and the room seemed to close in around me. "If it was straining her . . . I know she was old, but am I the reason she—"

Prudence's voice lashed like a whip. "Don't even ask that. Only Mother knew what her reasons were, but she chose her actions very deliberately, knowing more about their repercussions than any of us could." She shoved herself to her feet and began pacing, irritation clear in every line of her body. "But it's time to grow up, Fortitude. You are not Peter Pan, and this is not the end of the world. This is what is normal and natural for you, and I have no idea why Mother allowed this to continue." Her voice kept rising as she spoke; then she stopped herself, forcefully pulling herself back together. The bond between us felt too tight, and I could actually feel it as she shoved anger down and forced herself into an icy control. When she began speaking again, it was in a carefully modulated voice, her hand resting almost carelessly against the sideboard, but there was no hiding the glow of her blue eyes, or the weight of what she was saying. "If you're unable to finish it yourself, then Chivalry or I could take care of Henry."

"You mean kill him." Everything began to drain away from inside me, leaving me empty.

Prudence met my eyes, never flinching. "Yes. That's exactly what I mean."

I was the one who had to look away, from her, from my brother. I stared at the table instead—the pristine white tablecloth, the antique china that we ate off of with no regard because it had been in use in this family since it was new, the cut flower centerpiece that the staff members refreshed from our own greenhouse whenever the slightest hint of a wilt appeared. Here was all the beauty of the surface—the elegance and ease—and below us, down in the basement, was the reality, strapped to a table, fed from a tube. Henry's life had been in my family's hands, his death ours to deliver at a whim, since the moment that my mother decided, by whatever criteria she'd held in her mind and taken with her to the grave, that he would be her host, her Renfield, her means of creating one last child.

Prudence would do it, and with pleasure. He'd slipped through her hands once months ago, and I knew that she longed to finish the job. Chivalry would do it, if I asked him—do it with merciful swiftness, the efficiency that comes from always doing one's duty. If I wanted to, I could be weak, and neither of them would say a word against me. I took a deep breath and forced myself to look up at my siblings. "I'll do it."

"What?" They were both clearly surprised, but it was Chivalry who spoke first. "Fort, you know that I—"

I cut him off. "I know you would. I appreciate it. But it should be me."

"And when will this be?" Prudence asked, sarcasm and exasperation dripping from her words. "This is yet another attempt to stretch this out indefinitely, and I'm sorry to tell you, we simply do not have the resources to maintain—"

"No, Prudence." I stood up again, feeling numb and light-headed. This would be the day, then, when I finally had to let go of my deepest dream, that somehow the transition could be put off forever, that I'd never have to let biology win and become that thing that my DNA was programmed for. "He never recovered from what you did to him, and with Mother gone, now he never can." I forced the words out, and forced myself to accept them. "I'll do it today."

The process that transforms a human being into the particular hybrid that can create a vampire offspring is a punishing one. Over a series of weeks or months, the human's blood is removed and replaced with vampire blood, until eventually no human blood remains. The human's body is changed—it becomes tougher, stronger, and twisted all the way down to the DNA level, until the genes that are passed on are almost entirely those of the vampire, with only a few shreds from what used to be the human. The greatest changes, though, are in the mind. Sanity can't survive the process—whoever my host father, Henry, had been before my mother gave him her blood, it was long gone by the time I was conceived, replaced with a mind that was broken and craved nothing but death and destruction. There were shreds of lucidity in his madness, enough to recognize me, for example, and occasionally hold a level of cocktail-party conversation. My childhood finger paintings were framed on the walls of the room that contained Henry's cell, and, when it was on, the television was set to the weather channel. Henry seemed to enjoy seeing what the weather was doing—probably because he hadn't experienced anything but the sterile insides of his cell for over thirty years.

"He's in a good mood today," Conrad Miller, his keeper, told me. I was standing in the keeper's main room, with one side completely made up of the one-way glass that allowed Conrad to keep a constant eye on Henry's condition. The rest of the room was dominated by Conrad's computer setup, and of course Conrad himself, who was built along the lines of a gladiator.

"How can you tell?" I asked, looking through the window. Henry's prison was a clear cube of incredibly tough plastic, reinforced on the door and wall seams with enough steel to make it resistant even to a vampire. Inside, Henry was strapped to a gurney at all points, so that he wouldn't even be able to lift his head. His current physical condition necessitated the use of a feeding tube, and a catheter, and even occasionally some dialysis, and no one dared trust Henry around anything that could hold a sharp edge. The first time I'd seen a Hannibal Lector movie, I didn't realize at first that it was meant to be frightening and bizarre—after all, that was the kind of setup I recognized from every visit to my host parents.

"He was singing the Harvard fight song this morning." Conrad checked the charge on his stun gun carefully, then gave me a shrewd-eyed assessment. He hadn't been surprised by my announcement that I'd be going into Henry's cell today, even though I'd never done that before in my life, and for the entire few months of Conrad's employment, ever since he replaced the previous keeper, Mr. Alfred, the only people to enter the cell had been either himself or Maeve. But around Conrad's hugely bulging left biceps was a neat black band, a strangely old-fashioned gesture that I'd seen all the other staff wearing this morning, a dull black against the rich natural brown of Conrad's skin. As Conrad reached into a drawer and withdrew a small case marked with my name, I wondered how many final instructions my mother had left.

He opened the case for me and showed me what was there. "The bone saw is electric," he explained, "so you won't need a cord. I checked the charge yesterday, and you'll have everything you need. That's for the skull, of course. And the knife is for the chest—you'll want to start below the rib cage and go up. There are a set of tongs for removal." Conrad paused, then withdrew a long, full needle. "This wasn't in here originally," he said cautiously. "I thought about it, and then I asked Maeve to put it together for me."

"Morphine?" I asked.

He nodded. "Enough to drop a herd of elephants. Maeve put in triple what she usually gives Henry to knock him out when she's doing a procedure. You don't need to fumble around with a vein either—just use the needle to inject the whole thing into the top of his saline bag. He'll just drift off . . . and then you can do the rest of it."

"You know what I'm going to do, I gather."

Conrad nodded again, his expression calm. "Your mother explained everything."

"I'm sure she did."

He paused. "You know, of course . . . I'll be here watching, just in case anything goes wrong. But I don't think anything will."

"Why do you say that?" I took the case, feeling its lightness. It should've weighed a lot more, given what I was about to do. There was a carefully folded plastic apron, with a set of hospital scrubs, the kind that can go over clothing, plus a clear face shield, all folded and sitting on top of one of the tables. They looked much too big to be for Maeve, and I knew that they were for me, if I wanted them. But taking the case was bad enough—the last thing I wanted was to look like I was wearing a *Dexter* Halloween costume.

"He talks about it sometimes."

I looked at Conrad, surprised. He nodded. "If he's having a good day, and he can really talk. That's why I wasn't surprised when your mother gave me this, told me what to expect."

"He isn't scared?" I asked.

"Ask him yourself." Conrad opened the door and gave me an encouraging nod.

I could feel Henry's attention on me from the moment I walked into the room. He couldn't turn his head—it was strapped down too tightly—but I knew that he was aware. I walked across the room, passing over the thick red line that was painted on the otherwise pristine white floor—until now, that was the closest I'd ever come to the cage. This would be the second time that I'd ever touched my host father—and the first time had been during Prudence's murder attempt, when I was trying to haul him off Mr. Alfred while he'd been tearing at his keeper's throat with his teeth, ripping away with a savagery that had been wholly animal.

A harsh buzzing sound as Conrad remotely unlocked the door from his observation post, and I tugged at it. It opened easily, releasing a blast of air from the inside of the cell that was stale and reeked of rubbing alcohol and the faintest hint of feces. Three more steps, and I was over the threshold, beside the gurney, and within his eye line.

Henry had those Boston Brahmin looks, the aristocratic features, and the artfully present touches of gray in the hair just at his temples that made him look like an ad for Touch of Gray. His face was much more heavily lined than it had been a few months ago—his injuries had clearly taken a toll. But his eyes focused on me, and a slow smile spread across his face. The fingers of his right hand began to tap against the surface of the bed— and the tapping was in the same rhythm as my heartbeat.

"I felt her die, you know," he said, conversationally, as if we were picking up a conversation that had briefly been interrupted. Maybe, to him, we were. Henry's mind had always been like a nightmarish hedge maze to me. He laughed, softly, but with real amusement. "I never expected for her to die before me. It's very strange. Very peaceful."

"What do you mean?"

"Her blood would always whisper to me. It's in me, of course, and it doesn't like it. But when she died, the blood quieted. I think her blood is dying as well." He paused, and his brow slowly furrowed as he pondered. "I wonder what Grace would've thought about this. She always had interesting observations. She was studying medicine, you know. Quite radical. In her family, the girls were all expected to be debutantes, marry political men. That's why Madeline chose her, really. Chose both of us."

Grace had been my host mother, Henry's counterpart. She'd died when she stabbed herself to death with a homemade shiv, shredding her heart into enough pieces to kill even a host, and she'd done it for me. Somehow she'd known that, miles away in Providence, I was in a fight for my life against a vampire named Luca. Her death had begun my transition, had given me the speed and strength I'd needed to survive that encounter. I didn't know much about the origins of my host parents, besides what I'd picked up by inference or the occasional comment. I'd never really wanted to know, because when I was young I hadn't thought to ask, and when I was older, I'd known enough to be frightened and disturbed by them. I'd never heard either of them talk about how they'd ended up being Madeline's choices for hosts, and I paused where I was, curiosity tugging at me. "Because you were studying medicine?" I asked. When I'd been a student at Brown, there was a regular ad in the student newspaper, offering very sizable sums of money for semen and egg donations from young premed students—it wasn't unusual for childless couples of means to troll the student newspaper for their biological building blocks, often with a wish list of SAT scores and physical features, though it had been unusual enough to request a specific major that that ad had become the butt of a number of jokes around campus. A friend of mine, strapped for cash, had actually answered the ad, though he'd ended up being rejected for being less than their ideal height of six feet. I wondered for a moment whether Madeline had felt similar yearnings—if she had, she'd managed to conceal her disappointment extremely well when I declared my film studies major.

Henry laughed. "Silly boy. No, I came from a whole family of doctors. My father, uncles, brothers, both grandfathers. Great contributions to the field. That's what they expected out of me, of course. But I wanted to be a poet. Tried to change my major in college without telling them—of course the dean called my father anyway. They were old friends." He tried to tilt his head at me, and was stopped by the heavy strap around his forehead. But the dark eyes that focused on me were suddenly far too clear. "You see, then, don't you?"

"I'm not sure," I hedged. Honestly I didn't want to see.

"Madeline never explained it to us, of course. Why she chose us. At first I thought it was just a bit of snobbery—prominent families, good looks, that kind of thing. But Grace never agreed. She said that it had to be something more—all the fuss that Madeline had to go through to acquire us, particularly given the likelihood that either of us would die at some point in the process. Grace thought it was something in our temperaments that Madeline wanted. That she was hoping for something."

I shook my head. "Rebelliousness? That doesn't seem very likely." My mother had been experimenting with me—she'd admitted as much to my face. But this was just patently unrealistic.

Henry laughed again, from his belly. "You disagree now, but think it over. You don't get as old as Madeline did without being twice as crafty as a fisher cat." His laughter disappeared, and he was gravely serious. "You'll have time to think about it, of course. Centuries upon centuries. It does cheer me a bit, you know, my boy. When I'm dust and not one human even remembers I existed, there will still be that little scrap of me, that vestigial tail of humanity, walking around in you. Or flying. Do you think they'll have flying cars? I'm sure they will. You'll see them." A faraway look passed over his face, and a smile tugged at his mouth, one that had just a hint of his usual mania. "Or not. If they blow up the world, of course, even the vampires will die." Then, like a light being flipped, he was back to lucid and serious, the switch so seamless that it was downright eerie. "I know why you're here, son. Grace gave you the first half of it, and now I need to finish the job. By finishing me." A brief giggle, almost a titter, the kind you more usually hear when someone is half a dozen martinis to the wind, then painfully sane again. "You should do it now," he said, the tapping of his fingers stopping as he curled them into fists. "That blood is dead inside me—it's just sludge. I don't like it—too quiet. Go on, then." He frowned, irritated at me, snappish and upset.

I hesitated for just a second, then reached into the bag and took the needle out. He flicked a look over it, then back to me, that irritation remaining. I took a step toward his IV, then stopped. "I'm sorry, Henry," I said, feeling the uselessness of the words even as they left my mouth. What did you say to a person before you put him down like a senile ferret that was peeing all over the house? I couldn't even offer him a last meal, like a death row convict, since the only thing he'd been consuming for months was a protein-rich slurry being shunted in through his feeding tube.

The irritation melted from his face, and Henry smiled at me, sudden charisma and charm glowing off him like the sun for the briefest of moments before fading away, a small echo of the person he might've once been. "And what have you to be sorry about, son? Being born? I do appreciate you doing it yourself, though. Like Old Yeller, I guess." He snickered, then pitched his voice high, imitating a young boy. "Yes, Mama, but he was my dog. I'll do it."

Anger flashed through me. "You're not a dog, Henry," I said sharply.

"No, I'm not," he agreed, with the utmost gentleness.

"A dog is a loyal, loving thing. Maybe I used to be that, but I'm not anymore." He nodded at his IV stand. "Better go ahead and put that in, son. Sometimes I bite, you know. You saw, of course." Slow pleasure filled his eyes, a fondness as he lazed over old memories, and there was the quick flash of his pale pink tongue dragging unconsciously over his dry lips. "Saw me bite old Arnold. What a pleasure that was. I was sorry when you made me stop." His smile now was awful, nothing but teeth. "Is that what you need, son?" he asked conversationally. "To be reminded? Yes, I would kill him again if he was before me. And Conrad. And Maire. I would kill the whole world if I could—just bite and tear until it was nothing but an ocean of blood for me to wade through." His fingers started tapping again, much faster, and I turned away from him and walked quickly around the table until I was at the saline bag hanging on the IV stand. Then, not letting myself hesitate for a second, lest Henry continue talking, I pushed the needle into the bag above the saline line and pushed the plunger hard, injecting all the morphine to mix with the saline. There was no change of Henry's expression as he watched me, but he wrinkled his chin thoughtfully, and said, "Yes," and his voice was once again so calm and tranquil. "That was what you needed."

I watched the individual droplets of the liquid enter into the drip chamber, then into the IV line that led into Henry's arm. "Good-bye, Henry."

He watched me, thoughtfully, silently, for a long moment. Then his eyes relaxed, and the lids began to drift shut.

I relaxed then. Just a little, not even something that I even realized that I was doing at the moment that I actually did it, though of course that was too late by then. Because the moment my muscles made that infinitesimal movement, that my lizard brain decided that Henry was no longer a threat, that was the moment that he moved.

His left arm came up with a speed that wasn't human, and with a strength that he owed to alien blood, and the restraint on his wrist tore. How long he'd been working away at it, subtly and carefully, in those moments when Conrad wasn't watching, who knew? Who can say the patience that he must have exhibited, how much control he'd needed to restrain himself from attacking Maire or Conrad when they were in range, to wait until that moment he wanted, when I was near him, and my guard was down?

He'd surprised me, and I couldn't move back fast enough. His hand grabbed the front of my shirt, with enough force and strength that I could feel his nails rip at my skin, and he hauled me down, down onto the bed, so that I fell across his chest, face-to-face with him, unable to do anything but stare at his open mouth, at those teeth that I knew could rip muscle from bone. Time stretched—somewhere in the distance I could hear a door slam open, and I knew that Conrad was running out of the observation room, coming with his stun gun to protect me, but he might as well have been in another state for all the good he could do me in this moment, when I felt Henry's mouth against my cheek, could feel the heat of his breath in my ear, the power of the hand at my chest. I started to bring my own hands up, but I knew it would be too late, and I braced myself for the pain.

"I don't want you to feel badly about it, you know," Henry whispered in my ear, and I realized that the pain wasn't going to come. I froze, listening to Henry's voice. "I truly died when I was twenty-one, when Madeline changed me. This is just finalizing things, really." He lifted his hand out from between us, then reached up and, with exquisite gentleness, ran it over my hair. I felt him breathe in deeply. "They never let Grace touch you, you know. I think that's why she killed those doctors after they cut you out of her, handed you off to be carried away to Madeline. But I'm glad I got to do this, even if it's just now." His hand moved down, gave me a soft, affectionate pat on my cheek. "But do try to remember me sometimes, son. Just a little. Every now and again over the next half millennia. To a human, you know, that's practically eternity."

Henry's breathing slowed, and his hand slid limply off my cheek, onto my shoulder. Slowly, cautiously, I moved my hands up, pushed myself off him, and looked down. His breath was slowing, until I saw his chest stop moving entirely.

I looked left. Conrad was standing in the doorway of the prison cube, the stun gun in his right hand, and a Beretta sidearm in his left. He was staring at me, chest heaving as if he'd just run a marathon, a mixture of horror and wonder in his expression.

"I thought you were a dead man, Fort," he said, never taking his eyes away from my face, at the miracle of my unravaged skin. "Or that at least you would never be as pretty as that again." Conrad shook his head. "Anyone else in the world in that position, and Henry would never have let them come up again."

"I know." I swallowed hard. "Hand me the saw, Conrad. It's time to finish this."

I felt it the moment that Henry truly died—after I'd removed his brain, and the moment that I pulled his still heart out from its place within his chest. When Grace died, it had been like a snapping inside me, and I'd tasted blood in my mouth. This time, though, it was like a lock was turned in me, and every muscle in my body tightened into a rictus that left me crashing to the floor. My vision blacked out, my hearing was gone, and that was when the seizures started. Then there was a white nothingness, and my brain shut off, and the transition was finished.

Chapter Seven

A week and a half after Henry's death, I arrived home to my apartment after yet another meeting with my siblings in Newport. I took extra time when unlocking the front door—cautiously putting incrementally more pressure on the key until I felt the lock disengage, then turned the knob with the kind of caution that I would normally reserve for handling fine china. I'd snapped my key off in the door lock twice, and ripped the knob off the door once in the time that had passed since my transition. I was slowly figuring out how to handle the increase in physical power that had suddenly been present when I woke up from my transition, but it was a strange process. After Grace's death it had mostly been my reflexes that were initially heightened, with the increases in my physical strength trickling in slowly enough that I'd been able to adjust my day-to-day routine without really even being aware of it. This, however, had forced me to pay attention to all sorts of things that I hadn't had to consciously think about before—closing car doors, turning keys, unzipping zippers, breaking eggs without smashing the insides everywhere. So far Dan had been remarkably patient with my sudden morph in a Hulk-like creature of destruction in our apartment, but I was really hoping that this part of the process would pass soon—particularly after the previous night, where I'd broken the ON button on the remote by hitting it with apparently way too much force.

The most frustrating part, of course, was that it was the oldest skills that were most affected, the ones that I did largely on autopilot. Whenever I worked out or sparred with Chivalry or Suzume, I had no problems, because those skills were new enough that I was always consciously thinking about how much force to put into a punch or a block. Meanwhile, I'd broken half a dozen pairs of shoelaces, and managed to destroy one of the grommets on my favorite pair of sneakers.

Once the door was safely open, I trudged inside. I was absolutely exhausted, but there was nothing physical about it—it was the mental exhaustion of too many meetings that had gone absolutely nowhere, and left me feeling that I could've spent the entire day sleeping in bed and accomplished the same amount. The staircase decision remained the high-water mark of cooperation between me, Chivalry, and Prudence. When it came to actually dealing with the decisions of running our territory, we consistently deadlocked on everything. It was that meeting chaired by Madeline all over again—unable to agree on how to thoroughly address any issue, our days were actually spent on determining stopgap compromise measures that just kept everything in stasis on the assumption that more time would allow us to actually figure out a real way of dealing with the issue—something that seemed, day by day, more and more like a complete fantasy.

It was as if, terrifying as the thought was, my siblings and I were a microcosm of Congress.

The attaché request from Gil Kivela had been put off by an agreement to ask him to put it in a formal written petition, in triplicate, as a way to buy more time for us to continue arguing in circles, given that it didn't seem likely that Prudence would ever agree to it. The succubi issue continued to stagnate—I continued making regular phone calls to them, and there had been some bright news lately from Saskia when she'd reported that Nicholas had picked up some under-the-table work washing dishes at a local restaurant, and that she'd been putting up signs around town for housekeeping services at a cut-rate price. I'd told Saskia that it was still my goal to get them to the casino towns of Connecticut, but I knew that they'd started to give up hope of that when she told me, in a purposefully bright tone, that if they were still in the town in the spring, they'd figured that they could get some jobs doing basic yard work. Meanwhile, the adults were taking turns driving to the Newark Airport to hunt—which was something that no amount of forced optimism could make sound anything other than truly grim.

My mind was briefly pulled from the depressing state of affairs as I put the portable picnic cooler I was carrying on the kitchen countertop. The completion of my transition had altered my digestive system, meaning that I could now process human blood successfully—and was, in fact, now reliant on it for my continued health. I hadn't drunk directly from a person's vein yet—though I knew that it wouldn't be much longer before I had to, as adult vampires had to do that every fifteen days or so or risk dangerous effects—but I had been drinking human blood. Every other day I had carefully poured out an eight-ounce cup in the morning, then another in the evening, and drunk it down like a particularly disgusting medicine. I'd tried waiting three days between servings, which was the schedule that my brother was on, but quickly discovered that that wasn't going to work—I became absolutely ravenous, with a hunger that regular food just couldn't touch. Just as my sister had promised, blood was not something that benefited from sitting in a fridge—after just a few hours in the fridge the blood developed a distinctly unpleasant edge. After one day it was awful. And after two I would just spoon half the sugar bowl in it and try to just down it like cheap beer at a frat party. I'd attempted to freeze it to thaw later, hoping that would make the process easier, but that had tasted just like frozen and thawed milk—utterly foul.

The only silver lining to the whole scenario was that I hadn't had to try to find a human to provide the blood for me—my siblings were working overtime to keep me stocked up with the vampire version of take-home casseroles. I didn't want to think about how many people they were pressing into service to donate a pint here and there for me, which my siblings were then obligated to carefully agitate to remove the clotting factors in order to allow the blood to sit in my fridge without becoming a partially solid mass—right now I was just more than willing to accept the help, rather than attempt the process myself. They'd been slipping me their efforts separately—just today, for example, Chivalry had pressed the little picnic cooler into my hand as he was walking me to my car— inside had been one of those expensive double-wall stainless steel thermoses, with a sheet of reheating instructions carefully written out in Chivalry's beautiful copperplate and taped to the top. When I'd actually gotten into the Scirocco, I found Prudence's contribution on the passenger seat—a Chinese takeout soup container filled with blood, with DRINK ME written on the top in black Sharpie.

I unloaded the thermos and the take-out container. Out of necessity, I'd had to try to figure out a system to deal with my new nutritional requirements, and that had involved buying three plastic water pitchers from Walmart— one was blue, one was red, and the third was Hello Kitty (I'd run up against a selection issue). For today, I took the Hello Kitty pitcher off our drying rack from where I'd put it yesterday after I washed it. I popped off the top, then poured in the blood from the thermos and the take-out containers, putting those in the sink to wash and return to my siblings. Then I replaced the Hello Kitty lid, and put the pitcher into the fridge, behind the blue thermos, which had tomorrow's blood ration in it—the red pitcher was at the front of the row, closest to the door, and I knew that it had just a few sips' worth of blood left it in, just on the edge of being completely undrinkable, but enough to offer a quick supplement for what would otherwise have been my bloodless day.

It was definitely a very weird new normal. Though if I could've stuck with this level forever, I would've taken it. At least the minutiae of managing my blood, and figuring out how not to rip the tabs off my zippers, had some kind of frame of reference. But I knew that all too soon I was going to have to take that last step and feed directly from a human. It was my own personal Rubicon, which once I crossed I could never come back from. Both Chivalry and Prudence had offered to help me— Chivalry with all the delicacy and tenderness one could ask for, Prudence with all the blunt eagerness for expedience to ensure a truly scarring experience.

I'd turned them both down. I would handle it myself, I'd told them. In my own way.

I just didn't know exactly what that way was, or when I would be ready for it.

I started washing out the containers (for a guy who ate human organ meat, Dan had been pretty unrelenting in his proposal of a new apartment rule about the immediate cleaning of any containers that had previously held blood), then stopped and mentally kicked myself. I pulled open one of the drawers and withdrew a stack of Post-it notes, all of which had the following message pre-written on them:

FORT'S PROTEIN SHAKE — PLEASE DON'T
DRINK.

I pulled one off the stack and slapped it on the side of
the Hello Kitty pitcher.

Between my blood pitchers and Dan's human organ
meat, our fridge situation had become a little stressful
given Jaison's regular time in the apartment. Dan had
never been overly worried about Jaison delving into the
fridge drawer that contained his organ meats — all carefully wrapped in butcher paper and looking completely
innocuous from the outside — but the leftover situation
had been a concern. The ghoul's approach had been impressively straightforward — he'd labeled any leftovers
with human contents as "property of Fortitude Scott" and
had told Jaison that I was freaky when it came to personal
food properties, and relied on good manners to do the
rest. My one request in that situation had been for Dan to
use only opaque Tupperware containers to store those
items — both for my own comfort (I admitted to being
more than a little squeamish about shepherd's pie that
contained human liver), and to avoid the embarrassment
of Jaison thinking that I was a backsliding vegetarian.

I did sometimes stumble in my vegetarianism, but on
those occasions I tried to at least admit it. But I refused
to take the shame of the side-eye that nonvegetarians
were always eager to bestow on those they saw as back-
sliders when I had in fact not engaged in the practice.

The addition of the blood to our fridge had necessitated a serious roommate summit discussion, with the
outcome being the official lie that I had integrated a new,
absolutely disgusting, protein drink into my fitness routine. Dan had assured Jaison that I'd forced him to try it,
and that it had been like drinking raw sewage mixed
with Moxie soda — a description that we'd agreed would
keep any rational person from asking for a taste.

After one last check to make certain that the Post-it notes were prominently displayed in a way that could not be ignored, I pulled out the other addition to our fridge since my transition—the bag of baby carrots. Over the past several days, I had been unable to ignore the increasing soreness in my upper jaw and teeth. It had left me in a distinctly crabby mood, in addition to the personal surprise about the sharp increase in my saliva output (i.e., I was drooling like a leaky water hydrant). I was very unfortunately aware of the problem—I was teething. Specifically, my body was preparing to grow in my adult vampire teeth, which I'd been assured (by my siblings, with a notable lack of sympathy) would actually take a few months. In the meantime, I found myself preferring to gnaw on cool, hard things, like baby carrots, which I discovered was actually fairly soothing and distracting, in addition to adding to the healthiness of my diet. I'd also made a surreptitious trip to the grocery store and stocked up on frozen Popsicles, which were not healthy in the smallest sense, but were almost blissfully effective in numbing my irritated jaw. I'd stuffed them into the back of the freezer, and so far Dan had done me the great favor of pretending that he hadn't noticed their presence.

I checked the clock. This was one of my free evenings, and Suze had told me that she'd swing over after she ate dinner. Since it was also the night that Dan had his weekly dinner study group, I'd been looking forward to this. I'd found myself, surprisingly, still employed at Redbones. When I'd called Orlando to make arrangements for my final paycheck, he told me that the replacement that he'd hired for me had just quit—apparently she'd been something of a musical connoisseur and had been unable to last more than three nights on the job until the constant mangling of musical notes had finally broken her—and had offered me my old job back. So far it was an awkward balance with the daily meetings down at the mansion, but the truth was that I could use the money, and I knew that the alternative was taking money from my family. Also, in the midst of so many fundamental changes to both my life and my very physicality, there had been a strange comfort in continuing the old routine of heading to a crummy job.

I heard the rhythm of shave-and-a-haircut rapped into my door, and moved toward it with a big smile, knowing who was on the other side. Even after my mother's death vigil ended, I'd still been spending a lot of time down at Newport, so I'd missed seeing Suze a lot—some days the business of not agreeing on anything had lasted so long that all I had time to do was go to work, then come home, collapse into bed, then get up just a few hours later to repeat the whole process. And while Suze had kept me up to date by texting me every amusing YouTube video or Internet meme that caught her interest, it just wasn't the same as getting to drive around with her, focusing on territory business in my mother's name.

I pulled open the door, and there she was, a brilliant smile covering her face as she held out a brightly wrapped box, tied up with a neon yellow bow. "Hey, Fort!"

I stared at the box she held out to me, confused. "You got me something?" I racked my head. We were too early for Valentine's Day, and my birthday wasn't until June, so did that mean . . . "Are we doing anniversaries?" Panic rose inside me, and I immediately started trying to figure out what item in my apartment I could quickly wrap while her back was turned and present as a pre-bought gift. This would be made even more difficult given that I didn't think we even had wrapping paper in the apartment.

Suze snorted loudly. "Ew, fuck that madness. No, I just thought that since you've been having such a crappy few weeks, I'd find something to perk you up."

Relief rushed through me. Then I really processed what she'd said, and I smiled. We moved over to sit on the sofa, and while there was a part of me that remained cautiously prepared in case this turned out to be snakes in a can, the larger portion of me was just wallowing in the pleasure of having been given a present "just because." I unwrapped a corner of the paper, and laughed at what I saw.

"Peeps?" I asked, that unmistakable colored and shaped marshmallow delight peering up at me. I yanked off the rest of the paper and confirmed it unequivocally. "I thought you could only get them around Easter."

"Actually, it turns out that with the kinds of preservatives they pack into these things, Peeps can last for years. I got these on eBay. Apparently, there's something of a collectors' market. Oh, and as an additional surprise . . ." She reached into the pocket of her parka and, with full fanfare, removed something. After a pause, she opened her hand to reveal the second part of my treat—a tube of infant oral gel teething pain medication. As I stared, she grinned at me. "Yuzumi says that this is what she used on the triplets when they were teething." She looked at me brightly. "Cherry flavored!"

Then she raised her free hand for a high five.

I stared at her. "You told your cousin that I was having teething pain," I said slowly.

"No!" Suze denied immediately. "No, I would never betray a confidence. I definitely never even mentioned your name. I just mentioned that it was for an adult vampire." She paused, and pondered what she'd said for a second. Then, "Okay, bad news. It's possible that Yuzumi might figure out that it's for you. She has pretty good deductive reasoning skills."

I sighed heavily. Apparently hoping that the embarrassment of teething at the age of twenty-seven would remain a secret known only to those closest to me had been something of a futile dream. I reached over and closed Suze's hand around the ointment container again. "I'm offended," I said, "but I do appreciate the effort." I leaned over and gave her a kiss, which she returned with added interest. When we finally came up for air (it had been a while, after all), I reluctantly extricated myself from her and headed back to the kitchen to grab us each a beer.

"So, do you want a watch a movie, or watch a little TV?" I asked, pulling the bottles out. It had been Dan's turn to get groceries, which was why it was the good stuff in the fridge—Stella Artois. "I could make some popcorn if you want."

"If you're in the mood," Suze said, shedding her jacket and stretching lazily on the sofa. "But I actually did have something kind of serious to talk to you about."

"Oh?" I asked, popping the lids off, then handing Suze her beer. "Serious how?"

Suzume took a long sip of her beer, watching me steadily with her dark eyes as the movement exposed her long, pale throat. I noticed with interest that her sweater was rather aggressively scoop-necked for the season and the heating in the apartment, and reconsidered whether I really wanted to spend our time together watching TV. Suze finished her sip, then tilted her head slightly. "My grandmother wants to talk with you."

I shrugged a little—it wasn't exactly surprising. Most of the groups within the territory had kept their distance since my mother's death other than several very thoughtful floral arrangements, but it had been inevitable that they would eventually want to talk with what was essentially the new management, and it made sense that the kitsune would be the first to come forward, given that they'd been the group that had enjoyed the most freedoms and internal control under my mother. "Oh, sure. Well, tell your grandmother that she should call Loren Noka and make an appointment to see us, and I'm sure that a date can be found—"

"No." Suze slid onto her knees, folding her arms along the back of the sofa and watching me carefully—there was something in her body position that reminded me very strongly of when she was a fox and was crouched and coiled up just before she would spring to attack something—usually a paper ball. "You're misunderstanding, Fort. My grandmother, Atsuko Hollis, the White Fox, wants to see *you*."

"Ah." I considered Suze's expression, and comprehension filled me. "So, this is an off-the-record meeting? The kind that I don't mention to my family?"

Suze smiled slowly at me. "I knew you'd catch on."

"And when is this private meeting supposed to take place? I assume that you've told your grandmother about my schedule and availabilities, for example."

"Of course. My grandmother would be very flattered if you came to her house tomorrow, after your meeting in Newport. She'll have tea waiting for you."

I considered her. "You're not going to tell me what this is about, will you?"

Suze set her beer down on the coffee table with exaggerated care, then shot me a playful look and slowly tugged her sweater out of her jeans. "Church and state, man friend," she said, her voice throaty and rich. "It's not a good idea to cross those lines."

I walked slowly over to the couch and leaned over her, setting one hand at her waist and slowly pushing upward, feeling the soft heat of her skin as the sweater bunched up under my hand. "So I'll have to wait until tomorrow to find out, is what you're saying."

"Don't worry, Fort," she breathed against my mouth. "I'll help you find a way to pass the time."

Later that night I extricated myself from Suze's pleasantly entwined limbs and slid out of bed and into the bathroom. I yanked open the medicine cabinet, grumpily hunting for the bottle of over-the-counter pain pills that I'd been relying on to get a reasonable night's sleep, despite the frustrating ache in my jaw, and there, right in the middle of the shelf, I saw the tube of infant oral gel teething pain medication. Cherry-flavored.

I paused, considered resisting further, but the hour and the pain in my jaw decided the issue for me, and I squeezed out a healthy dollop onto my finger, then rubbed it against my gums.

It worked.

The next day, I dragged myself to the Scirocco and left the mansion at just after four in the afternoon. It had been yet another exhausting and frustrating day. After hours of arguing, all we'd managed to accomplish was to agree to cost-of-living wage increases for the staff members, and that, despite the death of Henry and the emptying of our basement prison area, we would keep Conrad and Maire on the payroll and in their current positions. With Maire, we'd found that in many ways it had been extremely convenient to have an in-house medical professional—she'd assisted Bhumika in her final illness, as well as Madeline, of course, and in addition to that had turned out to be very useful at giving Chivalry's wife, Simone, her regular blood transfusion without the fuss of having to use a local clinic. With Conrad, it had actually been Prudence who suggested keeping him—she'd pointed out that it didn't really cost us that much to allow him to continue staying in the basement apartment for now, and it saved us all the fuss of finding, training, and (most critically) getting the loyalty of someone with Conrad's particular skill set if we ever found occasion to fill the basement cells again. It was pretty clear that Prudence was looking ahead to a time when she would be attempting to make her own host, a thought that didn't exactly fill me with positive thoughts, given what I'd seen of her last attempt, but I'd agreed anyway. It had seemed a shame to make Conrad go looking for another job when this one suited him so well—plus, he'd turned out to be kind of like an on-site tech-support service.

Still, though Chivalry had spent a great deal of time at the end of the meeting enthusing about our progress, I hadn't been able to get much comfort from it. There'd been really no reason to disagree in those situations—the wage increases were something that had been done a hundred times before to keep up with the inflation rate, and keeping Maire and Conrad around was really just avoiding making any changes to our current routine. On any other topics, like the running of the territory, we couldn't seem to move at all.

I pulled into the driveway of Atsuko Hollis's farmhouse, with its neat little clapboard shutters and wings and additions that had been stuck on in every which way over generations so that the house itself became a kind of Euclidian nightmare—but with whimsy. The house had been in the Hollis family for many years—Atsuko had inherited it following the death of her husband, after she'd killed him.

I could hear the scampering of many, many small feet as I walked up the cobblestone steps to the front door. We'd had an inch of fresh powder last night, but these steps were pristinely swept, with rock salt generously applied. The sun had just set, and I could feel the temperature starting to plunge as I knocked on the door.

To my surprise, it was Keiko who opened the door. I'd gotten very used to seeing her in the context of her own house, where in lieu of maternity clothing she'd just started wearing really stretchy and low-riding yoga pants and topping herself off with Farid's button-down shirts or sweaters. Today, though, she looked like she'd walked off the pages of a magazine ad for the business chic pregnant woman, with charcoal tweed slacks and a matching blazer, and a forest-green silk blouse that was doing its best to achieve an elegant drape over the bowling ball–esque curve of her stomach.

"Fortitude," she said formally, extending her hand to usher me into the foyer of the house. "It's very good to see you again—it's been quite some time."

I lifted my eyebrows a little at her very pointed comment, but if that was how Keiko was preferring to play things, I certainly wasn't going to get her in trouble. I did my best to nod politely, as if she hadn't just recently been gleefully attempting to completely annihilate my chances of winning Small World by attacking me unceasingly with her Flying Sorcerers, and made the kind of polite noncomments that I'd make to any near stranger whose twin sister I just happened to be sleeping with.

Keiko led me through the twisting maze of the downstairs. Atsuko took a very minimalist approach to decoration—all the walls were painted white, with matching crown molding, and the floors were all the original wood, almost entirely free of the usual mishmash of area rugs or runners that would normally be seen, and showing the gleam of recent refinishing. Here and there were a few framed items—the occasional photograph of one or more of the Hollis women, some pretty nature paintings in the Japanese style, and one beautifully mounted and displayed antique kimono. I could hear the continuous scurrying of paws in the rooms around us, but I didn't see anyone except Keiko.

Finally I was led into the same living room that I'd seen on my only previous visit to this house. Atsuko Hollis stood next to a low table that was already set for tea, steam lazily trailing up from the pot. Suzume's grandmother must've been in her nineties, but she carried her years gracefully. Her hair was pure white, without a hint of gray to mute the color, and was still thick and healthy looking, twisted up on the top of her head with a single comb decorated with enamel flowers. She wore a dark blue kimono decorated with white cranes in flight, and as I walked in she gave a graceful bow of her head. I did my best to mimic the gesture, earning me a slight smile. Behind me, Keiko disappeared down the hallway, and Atsuko extended one arm with the sublime grace that hinted at her former career as a dancer, gesturing for me to join her for tea.

Just as on my previous visit, all serious discussion had to wait until the end of a precisely executed tea ceremony that lasted the better part of an hour. I did my best to be a more patient guest this time, watching Atsuko's gestures, allowing her to lead me in small, polite conversation, attempting to ignore the numbness that began to set into my lower legs, given that I was very unused to kneeling on a thin cushion rather than sitting on a sofa. As the ceremony continued, foxes began to trickle in from all parts of the house. Atsuko never acknowledged them, and they lined up against each wall and then sat perfectly still, a living honor guard of beautiful, delicately whiskered works of art, each furred tail adjusted just so. I was sure that I had probably met a number of these foxes in human form, but none acknowledged me, and I snuck glances at them from the corners of my eyes. Atsuko's descendants boasted a range of colors—the deepest russet red, to a range of grays, to blacks. There was one fox who left no doubt about her identity when she entered, though—Suze's fur was the perfect black ink of night, without a single spot of white except the frost tip of her tail. She sauntered in, her mouth lolling open with amusement, giving a saucy little flip of her tail as she passed me so that the tip of it trailed against my wrist. I smiled, and Atsuko gave her granddaughter a quelling frown that was met only with an added saunter around the table as Suzume made a show of deciding which side of the room she preferred to join. A little shiver of movement made its way along the watching foxes, a twitching of a tail tip, a quick licking of the jaws. Something in it made me think of barely suppressed giggles of amusement. At last, Suzume settled herself on the right side of the room and took on the same perfectly still stance as the rest, as if to dare anyone to suggest that she'd been less than behaved just a moment before. There was the slightest movement of Atsuko's mouth that made me think that she wanted to smile at her granddaughter but didn't dare encourage her.

At the conclusion of the ceremony, as Atsuko was carefully stacking the cups back on the tray, I noticed that all the foxes seemed to sit up just a little straighter, and a tension filled the room. They were focused entirely on me now as Atsuko made one last tiny adjustment, then said, "The last time you were in my living room, you told me very plainly that you were not fully a vampire yet, and that this was why your values were different than those of the rest of your family." One snow-white eyebrow arched delicately. "You are now most entirely a vampire, so may I ask—did you lose your tadpole tail, little frogling?"

I dipped my head slightly, acknowledging her point. "Just as you promised, Mrs. Hollis, it is now on the inside."

She nodded, looking pleased. "It is because of you that Suzume-chan earned her white," Atsuko said, surprising me. I knew that it had been the action of following me into the fight against Luca that had put the white fur on Suzume's previously entirely black tail, but she had always dodged around any of my questions, so it felt odd to have someone address the subject so overtly. "The two of you are changing each other, forming new shapes, like wax brought near a flame." Atsuko's expression changed ever so slightly, taking on a warning tone. "But do not forget what you are, Fortitude Scott, and what my granddaughter is."

There were a lot of ways to take that, particularly given the relationship that I had with Suzume. There were also a lot of conversations that I very frankly did not want to have with this extremely intimidating woman, so I chose the most diplomatic yet honest answer that I could—"I would never forget that Suzume is one of the kitsune." As I finished it, I wondered if what I'd said was idiotic, meaningful, or just fortune cookie nonsense.

Whatever it was, it at least got me off the hook for a moment, as Atsuko make a small "hrmph" sound, then finally got to the meat of the issue. "I did you a service once, young vampire, when you were desperate and on your own."

All too easily, the memory came back to me. I'd been trying to track down a European vampire, Luca, who'd been visiting my mother's territory and hunting the young girls of Providence. With my brother forbidden to help me and Prudence unwilling, it had been Atsuko who'd given me the information I'd needed. "Yes, you did. And I owe you a favor."

"You do," she agreed, her eyes gleaming.

"Are you calling in that favor?" I asked. It certainly seemed likely, but Atsuko also seemed entirely capable of just bringing me in and pointing out, godfather-style, that she still held my marker.

"Most certainly."

I waited for a long second, waiting to find out exactly what she wanted. Atsuko was in no hurry, however, simply watching me from across the table, her eyes slowly scanning over me, assessing my reaction. "Have you ever wondered why the kitsune have freedoms and power within this territory that other races can only dream about, though I was alone when I arrived on alien soil?" she asked, surprising me with the sudden whiplash change of topic.

"The question has crossed my mind," I said cautiously.

"I arrived here, and invited your mother to my house. It must have been a very long time since anyone dared ask Madeline Scott to go anywhere, and she came, I believe, partly because she was amused. She arrived at the stroke of midnight, and I sat and served her tea. We spoke of many things, for she had never traveled to Japan and was very curious. At the end of the evening, she asked me what I could offer in exchange for a place in her territory, and I invited her to come to tea again the following evening. Again, she arrived at midnight, and again we spoke and drank tea. Again she asked her question, and again I invited her." Atsuko reached one delicate hand, the skin wrinkled and hanging yet the skin almost luminously perfect from any mars or age spots, and lifted a teacup off the tray, balancing the thin china in her hand, tilting it this way and that and watching the way that the light brought out the beauty of the finish. "And we did this for a hundred nights."

I listened to her story, transfixed by the almost fairytale quality of it, trying to imagine my mother coming here and sitting where I was, and being served cups of tea by a young fox-woman who had just arrived in America.

"On the hundredth night, Madeline Scott did not ask me what I could offer—instead she made me her offer, one of protection in the shadow of her throne, and freedom for me and those who would follow me, for my daughter Izumi was already growing in my belly."

I stared at her. "Mrs. Hollis, I don't want to suggest in any way that I don't admire and appreciate your tea . . . but why would my mother offer you this?"

Atsuko smiled very thinly. "Your mother was a creature of centuries, and she understood the value of patience. She appreciated that I, though still very young, could appreciate patience as well." She tilted her head back, looking at the ceiling, or perhaps looking back at events of the past that now only she was alive to consider. "Your mother would have done well in Japan, for she was wise, yet cruel; thoughtful, yet also ruled by her heart when it came to her children. She was a creature of multitudes, and one who understood that, while so many in this land crave simplicity." She replaced the cup onto the tray with the slightest clink, a sound that nevertheless had a strange ring of finality. "The old way of your mother is gone now, however."

"Yes," I agreed, understanding washing through me. "I think I know what your favor will be." Exhaustion and despair warred.

"I believe you do, but I shall speak the words." The look in her dark eyes was pure steel. "Kitsune autonomy is to be protected at all costs. I know that your sister will seek to erode this, but you will be my wall and guard. My daughters, and granddaughters, and great-granddaughters, and all my line that lives in this land, shall be free."

"And you think that I can do this?" I asked.

She smiled. "I think that you will have to." Atsuko tilted her head in that particularly vulpine way and stared at me for a long second, then nodded, almost to herself, and said, "Your mother understood patience, little vampire, but you do not. Have a care that you do not leap into the fire because you fear not moving at all."

On that unsettling note our interview ended, and Keiko returned to walk me back out to my car. All of the foxes remained in the room with Atsuko, but I heard one small yip as the front door closed behind me, and I knew that was Suzume.

"I'm not used to seeing so many foxes in one area," I noted to Keiko, breaking the silence between us. "I've gotten to see a lot of your cousins at the bar, of course, but until now the only groups of foxes I'd ever seen were the triplets." Yuzumi's three-year-old triplets, Riko, Yui, and Tomomi, were rambunctious little bundles of fur and trouble that liked nothing better than playing fetch and getting tummy rubs. It was hard to compare my mental image of them, with Riko's ongoing fixation with chewing my sneakers, with the two poised lines of posed foxes that I'd seen today. "They seemed . . ." I hunted my brain for the right word, finally ending lamely with " . . . comfortable."

Keiko's eyebrows shot practically up to her hairline, and for a second she stumbled. I grabbed her arm just as she regained her balance, and between the two of us she stayed on her feet. She wrapped her hand around my arm, bringing her free hand over to rest on top of it, so that I was in the strange position of escorting her to my own car as if we were on our way to a cotillion. She was thinking hard for a second, then finally said, very slowly, "It's our true form, Fort. The human skin is the deception." Her dark eyes dug into me. "It can be easy to forget that about us. To the bears, for example, it is the human skin that they wear as the true face." We reached my car, and for a second she remained beside me, her hands still pressed against my parka-clad arm, a thoughtful expression passing over her face. "In some ways, Fort, I'm actually a little envious of my sister."

"Oh?" I asked, surprised.

Keiko nodded. "She can wear her true shape around you without fear, interact with you without burdens. It's the thing I most wish that I could do around Farid—have him see me as I really am, and accept it."

I stared at Keiko, shocked at the extent to which she'd just laid a part of herself bare to me, and completely uncertain how to respond. Apparently none was necessary, because she gave me a shallow nod, an echo of her grandmother's movement, withdrew her hands from my arm, and began a measured walk back up the driveway, the walkway, and inside the house.

I watched her walk away, not getting into my car until I saw the door close solidly behind her, despite the cutting wind that numbed the exposed skin of my face and hands. Then I unlocked the Scirocco, started it up, and slowly backed out of the driveway to start the drive back home.

I'd known that Suze's true form was the fox, of course—she'd told me very early in our friendship. But having her in fox form in my apartment had always seemed like a game to her, a way to scamper around and cause mayhem, and later, after we'd started sleeping together, it had begun feeling awkward when she wasn't in her human form, the one that I could recognize as not just my friend, but also my lover. But Keiko's words echoed in my head, forcing me to look through Suze's lens—that perhaps when I woke up beside a fox in the morning, it was because she felt comfortable enough with me that she didn't have to wear a mask while sleeping—that she could really be herself.

It was a lot to think about on my drive home, particularly given the massive headache of having to protect fox autonomy from my sister. Apparently Atsuko would not be open to any compromise measures either. I took a minor comfort in the thought that, given the complete lack of progress that the Scotts were making on important and pressing issues, the subject of the kitsune might never actually even come up.

That thought actually wasn't that comforting.

My phone rang, and I had to scrabble around in my coat pocket for it, barely avoiding rear-ending the car in front of me that had apparently decided that driving at night, even on roads completely clear of snow or ice, required going about thirty miles an hour slower than the flow of traffic. I managed to change lanes, and gave the caller ID a quick check. It was Lilah, so I answered it.

"Fort! Hey! Listen, I was so sorry to hear about your

mother—I meant to call you earlier, but I didn't want to intrude, and then I started wondering if I'd waited too long, and then I really got—"

I stopped her before she could continue laying out the convoluted thought process that surrounded the post-death phone call. "Hey, it's no problem, really. I appreciate it."

"Great!" she chirped brightly.

A long pause stretched, laden with awkwardness.

When neither of us seemed able to fill the silence, I said, "Well, I appreciate you calling, and we should definitely get together sometime."

"Yeah, yeah, we really need to," she replied, and the brightness was gone now, leaving just a wall of subtext that hit me like an anvil.

"Lilah . . . is there something you need to talk about? Like, business kinds of things?"

"Yes," she said, relief clear in her voice.

"Do we need to set up a time to meet?"

"Actually," she said, and now I could hear how stressed she was—definitely an 8.5 on the stress Richter scale. "I was really wondering if you could come over right now."

"Really? Now?" I checked the time. "It's going to be at least seven by the time I get to your house, Lilah. I'm driving in from Exeter." I liked Lilah—and since I'd made her the liaison between my family and the Neighbors, who were the human-mixed scions of the last elves on Earth, with the whole group falling somewhere on a sliding scale of psychopathy, she'd certainly had her hands full. But after an afternoon of tea ceremonies and double-speak, and a morning of political immobility, what I really wanted to do was go home, put on my sweatpants, and eat ice cream straight from the container while watching the original *Terminator* movie. That didn't seem like much to wish for.

The volume of her voice suddenly dropped dramatically, and I wondered for the first time if someone was with her. "It's not just me who you need to talk to."

"Is this about Iris?" I asked cautiously. Lilah's younger sister had been having a rough few months, ever since we had only barely managed to stop her from being forcibly impregnated after her parents had drugged her and handed her over for the process—and that was even discounting the whole issue of her actually being three-quarters elf and kind of creepy.

"No."

This was starting to feel like a game of twenty questions. I made sure to add considerable significance to my next words. "Lilah, do I need to bring anything extra with me?" I wondered whether that had actually conveyed my meaning. I resolved there and then to develop an agreed-upon panic code word with everyone I knew so that monitored phone conversations could still effectively be used to warn people that heavy ammunition was required to resolve a hostage situation. Something innocuous, like "pita bread." Or "Snuffleupagus."

"No, Fort, it's nothing like that," Lilah said, finally relaxing and sounding halfway normal. "I'm okay, and I'm not in danger, but it's Neighbor business, and it just can't get put off any longer."

I sighed a little, wishing that Atsuko's tea ceremony had been slightly more British in its approach to snacks. I had the definite impression that I was going to regret going to this meeting on an empty stomach. "Okay, I'll come straight over."

Lilah lived in a generic brick apartment building in one of the Providence suburbs, far enough away from the center of the city that there was a little space between apartment buildings, and that they weren't individually any taller than two stories, but also close enough that there was regular bus service at the stop on her corner. The perk of Lilah's building was that everyone had their own separate door, with no common hallways, just shared walls. Her door opened before I could even ring the bell, and I wondered how long she'd been pacing in her living room, peering out the window and waiting for me to arrive.

The first thing I noticed was that Lilah wasn't wearing her glamour, that haze of magic that allowed her to pass as fully human. The main work that the glamour did was on her ears—those sharply pointed ears, thinner at the base than any human ear, that twitched and rotated with all the versatility of a cat's ear. There was a soft hint of fur along its back, the same copper as her eyebrows. Lilah usually braided her hair over her ears, or wore stretchy hairbands that covered them up—not so much out of fear of her glamour failing, but almost as a security blanket. But today she'd tucked her brilliant copper-gold hair behind her ears and let it trail down her shoulders, and that seemed oddly significant.

She ushered me quickly into her apartment, giving me the smallest headshake when she saw me looking questioningly at her ears. I took the hint and kept my mouth shut, and she put one hand on my elbow and carefully drew me farther into the living room, where a man was standing just inside the room, perfectly positioned so that I couldn't have seen him when I first stepped inside.

I think he just wanted to see my whole reaction to him, because there was no way to look at him and not have a reaction. He was one of the scions of the elves, that was without a doubt, and carrying a lot more of the blood than Lilah did. Early to midtwenties, and tall, perhaps an inch taller than I was, and I hit the six-foot mark. Like Lilah, he wasn't wearing a glamour. I'd seen the Neighbors who were genetically close to their forebears before without their glamours, and the sight had not been a pleasant one—the almost reptilian cast of the Ad-hene features didn't mix well with human bone structure, and there was an awkwardness, almost a repulsiveness, in those Neighbors when they weren't wearing their glamours. They didn't have that certain something, that indefinable allure that the true elves had that made strange features compelling and attractive, that overrode the signals put out from the primitive, dark parts of our brains that rejected something as other, as ugly, and instead made it beautiful.

This man had that. His neck was just slightly too long for his body, his features cut at angles that no human would possess, but that weird fey beauty was there, making it hard to look away from him. His hair was pure black, but with a silkiness and a texture that reminded me of Suzume's fur when she was a fox rather than a human. His skin was pale, not in the translucent way that showed veins and blushes, but pale and glittering like morning frost, almost like a hard exterior. His eyes were the color of plums taken right from the tree, and his pupil was vertical, like a lizard's. It took me a long second to pull myself away from a stunned perusal of his face to take in what he was wearing—he had expensive black slacks, black shoes that had been polished almost to a mirror finish, and a black-and-gray-striped button-down that fit him sleekly and perfectly—the kind of button-down that was sold for clubbing, not actually wearing for business purposes, and didn't even have a useful breast pocket for sticking notes or cash, and was cut in a way that you weren't even supposed to wear an undershirt under it. In my experience, it was the kind of shirt most often worn by a complete douche bag.

Lilah touched my arm carefully, nudging me out of my thoughts. "Fort, this is Cole."

"Cole . . . I think Lilah mentioned you once or twice," I said, striving for politeness. After all, the way he'd positioned himself for surprise wasn't enough for me to dislike him—he had to know what he looked like, and I couldn't blame him for that. As for his shirt, well, there was no such thing as a perfect system.

"Only in the most positive context, I hope," Cole said, and there was no hiding either the silkiness of his tone or the way that he flicked a very warning look at Lilah.

I immediately hated him. Clearly the shirt remained a proven system for identifying douches. Because I was irritated, I asked, "Didn't you show up to a date wasted and have to sleep it off on Lilah's couch?"

Beside me, Lilah had to smother a small laugh, and I could see the sudden, gleeful amusement in her golden-brown eyes as Cole was momentarily thrown off balance. Apparently she wasn't a big fan of his either.

"Ah, that context," Cole said through gritted teeth. "I admit that I might not have been on my best behavior, though I'm sure that Lilah remembered to mention that it was an arranged date from the older Neighbors in the hopes that it would result in a pregnancy, which neither of us had any interest at all in partaking in." He paused and shot a glare at Lilah. "And I cleaned up the sofa the next morning."

"You *puked*? Lilah leaves all the fun stuff out of these stories."

I was starting to enjoy myself, but Cole suddenly leaped on my statement, with a sudden smoothness, a finesse. "That's true—sometimes Lilah leaves things out. Not intentionally, of course. We've known each other from childhood, after all, and I don't think that Lilah has a mean bone in her body. But sometimes, if one wants to make sure that all the information is being conveyed, it's important to be present. Make sure that nothing has been sugarcoated, or pieces of the story dropped out."

I'd surprised Cole for a moment, but I could almost feel him pulling together his equilibrium, planning his next move, shifting and muddying the conversational waters.

"So, naturally, I just wanted the chance to be here when Lilah talked with you about Neighbor issues, just to make sure that everything was conveyed correctly."

"Lilah is the appointed liaison to my family," I pointed out. Lilah had told me that there had been problems within the younger Neighbor community, factions emerging. It looked like I was now getting to meet one of Lilah's biggest problems, and I realized how crucial it might be to reinforce Lilah's position, and her authority. "If the Scotts need to know it, then Lilah is the person we trust to tell it to us."

"Of course. But it would make so many of us more comfortable to get a second opinion about these . . . consultations . . . that Lilah has with you. After all, so many crucial decisions rest in the hands of the Scotts, yet so few of us have even had the pleasure of meeting you." There was no mistaking his undertone.

Lilah stepped forward, putting herself just off to the side, forming almost a triangle between the three of us. Very carefully, watching Cole the way that someone would watch a rattlesnake, she said, "Fort, Cole and I have been working together on a lot of the recent issues that our community has faced."

"Yes, you've told me." I wanted to push him back a little, to not just let his earlier statement lie without some kind of reprisal. "So, Cole, how many of the Neighbors have died since October? My family likes to keep our records accurate—I'm sure that you understand."

I could see Cole recognize my implicit threat, and a sliver of caution flickered briefly over his face, disappearing all too quickly. "The Scotts have nothing to fear—tithes will still be delivered on time, and to the amounts specified. As for those who are dead, well . . . I don't think you and your siblings will be missing any of them. Troublemakers, rule-breakers, all of them, who flouted the rules that the Scotts have given us to live by."

He gave a very small, controlled smile, and I realized just how dangerous that certain something he'd inherited from the Ad-hene was—it was charisma, incredibly potent, and he knew how to use it. "We just saved you the trouble of their executions."

"How thoughtful of you. But in the future, do let us know beforehand. I'm sure an execution is no bother at all to my sister. I don't think you've had the pleasure of meeting Prudence, have you?" I deliberately looked him up and down. "You're all in one piece, so I guess you haven't." I turned entirely to face only Lilah. "Lilah, why don't we all sit down if we're going to talk business."

Lilah had been watching the interplay closely, and now she nodded slowly, a strand of her brilliant copper-gold hair sliding forward to lie against the freckled skin of her neck. We all settled around the small breakfast table that was bunched against the far wall of Lilah's galley kitchen, positioning our chairs awkwardly, with Lilah sitting between us, and Cole pushing his chair as far back as the cabinets behind him would allow, watching me without seeming to blink.

Lilah cleared her throat carefully and began. "Fort, you've met a few of our changelings, like Jacoby and Felix, the ones who were born to human mothers and didn't know about their heritage until the community reclaimed them when they were teenagers."

I nodded, wondering how much of this was for Cole's benefit, and how much was to make sure that I fully remembered my interactions with the weirdness of the Neighbor community from the previous autumn. "Yeah, I have."

"Jacoby's substance-abuse issues aren't unusual. The changelings are pretty much uniformly traumatized by what happens to them. One minute they're living with the only family they've ever known, with probably the biggest problem being puberty and acne, and the next minute they're being kidnapped by strangers, with their deaths faked, and told that they can never see their family members again, or a bunch of fairy-tale monsters will kill them. Oh, and that they're only fifty percent human."

Talk about a terrible facts-of-life talk. "I can see how that would cause some pretty substantial and long-term issues," I agreed.

"Exactly. So what we've been talking about is the idea of removing the changelings from their human families early—very early. Because of how aggressive Lavinia Leamaro was with her obstetrics program, we have almost sixty changelings living with human families right now—some are getting close to the age that we'd be automatically taking them, but the ages range right down to infancy, and a few possible pregnancies that we're monitoring."

I didn't bother to hide my surprise. "You want to take sixty kids at once?"

"Spaced out just for logistics, but ideally we'd like to have them all in our hands, and fostered in with Neighbor households, by the end of the year."

"That's a pretty big influx—can the community handle it?"

Lilah nodded firmly. "It will be a strain, but it would be worth it for the long-term health benefits. And in the future we would prefer to take the babies when they were born, to try to minimize the pain for everyone involved."

"You're taking the baby away from its mother," I pointed out. "A mother who, given her involvement with Lavinia Leamaro's clinic, would probably never be able to have another child, even if she was able to recover from losing her baby enough to even attempt it."

"We know the cost of what we're doing, Fort," Lilah said, her voice gentle, but also firm. "None of us are undertaking these issues lightly, and we've had a lot of conversations and discussion about this. But the changelings are our only source of fresh genetics, and while we aren't as dependent on them as we were a generation ago, we can't ignore that we need them."

I considered what she was suggesting, but I saw a lot of potential problems. "How are you going to get the changelings away from their parents? I know that before you were faking accidents—that's a lot of accidents to fake in one calendar year."

"You're right. It is a lot. We've accepted that we'd probably have to employ the kitsune for many of them."

"I've seen the kitsune prices—that's a lot of money you'd be putting in." Even if they could somehow convince Chiyo Hollis to accept a bulk rate, the kitsune put top dollar on their use of fox magic for other races—for good reason. The kitsune could fool not only the eyes, but all the senses. They could fool not just casual bystanders, but those trained to look and examine, like police and doctors. They could fool security cameras and print cameras, even instrument readouts. Fox magic could set illusions that most of the mixed-blood Neighbors could only dream about as they spent all their energy just hiding their own faces. If you wanted a body covered up in a way that ensured no awkward questions and no elaborate and convenient fires, you went to the kitsune. And they set those price tags accordingly.

"We have the money," Lilah said stiffly, clearly not wanting me to ask her to elaborate on the how of it.

From his seat across from me, Cole spoke, quietly and silkily. "The assets of those we executed, after all, are being held in a trust, to be used for the good of the whole community that was damaged by their reckless actions."

I could see Lilah wince—that was definitely not a happy memory for her, and probably suggested a previous disagreement between them—one that Cole had evidently won.

I deliberately ignored Cole and kept my focus on my

friend. "Apart from being very careful that no one starts noticing any patterns here, or realizes that the thing that all these children have in common is that their mothers got their infertility treatments at one place, I don't really disagree with you on any fundamental parts. I can't think of a way to let these kids know about their heritage and still let them stay with their own families, for example, not without taking a huge risk to too many people's safety. But is there any particular reason why the system was set up like this in the first place?"

"Tradition, I guess." Lilah gave a small shrug. "The Ad-hene always left their changelings with the mothers at first. They didn't have much interest in raising babies—they only valued the physically mature changelings, since they could be bred with or hunted for sport." Her voice was grim—after recent events, Lilah had no illusions left about the full-blood elves.

"Yes, dear old Dad and his buddies," Cole said icily. "And Madeline agreed with it, since she felt that adolescent deaths or disappearances were more easily explained than those of small children."

I couldn't ignore Cole anymore, particularly when he was actually making decent points, so I just sighed a little. "Yes, that does sound rather like my mother. Well, I can definitely promise to bring this up with my siblings. To me, at least, it sounds pretty straightforward and like a reasonable idea, but I can't make any promises about how my siblings will react." No promises at all, given the way that our meetings had been going lately.

Lilah gave me a warm smile, the kind that lit up her whole face. "I really appreciate you coming over, Fort, especially given the complete lack of warning." She pushed her chair back and got to her feet. "Can I offer you something for the ride home? I know I've got half a pie left in the fridge. Not that I baked it, of course, since I like my pie to be actually edible—"

Cole cut her off. "There was another issue that we'd discussed, Lilah."

She gave him an irritated look and snapped back, "Fort has already agreed to talk with his family about our petition—can't we wait to see how that one goes before we ask for something else?"

I glanced back and forth between them, and realized very clearly that this was the power shift within the Neighbors. Lilah was trying to slow things down, but it was all too clear that Cole was speaking for a majority, and that Lilah was on the defensive. I tried to weigh my words very carefully, looking for something that would satisfy Cole but wouldn't undermine Lilah. "If I don't think that my siblings will react well to multiple requests, then I'll only tell them about the first, for now. But why don't you tell me what you need, since then you can tell the rest of the Neighbors that you did pass everything along."

Cole paused, weighing my offer. "I suppose," he said carefully, clearly wanting more of a promise, but also considering whether that was enough for now. Then, with a quick nod of decision, he shifted forward, taking the reins of the conversation firmly from Lilah, and she knew it. She and I shared a look, but it was clear that neither of us could really do anything. "You know of course that the younger Neighbors, those who identify more with me, and Lilah"—though I heard the pause in his voice before he added her name—"have taken control of the breeding program away from those who were the creatures of our forefathers, the Ad-hene."

"Yes, by killing them," I pointed out.

Cole was completely unruffled. "Yes," he agreed. "Given the punishments handed down by your mother before she died"—I had to wince at the pun, unintentional or not, because part of the punishment of the Ad-hene was that Chivalry had cut off their hands, as well as other, more sensitive parts—"the Ad-hene are currently licking their wounds in Underhill, and haven't emerged from their hole since the last of their lapdogs were dispatched. But Lavinia had a great deal of their semen stored and frozen at her practice."

I could see very clearly where this was going. "You want to continue the breeding program."

Lilah interjected quickly, "With changes, Fort. Big changes. No more forced or pressured pregnancies—we still want to build our numbers, but only with women who are open to having a baby. We're going to stop the deliberate inbreeding—the Ad-hene were trying to exacerbate their traits, breed power and magic back in, but there are too many side effects. Bloodlust, a lack of real empathy, whole-scale psychopathy—these aren't things that we can deal with in the long term."

Cole nodded. "In this, Lilah and I are in complete agreement. The elves never cared about the costs, they just wanted to get offspring that were as close to the original as possible. The human side to our heritage is a moderating effect—the naturally born half-breeds, created from two changelings, like Lilah, are extremely stable, with just enough glamour to hide themselves. The five-eighths crosses that come from a half-breed and a three-quarter have a stronger magic, but are still stable."

Ah, fractions—the inevitable part of any conversation about elf genetics. I looked directly at Cole. "And the three-quarter crosses? Like you?"

Lilah put her hand on mine, giving a small squeeze, silently asking me to pull back. She sounded completely calm, though, almost detached, when she answered the question for Cole. "The most magic, but our most dangerous, with the least control. The most likely to crave violence and death, to get pleasure only from the pain of others." She nodded at the other Neighbor, and there was an understanding there—I didn't think that she liked him, but in this they understood each other—this was the viper's nest that they'd both grown up in. "Cole was, for a long time, the greatest success. His magic is strong, but he has as much control as a half-breed." Her voice softened. "You've seen my sister, Fort. She needs to kill—it's not a choice for her, but a real need. She can sate the need with animals, enough that she can mix safely with society, but I have to watch her carefully. Most of the three-quarter crosses are like her."

"And there's one more set, of course," I noted, not letting it go unsaid if we were going to have this conversation. "The seven-eighths crosses. The ones that the blood sacrifices were made for."

"Those babies are dangerous," Cole said clearly. "Allegra's son was the first, the other pregnancies still advancing, but I've already suggested that we kill them."

Lilah cut in. "Allegra loves her son, Cole."

It was clearly an old disagreement, and there was something wholly human in the irritation in Cole's voice. "He was born with teeth, and she had to stop trying to breast-feed him after only two days because he loved the taste of blood more than milk." While I was still internally wincing from that mental image, Cole turned directly to me. "You saw what was done to conceive them. They're too close to the Ad-hene."

As I looked at Cole, I suddenly realized something, something that set him completely apart from so many of the Neighbors I'd met before, the ones like Lavinia, who had worshipped and idealized the Ad-hene. "You hate them. You'd kill them all, if you could."

Cole's pupils contracted quickly, almost disappearing from those unbelievable purple striations of his eyes. "Of course I want them dead," he replied, his anger almost a palpable thing in the room.

"We're not talking about that," Lilah said, quickly. Too quickly, and I could see the warning on her face as she looked at him.

"No, of course not," Cole agreed, recovering with a clear effort, pulling himself together. "We're talking about the breeding program." Calmer, he continued. "We need the stabilizing element of fresh human genetics to help move us toward a strong, sane, and diverse population. The Ad-hene weren't just inbreeding to themselves—at times they would force full half-breed siblings to breed with each other, and those outcomes lacked any control at all. We need new changelings, and that means that we need access to human women in a controlled setting, with the ability to monitor them, follow their outcomes, and eventually take changeling babies. Lavinia is gone, and I hope that she burns in hell for what she did, but she'd been getting older, and was working on grooming her replacement. We have two different Neighbors of the younger generation who were being considered—one is in medical school right now, and the other is already in an obstetrics residency program. We can start making new changelings again."

I added things up in my head, and saw what they were deliberately talking around. "It looks to me like you're missing a pretty big piece of the puzzle. Lavinia used a witch to make sure that every woman who walked in that door conceived a baby with elf semen. After all, what was that success rate of the Ad-hene genes breeding true? Eight percent? Nine?"

"Seven. And yes, we need a witch." A disdain that almost equaled my own sister's dripped from Cole's voice when he mentioned the witches.

Once again, Lilah picked up the conversational ball, showing how often they had been around each other. "After what happened with Ambrose—" At the sound of his name, Cole's eyes flared again, and his lip curled. Lilah hastily corrected herself, which was definitely interesting. "With Lavinia's former witch, none of the other witches are even willing to talk with us. They all know that Lavinia was doing the forbidden, and died for it, and that her witch barely escaped a similar fate. We've been told very clearly that no witch in the territory will come near us unless we can show them that we have full Scott sanction on this."

"Well, I can certainly understand why the witches would be wetting themselves with you guys coming by," I noted. If I hadn't been present in the room and able to do some very fast talking, my sister would've ripped out Ambrose's intestines—and not because of the very morally gray components of his actions, but just because she'd been getting basic information out of him. The witches avoided Prudence for very good reasons. "I'll bring this up to Prudence and Chivalry, and if they okay things, then I'll talk to people on the witch side and see what they think about it. They're going to want full disclosure on this, you know. No more just cooking things up just because they're asked to."

"Really?" Cole asked coldly, his disbelief clear. "Well, how pleasant that they've finally located some ethics. I do hope that they used both hands and a flashlight."

Lilah got up and physically took me by the arm, towing me over to the door and leaving no question that this meeting was officially over. "That's everything we agreed that we wanted to talk about, Cole, so that's enough. I'm sure that Fort needs to get home." As she flipped the lock on the door, she paused and looked at me with deep sincerity. "Fort, thank you. I mean it."

I gave a small shrug. Lilah and I were the same in a lot of ways, given that we'd both run from our biology as long as we could. But when Lilah had seen bad things happening in her community, she didn't only just buckle down and do something about it, even if it meant risking her life, but she stayed involved, doing her best to try to help the weaker members of the Neighbors, to protect them. I respected the hell out of her for it, and couldn't say for certain that I would've been able to do the same thing in her position—at least not without trying to weasel my way out of it at first. "I should've checked in with you earlier, Lilah. I shouldn't have let it become an emergency. But give me a call sometime later—we'll do lunch, something that isn't about business."

She gave me a quick smile and a friendly peck on the cheek. "Thanks. I'll talk with you later. And do give my best to Suzume when you see her." A quick grin flashed across Lilah's face, and a hint of her old spirit. "I heard you two are dating."

I could feel a smile spread across my face, and I teased, "I thought there wasn't much talking between the races."

"Oh, there isn't," she assured me. "But this one was just too good for anyone to stay quiet about."

With one last wave, she closed the door, and I headed back to my car. Snow had started falling when I was inside—the eventual payoff from the heavy gray clouds that had hung in the sky all day, making everything moody and grim. It wasn't supposed to be a big storm, but I had to turn the car on to get the heat going, then pull my ice scraper out of the backseat and spend a few minutes brushing the fluffy accumulation off my windows, headlights, and brake lights, before I was finally able to get into the car and head home, mulling over all the issues that I would now have to present to my siblings and try to get some answers for.

In an effort to numb my brain to everything that was going on, I stayed up later than I had lately, and watched TV. Dan's parents had gotten him a subscription to Hulu for Christmas, giving us a sudden access to television that we'd agreed was both incredible and that we'd probably have to completely disable when he was in exam time again, so we spent the evening watching an older season of *Top Chef*, with Dan periodically complaining about how more challenges needed to focus on the use of organ meat so that he could get new ideas for the kitchen.

Around midnight, Dan headed off to bed. I watched one last episode, mostly just to have something to look at while thoughts chased around in my head like aimless mice. I unwrapped a Popsicle, the last of the orange ones, and began gnawing at it contemplatively, bliss filling me as the persistent ache in my upper jaw was soothed away. A knock on the door surprised me, surprising me even more when I opened it to find Lilah standing in my hall, her hair mashed under a dark green wool hat that matched her heavy winter jacket.

"Uh . . ." I said eloquently, the only thing running through my head being that I was in my pajamas and flannel robe, with a half-eaten Popsicle in my hand.

"I'm really sorry, Fort," she said in a rush. "I know that this is incredibly inconvenient." It was true, but agreeing to it seemed somehow a little rude, so I just gave a noncommittal shrug and opened the door wider so that she could come inside.

"Did something happen after I left tonight?" I asked, wrapping what was left of my Popsicle in a paper towel and tucking it back into the freezer. Unexpected guest or no, I was planning to eat that thing.

"No, nothing like that." Lilah pulled off her hat and coat, folding them carefully onto the side of the sofa. I suppressed a sigh. Apparently this wasn't going to be a quick visit. "I wanted to talk with you about Cole."

"Ah. Yeah, you'd mentioned him before as the one who pushed to kill the Neighbors who'd been working with the Ad-hene on the blood sacrifices." I sat down. "Kind of a surprise to find him waiting to see me, though."

"I'm sorry about that, but there was a big meeting

going down, and he backed me into a corner in front of a lot of the rest of the Neighbors." She ran her hands over her hair, patting the hair over her ears in an unconscious habit. Her glamour was back in place this evening. "But I'm sure that you're going to see a lot of him in the future."

"Oh? Lilah, don't get me wrong, but that it not in any way improving my night."

She gave me a quick smile, but it failed to make a dent in her overall anxiety. "Yeah, Cole can be kind of a dick, but he's not a bad guy overall. He really does want to protect us, to help with our new direction."

"But you don't agree with him."

"On some things, sure. Not on everything." She paced the room, looking around. "Oh, you got a new armchair. It looks nice."

"Lilah, seriously, it's after midnight," I begged. "I know there's something you don't want to say to me, but you came all the way over here to say it rather than texting me, so please just spit it out."

"You're right, okay." She plunked herself down on the new armchair, arranged her hands carefully in her lap, then looked up at me and opened her mouth. Five seconds later she was up and pacing again, and I threw up my hands.

"Lilah—"

"No, fine." She pressed her fist against her chin, then said, "You need to call the witches."

"Yeah, we were just talking about that this evening—"

"No," she snapped, then took a deep breath. "It's about Ambrose, Fort, the witch who cooked up those roofie potions that were given to the girls."

I sighed. "Listen, Lilah, I don't like it either, and I don't think that he's a particularly good person, but he didn't know what those potions were for. He should've asked, but he didn't, and I believe that he didn't know. If he was a doctor, I'd say to suspend his license or make him go before an ethics board, but he's not—he's a witch, and he was doing what Lavinia was paying him—"

"Don't defend him, Fort," Lilah said, her temper flaring enough that her eyes were significantly more gold than brown. "Iris was given that potion, and we both saw what it did to her. I know all the women who were given it, and I was the one who had to tell them what was done to them, because they still have no memories about what happened, but now they're having to deal with what was done to them, and that someone was murdered right in front of them when they couldn't do anything about it." Her knuckles whitened, and I could see her visibly rein in her temper. Her voice lowered, but the intensity was still there as she looked at me. "I want to hurt Ambrose. I want him to bleed. But I can't risk what would happen if a Neighbor killed a witch, and that's why I'm telling you this, Fort. You need to get him out of the city, hide him somewhere."

I looked at her and understood why she'd come here this late, and hadn't called me. "This is about Cole," I said. "He killed all the Neighbors who were involved, and now he's looking at Ambrose as well."

"He holds him responsible for what his actions contributed to," Lilah said dully. "Can't you understand that?"

"Yes, I can," I agreed. I leaned over and put a hand on her shoulder, squeezing lightly. "I know someone to call," I assured her. "I'll get Ambrose away before anything can happen."

She hesitated a second, then nodded, reaching her right hand over to pat my hand, nodding a few times. I could see the strain in her face, the worry, and it made me terrified to think about the things that she was still not telling me, and that frankly I wasn't even sure that I wanted to know about.

I hesitated, then said it. After all, she was my friend, and I knew that if Prudence got pissed about anything, she wasn't going to stop and ask questions before she started killing perceived ringleaders. "Lilah, I noticed what Cole said about the Ad-hene, and don't think that I also didn't notice you pushing that to a back burner."

She frowned at me. "You have to understand about Cole and the Ad-hene, Fort. His mother was a change-ling, one of Shoney's. When she was old enough to have a baby, Shoney was the father, and that's how Cole was born. And Cole was the best three-quarters that they'd ever produced—his glamours are the strongest, and he holds the glamours on almost forty of the Neighbors who are too weak to set their own. So Shoney wanted to re-create Cole—even after Cole's mother miscarried three times and had two stillbirths, he wouldn't give up. Finally Cole's mother told Shoney that she wouldn't do it any-more—no more pregnancies. And Shoney killed her—took her into the forest and just ripped her apart. Because to him she was just a changeling who was no longer useful, so she might as well give him the enter-tainment of her death."

We looked at each other grimly. The truth was that I wouldn't cry a tear if the Ad-hene were all killed the next day—they'd left too much of a trail of destruction be-hind them. And even though I still didn't like Cole, this made me understand him a little more, almost against my will. But understanding didn't change the truth that there was trouble brewing right now with the Neighbors—a lot of it.

As soon as the door had closed behind Lilah, I began muttering curses, circling around the room in much the same way that Lilah had done just a few minutes before. The last thing I needed was getting my sister involved—her answer would be to just start killing people and us-ing that as a way to discourage future problems. Calling

Chivalry was similarly problematic—given his fixation on following my mother's last directive, there was no way that he'd agree to keep this hidden from my sister, and that led right back to the first problem at worst, and at the very best, just yet another sibling deadlock that would result in all of us standing around arguing while Cole took out Ambrose.

I pulled my phone out of its charger in the bedroom and called Suzume, but she didn't pick up—it was entirely possible that she was out running around the woods behind her grandmother's house on four legs, hunting bunnies and mice, or knocking over her neighbor's trash cans for the umpteenth time. I cursed, checked the time, and cursed again. As I scrolled through my contacts, I hoped to hell that Valentine Sassoon was a night owl.

He wasn't. Valentine Sassoon might be the would-be Norma Rae of the witches, but he was also a doctor with a thriving practice in sports medicine and orthopedic surgery, which apparently meant that he followed the practice of early to bed and early to rise. After he'd woken up sufficiently to realize that this was important, and that it really couldn't wait until morning, he asked if it was possible to meet to discuss it. I ground my teeth at the thought of having to actually drag myself out somewhere, but the truth was that this was probably something that merited a full face-to-face conversation. There was a twenty-four-hour diner that I knew on the edge of the College Hill neighborhood that had decent parking and wouldn't be far for him to get to, so I asked if he could go there. He agreed, and we both hung up.

I looked out the window—an inch of powder, snow still coming down, and other than the tire tracks from other cars, it was clear that the plows weren't going to bother getting to work for another few hours. I cursed loudly and changed my sweatpants for jeans, and pulled a sweatshirt over my usual pajama top. The diner had undoubtedly seen worse. Yanking on my shoes, I went back into the kitchen and gnawed my way quickly through the Popsicle—it was probably a dumb thing to do before heading out into the cold, but damn it, this night was not going my way.

As I trudged down the apartment building steps, I passed Jaison coming up. I waved at him in passing, and grinned. "Hey, Jaison. Dan get lonely?"

Jaison gave me a lazy smile and gestured to himself. "Hey, who could blame a man for not being able to resist this?"

I laughed and continued to head down. "Did Suze booty-call you too?" Jaison called to me, pausing in his own trek up the stairs.

"I wish," I grumbled. "No, I just have to meet up with someone, then come back. Family shit."

Jaison reached into his pocket and withdrew his keys. "If you're coming right back, then take my truck," he advised. "Those tires that you have on the Scirocco are crap, even in baby snow like this."

"Thanks, I really appreciate it," I said, catching the keys as he tossed them down to me.

"No problem. Just remember—I want the same number of dents in my bumper tomorrow as there are right now."

"Forty-eight, gotcha," I said. "Thanks, and have fun."

"You know it," he said, heading up the stairs again with a definite jauntiness in his steps.

There's a certain point of the night when a twenty-four-hour diner becomes a very weird intersection of humanity. People on dates who like each other enough to keep talking to each other, but aren't ready to go back to someone's house and possibly end up in bed. People who are in the middle of breakups. People who work weird work shifts, and are actually having their dinner, or possibly breakfast. People who you are almost entirely certain are prostitutes. People who are probably homeless, nursing cups of coffee as an excuse to sit somewhere nice and warm rather than being outside in the cold. People who have nowhere else in the world to go, and just look like the universe really needs to cut them a break for once.

But when it comes down to it, twenty-four-hour diners are wonderful, because where else can you walk in and get French toast at any hour of the day? If nuclear fallout ever ended up happening, my plan was to hole up in a twenty-four-hour diner and just eat French toast.

Since I was hoping to get out of this meeting as soon as possible and actually get some sleep, I avoided the siren song of French toast and just ordered a cup of hot chocolate—and given the level that my night was sucking, I felt entirely justified when I asked for extra whipped cream on top. Perhaps my waitress picked up on something with that sixth sense for sadness that all good service personnel are able to develop (I, for the record, had never developed this), or was just incredibly bored, because when she brought it to me, it was also jazzed up with a whole bunch of sprinkles.

This improved my night right up until the moment that Valentine Sassoon, looking more put together than any man apart from my brother had any right to at this hour of the night, sat down across from me, catching me midslurp of my delicious, whipped-cream-and-sprinkle-covered hot cocoa. He didn't say anything, but there was no doubt that the subtle arch of his eyebrow was providing commentary on my choices.

It was of small comfort to me that I'd had much more embarrassing moments.

The waitress looped around again, long enough to take Valentine's order of a small bowl of chowder and pretty much fall in love with him. Right there in the middle of a shift in the absolute dead of night, there had appeared a man who not only didn't reek of alcohol or despair, but looked like he could be a model. Plus, he smiled extremely politely at her and even repeated her name after she'd introduced herself. I had a feeling that someone was going to get some extra crackers with his chowder.

That actually wasn't a euphemism.

Once the waitress had managed to pry herself away from our table, I filled Valentine in on what Lilah had told me that evening. He listened without interrupting, his fingers carefully steepled as he gave me his full attention, his handsome face intent, but not giving any hints about how he was reacting to what I was telling him.

After I'd finished, Valentine placed his hands down flat on the table, the faded beige of the plastic top contrasting the dark skin of the long and elegant fingers that would make piano teachers and surgical instructors alike swoon.

"You know," he said thoughtfully, "I've been worried for a while that the other shoe was waiting to drop on Ambrose, but I've got to say that I wasn't expecting it to come from this direction. Honestly I didn't think that the elves even gave a crap."

"The Neighbors aren't like the Ad-hene, at least not this group," I reminded him, "and they are not happy with what happened." I took another sip of my cocoa, which was really very good. "Frankly, a lot of people should be unhappy."

At my tone, Valentine's eyebrows arched again. "I'm not arguing with you, Fort. Ambrose got very used to just doing what Lavinia asked him to, with no questions asked. But this is about a bigger issue, the problem of—"

"It's one in the morning, and you would not even believe how many plates I'm already keeping in the air.

Can we please, just this once, only focus on the issue of what's happening right now?" I begged.

The witch sighed heavily. "Fine, we'll do it your way. Treat the symptom, not the malady. But hey, what would I know about that? I just have a medical degree."

"Ha-ha." I rubbed my hand across my eyes, which were doing that overly moist almost-teary thing that happened when I was really tired. "Ambrose needs to get out of town, and given what's going on with the Neighbors right now, I don't think he should plan on coming back. So how do we relocate him?"

"It's not just him. Ambrose has a wife who is also a witch, and their youngest child is still at home. You're looking at relocating a family of three."

"Shit," I said. "Okay, do they have family that they can stay with?"

"You're forgetting the system, Fort," he said, at least doing me the favor of not gloating as I walked right into his hands about the bigger issue topic. "Witches need Scott permission to relocate anywhere in the territory—if a witch wants to move one town over, she has to put in a request. Plus, your family doesn't want witches grouping in an area—there's a quota system in place for how many witches can be in one place. If Ambrose and his family goes to stay with another set of witches, then they're risking someone dropping a tip to the Scotts. Best-case scenario, a hell of a fine. Worst-case, Prudence shows up on their doorstep."

I shoved my hands hard through my hair, frustrated. "I get your point, you know, Valentine. Yes, this system is deeply flawed. Yes, it really needs to be overhauled. None of which helps us keep Ambrose safe right now and prevent a huge interspecies incident. He needs to make a transfer request to somewhere that has room in its quota for more witches. Okay, how long does that kind of request usually take?"

Valentine took a spoonful of chowder and swallowed it slowly. "Last time I checked, eleven months was the average."

"What?" I shrieked, making every head in the diner turn in my direction, even those of the couples who were in the midst of painful breakups. Our waitress gave me a quelling glare, and I made one of those little apologetic hand waves and lowered my voice. "It takes *that* long?" I hissed to Valentine.

"Yes, it really does," he replied, his expression grim. "There were witch families that lost their houses during the last recession, and they had to stay in hotels for months before they could get permission to go anywhere else, even though they had families that they could've stayed with, or sometimes could've rented cheap apartments in different areas of the city rather than pay out the nose with money they couldn't afford to spend. But there's no appeal process, no way to prioritize emergency requests over those that could wait, or fast-track requests from people who need to move to accept new jobs, and don't get me started on what a headache college applications are to kids who don't know if they'll even be allowed to live in the area where their college is. Most witch children end up taking gap years just to give the paperwork time to go through."

"Shit." Something else that needed nothing more than immediate attention and overhaul, with a thoughtful implementation of better rules, and was instead going to get stuck into committee hell courtesy of the Scott siblings. I scrubbed my hand over my forehead, wishing that by friction alone I could force out some idea on how to get Prudence and Chivalry to agree with me when I finally brought this particular issue to the table. "Okay, I need you to tell Ambrose that he needs to be on the lookout for pissed-off elflings, and I'm going to have to go down tomorrow and make something work."

Valentine stared at me, caught somewhere between the extreme hope of his idealism and the extreme cynicism that was no doubt the by-product of a life spent subject to the Scott rules dictating witch behavior. "Do you think you can?"

"I don't have many options, do I?" I said, irritated.

"You could do nothing, you know," Valentine pointed out. "It's what plenty of people might do in your situation."

"For Christ's sake," I grumbled, pulling out my wallet and thumbing through the contents of a billfold so meager that I was half surprised that a moth didn't fly out. "Let's not give me a medal for just deciding not to act like a complete dick and ignore problems. I mean, I haven't gotten a damn thing done yet, Valentine. I don't think that 'good intentions' counts as an accomplishment."

Valentine reached over and pushed my wallet back, stopping me from pulling anything out. "I make good money, Fort. Let me get this one." He gave me a searching look. "You're angry at Ambrose. You think that he deserves some kind of punishment on this. But you're working pretty hard to keep him alive here. Can I ask why that is?"

I was broke enough at this point that I wasn't going to make a fuss about being treated to a cup of hot chocolate, so I got up from the booth and started yanking on my jacket. "Something needs to be done, Valentine, but the last time I checked, vigilante lynching squads are very rarely the answer to anything." I pulled on my hat. "Call me if anything happens."

I could feel Valentine's eyes on me as I left the diner, but I didn't look back. I couldn't handle knowing that the hopes of yet another group were pinned on me.

It was just too depressing to think about.

The snow had stopped, and the plows were finally starting to make their rounds when I pulled into the parking lot of the apartment building. I'd ended up turning on the radio to help keep myself awake, and had made the strange discovery that all of Jaison's radio presets were to country stations. If that wasn't an example of musical crossover appeal, then I didn't know what was.

I opened the apartment door, and was met with the strange sight of Jaison, dressed only in a pair of flannel pajama bottoms, leaning over the sink, flushing his mouth out with water. My eyes slowly drifted over the items on the counter next to him—my blue pitcher of blood, a glass with a distinctive residue stain along the inside—and I froze in horror.

Jaison lifted his head up from the faucet and caught sight of me. "I'm really sorry, Fort," he said quickly. "I was just curious and . . ." He made a brief retching sound and went under for another mouthful of water. "Sweet mother of *God*, that shit is *rank*."

"Yeah. . . . Yeah, it is," I replied slowly, my heart beating practically out of my chest. "Let's . . . let's just pretend that it didn't happen, okay?" I paused. "And maybe not mention it to Dan?" The ghoul would absolutely freak if he found out that his boyfriend had just swallowed a mouthful of A-positive. Frankly, I was feeling somewhat nauseated myself, and I wasn't the one who kissed Jaison on the mouth.

"Fine by me," Jaison agreed. "How you do it, Fort, I have no idea. I don't think any amount of muscle gain is worth having to drink that shit." He turned to the fridge, pulled it open, and started hunting through it. "Now how the hell do I get that taste out of my mouth?"

"Try some orange juice," I said blandly.

Chapter Eight

Suze called me back late the following morning, as I was driving down to Newport and feeling the burn in my shoulders from having to shovel the majority of the parking lot out by myself, Dan only being able to shovel with me for a short time before he had to leave for class.

"Hey there, Mr. Thirty-seven Text Messages," she said, amusement clear in her voice. "I hear that you got up to some shenanigans last night."

"Yeah, I did, thanks for asking." I was feeling distinctly grumpy, and I hadn't even laid eyes on Prudence and Chivalry yet. "Do I even dare ask why you weren't answering your phone?"

"Urban chicken-hunting." She was obviously feeling very pleased with herself and life. "There's a rooster half a mile away from my grandmother's house, and we took him out last night."

I sighed heavily. "Suze, you have access to sharp weaponry and opposable thumbs. I'm not feeling impressed right now."

"Don't denigrate the ways of my people, Fort. This was done entirely on four feet. And let me tell you, that rooster's owner probably lost his shit when he saw that we'd gotten into his coop. That guy had it locked up tighter than Mother Teresa's panties."

"I'm not even Catholic, and I found that offensive."

She ignored me. "Four different layers of wire, Fort! Four! And a layer that ran under the coop itself, so that we couldn't dig our way in. Plus a surveillance system. This is a person who is serious about his omelets, man friend."

I paused, picturing this kind of backyard setup in a town like Exeter. "Okay, that's starting to sound somewhat impressive. But can I at least tell you about my night first, before you tell me about the great rooster heist?"

"Fine," she grumbled, "though I got the gist of most of it through your test messages. Also, emoticons, Fort? Really, it's all about emojis now."

I spent the rest of my drive filling her in, finishing just as I drove through the E-ZPass lane on the Claiborne Pell Bridge and spared a moment to consider exactly what kind of toll bill was currently racking up for me. It was not a comforting thought.

"So?" I asked her. "What's your thought on all this?"

"That's some pretty deep shit you're wading in right now," she said.

I waited.

She said nothing.

I waited some more.

Finally I said, "That's all you have to add to this? I'm about to go in and present this crap situation to my siblings and attempt to actually address this and get tangible decisions made, and you've got absolutely nothing for me."

"Oh, crap, you were expecting actual help?"

I rubbed my jaw and regretted not bringing a bag of carrots with me. "If it's not too much trouble for you, yeah," I said sarcastically.

"Get them drunk. I'm not sure what vampire age does to alcohol tolerance, so you're going to want to find a way to get Prudence to drink at least three full bottles of brandy. At that point, she'll probably agree to whatever you suggest."

"I'm going to hang the phone up right now."

"That might be the best way out for both of us at this point. But if you come up with some kind of solution that involves punching, remember that I'm your girl."

Sitting around the sofas in the drawing room, with a toasty fire roaring away in the fireplace and a thoughtfully provided selection of hummus and cold vegetables, I told Prudence and Chivalry about my meeting with Lilah and Cole, with a few careful edits. I didn't mention the threat against Ambrose at all, or my meeting with Valentine. Even if the thought had been in my mind, the complete train wreck of the Neighbor conversation would've prevented it.

"After what happened in the autumn, the Ad-hene are lucky that we restricted their punishment to slicing off things that will grow back," Prudence growled, slamming her teacup down onto the coffee table with enough force to send tea sloshing through cracks in the china, which she ignored as she shoved to her feet and started pacing the room. "And now they actually have the balls to make *requests* of us? Clearly Chivalry didn't cut enough off."

"This isn't coming from the Ad-hene," I said, for at least the fifth time. "This is a group of the younger Neighbors who are making separate decisions, and need to be regarded as a different group entirely."

"Fortitude, I know that you're fond of Lilah Dwyer, and that she was helpful to both you and Prudence during your investigations, but I really think that you need to take that with a grain of salt," Chivalry said, looking irritated. "The Ad-hene have always kept a tight control over their scions, and I find it rather hard to imagine that something is occurring that I've never seen before in the entire time that the Ad-hene have been within our borders."

"The situation *is* different," I insisted, feeling the distinct urge to tear my hair out. "Lavinia Leamaro's success in creating more than just half-breed offspring has created a whole group of Neighbors in their twenties who are different than any generation that came before them, and thanks to a real push on their breeding program, this is also a group that has a significant numbers advantage. It's a change in the basic demographics of this group, Chivalry, and you just can't keep ignoring that."

"If the numbers are the problem, then we can take care of that." Prudence flicked an imaginary piece of dirt off the sleeve of her cream sweater and took a moment to adjust the level of one of the paintings. "They want approved witch assistance to continue this breeding program of theirs? We simply forbid the witches to even go near the elves for a minimum of twenty years. That should teach the Ad-hene a lesson that will finally make an impression, since apparently ball slicing didn't."

"We're not talking about the Ad-hene here, Prudence," I said, my voice raising. "And this other group isn't even a problem—it could be a *good* thing if we would just work with them, rather than refusing to acknowledge that they even exist."

"Perhaps we could find a compromise here," Chivalry interjected. "We could put a yearly quota on how many times a witch could assist with a changeling conception, which would put some control on this numbers increase and also reemphasize who is in control here."

"A quota? On something as basic as reproduction?" I stared at my brother, my jaw dropping. "And that will in some way settle this issue? That's just going to throw fuel on the fire. Besides, they're asking us to intercede to reassure the witches, not because they actually even need our permission for something like this. We don't forbid the races to interact, after all. They can do business with each other without our okay."

"They should've asked us, regardless," Prudence said icily. "And as for collecting their changelings all at once, I'm not sure we should be letting them engage the services of the kitsune at all."

"What do you mean?" My head was beginning to pound, and I wasn't sure I could blame even part of it on my teething issues. "Collecting the changelings earlier is a good idea—it would result in more emotionally stable adults."

"I strongly doubt that," Prudence snorted. "There's madness in that blood, Fort. I would trust in nature over nurture. The only thing that collecting the changelings early will do is stir this group up even more, and provide a financial windfall for the kitsune that they frankly do not need."

My expression must've been a sight to behold, because Chivalry gave a heavy sigh, put his coffee cup down gently, and said, "Sister, in the possibility, however remote, that Fort is right about there being separate groups, we could act in a way that shows our willingness to be generous, despite past indiscretions. What if we drop the allowed collection age from fourteen to thirteen? I think that could be a workable compromise to your two positions."

I sputtered, and I couldn't hide the anger in my voice. "Fourteen to thirteen? Chivalry, that's not a change— that's just the status quo wrapped up with a pretty bow." By the end, I was nearly yelling.

Chivalry's face darkened, and the pupils of his eyes flared, all clear signs that his own temper was now well and thoroughly engaged. "And what's wrong with the status quo, Fortitude? And you as well, Prudence?" He turned to include her, clearly surprising Prudence, who had been standing back and enjoying our argument. "Mother's system has worked more than well for many years, yet all either of you wants to do is change things that would be better left alone." Chivalry shoved himself to his feet and stalked out of the room, slamming the door behind him with enough force to rattle all the cups and cutlery, as well as a dozen porcelain figurines.

Prudence and I both stared after Chivalry, mute with wonder. Over the past days we had each stormed out of the room multiple times, but Chivalry had been the one with patience, the one arguing for the middle path, coaxing us back to the table and reminding us of the critical importance of working together. Through the bond we shared, I could feel Chivalry leaving the house, and then quickly fading into the distance.

I looked over at Prudence, who was looking deeply thoughtful at our brother's action. She slowly slid her blue eyes over to me and raised her eyebrows. "Well, I'd say that we're adjourning early today." She checked the clock on the mantelpiece, and looked pleased. "I might actually be able to get some real work done today at the office, thank heavens." And with that she strolled out the door.

I looked down at the wreckage on the table, Prudence's teacup continuing to slowly ooze tea onto its saucer, and the overloaded saucer dribbling onto the rest of the tray. I got up slowly to my feet. Despite my brother's longing for the old ways, those just hadn't worked either. I walked down to the office, where I caught up with Loren Noka while she was sorting through the mail. Between the tithing money coming in, the general business of being a hugely wealthy family with fingers in lots of pies, and issues that pertained to the supernatural community, mail sorting was actually something entrusted only to the most high-level staff members.

She smiled at me as I came in, and held up a beautifully embossed invitation. "Any interest in a black-tie charity dinner, Fort?" she asked. "Just five thousand dollars a plate."

I snorted. "Suze will have to content herself with going to the movies and paying for her own ticket." I glanced over the invite. "But put it at the top of Chivalry's pile. He loves those things, and it'll perk him up when he finally comes back."

Loren's face was very professionally neutral, but there was no hiding that she knew the extent to which things were backing up. She tacitly said nothing, just putting the embossed invitation to one side.

"Loren, you know where the files on witches who want to change residence are, right?"

She nodded. "That was something that your brother would generally go over every quarter or so with your mother, but of course I know where they are." She paused. "Did you want to see them?"

"If you have a moment, I'd appreciate it."

Loren looked a bit surprised, but, with that incredible professional decorum, she restrained herself from asking any questions as she led me to a corner filing cabinet and pulled open a drawer. The files were as carefully organized as everything else in the office (clearly Loren would tolerate nothing less), but there was no hiding it — there were a *lot* of requests for movement, and judging by the dates listed, not much of an effort to get timely responses back to people.

After taking a minute to walk me through the system they were using, Loren politely excused herself and left to head back to her own personal workstation in the smaller support office that had previously been the mansion's music room, back in the days before radio, when entertainment had either been hired in or the family had suffered through Prudence's very tortured piano playing. (In fairness, Chivalry was just as weak on the harp.)

I sorted through the files. Luckily for me, they were organized by intended location, so I just flipped my way over to the P section and began poking around. Lots of students trying to get to college, and individual witches who had just been forced to leave the family group because they'd hit the age of twenty-two, and were trying to get to a city that could promise potential work plus livable rates of rent. None of those were what I needed, so I continued sorting until I'd pulled out the files for the families that were trying to move here. What I was hoping for was a family that had already had their application in, so that I could just get Chivalry to approve it, then shove through paperwork for Ambrose and his family that put them in the newly created opening wherever the other family was from. It certainly wasn't ideal, but I was pretty certain that Ambrose would take a blind move over possible death by elfling, even if it meant moving to Bangor.

There were three in total, and once I was sure that I had all of them, I pulled out my phone and called Valentine. He picked up immediately, and I could hear him apologizing his way out of an appointment. As soon as he gave me the okay to talk, I read through the list of families who had official requests in. Pulling open each folder further, though, revealed that all of them had already received some attention—on the second page, next to biographical information, was a clear stamp—LOCATION AT CAPACITY.

"What the hell?" I muttered. "This isn't just backlog."

"How big are the families that were trying to come in?" Valentine asked.

I checked. "Um. . . . smallest one has five members. Two adults, one dependent elder, two children."

"Yeah, the cities are hard to get into. If you're born in Boston, say, you get grandfathered in, but the old quotas for how many witches can live in an area were set over two hundred years ago, and they don't exactly reflect current population density, or the growth of the witch population, or even that we just don't stick out as very weird anymore, especially in cities. A lot of people end up in the suburbs or rural spots and having pretty long commutes, even though we actually are a bit more at risk for exposure in little communities where our neighbors get to know us too well." Valentine paused. "I can see what you're trying to do, Fort, but isn't there any way to just convince your brother or sister to do an emergency approval of moving Ambrose and his family? I know that there are lots of open spots in Manitoba." From Valentine's tone, that was a fate preferable to death—but not by much.

"Asking them to actually agree with me on something is not exactly going to work, especially today," I said grimly. I paused and considered the files, flipping around. Behind the transfer requests was the overall listing of witch locations, divided by town and city, with a precise number of residents beside each name.

Numbers. Not who, just the total. I could feel the seed of an idea start tugging at my brain. I paused, felt at the edges of it. Trying to do anything behind my siblings' back had an element of danger to it, especially with witches, who my sister was always eager to kill. But if I could do this in a way that kept it completely under the radar from her, and never produced a paper trail that she'd notice, it would be safe. Or at least, as safe as it could be.

"Valentine," I asked, "do you know a family of three that would be okay with moving to Providence? Or even just three people from the same town who would be okay with moving? Doesn't matter if they live together, they just need to be from the same location."

"Oh . . . so like a swap?"

"Exactly. Three people come into Providence, at the

same time that three people from Providence replace their number from the origin location. If we do it fast, then the reported numbers won't change at all, and no one at the top over here will even register that something happened."

"Let me think. . . ."

I could hear a rustling of paper over at Valentine's end, and pictured him shifting through piles of notes.

"Oh, okay, here's something. I was talking to a young couple in northern Vermont. New baby, and they lost the primary income a couple of months ago and haven't been able to replace it. Things are pretty sluggish up there. They would like to move to an urban area, but they haven't even bothered putting in a transfer request because they knew they weren't going to get it."

"Family of three, Vermont, perfect. What's the name?" I wrote it down quickly. "Listen, I need you to call them right now. They can come to Providence, but it has to happen right now. We're going to switch these two families, and everyone needs to be in their new area by tomorrow morning. Tell everyone to pack just the things that they need—fill up their cars, rent a trailer, I don't care, but they're on the road. They can stay wherever the other family was living while they figure out other housing. If they're going to sell, go somewhere else, all those details can wait, and they'll finish the packing for the other family."

"I know that Ambrose and his wife will do this, but . . ." Valentine hesitated. "I can't promise things for the Vermont couple. This is pretty sudden, and they don't have a death threat like Ambrose heating things up."

"Then you need to call them up and convince them," I said, knowing that I was being a hard-ass here but knowing no other way. "This is their one chance to get to a city, and I'll be honest, this offer probably won't be on the table tomorrow. If they want to move, it has to be now."

"They'll want to hear this from you, Fort. They'll need a Scott's confirmation, beyond what I'm saying."

"Give them my number, then. When they call, I'll tell them myself. Now get this moving—everyone needs to be hitting the road either tonight or in the wee hours tomorrow, and we need to do this as quietly as we can."

I knew that Valentine was mulling it over, that this wasn't what he'd expected, but when he said, "Okay. I'll make the call," I knew that he would make it happen.

We exchanged good-byes and hung up. I wrote down the names of both families, then swallowed hard. I'd had adrenaline in my favor when I told Valentine what to do, but now I had to do my part, and hope that things worked. Because if they didn't, I knew that I'd have both my siblings breathing down my necks, and both Ambrose and the Neighbors would have a lot more attention focused on them then they could really afford right now.

I went to Loren's desk, where she was working at her computer. One of the human accountants was out of the room, and the other had on a set of seventies-style vintage headphones and was apparently rocking her spreadsheets out to Black Sabbath, judging by the portions of sound that I could hear even across the room. Taking advantage of the momentary privacy, I handed Loren the paper with both names on it.

"Loren," I said softly, looking her directly in the eye and hoping that what I'd seen in her during the trip down to the succubi was something real. "I need you to swap these two witch files. Off the books, just move the files." If the files had solely been print, then I would've done it myself, but there were backup lists on the computers that were used to make up the tithing lists and bills that the accountants handled, and she would almost certainly notice if I started trying to mess around with those with all the grace and subtlety of a water buffalo in a marsh.

She stared at me. "Off the books?" she asked slowly.

I nodded, my heart pounding in my chest. I could see her hesitation, and her very real worry. She knew who she worked for—she'd probably been one of the staff members who had made arrangements for the bodies on the night that Madeline died, with those most faithful of her retainers. Loren knew exactly what was at stake—for all her years of dedicated service, all the extent to which we relied on her to keep things running smoothly, just one careless blow from Prudence and she would break.

She inclined her head, just once. "Of course, Mr. Scott," she said, her voice shaking just a fraction as she spoke. "I'll handle it right now, and you can rely on me."

"Thank you," I said, relief palpable in my voice. "It's really important. You know that I'd never ask you if it—"

"I know," she said, cutting me off. She glanced quickly around the room, taking in her office mate's complete distraction, then looked back at me. "You can trust that it will be taken care of immediately." Then, worry breaking into her expression and made all the more shocking for how controlled she normally was, she said, quickly and nervously, "But you know that this can't be usual. There are too many things—"

This time I was the one to cut her off, nodding. "I know. I know that. And I'll tell Prudence and Chivalry about the switch—eventually. After it's settled and everyone is safe. It'll be easier then, to just agree with what was done, rather than have to actually agree to do something."

As I walked out of the room, I really hoped that was true.

The temperature continued to plunge throughout the day, leaving any snow that had partially melted at some point or been turned to slush by passing cars or feet to freeze into the kind of ice that caused sidewalk falls and multiple car pileups. Between the weather and the fact that it was Thursday, the scene at Redbones after we opened for business started dead and pretty much stayed that way, with our few customers consisting primarily of extremely drunk frat guys from the local colleges, who, fortunately for me, were in the "I love you, man" oversize-puppy state of inebriation, which made them easy to handle. After my long days at the mansion, there was an odd sense of comfort in my evenings at Redbones. Sure, I was filling snack baskets and sprinkling sawdust on vomit, but I was at least *accomplishing* something.

I wondered if that said something awful about the current state of Scott family affairs.

Hoshi sauntered into the bar a few hours in, but was quickly eyeing up the goods in the bar with a distinct air of dissatisfaction.

"I thought the blond was working out?" I asked as I delivered her gin and tonic.

She shook her head sadly. "I had to eliminate him from the running after I found a copy of *Atlas Shrugged* on his bedside table."

I paused, and considered. "You know that enjoying Ayn Rand isn't genetic, right?"

That earned me a horrified glare. "Why would I potentially risk my future daughter's health and safety, Fort?" She shook her head, sending her curly hair flying. "Jeez, think these things through."

At just past eight, with the bar continuing to empty out, I headed into the back room to officially freshen up some snack baskets, and unofficially to escape the frat boy who had apparently been dumped recently and was currently working out his feelings by singing a whole lot of Adele songs, badly. After a quick glance out the door to make sure that no one was looking like they were trying to get table service, I walked over to where my heavy parka was hanging and pulled my phone out of its pocket. I'd long since learned that as a bar waiter I had too many drinks spilled on me in the course of an evening to risk keeping my phone in my apron pocket.

Pulling open the phone, I was surprised to see that Lilah had tried calling me over a dozen times since my shift started. I didn't bother to listen to her messages, just called her back while checking out the back door porthole to make sure that Orlando wasn't looking in my direction. For once, luck was with me, and I could see that the frat boys had apparently reached the point in the evening where they thought it would be hilarious to order a whole tray of elaborate girlie drinks, which would keep my boss well occupied for a while.

Lilah picked up on the first ring. "What's going—" was as far as I managed to get.

"Fort," she said urgently. "Cole's moving tonight. I talked with him this morning, and I thought that things were fine, but someone tipped me off that he called a meeting without me, a meeting that only the three-fourth mixes were invited to, and that he's going to take a small group over to the witch's house and kill him."

"Shit," I said with feeling. "What the hell is he thinking?"

"He's rolling the dice that Prudence won't care if he kills a witch, and that even if you do, it won't make a difference." She paused, then said, "Fort, my sister is in the group, and she isn't answering my calls."

"Okay, I'll handle it," I promised. "Stay where you are and don't get involved."

I hung up and cursed. Pacing the room, I immediately called Valentine and filled him in on what was developing.

There was no hiding Valentine's anxiety. "I checked on Ambrose earlier—they packed one car, and their son is driving that up now, but Ambrose and Carolina were still packing the second car, and they said they didn't expect to be done until at least after midnight. Listen, I'm at a patient's house right now in Boston, so I'll leave now, but it's going to take me at least forty minutes to get there."

"Crap." I gave a pile of neatly stacked plastic food baskets an irritated shove. "How did they even find out where he lives?" I asked, frustrated.

". . . . well, probably the Internet. His address is on his Web site."

"What?" Once again, technology coming around to bite us in the butt. I momentarily longed for the days when people had been reduced to rooting through the phone book. If the *Terminator* movie had happened today, Sarah Connor would've been dead.

Valentine was still talking. "His wife does Reiki massages out of their house, and Ambrose has been helping out a little since he lost the work with Leamaro. I know that they've updated the Web site, so—"

"Shit, fine, okay, it doesn't even matter. You call them up right now and tell them that they're hitting the road—I don't care what they have to leave behind. They're in that car and driving in two minutes. Text me the damn address. I'll go right over."

"Okay, but, Fort, the Vermont couple is already heading down, and they're going to need to stay in that house for a month at least. If the elves are—"

I could see what Valentine's concern was on this, and I cut him off, grimly. "They can keep coming. I'm going to make sure that everyone knows that the witches are not fair game. Now text me the address. I need to get going." I hung up, and Valentine's text came through almost immediately. In the first break I'd caught in a while, it turned out that Ambrose lived in the College Hill neighborhood, in an area that I actually recognized. I forwarded the text to Suze, then typed out "if you want to punch someone, MEET ME HERE RIGHT NOW" and hit SEND, figuring that would get her moving faster than anything else.

Now came the undeniably sucky part. I pulled off my waist apron and yanked on my jacket, and hurried out of the back room at double pace. A few of the frat guys were starting to look around in a way that I immediately recognized as the classic "searching for waiter" presentation, and I hustled over to the table where Hoshi was currently enthroned, pouting over the fact that the tabletop was only half-filled with the drinks that other people had bought her.

I shoved my waist apron into her hands. "Listen, Hoshi, I need you to cover the rest of my shift."

"Wait, what—"

"No, seriously. You can tell Orlando that I quit, but I need to go and protect some witches, and I just don't have time for him to scream at me. Tell him that I'll send someone over to get my last check."

Recovering much faster than I would've given her credit for, Hoshi shot back, "I get all your tips from tonight."

"What—Jesus, Hoshi, I'm just trying not to be a complete dick and leave Orlando with no waitstaff, not actually—"

"And whatever you'll be paid for tonight."

"*Oh my God, woman*—you know what, fine, just fine." I realized that any extension of this conversation would just end even worse for my wallet, and I ran out the door. As the door swung shut behind me, I finally attracted Orlando's attention, and I could hear him bellowing my name behind me.

I'd had a lot of ignominious ends to employment, but this was definitely breaking my Top Five.

Thirty minutes later, Suze and I were waiting in Ambrose's tiny two-story house, hedged in on both its sides by identical homes on equally postage stamp lawns. I'd arrived in time to tell Ambrose and his wife that, no, they really and truly had to hit the road now, and could not put fresh sheets on the bed for the couple driving down, and I didn't care how late it would probably be before they arrived. Carolina was apparently one of those dyed-in-the-wool nurturers who was also slightly skewed in where she put her priorities, and so the emergency rush out the door had also been slowed by her insistence that they go up in the attic and bring down their own children's old crib for the Vermont couple. Whether this was a common witch trait or that this was just a woman who Darwinism somehow missed, I didn't know or care, just promised her faithfully that, yes, I would keep an eye on the pie that she had going in the oven while she and her husband fled from the people coming to kill him.

Suzume showed up, lured by the possibility of violence, and together we shut off all the lights in the house and waited, me by the back door, her manning the front, for the attack to come.

After all the creeping around, I was alerted to the incipient danger when I heard Suze bitching loudly from the front hallway. "Idiots. Fort, you've got to come see this. They're going full lynch mob here. Just coming up to the front door! This is completely amateur-hour."

I came up behind her and looked out the pane of glass set in the middle of the front door, coated with those faux stained glass decals that were sold down at hardware stores. Sure enough, there was Cole, at the head of a phalanx of seven other people, whose features in the light from the neighbor's motion-activated deck light were just off enough that it was clear that we were dealing with almost entirely three-fourths Neighbors. "Suze—"

She was too busy being offended on the part of murderers everywhere to listen to me, and continued. "If I was going to murder someone in their home? Full-out fucking fox ninja actions. I'd wait in the bathroom, kill whoever was first in there with a garrote so there'd be no noise, then I'd hide in the tub with the curtain drawn and wait for them to find the body. I'd wait for them to scream, then I'd jump out and stab them. Then for the third—"

"Wow, can we just stop right there, Suze, and be really grateful that elf gene sociopathy apparently doesn't include crazy murder planning?" She leveled a glare at me, still very annoyed. I sighed heavily, wondering exactly how my night had come to this point. "Yes, Suzume, you're the greatest that there is, and no one else can possibly hold a candle to your badassery."

"Damn straight." She nodded, and finally settled down enough to focus on the actual situation. "Now, how do you want to deal with—"

I walked out the door and onto the porch, while behind me I could hear her say, "Oh, so you're just going to do that. Well, okay. Straightforward it is."

The Neighbors had made it about halfway up the brick walkway, hemmed in at either side by about half a foot of crusted snow, and while some looked a little uncertain when I walked out, Cole's shining white face was unmistakable, as was the rage that burned in his dark purple eyes.

His mouth twisted as he realized who must've told me what had been planned. "Lilah—"

"Is the appointed liaison to the Scott family," I warned him, my voice so cold that I almost didn't even recognize myself—I sounded too much like my own family in that moment, but it was what was necessary to keep these idiots alive, so I accepted it. "I'd be very careful what you say, and what you do. And right now she's got a much better sense of wise moves to make."

Cole sneered. "Like the Scotts care if a witch dies."

I could hear the sound of Suzume's boot heels as she

walked up behind me, and knew that I could only hear them because she wanted me to. "Of course they wouldn't, Legolas," she said disdainfully. "But they probably care a lot about Neighbors killing with impunity—if you broke a plate that Prudence Scott hated, she wouldn't give a damn about the plate, but she'd rip you apart for daring to break something that she owned."

"Ambrose is gone," I warned them, but it was all too obvious from the group dynamics who was the ring-leader. All those faces with their strange bone structure—the kind you'd see on runway models or CGI characters that looked just wrong enough to give you the shivers—were sneaking glances over at Cole, looking at him for what would happen next, grateful that he was there to talk with me. And after they'd give him a long look, they'd turn back to face me and Suze, and all that nervousness would be gone again, replaced with righteous anger and certainty—for a minute. Then they'd have to look back at Cole again. "And I'm telling you now—don't you dare try to find him or go after him."

"So he gets away with it?"

I didn't like Cole, but there was no doubt in my mind that the rage in his voice right now was real.

"With what he did? With what happened because of him?"

He saw the answer in my face, and his anger carried him forward across the two feet that separated us. He was throwing a punch before I think he even knew that it was what he wanted to do, but it was coming anyway, and faster than any human could've been. But I was fast as well now, with speed that might've been the slowest of any vampire on the continent, but it was full vampire speed now. I moved away, dodging enough that I was only lightly clipped in the shoulder instead of smacked in the mouth. I realized as it happened that it was probably a good thing that I'd moved rather than tried to block in the boxing manner that Chivalry had taught me, because I could feel the power behind that punch, and it was more than a human's, and more than that of any other Neighbor that I'd ever encountered, even on the night that we'd fought against the handpicked loyalists of the Ad-hene.

But I'd gone through my transition, and almost all of what had kept me human had burned away with Henry's death. I got a hand on Cole's shirt collar and gave him a shake hard enough to make his head snap forward, but it wasn't enough to make him think twice, and then we were locked close in a scuffle, hands kept low enough by our proximity that we were landing short, shallow punches to each other's ribs, without enough room to maneuver. I gave a sudden shift, enough to get room to swing my elbow up fast and pop Cole in the nose with enough force that blood came pouring out.

I wouldn't have been able to do that a month ago. Before my transition, Cole would've been too fast, too strong, to inhuman for me to keep up with. But now we were almost evenly matched, and I didn't know if it was the old me or the new me, or both, that felt that thrill and triumph when blood that was just slightly not red flowed out of Cole's nose.

All of this had taken mere seconds, too fast for others to be reacting, and it was only then that the other Neighbors reached us and were yanking Cole back and away, all of them straining to hold him as he pulled forward, trying to get at me. For a second, my own blood churning, nothing but a roaring sound in my ears, I took a step forward, but then Suze's hand was around my wrist, urging me back and reminding me what was happening and where I was. I looked at the Neighbors urging Cole back and saw the unmistakable brilliance of Lilah's sister Iris's hair, like a newly shined copper teapot, and looked at her inhuman face. It calmed me, reminded me why

Cole was doing all these things, and for just a second I felt regret.

"Cole," I said loudly, but staying exactly where I was, "I don't think Ambrose shouldn't have some kind of accounting. I'll talk with Lilah. Then I'll talk with my siblings—"

"And nothing will happen," the elf scion said harshly, his eyes brighter in the darkness than they should've been, his skin gleaming with that otherworldly hue that seemed to suggest that the moonlight was seeking him out specifically. He stared at me, and I could see his anger, but also his despair. "You can't make promises for Prudence and Chivalry. Neither of them will give a shit, so whatever you say now to make it seem like you want to help us, you know exactly what I know—this won't go anywhere."

He was right, and we both knew it, and everything seemed to drain out of us in the long minute that we stared at each other, leaving just dull emptiness behind. Then he turned and began walking away. Behind him the Neighbors glanced between us before falling, one by one, into line behind him.

I started to go after him, not even knowing what I would say, just that I had to try to at least say something, but then Iris stepped into my path, blocking me. She put out one hand, unmittened and painfully pale in the cold night air, coming within a hairbreadth of touching my chest for just a second, then jerking back before she could touch me with as much aversion as if she'd just been burned.

"Don't worry about my sister," she said quickly, quietly. "Cole will be pissed, but none of us would hurt her." Her mouth pressed together and she pressed those pale fingers against her own face, almost yanking at her own skin as she looked at me with eyes that were far too empty. "I know why she told you. She says that we have to be careful to make decisions based on what all of us need."

A deep, painful pity filled me, reminding me of my own helplessness in this situation, looking at a young woman who had been so deeply betrayed by the ones who should've been fighting the hardest to protect her, instead just trying to turn her into a vessel to be used. For the barest of seconds I could almost understand why Cole would be desperate to continue to find targets for the young women like Iris, rather than have to face that feeling of helplessness. "I know you want Ambrose to pay, but I can't let you kill him," I said, as very gently as I could. Then, seeing nothing in her face, I continued. "Lilah already told me that you killed the Neighbors who knew, the ones who were helping the Ad-hene."

For just a second, Iris's glamour flickered, and I caught a glimpse of her inhumanly golden eyes with those long, reptilian slits, and the true brilliance of her hair before it was covered again by that hazy illusion. "You're like Lilah—she asked me when there would be enough blood for me to start healing." Anger flicked across her mask-like face, tied to hurt, painfully real and human. "She told me that killing Ambrose wouldn't help me, or any of us, and that if it would've, then she would've found a way to let us do it. She promised, and I believe her."

"What would help, then?" I asked softly.

Even with the illusion, there was no hiding how very eerie the expression in her eyes was, as her face emptied entirely. "Killing the ones who are really responsible, of course." Then she turned and left, disappearing into the darkness, following the others.

As I looked out into the darkness of the little residential neighborhood, spotted up and down the road with its identical houses, Suze stepped up beside me. "You know who she really means, of course," she said, her tone conversational.

"The Ad-hene. And can you blame her?"

Suze tucked her hands into the front pockets of her thin fleece jacket, and tilted her head to one side, considering the question for a moment. "Nope. Not one bit." She gave a loose shrug, then nudged me playfully in the side, somehow managing to avoid all the places where Cole had connected, which were already, now that the adrenaline had filtered out of me, making their presence known in a dim, annoyed way. "Nice moves there with Cole, Fort. I got so proud when you tried to dodge that punch."

"Oh, is that why you just stood there?"

"You were handling things," she said calmly. She looked pensively up at the moon. "Real bummer about the karaoke job. If all you're drawing for cash is that couch money you get for doing Scott work, then I guess you'll have to take your trust-fund stipend this month. Of course, with the way things are going with the territory right now, I guess this is more your job anyway, right?"

"I don't want to talk about it," I grumbled. I would almost welcome another rumble with mixed-breed elf offspring if it meant that I could continue not having to think of the amount of crow that I might end up eating regarding my financial situation.

There was just the barest hint of sympathy on Suze's face when she looked at me. "We all have to get real jobs eventually, Fort. No one can do shitty postgrad jobs forever."

Another long pause passed as we both pondered that nearly philosophical statement, until it was broken by Suze's sudden, extremely annoyed realization. "Hey! I didn't get to punch a single damn elfling!"

Like my own personal *Groundhog Day*, the next morning found me back in the drawing room of the mansion, having what felt like the same conversation with my siblings, as useful as digging holes on the beach right at the wave line.

"This entire territory is a powder keg waiting to blow, and we're not doing a damn thing!" I yelled.

"You are overstating things, Fortitude," my brother said mildly, leaning back into one of the leather armchairs and steepling his fingers, looking very much the captain of industry this morning. "Last night's situation proves that our system is working entirely adequately, despite recent pressures. You defused and dispersed the Neighbors, and by taking the action of switching the witch families, you managed to clear up the whole problem."

Prudence's response was significantly less mild, as she practically did a spit-take into the cup of distinctly Irish coffee that she was nursing. "Chivalry, how can you think that? We nearly had an interspecies brawl in the middle of Providence. What we should be doing right now is stringing up enough bodies that the races focus on preserving their lives and stop causing trouble—I suggest we start with everyone involved in this sordid little incident, and then just expand from there. I doubt anyone would be crying over the loss of a few witches and elf brats."

"Prudence, are your suggestions ever *not* based on mass murder?" I asked with biting sarcasm. "What we need to be doing is figuring out a way to actually address the underpinning issues that are coming up here, rather than waiting for things to boil over so that I have to quit my job and run around the city putting out fires."

At the update about my employment status, my brother looked extremely pleased. "See? That's yet another good thing that came out of last night's fracas. Fort, by quitting that demeaning excuse for employment, you can finally fully focus on the business of the family rather than busing tables and folding napkin swans."

"As thrilled as I am that one of our family is no longer debasing himself for minimum wage," Prudence interjected in icy tones, "I'm not as sure about the directions that Fort is putting his efforts. You certainly did not ask for our agreement when you went ahead and validated travel plans for two sets of witches."

Tempers were on edge all around the table, and I glared at my sister. "If I'd brought it up, then we'd still be sitting here arguing, and there would be bodies on the ground. And not even ones that you put there, Prudence."

Chivalry had apparently decided to try to put his walkout from yesterday's meeting entirely behind him, since he frowned at both of us. "Prudence, I have to side with Fort on this one. He found a way to work within the existing system—our population quotas remain entirely undisturbed, yet the witches are probably more content today than they were yesterday. If anything, our brother had a stroke of brilliance, and we should put someone on the task of implementing this idea of location switching as part of our overall system. Perhaps we can ask Loren about the possibility of a Web site."

I broke in before the train to Delusionville could leave the station. "That's just another Band-Aid, Chivalry. And if we want to talk about things that could actually use a discussion from the group, *Prudence*, then how about the succubi who are still in complete limbo down in New Jersey?"

My sister's monumental irritation with me was clearly evident as I brought up one of the least favorite subjects yet again. "Yes indeed, a group that will bring us all trouble and no income. The last thing we actually need, given that when I popped my head in to check on the accountants this morning, one of them informed me that one of the primary ghoul businesses completely missed its final quarter tithe payment."

Chivalry lifted his eyebrows. "Well, that's rather a surprise. The ghouls are usually so reliable about those things."

Prudence made a small moue, as if she expected so little from any of the other races that she was incapable of being surprised over yet another failure. "I'll go over today and get the money, and remind them about their duties while I'm at it." And from the look in her eyes, there was no doubting about what form her "reminder" was going to come in.

"No, Prudence, I'll go over and talk with them," I said quickly, hoping to derail the one-woman traveling production of *The Clockwork Orange* level of ultraviolence.

Temper flashed across her face. "If this territory is a powder keg, as you've just claimed, then perhaps our residents need to be reminded why it is a poor idea to cause troubles—and right here at hand is an excellent opportunity to set an example."

I refused to be deterred. "Prudence, you're going to go straight in there and start ripping people apart. This isn't a business that has missed payments in the past. Well, that suggests to me that this should be handled by talking—"

Clearly yet another reference to talking was enough to break her control entirely, and she half rose from her sofa, her voice heading for the rafters. "Little brother, you are—"

"*Hush*, both of you," Chivalry snapped loudly, startling both of us into a momentary pause. He nodded at our result. "Good. Sister, we might as well send Fortitude over there and see if we can get the money owed the soft way. For one thing, the forecast today is for very sunny skies, enough that I was planning to stay inside, so you will definitely be unable to drive up to Providence in any comfort at all until at least the late afternoon, and by then our brother could already have gone up and ascertained the lay of the land, so to speak. If our brother is able to sort this out his way, then he has saved you a trip, and if not, you wouldn't be getting up there any earlier anyway."

Prudence did not look remotely appeased by his logic, but a glance at the sun streaming through the windows had her reluctantly acknowledging the truth of it. "And I notice that you are showing no interest at all in undertaking this yourself?" she asked pointedly.

"Certainly," he replied, looking not even remotely sorry. "Simone was just employed to guide a group of hikers up Mount Washington next week, and I would far rather spend some additional time with her than listen to excuses about how the check is in the mail or some idiocy like that."

Prudence made a wordless sound of frustration. "You are always the same in your honeymoon period, Chivalry, do you realize this?"

My brother flinched at her comment, and his expression was profoundly insulted. "There's no reason to be rude, sister. Simone is an utter delight, and if you would just make an effort to get to know her, I'm sure that you—"

She cut him off with a gesture, then swept her cutting gaze over both of us. "I hope that you are not as dense as you are attempting to appear, brother, and that you are realizing what I am more than certain that Fortitude has already long comprehended."

Chivalry's expression changed between one breath and the next, his eyes suddenly very dangerous, and in that moment I was abruptly reminded that my sister was not the only predator in the room. "And what is that, my darling sister?" he asked, his voice very low.

"That despite all of Mother's hopes, and all the vows she made us swear, this *is not working*."

For a long second, no one even dared to breathe, even Prudence, at what had been said. A muscle in my brother's cheek twitched, just once, and he got up, very silently and deliberately, and walked out of the room for the second day in a row.

I looked at my sister. I agreed with her, but we were coming at this whole situation from such polar opposite directions that it didn't even seem to matter that we were meeting at this point—it was just the happenstance intersection of two lines that would otherwise have nothing else in common. Frankly, that we were agreeing at this point seemed like a pretty bad thing. I got up and slowly began to head out myself, saying to her as I went, "I'll get the tithe information from the accountants, and I'll drive up—" Just outside the door, I froze. Sitting patiently on a small chair in the hallway was Jon Einarsson, reading a copy of *Wired* magazine, looking like he was in a doctor's waiting room. I hadn't seen Jon since the day that Prudence invited him to her town house in order to use him as a live feeding example for me. He still had that fit and square-jawed appearance of a former college athlete that no amount of legal education could completely exorcise, but there was a slight change in his pallor. Perhaps no one who didn't know what they were looking for would've seen it, but while Jon was still blond and handsome, there was a hint of sickness to him, an air of vulnerability that hadn't existed a month before. Being my sister's source of fresh human blood was taking its toll on him.

He caught sight of me, and set his magazine down immediately. "Fort!" he said cheerfully, and reached out to give my hand a firm shake. "Good to see you doing well!"

"Yeah . . . so, are you here to see my sister?" Inwardly I cringed a little—somehow that felt even more awkward than if he'd been my sister's hired gigolo.

"Oh, Prudence asked me to come by today," he said, that friendly smile almost welded into place.

Behind me, Prudence emerged from the room, looking very pleased with the situation, her previous irritation set aside. "Jon, punctual as always," she complimented him. "Yes, I was wondering if you'd be willing to let my brother drink your blood today."

"What?" I squawked, taking an automatic step backward.

Jon's eyes never left Prudence's face. She'd tricked him into ingesting some of her blood, which at her age created a powerful sense of unwavering loyalty in his regard of her. It was a frightening, insidious thing, which made him so willing to give up all sense of self-preservation and allow her to feed on him, and even hide the evidence of it from anyone else in his life as she slowly killed him, one bite at a time. "Oh, if that's what you'd like, Prudence," he said, as if she'd asked him to let me borrow a pen, rather than open up a vein. "It doesn't seem like it would be a problem."

"Prudence," I started, then looked at Jon's open, friendly expression, and just couldn't take it. I grabbed my sister by the elbow and towed her to the other side of the hallway, then turned my back to Jon and hissed, "Prudence, what exactly are you doing here?"

She looked at me very seriously. "Little brother, you will need to drink from the vein very soon to maintain your health, so why not do so with Jon? He is present, and I have already made certain of his loyalty, which you will be unable to do with your own victims for many years yet."

My sister was never more terrifying to me than when she was showing her affection. I knew that, in this instance, there was no ulterior motive—that her primary concern was for my physical well-being. It made me want to vomit, but I forced myself to be calm as I answered, "I appreciate the offer, but I'm going to handle this in my own way."

She sighed, the perfect image of a put-upon sister with a bratty little brother. "I wish you wouldn't be so stubborn." Her expression turned sympathetic. "And how are your teeth today? I know that Chivalry was looking around online for remedies, and purchased some kind of small terry cloth octopus that can be put right into the freezer for when you—"

"No, no, I don't even want to know. I'll talk with you later." I turned and left.

As I walked away, I could hear Jon ask Prudence, "Well, if he isn't interested, would *you* like to drink my blood today?" and hurried my steps so that I couldn't hear her response.

After collecting the tithing files from the accountants, and double-checking the location of the ghoul-owned business in question, I drove up to Providence and picked Suzume up from the downtown area, where she'd just wrapped up a business lunch on behalf of her grandmother.

"Was this one of *those* business lunches?" I asked her as she carefully maneuvered herself into the Scirocco. All I could see of her was a long black wool coat that came down to the tops of her calves, and a pair of black stockings ending in a pair of perfectly acceptable business pumps, but I could tell from her movements that she was almost certainly wearing her usual business uniform of a knee-length pencil skirt and a silk blouse.

"Silly vampire," she said affectionately. "I told you that Midori got the short straw and is doing client interviews now. That was a meeting with the state attorney general about how happy Green Willow Escorts will be to make a sizable donation to his campaign fund when he announces his candidacy for the Senate in a few months."

I snorted. "Another great example of money in politics."

"Don't be grouchy," she replied. "Look, I even brought you my leftovers." She held up a leftovers box. "Scallops!" Withdrawing a napkin from her pocket, she unrolled it to reveal a clean fork, then popped open the top of her container and was in moments holding out a forkful of incredibly decadent-smelling scallop to me.

I was admittedly kind of hungry, so after I had merged the car safely back into traffic, I leaned over and begrudgingly ate the bite she was holding out to me. It was delicious. "I'm surprised you aren't taunting me with surf and turf," I grumbled as I chewed. "That's what you used to always go for when someone with deep pockets was footing the bill."

"I normally would've," she agreed, "but I got your text about going to shake down the ghouls right before I ordered, and given where we're going to end up going, even for me it seemed like a good day to avoid red meat."

I made a face and had to agree.

The era of the local butcher shop—where professional butchers took huge sides of meat that were delivered to them directly from the slaughterhouses and broke them down themselves for customers, able to answer any and all questions about the meat in question—was one of the sad casualties of the modern big-box grocery store, where precut, packaged, and frozen meats were shipped in from hundreds of miles away to be thawed and presented for sale by glorified stocking clerks. The small butcher shops that remained were fighting the long defeat against an opponent that would always be able to undercut them on price, and whatever edge the butcher shop had in terms of customer service or basic competence was invariably lost when customers weighed that against the ability to also be able to buy eggs, panty hose, laundry detergent, and just-released DVDs while they waited for their order to be put together.

The butcher shop that we entered was one of this dying breed. With no frills or shiny pizzazz, it nevertheless had a long and gleaming selection of meats, and the chalkboard that ran the entire length of the counter showed a rather staggering breadth of both meats and cheeses. Looking over the counter gave the customer a full view of the three men currently working. One was breaking down meat from the full half of a cow into specific cuts to be sold, another was mixing ground meat in a large bowl, and a third was at the slicer making deli cuts. The only woman was standing at the counter, waiting on an elderly customer, but from her red-flecked apron, she was also no stranger to the butcher's knife.

If I hadn't known that this shop was owned and entirely staffed by ghouls, and that some of the offal meat that was cut, ground, or sliced on those workstations was from animals that had walked on two legs, I probably would've bought as much cheese as my budget could allow out of the sheer desire to express solidarity for the locally owned store. As it was, of course, I had to work to keep my stomach under tight control. Even living with Dan couldn't shake me of the feeling that it was just kind of gross to eat human organs.

I was aware of what a hypocrite that made me, given my very regular consumption of human blood smoothies (the crushed ice and fruit didn't exactly improve the flavor, but it did distract me a little more than when I warmed it). However, that didn't make it any less true.

The ghouls knew who I was. From that mixture of outright terror and pants-wetting relief that crossed each of their faces, it was also clear that they'd known this visit was coming, and that they were aware just how lucky they were that I was the one to show up rather than my sister. I'd never exactly wanted a reputation—frankly, I'd spent most of my life just trying to fade into the background of almost every situation I was in—but I'd apparently, despite my best efforts, secured one for myself. Fortitude Scott—Holy Shit, We're Glad You're Not Your Sister.

Suze and I were hustled immediately to the back room, given the nicest seats, and then spent the next half hour trying to get everyone to stop promising speedy repayment and repeating babbled apologies so that we could actually figure out what was going on. After they finally caught on that—just as they'd barely even dared to hope—I wasn't planning on using my sister's method of persuasion, they calmed down enough that I could get them to actually walk me through the background.

What finally came out was that a year earlier, a large supermarket chain had bought up some defunct warehouse just one street over from the butcher shop, and had announced plans to raze the old building and construct a beautiful new grocery store with an emphasis on environmentally sustainable practices, excellent foods, wide varieties, and, among other things, its own in-store butcher station. Realizing the danger that this posed to their business, the ghouls had sent an appeal to my mother to use her political connections to make certain that the supermarket never moved in. They had received assurances that this would happen and had settled back, certain that Madeline Scott's hands would soon be manipulating the levers of power like a seasoned organ player.

The problem came, however, when that never happened. Why my mother never became involved was unclear, though I wondered if many small items might've begun slipping through the cracks as my mother's health trickled away over the last months, but the ghouls realized too late that Madeline Scott wasn't going to intervene as promised. They attempted a local protest against the plan, and made quite a lot of fuss at city meetings, but they were simply the owners of a small, threatened local business, and without a big and powerful ally in their back pocket, they ended up in the situation of every other small but beloved local business since the beginning of time—steamrollered by the incoming supermarket chain with its very deep pockets and slick advertising campaign.

The supermarket had opened five months ago, and the butcher shop had lost half of its business virtually overnight. At first, the ghouls had put their savings into the shop to try to ride it out, hoping that those who had gone to try out the new supermarket got tired of getting a much lower quality of meat in exchange for a little bit of savings and convenience, and would return to the store. That didn't happen. They had to cut back on some of the variety that the store offered, and lost more customers as a result. They still had the local ghoul population, which relied on the store to break down and distribute the human organ meat that they needed to maintain their health, but the problem there was that the ghoul community treated the human meat as a shared commodity—it was obtained by those who owned funeral homes or worked in professions that gave them access to the organs, then passed along to the butcher shops, then distributed to all the households, all without money changing hands. The ghouls of course did do all their other meat purchases at the stores that were ghoul-owned, but that wasn't enough to offset the loss of the human patronage that had made up such a vast percentage of the customer base.

When the autumn tithe to my family was due, the butcher shop had already been struggling and didn't have the money to pay the bill. They'd turned to others within the community, who had gone around and raised the money by each business and individual household putting forward what they could spare, which had allowed them to get by that time. But when the winter tithe had been due at the end of December, the butcher shop's profits plunged even further, and on top of that the other businesses were facing tight times as well, and hadn't been able to offer an equal amount as in the autumn, leaving the butcher shop owners with a large shortfall to make up. They'd stretched as long as possible, and were in fact in the middle of acquiring a loan, with the owner using his house as collateral.

"That's completely unacceptable," I said bluntly.

"No," the owner said frantically, "if you just give me a few more days—"

"That's not what I mean at all!" I replied. "That grocery store isn't going away, and the last thing that should be done is for the tithe to be the deathblow to your business. No, what I mean is that I'm going to have one of our accountants come up here today, and you're going to go over all your records from the five months since the supermarket came in. The tithe is going to be readjusted to reflect the difference in what is a real-case bottom line in the current market conditions, not what existed before in the best times."

The owner looked at me, so incredibly grateful that it hurt to even see it. "That's amazing, Mr. Scott," he stammered, "and we're so—"

I cut him off, anger filling me. "No," I said. "We dropped the ball on our end, and you've had months of stress and hard decisions as a result. If we hadn't been able to stop the supermarket, then adjustments should've been made to the tithe immediately. So I'm also going to be telling the accountant that you need to be issued a credit for the tithe amount that you essentially overpaid. I also want credits issued to all the businesses and households that put money forward to help you when you almost went under in the autumn."

They stared at me, unable to process what I'd said at first. "You mean," one of the younger men said finally, almost forcing out the words, "that you'll be talking to your family, and that this is your recommendation that—"

"No. This is what's happening, and I'm getting that process started today."

The owner began to cry, fat tears sliding down the deep wrinkles in his face. And I was suddenly surrounded by all four of the ghouls, all of whom were clasping my hands and thanking me in as many ways as they could say it. I nodded, uncomfortable but knowing that they needed to do this, studiously ignoring the expression on Suzume's face.

We didn't leave the butcher shop for several hours, not until Dulce Scarpati, the accountant who was the Black Sabbath fan, had arrived, somewhat surprised at my unexpected call, but well conditioned to follow Scott orders without question, and had made as much headway as she could on the numbers and tithe recalibration for the day. I signed off on everything, making my signature large and unmistakable, the whole time trying to hide from the euphorically relieved ghouls just how unbelievably pissed I was.

Once Suze and I walked back to the car, and were out of sight of both grateful ghouls and a mildly bemused accountant, I tried to get out some aggression by kicking at a wall of iced-over snow that had been created by multiple plowing passes through the parking lot. Suze watched silently as I chipped away at it, not commenting. Finally I felt at least ready to get into the car, if not exactly drive safely, and unlocked the Scirocco.

We sat silently beside each other as the car slowly warmed up. After several minutes, Suze slowly turned to look at me, her face very grim. "So, you know that your family is not exactly going to take this well," she said at last.

"I don't give a shit about them right now," I said through gritted teeth.

Suze continued as if I hadn't spoken. "Even if they end up agreeing with you in the larger sense about reducing the tithe and attempting to keep the business alive in order to maintain a long-term stream of revenue, you should've brought this one back to the group to discuss and agree on."

"We couldn't agree on whether or not to eat ice cream at this point."

"They're going to be pissed, Fort. Pissed at you."

"It doesn't matter," I said, fed up at last. "This is an unsustainable situation, and I know it, Prudence knows it, and Chivalry is trying as hard as he can to not know it." I took a deep breath and looked out the window at the ice and snow for a second, then turned back to Suze. "It's time to just accept what things are, Suze, rather than what we'd like them to be. So that's why I actually did something for the ghouls, even though I know it's going to cause trouble with my family."

Suze watched me steadily. "If that's true, Fort, and how you really feel, then how far does it go?"

I frowned at her. "What do you mean?"

"Your hands are restless when you're listening to someone. Your pupils are wider than they should be. I don't think you even notice it, but I've seen the way that you're tracking all the people around you today." She reached over and touched my arm, very gently. "In another day or so, you'll notice it yourself. But by then you might be getting dangerous."

I wanted to yell that this wasn't true. I wanted to beg for just a little more time. I didn't do either, because she was right. "You're saying that I need to feed," I said, forcing the words out.

"I'm saying," she said, her eyes so brilliantly dark and lovely, so sharp and knowing, "that you need to accept what things are, rather than what you'd like them to be. And accept that it's not your fault that you are what you are."

I couldn't say anything at first, and I just moved my hand over to hers and twined my cold fingers through her warm ones. We sat together, watching the movement of people and cars and the whole city around our tiny oasis of the parked Scirocco.

"Will you help me?" I asked finally.

"You know I will."

"Okay. Then it will be tonight. Before I'm dangerous. Tonight."

It hurt to say it. To lose that last dream and illusion. But this was the path that I'd started down from the moment that a collection of multiplying cells suddenly created a heart that could beat. And after all that fighting and terror, it finally came down to this—that tonight I would feed on a human.

Chapter Nine

We waited until well after nightfall before we went out. It wasn't for solely atmospheric purposes, though it didn't escape my notice that we were going out on a Friday night for the same reasons as muggers and rapists—we were looking for a certain kind of inebriated and potentially vulnerable individual, and it would be easier to get that person alone and unobserved if we waited until most people were well into their third or fourth drink. Also, Suze wanted to have dinner before we headed out, arguing that she did her best work on a full stomach.

It was after ten when we found a parking spot for the Scirocco about two blocks away from one of the revitalized downtown areas where derelict warehouses had been transformed into lofts, boutique shopping, and trendy nightclubs. Given the weather, most people had sprung for the valet services, or had paid up to put their cars in the nearby lots, so there were plenty of spaces available. I took my Colt out from its usual place in my duffel bag and ejected the clip to see how many bullets I had left. I was certain that I had put a full clip in before we'd left the apartment, but my foster father had always emphasized staying in the habit of verifying exactly what was present as often as possible. Just as I'd expected, it was a full clip with eight rounds, and I reloaded it and flicked on the safety. Beside me, Suze gave a loud snort.

"What are we doing, holding someone up at gunpoint, Fort?" she asked derisively. "If so, I forgot to pack my niece's Princess Elsa mask from Halloween."

I put the Colt in my parka pocket and zipped it closed. It was a sizable handgun, but my parka had been a Christmas present from my brother, one of those long, wonderful concoctions of goose down and rainproof material, with a removable hood and at least a dozen pockets of various sizes, one of which was not only long enough and deep enough to contain the Colt and save me from having to fuss with trying to access a hip holster on a knee-length coat, but also didn't even show the shape of what I was carrying. "No, I think we've got a workable plan," I said, "but this is just an insurance policy."

Suze shook her head. "I'm the mastermind behind this plan. Insurance is unnecessary."

I looked at her patiently, making no move to remove the Colt from my pocket. Finally she stuck her tongue out at me and wiggled out of her own jacket, tossing it to me, revealing her sparkly backless club top and black leggings. "Hold that," she instructed. "I'm practically going to be hypothermic when I get back."

We walked together to the club, separating at the front. She strutted up to the entrance and was ushered inside, no cover charge, while I circled around the building until I was at the back door, right beside the Dumpster. It was one of those doors that only opened from the inside, so anyone coming out and intending to get back in would've had to prop it open, but I wasn't worried—after all, no part of this plan involved me actually entering the club. I stood slightly behind the Dumpster, ready to duck behind it if someone just came outside to dump trash or vomit their guts out (which several frozen piles revealed to be a pretty standard activity choice), shifting from one foot to another in the frigid night air. I could hear the muffled thudding of the music's bass line from where I was standing, and it provided a strange counterpoint to the utter stillness around me. Every time I breathed out, I could see the steam of my breath curl in the dim security light on the back door, a small pool of weak light surrounded by the dimness of branching alleys and the complete darkness around several stores that had closed hours ago.

Thirty minutes after Suze entered the club, the back door opened and she emerged, towing a blond college-aged guy built like a defensive linesman. There was a glazed look on his face, and his eyes were tracking strangely, not following either of us, even as I stepped out to meet Suze, but looking at things that weren't there, silently mouthing words and then listening intently as if to another side of a conversation.

"Here," Suze said, looking pleased. The club must've been incredibly hot inside, since there was sweat streaking down her forehead, and for a moment she looked refreshed by the night air rather than frozen. Somewhere she'd acquired a great deal of glitter in her black hair, and between that and the sequins covering her top, she caught and reflected the meager light. "He's the rapeyest one in there."

"What?" I handed Suze her coat before she could start developing frostbite and took over the job of leading the young man away from the club, down the increasingly dark alley to a spot where no one would see and potentially intervene with what was about to happen.

"You're about to take a bit of a nip off his life span, right?" Suze asked, tugging on her coat and zipping it up as she followed us. "Well, I'd personally like to have that happen to an ass-grabber who was trying pretty hard to distract me from my drink, if you know what I mean, and

I'm sure that this will make you feel better as well if you find yourself inclined to postmeal remorse."

I considered for a moment. She was, it had to be said, entirely right, and I was already feeling substantially less guilt over what I was about to do. Actually, taking into consideration that he'd apparently tried to roofie Suzume, I was suddenly feeling rather eager about what was going to happen, even beyond that instinctive part of my brain that was A-okay with everything, so long as it ended with a mouthful of blood on my part. I gave the guy one last yank as we reached a corner, behind some old discarded pallets of wood and trash, where only my sharpened vampire eyes were allowing me to see at all, and our companion was blinking, confused at where the light had gone. "He looks pretty out of it," I noted to Suze. "Will he remember any of this?"

"No." Suze's mouth curled into a very mean smile. "I was touching his skin when I started working on him, and the only person whose perception I'm affecting right now is him—so I'm definitely cooking some A-level fox mojo here. He thinks he's going home with me right now. But"—the blond made a sudden, very hoarse, very frightened sound—"he's not going to like what happens in this memory." Suze gave him a hard shove, and the guy fell backward onto the ground, scooting himself away from whatever was frightening him until his back hit the brick wall and he couldn't go any farther. She crouched down smoothly, tilting her head and watching him consideringly. "I'm an educator at heart, Fort," she mused. "And I think this one is going to end up with a lot more respect for women after tonight."

I eyed the look on the guy's face. "Respect? Or fear?"

She smiled. "I don't argue with results, man friend." And with a quick motion she flicked out her switchblade and made a deep slice across his wrist, bringing a thick wave of blood out. I hesitated for barely a second before

I was down on my knees, grabbing the wrist with both hands and locking my mouth around the wound. Instinct had pushed me forward, but the moment the blood hit my tongue, I didn't need instinct anymore. It wasn't the same as drinking from my mother, but it was so far from the experience I'd had drinking the stale, refrigerated blood that my siblings had brought me that it was like slicing into a piece of perfectly cooked and sauced filet mignon after a lifetime of eating nothing but twice-reheated meat loaf. I never lost awareness of what was around me, and was comforted by Suze's alert presence beside me, but the blood demanded my attention. It was hot, and alive in an indefinable way, fizzling down my throat delightfully, and the first few swallows just whetted my appetite for more. I knew that Suze was watching me, and would stop me from taking too much, so I just did what my body demanded, drinking and drinking, until finally I got the "that's enough" full signal from my belly, and I stopped. I lifted my head back, warm and replete as if I'd just finished a good meal in a fine restaurant, and watched benignly as Suze slapped a square of gauze over the slice on the guy's wrist and pressed down hard to stem the bleeding. I blinked, utterly content; then suddenly my body was sending me a whole different signal. I jumped to my feet, looking around desperately, but we were in an alley and the sudden screaming warning from my bladder left no doubt at all that this was a code-red emergency, and it was a question of either taking action or suffering an indignity that I hadn't experienced since potty-training.

I shuffled around fast, putting my back to Suze, whipped my fly down, and held my parka hem up with one hand as I peed against the alley wall, panting with relief.

Behind me, Suze was laughing hysterically. "Holy shit, it's really true," she gasped, and continued into a series of such belly laughs that if I'd been able to really take my attention away from my current predicament, I wouldn't have been surprised to see her rolling on the ground. As it was, though, I was in the middle of an epic pee break, and was doing my best to make sure that my shoes and pants were spared. "I was wondering if that would happen," she chortled.

"What?" I said, without much tact or patience, but, honestly, I was having to pee in an alley in front of my girlfriend. I deserved a pass.

She was still snickering as I zipped up and turned. "You're an obligate sanguivore, Fort. Just like a vampire bat."

"I'm aware of that part," I grumbled.

Her grin widened even further. "I did more research than you did? Oh, *Fort.* Come on, good buddy. Blood feeding is just about the most inefficient feeding process that there is. You have to suck in all that liquid, and your body needs to separate out the water from the good stuff as quickly as it can to make more room for the blood. Judging from McAssGrabberson's face here, I bet you just guzzled down three, maybe three and a half pints. What did you think your body was going to do?"

I stared. "You mean that bats—"

"Start peeing halfway through a feeding? Hell yeah." She snorted. "Watch a nature program sometime."

"Oh my God." Of all the things I'd thought about when it came to feeding on humans, my bladder had honestly never even crossed my mind.

"It's cool," Suze assured me. "And if I can keep finding douches for you, next time just take a piss right on him." She leaned down to my silent victim and punched him hard across the face, breaking his nose audibly and looking deeply satisfied. "Now, let's go dump this asshole in his car. He'll get home on autopilot. Then, in a couple of hours, he'll wake up with a memory of a deeply character-building experience, and a need for a tetanus shot."

"A what?" I asked, hoisting the guy to his feet.

Suze was smug. "He'll think that I sliced him with a dirty knife when he got too pushy. And then things got *really* interesting."

We hauled the guy back to his car, but by the time we got there it was clear that, between some minor blood loss and whatever psychological trauma Suze had just put him in, he was in no shape to drive. A quick check of his license revealed his home address, and we deposited him in his backseat and Suze drove his car, with me following in the Scirocco. From the looks of where we ended up, it was his parents' house, with everyone inside tucked neatly away in bed, so we left his car running in the driveway with the heater on high. He had an almost full tank of gas, so either he would wake up on his own at some point and stagger inside, or his parents would find him the next morning, asleep and in need of a low-priority trip down to the ER. Suze also fished through his pockets and confiscated a breath mint tin that contained several very suspicious pills that were definitely not mints.

She also took all his cash, assuring me that she had extremely important reasons for doing so. *Continuity* reasons for her fox trick, apparently.

We were less than a mile away from Suze's house, and she was insistent that only her own shampoo had, as she put it, the balls to get all the glitter out of her hair. I was informed pointedly that men's shampoo was completely weak, and got quite a lecture about it as I drove her to her own door.

"Thank you," I said, very seriously, just as she was about to leave the car. "You made that not awful, and I don't even know what to say to really thank you."

She leaned back toward me and cupped my cheek with one palm, pressing her forehead against mine and looking deeply into my eyes for a long second. Then she pulled back and, giving my cheek one gentle pat, said, "You don't have to thank me, Fort. It made me happy to help you." A small smile played at her mouth. "Isn't that something?"

Then she was out the car and giving me a jaunty wave as she walked up to her door and disappeared inside her house.

I got home to my apartment about twenty minutes later, and by then I was discovering that as good as that blood had tasted on its way down, it still left a distinctive funky taste in my mouth after some time had passed. I was definitely looking for some quality alone time with my toothbrush and half a tube of toothpaste. And maybe a Popsicle afterward, just because I'd earned it, and the blood in my stomach had put a definite pep in my step, but had failed to make the slightest impact on the achiness of my jaw.

The only light on in the apartment was the small one just by the door that we usually left on if one of us went to bed and the other wasn't home yet. We called it the courtesy light, since by leaving it on you did the other person the courtesy of not having to fumble around for a light switch while also attempting to take off his shoes.

There was a movement in the darkness of the living room as I closed the door behind me, and I saw that it was Dan, sitting in our new armchair. He must've been waiting for me. Jaison's heavy boots were on our shoe mat, so he was probably the reason that Dan's bedroom door was closed. There was something in Dan's face that I hadn't seen before, and it silenced me before I would've greeted him, or asked why he was sitting alone in the dark.

He walked up to me, stopping just far enough away that we were almost touching, and when he started talking, it was barely above a whisper. "Jaison is sleeping, but, Fort . . . I just wanted to say . . ." He paused, then cleared his throat and took a deep breath. "Everyone is talking about what you did today. And it's just . . ." He was forced to stop again, and for a second it looked like he was actually fighting back tears. "I know how that could've gone down if it hadn't been you who went there today. That, honestly, you could've just done things the way your family has always done things, and no one would've been surprised. So, I know they already said this, but *I* need to say this—thank you."

I closed my eyes as all those things that I'd felt in the butcher shop came rushing back, despite all my efforts to forget them in the confusion and rush of feeding from a human victim for the first time. "This can't keep going, Dan. I mean, we can't possibly stay in a situation where people have to *thank me* for not massacring them." I opened my eyes, and Dan was looking back at me solemnly.

"Then what's the alternative, Fort? Really?"

We stared at each other for a long second, and then Dan gave a small shrug of his shoulders. "You did a good thing today. Come on—let's bro-hug this one."

A small laugh escaped me, and I accepted the manly hug, with its requisite slaps on the back and nods at the end. There was another pause, and then Dan said, "Okay, now go gargle a bottle of mouthwash, because that is some *Guinness*-level bad breath."

I laughed again, because I knew that was what he'd intended, because for Dan there was no way out, and no other options beyond leaving the Scott territory entirely, which, as I'd learned with the succubi, carried its own risks. So he was trying to distract me, to give me something else to focus on, even if that something was my own utterly fetid breath.

When the illuminated numbers of my clock turned over to five a.m., I was awake and watching them. I'd been awake for most of the night, thinking. I was thinking about everything that had happened since my mother's death, and quite a few of the things that had come before it. But mostly I was thinking about how incredibly angry I'd felt that the ghouls had thanked me so sincerely. The sly gamesmanship of Atsuko Hollis, the rage of Cole, and even the careful maneuvering of Valentine Sassoon had all felt somehow easier to handle than that relieved gratitude from the ghouls. But when I put all those things together, I felt one overwhelming certainty—this couldn't go on.

Lying there in my bed, watching the darkness in my room lighten infinitely slowly, until finally the sun begrudgingly began to emerge, I finally believed that enough to do something about it. I also accepted the truth—because of what I'd done on behalf of the ghouls yesterday, Chivalry and Prudence were going to be pissed off at me.

And the thought emerged—if they were going to be pissed off at me anyway, why not really earn that, and do some real good while I was at it?

As soon as I weighed that thought, I realized the rightness of it. I rolled out of bed and dressed in a hurry, yanking on clothing without caring whether it came from the dirty or the clean piles, and rushing through my business in the bathroom without even glancing at my appearance in the mirror. I ran a quick hand through my hair, then stuffed a knitted hat over whatever nightmare was currently occupying my scalp and took the steps two at a time as I hurried down to my car.

Suze's voice was still warm and mushy with sleep when she answered her phone, her greeting so mashed together that it was only from its context that I knew that she was saying my name.

"I'm on your doorstep," I said. "Come let me in."

There was a pause while she wrapped her sleep-foggy mind around that, and her answer was searingly filthy even by her standards, but she padded her way to the door anyway and opened it. She must've been sleeping in fox form, because she had wrapped herself in one of the snowflake-patterned flannel sheets from her bed, and was giving me a distinctly unhappy glare that suggested that if I didn't have a particularly good reason for waking her up in this way, I was quickly going to find myself mauled.

I walked straight into her living room, hearing the sound of the door shutting behind me, and immediately started talking. "I'm going down and getting the succubi," I told her, pacing the floor, unable to stand still. "Chivalry and Prudence can go screw themselves, because I'm not letting them spend one more day in limbo. I'm going to hand them the paperwork, bring them up to Connecticut, and find them a hotel or something to stay in while they settle in. My sister might blow a gasket, but once I have them in this territory, Chivalry won't be willing to go against signed agreements, and Prudence won't be able to kick them out or kill them. Because the succubi are going to belong here, damn it, and get all the protections that we can give them." I spun around to look at her. "And I'm here to ask if you'll go down with me, Suze."

She blinked twice at me, her mussed dark hair half covering one eye. "This is going to require some coffee," she said slowly, and began walking toward the kitchen.

I stopped her when she would've passed me, wrapping one arm around her waist, feeling the soft flannel that draped over her, and the heat and curves of her body. "No, I need your answer," I said, never taking my eyes away from her face. "Because I'm getting in that car and I'm doing this, with or without you, but—"

She reached out one hand and smacked my cheek,

hard enough that I stopped talking. Then she clicked her tongue and said, "You idiot. Of course I'm coming with you. But it's an ass-long drive to New Jersey, and I'm going to need some coffee." I stared at her, and she smiled. "You're my buddy to the end, Fort, and if you've come up with this insane idea, then I'm with you until the wheels come off. But I expect a cup of coffee first."

There was nothing I could say in answer to a statement like that, so I leaned down and kissed her, trying to put all my gratitude and respect and love in one gesture that felt both utterly inadequate and at the same time wholly right.

Our first stop was Dunkin' Donuts, because their coffee was a lot better than anything that Suze was capable of brewing, given that I was fairly certain that new iPhones were produced more regularly than she changed her filters. The next stop was at my mother's mansion, where at six thirty Suze kept the car idling in the driveway while I slipped inside and made my way into the office. I knew from the bond between us that my brother was upstairs in his suite of rooms, probably snuggled next to Simone, and that Prudence wasn't present at all—she was almost certainly at home at her town house.

The succubi file, with all of its requisite paperwork for immigration and tithing, was in the increasingly over-stuffed drawer marked PENDING DECISION, and I slid it out in its fat entirety and flipped through it. With Loren Noka's trademark efficiency, and also what I couldn't help perceiving as a certain relentless optimism, the elaborately worded documents were already completely ready, awaiting only the signatures of the succubi spokes-man and a member of the Scott family. An oversight, of course, and one that I was sure would be immediately corrected when I came home and shoved the document into my siblings' faces—surely future documents would require all three of our signatures, but here was that shining loophole, and if I was only going to get to exploit it once, then I was going to make it count in people's lives.

I made it back out to the driveway without being detected, though I could already hear the sounds of the house starting to come alive, with the staff coming in from their own tucked-away parking area and starting their days of cleaning, or cooking, or data crunching. As I got back into the car, Suze took off the parking brake and moved the clutch to its slipping point, allowing my manual transmission car to ghost down the driveway, the light layer of snow on the gravel muffling the normal sounds.

"You know, you could turn the car on all the way," I said. "It's not going to attract any attention, since they'd probably just think that it was the woman who delivers the newspapers."

"I'm in a spy film right now, Fort. Don't ruin this."

An hour later I called Loren Noka from the road and told her that I'd handled all of the ghoul issue, but that I wanted to have today's meeting canceled, because I had things to handle, and that she could inform my siblings that I'd discuss everything fully with them tomorrow. She paused, and I knew that she'd picked something up in the way that I'd phrased that, but then she calmly assented and assured me that she'd pass the messages on.

"They'll probably enjoy a day off anyway," I said to Suze as I hung up the phone.

"I sure hope so," she replied around a mouthful of chocolate munchkins—after all, what was a stop at Dunkin' Donuts without also getting some pastry— "since after they find out what the hell you've been up to for a day and a half, they'll probably never let you go anywhere on your own again."

At just after ten in the morning, the Scirocco pulled

into the driveway of the wheat-colored Colonial that the succubi had been staying in. Their repurposed church youth group van was still in the driveway, with a new set of New Jersey plates. Beside it was a new car, a plain Honda Civic with a Nevada license plate.

"Did another of the succubi end up making it out?" Suze asked as we got out of the car.

"Saskia didn't mention it the last time we talked," I answered, "but I know that she hadn't given up hope, especially for her brother. Maybe we'll each have some good news to share." But I reached my hand reflexively into my pocket to touch the Colt, just to make certain that it was there.

There was no movement at the windows as we came up the walkway, but as we got closer we both saw at the same time that the front door was ajar. It wasn't anything that was unexplainable in a house containing that many small children, but the silence in the air suddenly felt much less like the New Jersey suburban dream, and much more threatening. Suze put her finger to her lips and slipped in front of me, glancing inside quickly, then nudging the door all the way open with her shoulder, both of her hands now wrapped around the handle of her longest knife, the one that was nearly a machete.

We both went in silently.

What was left of Milo, the adult succubi who had held so tightly to his young son, was halfway down the staircase. His left arm was separate from the rest of his body, resting two steps above a single toddler's flip-flop. I froze at the sight of the tableau, realizing with a deep, crushing knowledge that I'd acted too late, and they'd paid the price.

A sound broke the silence—a low mewling, followed by a crunching. I could feel Suze's hand on my shoulder, urging me back, but I was already moving, and I was no longer even thinking at all, except that whatever had done this was still in the house, and I wasn't going to let it walk out again.

A tall man with light brown hair and good looks was in the living room, crouched over a bloody, mangled pile of something that I knew had been a child only by the size of it, and realized was still alive only from that tiny, lost, empty mewl, the last sound possible from a throat that had already screamed itself out when the skinwalker started to feed. Because that was what it was doing— leaning over what had been a child's stomach, his mouth impossibly wide, pushing back the skin of the dead man that he was wearing so that long black mandibles could emerge, slice flesh off its prey, and pull it back inside.

I'd aimed the Colt at his head and squeezed off three rounds as soon as I registered what I was looking at, but even that had been too slow, as it either sensed my movement or caught sight of me, and it was moving before the bullets could reach it. It moved even faster than Soli, the last skinwalker I'd faced, had moved, so fast that even my vampire eyes had trouble tracking it. The first shot took off a chunk of his cheek and jaw, and he screamed as he ran, a high, painful sound that raked down my brain at a decibel level that I wasn't even sure I was fully hearing. His victim's skin tore, but what came out wasn't blood, it was a foamy white substance, and the puncturing of the skin released a smell that was worse than maggoty garbage in the summer, a putrescence that filled the room.

My second two shots had missed, but I was already moving, trying to get another shot, when it slammed into my side, throwing me across the room and into a wall, missing the stone fireplace by mere inches, the Colt knocked out of my hands. He would've come after me, but then he had Suze to deal with, the long knife in her hands whipping with deadly accuracy and kitsune speed, but each time she slashed out he was already gone, dodging with terrifying ease, and she'd learned from her last fight with a skinwalker to keep her cuts shallow, to never overextend herself.

I rolled to my feet. The Colt was gone, so I grabbed at the cast-iron fireplace tools that were beside me, tossing aside the brush and the short shovel and rake, coming back with the long, heavy poker. This time, when the skinwalker dodged to avoid Suze's knife, he found himself bashed with the metal poker that I brought down with all the strength I had onto whatever I could hit, which in this case was his left shoulder. There was an explosion of more of that foamy white fluid, and I could feel the reverberation and sting up my hands and arms from what I'd just connected with—it was if I'd just slammed the poker broadside against a cement wall, but there was no doubt that the skinwalker was affected, because the scream was even louder this time, and there was a sudden ripping sound, like what a wet grocery bag would make as the gallon of milk finally makes its escape, and an explosion of the smell was so extreme that it made me double over, gagging, my eyeballs burning and tears running down my cheeks, the inside of my nostrils and throat feeling like sandpaper was being scrubbed against it, as if this wasn't just a smell, but mustard gas from World War I.

Suze, her nose so much sharper than mine, was affected even worse, falling to her knees, barely able to hold on to the handle of her knife as she vomited helplessly. And in front of us the skinwalker shed its stolen mask, shreds of rotting human flesh falling around it as the hardened black carapace of the true skinwalker emerged, shoving its way out of the dead man's skin to reveal a full height that had its head brushing against the ceiling of the room, an insectoid face with steadily working mandibles and shining refracted black eyes that reflected my own face a hundred times.

It knew that Suze was the greater threat, because it

moved for her first, even faster now that it had fully shed its facade, the inch-long, curving black claws that were serrated like shark's teeth slicing down with deadly intent. I forced my arm to raise the poker again, but too slowly, because it had already reached Suze, and those claws sliced through skin, searching for vital organs. I slammed the poker down onto the left arm, and as it slid over that glossy hard carapace I was able to twist it, pulling and engaging one arm long enough to get those claws away from Suze and give her just an instant of an opening.

Between one breath and the next, the woman was gone, leaving a wounded fox that leaped away as the skinwalker hesitated for just an instant, thrown off by sudden air beneath claws that just a second before had been trying to tear flesh from bone. I threw my whole body forward, knocking the skinwalker onto its knees, and screamed when I felt those mandibles rip into my shoulder and chest, grabbing and slicing as if they were knife-tipped fingers searching for the softest, most vulnerable areas, even as its free arm now found its way right to my side, his fist slamming into me hard enough that I could feel my ribs crack. I shoved my left hand up, catching the bottom of its chin and trying to force that mouth away from me—whatever was happening at my side, there was no mistaking that the true danger was his mouth. I could feel the edge of Suze's knife beneath my knee, but it might as well have been on the moon for all the good that it could do me in that moment.

I caught the movement out of the corner of my eye as a black fox, her fur wet with blood in a dozen places, jumped with pinpoint accuracy, landing just so on the shoulders of the skinwalker, her delicate clawed feet fighting madly to find purchase in the smooth surface, and the white of her teeth flashed as she brought them down into the skinwalker's right eye. Its scream filled the

room as the surface of the eye was pierced, a yellow vis-
cous fluid exploding outward, and Suze was thrown off
the shoulders, but she snapped her jaws tight and swung,
her teeth embedded in what was left of the eye. The skinwalker abandoned me completely, desperately bringing
its free arm up to try to get Suze off it, and that gave me
the opening I needed to drop the poker and dive down
for Suze's knife. I brought it up with all the strength that
I had into the main body section of the skinwalker, and
I could feel the tip scrape against that carapace until it
finally found a seam, a tiny joint between plates, and I
shoved Suze's knife in all the way until its hilt was the
only thing emerging.

The skinwalker fell backward, its limbs spasming un-
controllably, and the black fox rode it all the way down,
growling like a creature possessed. Half-hidden beneath
the remains of a coffee table, I saw a familiar handle, and
I moved without hesitation, grabbing the Colt, straddling
the skinwalker, pressing the muzzle of the Colt into its
mouth (uncaring about the way that the mandibles sliced
my hand), and I squeezed off all the remaining five shots.

One final shudder ran through the skinwalker after
the majority of the back of its head exploded from the
inside out, and it went limp, well and truly dead. For one
long second I stared at it, still processing what had happened, and then every injury on my body seemed to register itself with my brain in the same instant, and I gave
a guttural yell that was practically a scream, then started
crawling, because standing up was not even an option at
this point, toward the black fox whose jaws were still
lodged in the remainder of the skinwalker's eye.

"Suze?" I asked hoarsely, reaching out my bleeding
hands to touch her, shuddering at how deep the slices on
her body were as they bled freely. "Suze?"

She opened her mouth almost delicately, her pink
tongue liberally coated with the yellow ichor from the

eyeball, and turned to look at me. Her back arched suddenly, and she made a deep, whole-body hack, like a cat about to expel a hairball, and several chunks of strangely colored eyeball emerged, along with a whole lot of sputum. She focused on me again, still covered with blood, and flipped her tail back and forth as if to say, *A-okay*.

I dragged us both to the downstairs bathroom, Suze tucked under my arm and clearly grateful for the ride. I was just glad that in this form she weighed less than twenty pounds. There was a fully stocked first aid kit under the sink, and I broke it open and hauled out the three full rolls of gauze. Suze's slices were so deep that on one of them I could actually see the white of bone, but all she let me do was wrap up her torso with gauze, trying to put enough pressure on things to slow the bleeding, before she gave a small growl and used her nose to nudge one of the rolls in my direction. Then she lay down on the bath mat and watched me through partially lidded eyes.

My left shoulder and upper chest were a mass of blood, but the flow was already slowing as I fished out a few bags of those heavy gauze pads that were meant to be cut down to size to go over skinned knees or burns, and just slapped them onto the area and secured them with half a roll of medical tape. The mandibles had been sharp and terrible, but fortunately they hadn't been able to slice too deeply, though the web of tiny, precise cuts hurt even worse than my ribs, which burned with every breath that I took. My right hand was also bleeding from a lot of cuts around my fingers and wrist, and along the back of the palm, from where I'd basically shoved it into the skinwalker's mouth while I was shooting him, and I wrapped it as best I could, given the awkwardness of using my left hand.

I looked over again at Suze, who had clearly taken

much more damage than I had. "What do I do, Suze?" I asked. "Should I take you to a vet?"

She whuffled a little, amused, and shook her head. Then she lifted her face imperiously and gestured at the door.

"You need me to get something for you?" Shaking.

"I need to look for something?" Nodding.

"Something you need?" Shaking.

I paused, and considered. "Oh," I realized. In the fight for our lives and making sure that we weren't going to completely bleed out, I'd almost managed to forget what we'd seen. "I need to check to see if there are any survivors," I said bleakly, and she nodded.

There weren't.

He must've arrived early in the morning, before the succubi had woken up, because it was upstairs, in the bedrooms, where I found most of the bodies. From the looks of it, he'd killed the adults first, taking them out quickly. It was with the children that he'd taken his time, and the sight of those tiny, tormented bodies was something I knew that I'd never be able to forget, however many centuries I lived.

I didn't know what else to do, so I simply laid each small body out and then covered it with a sheet. Saskia and Nicholas had both died in the master bedroom, in front of a large walk-in closet. There were tiny footprints in their blood, making me wonder if they'd realized that the skinwalker was in the house, and had tried to hide some of the children. I arranged them beside each other, with the remains of their daughter between them.

For Miro, I carried him downstairs, ignoring the screaming protest of my cracked ribs and the slices on my torso. By process of elimination, I'd realized that it was his son, Kirby, that the skinwalker had been eating when we came in. He'd been the youngest of the children, and he was the smallest of the corpses. I put him down in the living room, beside what was left of Kirby, and covered both of them with a throw rug from the sofa.

I heard footsteps, and turned to see Suze limping into the room. She'd returned to human form, and while I'd been covering the bodies, she must've been wrapping up the worst of her slices. She'd put a few butterfly bandages on the cut that had run across her muzzle as a fox—as a human it sliced across her cheek, barely missing her right eye. She was covered in blood, and gave a small groan as she reached down to snag her shirt off the floor where it had fallen when she changed into a fox.

"How are you even walking?" I asked.

"'Kill me fast or start running like hell' is practically our motto," she said, wincing as she eased herself down onto the sofa. "I heal faster than you, vampire boy, or at least faster than you will for another few decades, so after you helped keep me from bleeding out, it was just a matter of waiting for the worst of things to knit together enough that I could grit my way through it." She started to tug her shirt on, but even with excessive care she almost immediately made a wrong movement and made a half-smothered scream of pain. She paused, panted, then said, "Though I might be taking it easy for a few days. Slacking back, eating ice cream, watching reality TV. Doing some laurel resting while this heals up."

I looked down at the bodies at my feet. "What are we going to do about this, Suze?"

She ignored what I'd really meant. "I can't disguise this many bodies, even if I hadn't been devoting so much energy to healing." She dropped her shirt onto her lap. "Fuck that, I'm just going to ride home fox. You can throw some towels down on the seats." She gestured broadly at the house. "We'll disable all the fire alarms and burn the place to the ground. If we siphon some gas from the tanks of their cars, we can get things cranking and make sure that there's almost nothing left for anyone to examine. We'll throw the cars in the garage, let the fire take them as well. I can set enough of a fox trick that everyone who comes to investigate this will agree that the fire started naturally—probably an electrical fire, and that it started when whoever was in the house was asleep. Enough smoke inhalation, fire spreading too fast, and no one got out." She nodded grimly. "That's what we'll have to do."

"Suze, that's not—" The sudden sound of a phone ringing cut me off. It was loud—definitely coming from this room, but it wasn't my phone or Suze's. I looked around, then recoiled in disgust. It was coming from the remains of the skinwalker's human flesh—the phone had been in his pants pocket, and had ended up among that twisted wreckage of nasty rotting meat. Suze's discarded socks were lying near it, and I tugged one of those over my hand and poked cautiously among the pile until I pulled out the phone.

"What are you doing?" Suze watched me from the sofa.

"Have you wondered," I asked slowly, scrolling down through the list of recent calls received, "how the skinwalker knew how to come here? The succubi changed the plates on their van more than a dozen times, and were using nothing but cash so that they wouldn't leave a trail. So how did the skinwalker find them? How did it enter Scott territory and go to the one house where its quarry was?" I saw the number on the skinwalker's phone, and my heart sank. I looked up at Suze. "He was invited, and told exactly where to go."

She stared at me, comprehension dawning, but I had to say the words myself. "I wasn't the only one who was frustrated with the stagnation of things that had to be dealt with," I said. "Prudence was angry. And she moved faster than I did—she got this skinwalker's phone number— who even knows how—and she called him so that he would come here and kill all the succubi and remove a point of discussion from our list." For a moment I felt light-headed and wondered if I was going to pass out, whether from blood and injuries or just the sheer weight of this knowledge, crumpling down like a Southern debutante in an old movie, but it passed, leaving me still standing with what I knew. I opened my eyes again and focused on Suze. "All these people . . . This can't happen again, Suze. I can't let this happen again."

"What are you going to do?" she asked, very softly.

"Something," I said. "I'm going to do something." I looked down at the throw blanket that I'd put over the bodies, at the way that it was slowly wicking up blood and forming stains. "Something big."

I arrived at the mansion the next morning, ten minutes after the beginning of our scheduled meeting. One of the staff members was refreshing the floral arrangement beside the base of the stairs, and I asked her to go get my siblings and to please bring them here, to the main entryway. Her surprise was clear, but she was well trained and did what I asked without question. After all, I was a Scott.

Prudence and Chivalry walked in together, and stopped dead at what they saw. Because I was standing there, of course, but arrayed behind me were Atsuko and all her living daughters and granddaughters, in human and fox forms. And Gil and Dahlia Kivela were there, with a dozen of the *metsän kunigas*. The ghoul elders were there, along with their strongest members, the ones most ready for a fight. Lilah and Cole stood off to the side with several of the Neighbors, their glamours dropped and their hair gleaming like metal threads, and finally there was Valentine Sassoon and over fifty adult witches. The kitsune had hidden them all as they came in. Because the kitsune worked at their strongest within expectation, and who would ever have expected to see these groups together, arrayed as one body, filling the whole of the massive entryway of Madeline Scott's mansion?

My brother recovered first. "Fort," he asked carefully, "what is this?"

"This is called a coup," I said, and I looked directly at my sister. "We're not going to keep doing it the old way anymore."

Prudence was absolutely cold, rigid and controlled. "And how do you suggest we do it?" She scanned her eyes over everyone in the room, her expression promising death. "What promises have you made, baby brother?" she hissed.

"Everyone has a seat at the table now." I nodded behind me, indicating those who stood there. "We all live in this territory, and we all have a stake in it. Every group will have a representative, and every representative will have a vote."

Chivalry's expression was despairing. "You think it's that simple, Fortitude?"

"No, I know it isn't. But that's where we're starting. We'll work it out, all of us." I stared at my family, and the heat of my anger and rage was just as strong as it had been the previous day, when I saw Prudence's number on the skinwalker's phone. "We live in America, and it's time for a motherfucking democracy."

My sister stepped forward, and she wasn't cold now—her eyes were glowing, and an unholy rage was almost rolling off her. "This country won its democracy through blood, brother. I remember—I was there to see it. How much will your little group sacrifice for this? How much blood will they shed?" Her fangs slid out, white and sharp.

Everyone around me tensed, but no one ran as she

moved closer to us. I drew my sawed-off Ithaca and sighted down on my sister, bracing myself to pull the trigger and shoot her.

For a long minute, I don't think anyone in the room breathed, as everything hung by a thread.

It was Chivalry who suddenly reached out and caught Prudence's arm, keeping her from taking that one final step that would've sent violence exploding throughout the room.

"Stop, sister," he said.

"Even you, Chivalry?" she asked, shocked.

"Yes." He nodded, but there was a world of sadness in his voice. "If a side must be chosen, here and now, then I choose to follow Fortitude's path rather than to fight him."

"Even if that means fighting me?" She reached over to touch where his hand was holding her, and her grip tightened, making his jaw clench with pain, but he didn't waver, just held her gaze and refused to look away. Something passed between them—and it was Prudence who looked away, and who stepped back.

"Very well, brother," she said, so low that I wasn't sure how many in the room could even hear her. "Since you have at last made a decision, I will agree. Two votes to one, after all." She looked around the room once more, disgust curling her lip. "Though perhaps the staircase remains our best moment of unity."

The race factions all filed into the dining room for the first official discussion. Staff members hurried among them, making certain that everyone had chairs and glasses of water. Loren Noka had dug out a stenographer's typewriter, and was setting it up so there would be an official record of all statements made, though I noticed that she'd also downloaded a recording app to her phone to augment it.

Chivalry stood beside me, watching silently. Finally, as the last entered the room, and they waited for us to join them—not as their rulers now, but as the last of the voting factions, my brother turned to me and asked, "Do you understand what you've begun, brother?"

"Something better, I hope." I answered.

"Hope," Chivalry said, disgusted, and shook his head. "This wasn't what Mother wanted. She foresaw problems coming and wanted us to share control between the three of us, and she must've wanted that for a reason." Urgently he whispered, "We're moving off her path, Fort, and into the wilderness. And without knowing what she knew."

"There's no real vision into the future, Chivalry," I insisted. "The future is what we make it."

My sister joined us, and gave a slow nod at my statement. "Indeed, brother." Her blue eyes glowed. "The future will continue to come, no matter what you do. You make this deal today, with these individuals who you seem to trust so much. But remember that you'll be dealing with their children someday. And then their grandchildren after that. And their great-grandchildren. You're not even thirty yet, Fortitude. You don't understand that we—your family—are all that will stand with you against the wave of time, as all others get crushed into the sand."

I could feel my mouth twist. "That's why you let Chivalry stop you. Because you think that I'll change my mind."

"I have time, baby brother," she answered. "Centuries of it, and enough to have learned the true value of patience."

"Time goes both ways, Prudence," I reminded her. "Now, I'm going to go make a future that I'd like to live in, whether you like it or not."

I entered the room, hearing the footsteps of my siblings as they followed me. All the eyes were on me, but the ones that I met belonged to a small black fox, swathed in vet wrap bandages and held in the arms of one of her cousins. She wagged her tail at me and yipped, just once.

ABOUT THE AUTHOR

M. L. Brennan lives in Connecticut with her husband and an assortment of extremely spoiled cats. Holding a master's degree in fiction, she teaches basic composition to college students. Her house is more than a hundred years old, and is insulated mainly by overstuffed bookshelves.

CONNECT ONLINE

mlbrennan.com

@brennanml